M000112064

Christopher Lehmann-Haupt

A CROOKED MAN

A NOVEL

SIMON & SCHUSTER

New York   London   Toronto   Sydney   Tokyo   Singapore

SIMON & SCHUSTER
Rockefeller Center
1230 Avenue of the Americas
New York, New York 10020

SIMON & SCHUSTER and colophon are registered trademarks of Simon & Schuster Inc.

Designed by Hyun Joo Kim
Manufactured in the United States of America

1   2   3   4   5   6   7   8   9   10

Library of Congress Cataloging-in-Publication Data

Lehmann-Haupt, Christopher.
A crooked man: a novel/Christopher Lehmann-Haupt.
p.   cm.
I.Title.
PS3562.E435C76 1995
813'.54—dc20   94-34247
                                  CIP
ISBN: 0-671-73444-X

ACKNOWLEDGMENTS

The story that follows is entirely fictional, of course, but many people helped me to build the factual foundation that supports the fantasy. I am particularly grateful to Judith K. Keenan for help on the legislative details and on other Washington arcana, to Senator Carl Levin for showing me around the Capitol Building and the United States Senate, and to Michael Korda, Chuck Adams, Donald A. Ritchie, and Steven M. L. Aronson for their painstaking readings of the text at various stages. However, any missteps that may have occurred are exclusively my own.

Also helpful in more ways than I can detail were Harold Aks, Nelson Aldrich, O. P. Anders, Bennett Ashley, Richard W. Baron, Zerina Bhika, Willie Blacklow, Marty Blane, Dr. Philip W. Brickner, William F. Buckley, Jr., Wade Burkhart, Robert A. Caro, Elliott Carroll, Don Caswell, Albert D'Annibale, Donald N. Ebright, Mabel M. Eckels, Joni Evans, Maria Gallacher, Helen Galen, Ben Gazzara, Dan Green, Tom Harris, Julie Harston, Rebecca Head, Marsha Hilsenrad, Norman Hilsenrad, Patrick Hines, George F. Hoffman, Dr. Georgiana Jagiello, Gordon Kerr, Nicola Khuri, Rachel Lehmann-Haupt, J. Robert LeShufy, Devera Levin, Ellen Levine, Dr. Richard U. Levine, Ira Lowe, Sebastian Marinaro, Frank Metz, Lester Migdal, S. A. Miles, Boyd L. Myers, Jr., Lynn Nesbit, Hugh Nissenson, Marilyn Nissenson, Allen Peacock, Eric Rayman, Jonathan Rinehart, Ronnie Scharfman, Dr. I. Herbert Scheinberg, Sophie Sorkin, Betty Stram, Thomas Thacher, Martin Tolchin, Calvin Trillin, Clare Walker, Cheryl Weinstein, Lydia Wills, and Jackie Yeager.

FOR NATALIE ROBINS

MY COMPASS

There was a crooked man, and he walked a crooked mile,

He found a crooked sixpence against a crooked stile;

He bought a crooked cat, which caught a crooked mouse,

And they all lived together in a little crooked house.

There Was a Crooked Man

anonymous

PART ONE

Saturday, April 12th

I

The Dummy

It was bright morning in the dream, and Nick Schlafer was standing against the giant woman's thigh. The rocks and water seemed bathed in brilliant light. Yet the pool looked to him as it usually did at nightfall, when the trees and shrubbery turned to shadows, when only the rock face reflected the dying light, and when the opposite shore appeared like a huge flexed leg, the knee the outcropping of stone high above, the thigh the smooth in-sloping wall that dropped to the water's edge.

Something felt wrong. He was standing on the ledge, leaning back against the boulder face behind him, as if he were resting against the woman's other knee. He could hear the crash of the waterfall upstream; he could smell the earth of the stream bank; he could feel the current flowing against his waders. But he was uneasy. Something was in the water. Something was struggling to the surface. He was not holding his fishing rod, but the thing in the water was fighting and breaking the dark surface.

He leaned from his perch and peered down at the water.

He leaned too far, lost his balance, and began to fall. He put out his hand to meet the surface of the water.

He kept falling and falling.

• • •

He opened his eyes. Sunlight flooded the porch. He lifted his right arm to look at his watch. It was 6 A.M. His mouth was sour from the brandy he had drunk the night before.

He sat up on the mattress, groped for his eyeglasses on the ledge next to the screening, and worked himself free of the sleeping bag twisted around his legs. Naked, he turned the corner of the porch, walked past the wooden picnic table, and pushed open the door. Inside the house, he went into the kitchen to the left and lit the burner under the kettle of water on the stove. He yawned and removed the breakfast fixings from the small plastic cooler he had brought with him from the city and set them on the counter. He moved out onto the porch again, pushed open the screen door, went down the steps, and trotted over the floor of hemlock needles to the stream, where he shocked himself awake by splashing his body with the icy water. On the way back he passed the grill that stood some fifty feet from the house. He thought of cooking his breakfast there. But it would take too long for the coals to heat.

Back on the porch, he rubbed himself dry with the faded bath towel he had found the evening before inside the cedar chest in the living room. He put on frayed boxer shorts, old army fatigues, and an olive drab sweater. He went back inside to the kitchen. Using two separate pans, he fried sausages and eggs. He scooped them into an army mess kit and mixed a mug of instant coffee.

He carried his breakfast outdoors to a familiar spot where the roots and the trunk of a huge hemlock formed a natural armchair: "the little bear's throne," his grandfather had named it. A slab of rock beside the seat formed a natural table. From the seat he could see either the water off to his right or the cabin to his left. Leaning back, he thought of how as a boy he used to sit there late at night and listen to his grandfather, Big Stash, and the other old men. After dinner they would play cards at a table set up by the campfire. Later they would sing and tell jokes and talk about their long-ago days working as railroad experts in the Hoover Administration—before Franklin Roosevelt, "*that son-of-a-bitch*," had come along and taken the country away from them. Listening to the old men, he would fight to stay awake, until the bang of the screen door and the bobbing light of the kerosene lamp told him his grandmother was coming to fetch him off to bed. Years later, when he was at Princeton, he would drive down here with his roommates and buddies, and whatever women were game enough to join them, and put in an afternoon of fishing. In the evening, when the catch had been cooked on the grill that his grand-dad had built out of cinder blocks, and had been washed down with too many six-packs of beer, his friends would retreat to the porch. He would go to the bear's throne and sit listening to them.

He ate the last of his eggs and began to sip the coffee. Those occasional times when he had been able to get his wife and children to come down for a weekend all together—they disliked the isolation of the place, most of all the lack of a telephone, which he refused to install—he used to like to get up early and catch enough trout for breakfast. The smaller ones were the best, about seven inches. He would cook his share and eat them while the family was still sleeping. He liked to linger over his coffee and take stock of the place: the firewood stacked under the porch; the shingles all nailed down; the screens properly patched. Yet it also faintly saddened him that thinking about such chores, which had been his responsibility as a boy and had seemed to him then an unbearable intrusion on his freedom, now served as a way of putting his world back in order.

He looked off at the stream. Wind ruffled the surface of the water. There were no fish rising this morning.

He drank the rest of his coffee and pushed himself stiffly from his seat. As he leaned to pick up his utensils from the stone shelf, a shred of whiteness caught his eye. It was a small strip of paper that appeared to be stuck to the outer edge of the stone. As he stooped to examine it, he caught himself thinking that it might be a clue left over from the Easter treasure hunts he used to make up for his daughter, Lore, when she was little. But the last one of those had been—when?—six or seven years ago? Lore had lost interest when she was about twelve—had stopped coming down to the camp with him when she was fifteen or sixteen, when the trouble had begun—and, except for her occasional sarcastic repetitions of her father's favorite treasure-hunt phrase—"You have to ask the right question, Lor-ee!"—that had been the last of that little ritual.

Another tie between them had broken. Now she was dead.

He said the words aloud: "Now she is dead."

He squatted and with his thumbnail scraped the edge of the paper strip until enough of it came free to grasp between his thumb and fingers. It pulled away easily, as if stuck on with rubber cement. He pushed his eyeglasses up onto his forehead and examined the paper closely. It looked fresh and unweathered, as if it had been pasted to the stone only hours earlier, certainly since the rain had stopped falling. On it were typed four words: "WHY DON'T WE MEET?"

He flicked his glasses back in place, removed his wallet from his hip pocket, folded the paper in two, slid it into one of the credit card compartments, and repocketed the wallet. He bent, picked up the mess kit and mug, and started back to the cabin.

"WHY DON'T WE MEET?" The message was mild enough; the place where he had found it, however, made it threatening.

He set the utensils on the counter by the kitchen sink and went back out to the porch. There were any number of people who might want to deliver such a message, but he was sure that only Rizzo would have had the daring and insolence to do it. To steal into the fishing camp and paste the message right under his nose.

Salvatore Rizzo. He thought of his first encounter with the man. Rizzo had been almost unreal with his slicked-down blue-black hair, his Prohibition-era style of dress, and his nearly comic pantomime of menace. His appearance suggested the line from the first *Godfather* film, the movie director yelling about "greaseball goombahs" coming out of "the woodwork." Rizzo was hardly to be taken seriously, except that he had somehow managed to get past the barriers that discouraged most intruders. First he had telephoned the office on the private line. Then he had shown up in person, having run the gauntlet of secretaries and assistants. He had even gotten past Abby. He was suddenly there, strutting, glowering, flaring his nostrils.

What had Rizzo wanted? That too was hard to take too seriously—his elliptical talk about "my client's interests" and wanting "to do biz-i-ness."

"I represent a man would like to have a meeting with you," Rizzo had said.

"Represent?"

"I'm a counselor. At law."

"What kind of meeting do you want?"

"My client will explain."

"Who is your client? How did you get in here?"

"All that will be explained."

"I don't think so, Mr. Rizzo."

Recalling this, Nick's face flushed with anger.

Don't think about it now.

Try to relax.

Out on the porch, he stood at the end of a wooden table covered with fishing and camping equipment. What troubled him most was that he was sure that Rizzo's client had something to do with drugs. There was nothing he could put his finger on, except a veiled reference to Lore. "We could have helped your daughter," Rizzo had said as he was firmly led to the door. Again, his menacing insinuations had seemed laughable at the time. But if he was responsible for the message on the rock, there was no telling how far he might go or what he would do next.

They could even be watching him right now.

Looking at the fishing equipment on the table, he used his body as a map, beginning with his feet. There were woolen socks; an old-fashioned pair of chest-high rubber waders with booted feet; a vest lumpy with pockets full of paraphernalia like tippet spools, fly floatant, and a tiny gooseneck flashlight for tying flies on after dark. There was a landing net, a battered felt hat, half a dozen fly boxes, two reels, and two rods in metal tubes, one graphite, the other split bamboo.

He removed his shoes, pulled on the socks, and clambered into the waders, balancing himself on one leg at a time until the opposite foot slipped snugly home. After tightening the suspenders, he twisted himself into the vest and pushed the old beige hat onto his head until he could feel the cool of its sweatband against his forehead.

From a pocket of his vest he removed a small plastic bottle of insect repellent. Old Woodsman Fly Dope. He wouldn't need it; the air was too cool for insects. Anyway, the stuff was obsolete because of all the fancy new chemicals that had come on the market in the past thirty years—you couldn't even buy it anymore. But he had an old bottle and he liked the smell—a powerful mixture of camphor, pine tar, and citronella. It reminded him of Big Stash.

There was no question about it: Rizzo's so-called client had to be connected to drugs. That for damn sure was his "biz-i-ness." So now a narcotics kingpin wanted to consult with him. Great. One more reason why it was crazy to go ahead with his drug bill.

He looked out at the stream. Its surface was still flurried. He took the longer of the rod tubes, unscrewed its lid, upended it, and shook it until its cloth cocoon slid out. Setting the tube aside, he pulled loose the knots that secured the three rod pieces inside the cloth case and slipped them free of their sheathing. He pulled the cork stoppers from the female ferrule sections, dropped them back into the tube, coaxed the empty cloth case in after them, and screwed the lid back on. From the pile of silvery fly boxes he took those containing nymphs, streamers, bucktails, and the gaudier finder flies and slid them into the lower pockets of his vest. It was too cold for hatches this morning; no subtle imitations would be needed. He took the heavier of the reels, unzipped it from its chamois case, checked to see that it still held the spool with the dark green sinking line, and secured it to the butt end of the rod.

At the bottom of the porch steps, he pieced the rod together, first rotating the ferrule butts against the side of his nose to lubricate them. He stripped off line from the reel. The ratcheting screamed in the air. He bent a piece of the line against itself to form a loop that could more easily be pushed through the rod guides. When the loop came through the guide at the rod tip, he pulled the doubled section free and checked the leader tip to be sure it was thick enough for the heavy flies he would be casting. He removed one of the fly boxes from his vest, opened it, and picked out a Letort Hopper, a highly effective brownish grasshopper pattern named after the famous chalk stream not far from his home in Pennsylvania. Setting the rod butt on the ground with the tip against his shoulder, he tied the fly onto the leader tippet.

He picked the rod up and secured the hook to a tiny ring next to the rod's cork handle. Flicking the rod in the air, he set off for the stream.

The list of negatives surrounding his legislation was growing by leaps and bounds. He had not yet gone public with the specifics of his bill; he would be appearing on CNN tomorrow morning to outline his plans, and he would be introducing the bill as a joint resolution sometime next week. But already word had begun to spread and stir up a furor. Constituents had called to protest. Colleagues had stopped to harangue him. Telephone calls had come in from AMA lobbyists and a dozen watchdog organizations. The brickbats were darkening the sky.

Did he want this for his epitaph? Nicholas Stationer Schlafer III, Junior Senator from Pennsylvania: he fought to legalize drugs. He tried to fry America's mind.

Not to speak of the threat to his family. Did he want to put Matty at risk after what had happened to Lore?

And he didn't even believe that his bill had any chance of passing.

When he reached the stream, he waded a few feet out in water no deeper than six inches. Tiny minnows flickered among the rocks. He stepped onto the back of a large stone that sat where the stream bed began to drop off. Beyond the still water where he had bathed an hour earlier there lay a channel about ten feet wide where the current raced in a curve. He would fish only the deeper runs today. A gust of wind rippled the surface again and stirred the branches of the hemlocks on the far shore. He stepped off the rock and waded to the edge of the faster current. The water, swollen from spring rains, came up to his knees.

But yes, he damn well did want to go ahead with his bill. Why? It would be a memorial to Lore, for one thing. That was important to him, though it was hardly a reason.

They would accuse him of doing it for her. Fair enough.

Still, the great war on drugs that the country had been waging for decades had proved a dismal failure. Not only had it not solved the problem, it had made it worse. Every drug bust that looked so good on the evening news only served to drive up the price of whatever remained in the dealers' predatory clutches. Every interdiction of a shipment or arrest of a supplier only cleared the way for others lying in wait to take over a territory. And where did half the stuff go that was laid out on tables for police publicity photographs? Back onto the streets again, through the hands of dishonest cops.

And then there was the violent crime involved. Did anyone really know how many robberies and murders could be traced back to drugs? Drugs cost the country upwards of a hundred billion dollars a year now. What was that buying except corruption and death?

Holding the rod in his right hand, he pinched the brown lure between the finger and thumb of his left hand, spread his arms, and moved the rod tip outward until the line and leader came taut. Whipping the lure into the air, he began to strip line from the reel. It was no use trying to false cast in the wind. He let the hopper settle on the water and unreeled line until the fly had become a dark speck thirty feet downstream. He waited for a gust of wind to die. When the water calmed, he raised the rod tip, pulled in line with his left hand until the lure had come back to him, and then snapped the rod sharply sideways back and forth. The fly came clumsily off the water, danced in the air, and flew to the far edge of the channel, where it slapped onto the water. When the line had settled in the current and begun to bow downstream, he gave the rod tip a flick to pull the fly under. He could just make out its dark form swimming beneath the surface. He waited

for the drag to tell him that the line had been pulled straight by the
current. Then he began to tug the rod sideways to make the lure come
alive and dart across the current.

Nothing.

He moved upstream a few steps, removed a pair of clip-on Po-
laroids from a pocket of his vest, and attached them to his eyeglasses.
Now he could see the lure better below the surface. He waited for another lull in the wind and cast again. Nothing. Not a sign of life.

He pulled the line in and let the lure flutter in the wind. His only
real prospect was the Woman's Pool. He would work his way up the
stairway of pools quickly, skipping the usual pockets and fishing only
the deeper runs.

He turned and began the climb to the next pool.

What mattered most to him was that he considered drug legalization a cornerstone of the libertarian political philosophy on which
he had run for office and gotten himself elected. If ever there was a
case where free-market forces would work to the benefit of people!
Just liberate the supply and demand of hard drugs and the price of
them would drop like a shot duck, and all the need for crime and vio-
lence would disappear.

Of course the market could not be completely free. The state
would have to control the supply through the licensing of dealer-
ships. Just like booze, a more dangerous drug than heroin or coke or
marijuana when you came right down to it. The state would have to
control the supply and channel the profits into educating the public
against the use of drugs. There would still be a black market, just as
there was betting outside of legal parlors. But the black market would
be negligible compared with what existed now.

Anyway, this would be his last chance to accomplish anything
notable. Graced with his grandfather's name and all it meant, he had
been swept into office on a tide of Republican conservatism. But after
nearly a decade in office he had not greatly distinguished himself. He
had followed faithfully but rarely led. For the past year he had hardly
functioned at all. And now the tide was going out again. The country
was weary of conservatism. He was not likely to be reelected, and
while he did not for a moment believe that he would succeed with his
bill, he would fight to get it voted out of committee and onto the floor
of the Senate for debate and consideration. The battle over drug legalization would be joined. He had the votes in the judiciary subcommittee that he chaired. That much he had accomplished. Members

had even encouraged him to introduce the bill. Of course he knew they were using him to send up a trial balloon. If reaction was too negative, they would scurry for cover, leaving him to take the fall. But that was okay. The debate itself would be his monument. And some-day when Americans decided to stop tearing themselves to pieces over drugs, maybe he would be remembered as a pioneer.

An hour later, after he had fished the mile of water between his cabin and the Woman's Pool, he came to the channel of white water that lay just downstream from his destination. Here the current was too deep and fast to trouble wading against, so he headed for the shore to his left. In the distance he could see the wooden bench that his grandfather had set up next to the Woman's Pool so that he could fish it in his old age.

When he reached the crescent of dirt and pebbles that ran along the right ankle of the pool, he stepped onto it. Once more, he checked to be certain that his leader was strong enough to bear a hard strike and began to make his way toward his perch next to the right knee.

The next step was tricky, even dangerous. He had to step into the stream and slide down the steeply inclined bank until the water came up to his waist. At exactly the right moment, still sliding, he had to launch himself forward and feel with his foot for the stone that he knew lay submerged about a yard away. He had to step onto it and from there, without stopping to catch his balance, he had to leap to the submerged ledge from which he liked to fish. After his leap, his momentum should have caused him to slide across the ledge's mossy surface and to plunge into the deep current beyond, but a layer of felt cemented to the soles of his boots gave him traction to recover his footing and regain his balance.

He had the maneuver down pat by now, though he still felt re-lieved each time he completed it successfully. He could not help imag-ining what would happen if he ever did fall into the water. His waders would quickly fill and he would not be able to touch bottom for at least twenty yards downstream. Fishermen had drowned under less treacherous conditions.

But his anxiety was quickly overcome by anticipation. Even on a bad day like this, the pool seemed rich with promise. Three years ear-lier, on a similarly cold and windy day, he had cast a streamer to the opposite shore, where the woman's thigh entered the water, and hooked what at first had felt like an underwater log. Certain that he was snagged, he had all but given up on saving his fly and leader when the log began to move. Relentlessly, it had swum downstream, gathering speed and pulling off line as it went, until his reel was screaming. When the line had run all the way out and the backing began to show, he had tried to cup his hand over the spinning reel handle and apply enough pressure to slow down the fish, but he hadn't had a chance. The instant he had halted the spool's crazy spin the line parted, and he had been left with the sad conviction that he would never again be so close to such a fish. When he reeled the line in he found that he had been fishing with too fine a leader tippet. He had forgotten to replace it when he'd switched from a dry fly to a heavier lure. The experience had never left him. At the edge of a hundred nights of sleep he had relived the moment.

Though he had never again had so much as a nibble in the pool, it still held magic for him.

He closed his eyes and let the roar of the waterfall fill his mind. There was a rhythmic throb to it that he had never noticed before. The wind had died and the air had warmed a little. He could even feel the sun on his shoulders.

He raised the rod and began to false cast and strip off line from the reel, making sure to keep his backcast high and out of the shrubbery on the shore behind him. When the line in the air felt heavier than the rod, he thrust his arm forward, as if he were throwing a baseball from the outfield, and released the extra line that hung looped in his left hand. The lure sailed out, hit the wall on the opposite shore, and plopped into the current. He gave it a moment to sink, then began to whip the rod and tug in line so the lure would dart like a minnow.

Now it might happen.

He let the lure drift into the faster current, then jerked the rod again.

Nothing.

"WHY DON'T WE MEET?" If he was right about whoever Rizzo represented—that they were somehow connected to the drug business—then it was pretty obvious why they wanted to meet with him. Since the point of his legislation was precisely to cut the ground from underneath the big drug operators, it would be in their interest to stop what he intended to do.

They might not take the risk of hurting him, but they might try to buy him or blackmail him, if they could somehow find the leverage. It would not be the first time that an elected representative had fallen into the hands of the mob. Or if they didn't lean on him, they might offer him protection from others. The good cops playing themselves off against the bad.

Or they could try to get at him indirectly, through someone close to him. Despite the official conclusion that Lore's death had been a suicide, he still believed in his heart that it was far from that simple, that others had somehow been involved, and that those others might have had something to do with drugs.

"WHY DON'T WE MEET?" He could not afford to ignore the message. He had better give Rizzo a call when he got back to the city.

The pulse of the waterfall seemed to grow louder. He lifted the rod tip. The lure came to the surface downstream and danced along the surface. He gathered slack line in his left hand. Halfheartedly, he cast again. This time the feather fell short of the wall and was quickly swept under. He began to retrieve it, wondering if he should quit now and head back to the city. He would get there early enough to stop by the office before lunch.

Wait!

There was something on.

It felt like a snag, but he wasn't going to be fooled again.

Cautiously he lifted the rod to make sure the hook was set. Something was on, and it was moving downstream. A shiver went through him. At last. He lifted the rod higher to apply more pressure. There was no give, but strangely there was no tension either, no fight. Maybe with more pressure he could lead the fish out of the current into the slow water near the shore.

The reel began to click sporadically as the last of the line in his left hand paid out.

Click . . . click . . . click. There was something peculiar about the slow rhythm.

Grasping the rod butt with both hands, he raised his arms and pulled the rod to the right. The line ran taut to the bubbling surface. As he sighted down it, he could see pearls of water explode from it in the sunlight. It was responding to the sideways pressure. Just by holding it steady where the current swerved to the left, he might be able to lead the fish into stiller water. He would fight it there. Yes, the drag was easing; the fish was moving out of the fast current. Better get off his perch now and find a place where he could maneuver. The fish would soon sense what was happening and begin to panic.

Holding the bent rod high with his right hand, he stooped and braced himself with his left hand. He lowered his feet into the water, feeling for his stepping stone. When he found its jagged edge, he pushed away from his perch and, regaining his balance, began to reel in the slack line he had gained by moving closer to the fish. Still tugging the rod and reeling in line, he moved slowly up the sandy embankment and stepped onto the crescent of beach. His legs were shaking. He strode as quickly as he could to the lower end of the beach, yanking and reeling as he went. The fish was quiet in the water now, maybe fretting and getting ready to run. Any moment now he would get a glimpse of it.

He splashed his way into the water below the beach and gave a harder pull on the line. The weight gave easily. Too easily, he thought. Now that it was free of the current, it seemed unnaturally light. He flipped his sunglasses up and craned his neck to see beneath the surface. There it was! Just a few feet below. Something darkish, and not a log. There was something white on it too. A dark shape with something white on it. He could see the outline of his lure.

He let out an involuntary cry. He leaned closer to the surface and gave another pull on the rod.

He could swear . . . but it couldn't be. It made no sense.

Another hard tug of the rod, and the thing turned slowly over. He stared and tried to grasp what he was seeing.

A face. A small face.

A human face.

It was floating on its back now, its arms outflung, its pale face tipped back.

His stomach heaved and his legs went weak. He staggered back, felt with his free hand for the low embankment, slipped on a submerged stone, and involuntarily sat where the shore formed a ledge. The pounding of the waterfall seemed unnaturally loud.

The face of his daughter came to him, her lifeless stare, which he could never forget, never wanted to forget. The unnatural pallor. And always the blood. But this was not Lore. It wasn't Matty either; it could not be Matty.

He felt sick.

Why was the waterfall pounding like that?

He bent forward, thrusting his head against his knees. The pounding grew hollow. His hands and face felt clammy.

What in hell was he doing? The child could still be alive.

He forced himself up and splashed to where his line entered the water. He thrust his hand down toward the whiteness, felt slippery cloth, grabbed it, and yanked upwards. The thing was eerily light in his grasp. It broke the surface, its head lolling, its face grinning as the water ran off it.

Grinning.

It was a large doll.

Charlie McCarthy.

It was that old-time comedian's dummy, wearing his tuxedo and monocle, grinning at him insolently. The brownish lure was hooked into the suit's lapel.

A ventriloquist's dummy.

What in hell . . . ?

He turned and stumbled back toward the shore, trying to re-move the hook from the cloth as he went. The doll was heavy now that it was out of the water. Holding it by the neck, he ran his free hand down the front of the torso as if he were frisking it. Heavy lumps bulged at the hips. Reaching dry ground, he laid his rod down, took a seat on the shelf of embankment above the strip of beach, and began to examine the dummy.

The heavy lumps were large lead fishing weights that had been jammed into the tiny pockets of the jacket. One of them had a scrap of cloth wrapped around it. He unwound it and flattened it against his knee. He could make out the remains of crude lettering, but what-ever it had said was indecipherable now. The face leered at him with its look of mock expectation. He yanked the hook from the lapel, tearing cloth, and flung the doll down.

What the hell was going on?

It was a one-in-a-thousand shot that he'd hooked it. So it couldn't have been intended for him. Pure, frightening chance. Still, what was it doing in the stream? His mind drifted as if searching for something it could never find. He shook his head like a dog drying itself and glanced upstream. Nothing there except white water bubbling over rocks as it had for a thousand years. The pounding of the waterfall had stopped now. Had he been imagining it?

How had the dummy gotten into the water, and why? He picked it up again and stared at it. Why had it scared him so? Why had he thought it might be Matty? Was he supposed to think that? No, that was crazy. He wasn't even meant to have found it.

A twig cracked somewhere in the woods in back of him.

Instinctively, he picked up his rod and moved to the upstream end of the sand where the taller shrubbery would conceal him from anyone in the woods.

Another sound. A rustle of leaves.

He thrust the dummy deep into the weeds on the bank, marked the spot with a rock he dug up from the beach, and turned to move downstream again. He caught sight of movement on the opposite shore, high up at the top of the knee.

He froze.

A man dressed in tan stood there with his hands on his hips. He was wearing reflector sunglasses.

There was another movement upstream. On the boulders above the waterfall, a similar figure appeared. His eyes too flashed silver.

It was no use trying to hide. They had spotted him.

"Senator," a voice called from somewhere behind him.

"Yes, I'm here," he called out absurdly.

More rustling and then a form appeared from the trees. It was dressed like the others in tan slacks and windbreaker.

"Senator Schlafer?"

"Yes," he said.

"Sorry to sneak up on you, sir."

"Jesus."

The man stepped lightly down onto the sand and signaled with his arm to the others.

"What in hell are you doing here?"

The man came halfway to attention. "Lieutenant John Molloy, Senator Schlafer. The President wants to see you. Right away."

"The President?"

"Didn't they call you?"

"My only phone is in my camper. How in hell did you get here?"

"You didn't hear the chopper? We thought we'd spooked every fish in the river." He whistled sharply and signaled once more to the men on the opposite shore.

"They didn't need spooking. Look, Molloy, I need ten minutes to change and stow my gear."

"No, sir. The President wants you right away. You can go as you are. We've got permission to land on the White House lawn.

"Jesus, what's the rush?"

"One of the men will take care of your fishing gear. You can give him your waders and stuff. We'll have you back out here again by this afternoon, if you want. Though frankly, sir, it seems a bit cold for the trout."

"You have the helicopter right here?"

"Marine One. Up in Big Meadows. We drove in from there. It's amazing you didn't hear us."

"I guess I did."

"Come on, then. We have to hurry."

"I'm right behind you."

He looked once more at the stream. The men on the other side were gone. Feeling like a child caught playing hooky, he turned and followed Molloy into the woods.

2.

The President

They banked to the right until the sun was directly ahead of them, a painful yellow blaze just above the horizon. Nick clipped his sunglasses on. He thought he knew why the President wanted to see him, but as he scanned the city below for familiar landmarks—the Pentagon and Arlington Cemetery lying side by side appropriately, the Potomac River winding away on the left into the hazy distance, the White House gleaming up ahead like a slightly used bar of soap—he could not focus his thoughts. The helicopter dipped, and Molloy's handset burst into unintelligible squawks. Nick shrugged to himself. It was not exactly as if he would be meeting a stranger.

The aircraft slowed, tilted, and steadied; the people waiting on the ground expanded to normal size. Nick leaned closer to Molloy and shouted in his ear, "Can you really land me here, on the lawn?"

Molloy turned and shouted back: "You're one of the few from the Hill to do this since Hale Boggs during the Cuban missile crisis. They flew him straight from the Gulf of Mexico and choppered him here from Andrews still stinking of fish."

"At least those fish were biting," Nick yelled. Following Molloy, he clambered through the hatch.

Just beyond the landing pad, Molloy introduced Nick to a Navy admiral. Nick failed to catch his name above the pounding of the rotors, but his nameplate said Turner. He led Nick briskly across an expanse of lawn bordered by thick clusters of daffodils still swaying in the wash of the prop, and through an entrance beneath a canopy. They climbed the grand staircase and went down a long corridor to a small cluttered room off to the right.

Stepping to the center of the room, Nick turned to face his escort, ready to make conversation. But Turner was gone and a man in civilian clothes was standing next to the doorway staring into the distance. Nick moved to the far end of the room, where he saw an advance copy of the latest *U.S. News & World Report* lying on a shelf in front of the window. He looked closer at the cover. The drawing on it resembled the illustration of the caterpillar on the mushroom in *Alice in Wonderland*. But instead of the caterpillar holding the hookah pipe, Nick saw what he realized was a caricature of himself.

He picked up the magazine and examined the drawing by the light from the window. Clouds of whatever he was sucking from the hookah wreathed his head, which was tipped back and turned to the right so that the viewer could make out his image. Leaning against the stem of the mushroom was a fishing rod and a clutch of dead fish. Alice, on tiptoe, was peering above the edge of the mushroom and asking through a word balloon filled with old-fashioned script, "Sir, do you really intend to make drugs legal?"

His features had been savagely exaggerated: the shock of steel-gray hair that fell across his broad forehead, his downward drooping eyes behind his aviator glasses, his aquiline nose and sharp, dimpled chin. His face was an inverted triangle. By drawing him with his head tilted back the artist had given him an absurdly haughty look. But he had caught the essence of Nick's face, the slightly helpless smile and raised eyebrows that made him look, Nick had always thought, like a handsome lightweight.

"Admiring yourself, Nick?"

He turned to see the President coming toward him, his broad face radiant and his arms flung wide. He was casually dressed in gray corduroys and a dark-blue V-neck sweater over a light-blue shirt with an open collar. Nick put the magazine back and stepped to meet him in the center of the room. For a moment it seemed right to embrace him, but he ended up grasping him stiffly by the shoulders.

"It's great to see you . . . Mr. President."

"Cut the formality, Nick," he said, grasping him by the upper arm and guiding him to a black leather armchair in the corner. "Sorry to spoil your fishing."

"There wasn't much. It's a cold April."

The President narrowed his eyes. "Is the American public aware that the Junior Senator from Pennsylvania owns a private cabin next to Camp Hoover? Isn't your place in a wildlife preserve?"

"Actually not. It's different land, upstream."

"But it's in a national park. Shenandoah."

"It's private land. My grandfather bought it legitimately."

"Thanks to his friendship with a President. I don't know, Nick. That smells a lot like special privilege to me." He squeezed Nick's arm. "But don't worry about it."

"I'm not."

"I'm just looking for a little leverage in case I ever need it."

"All's fair in politics, huh?"

"What was that thing called? The bear's throne?"

"My God! You were down there once. I forgot."

"Hard to believe you would have entertained a shabby liberal, huh?" He pushed Nick to sit down. "A near pinko!"

"I was just getting to know the enemy."

"You were something of a hippie yourself back then, if memory serves."

Nick found himself sitting, with the President standing over him, too close to allow him to get up again. He felt like a child looking up at a grown-up. "Well, it was a long time ago."

The President shook his head and rocked back on his heels, grinning lopsidedly. "Seems like yesterday to me." His dark eyes flashed amusement. After a moment, he moved to a black leather couch next to Nick's chair. He sat down, folded his hands over his right knee, and looked at Nick.

Nick spoke to break the silence. "So how is it, Mr. President?"

"How is what?"

Nick looked around and extended his right hand. "All this. Being President."

"You mean we haven't talked since the inauguration?"

"A dozen times. But never alone."

"Forgive me, Nick. So many people. One loses track." He shook his head. "No, that sounds like—"

"Please. I understand. I've kinda been . . ."

The President nodded. "Anyway, how is it? I'll tell you: It's light years from Princeton." He patted Nick's arm. "Now, how are you? How's Josie?"

"Holding together. I've been more or less out of circulation since—"

"We were so sorry."

"We were grateful for your note."

The President nodded.

"We're separated, you know." Nick said.

"Yes, we heard."

"Temporarily, I hope."

The President shook his head. "Incredible thing. How old was she?"

"Seventeen. She would have been eighteen last month."

"A child."

"It was suicide."

"Really?"

"That's what they say."

"You don't believe it?"

"Not really."

"Why, Nick?"

Nick sighed. "Lore just wasn't a child who'd kill herself."

"What was the cause of death?"

"Either blood loss or a heroin OD. They couldn't say for sure."

The President nodded.

"But she did leave one clue."

"Yes?"

"Something she wrote on the wall. The word 'Red.' And then the letters 'H' and 'O' and an indecipherable line. With her own . . . blood." He squeezed his eyes shut and bit his lip.

"Hope. Hole. Home," the President said. "House. Red house."

"Maybe."

"What does it mean?"

"I don't know."

"Why wouldn't she have tried to write the name of her killer?"

"Because she didn't know him?" Nick shook his head. "That's another mystery. There was no sign of a break-in, obviously."

"What do the police say?"

"Nothing. A dead end. Suicide."

"The FBI come up with anything?"

"Nothing," Nick said.

"How long has it been?"

"Since it happened?"

"Yes."

"It was last February eleventh." Nick looked at his watch. "One year, two months, thirteen hours, and fifty minutes." He looked up. "Approximately."

"A bad year for you."

"To put it mildly. She was pregnant, you know."

The President studied him. "Yes, I'd heard," he said softly.

Nick nodded. "It's true. About four months."

"Any idea by whom?"

"None. But we have DNA samples."

"They can fingerprint the father from the fetus?"

"That's what they tell me. Apparently the sequences remain unique even after they combine in the child."

"Amazing."

"Yes, but you've got to have someone to match the samples up with, so how do you find him?"

The President was quiet for a moment. Then he said, "Anything I can do, just give me a call."

"Thanks."

"I mean it, Nick. Call me."

"I appreciate it," Nick said. He averted his eyes and let them fall on a ship model in a glass case on the windowsill. It was a whaler, he thought. Somewhere he could hear the sound of a clock ticking.

He looked back. "Well, Mr. President, I'm sure you didn't send for me to make small talk."

"This isn't small talk, Nick." He sighed and pounded the fist of his right hand against the palm of his left. "But you're right." He looked over at the doorway. A steward in a white jacket was waiting. "Something to drink?"

"Coffee would be fine."

"Coffee for both of us," the President said.

Nick leaned back in his chair.

The President looked at him again. "Nick, this drug bill of yours. I don't like it."

Nick let out his breath. "Well, I didn't really expect you to."

"It's not going to work."

"Prohibition hasn't worked, Mr. President. Before the Harrison

Act was passed in 1914, drugs were a middle-class thing. And not a terrible problem."

The steward reappeared, followed by another white-jacketed man wheeling a table laden with dishware. The steward set a tray down on a table between the armchair and the couch. He poured coffee.

"Thank you, Lewis," the President said. He poured cream and stirred.

"The irony," Nick went on, "is that Harrison wasn't meant to prohibit. It placed discretion in the hands of doctors. Then Harry Anslinger and his enforcers moved in."

The President sipped his coffee and put up his hand.

"I didn't mean to make a speech," Nick said. "Forgive me."

"I've been very strong on drugs, Nick. I've brought Emery Frankfurt over from the CIA and made him Drug Czar. I've made him a member of the National Security Council—the only Republican on it, I might add. I've transferred the entire drug-fighting bureaucracy to his jurisdiction—every last agency including the relevant parts of the FBI, which hasn't been easy, believe me. Even got the Congress to make it an executive department. And I've asked for all the money he wants. So it's up to you people now."

"It's just the wrong approach," Nick said. "Enforcement isn't going to work. The English tried it. They've gone back to legalization. Here even Federal District judges are in rebellion. They're refusing to take drug cases."

The President put down his coffee and steepled his fingers. "Aside from disagreeing with you, I'm concerned about your bill being a distraction. We have other priorities."

"I won't dispute that."

"We have a budget to prepare and a deficit to cut."

"My drug bill contributes to that. It cuts the costs of the enforcement bureaucracy."

The President looked at Nick. "We have a tax bill to pass."

Nick smiled. "Well, of course I'm opposed to you there."

"A progressive tax bill," the President added.

"You're not going to get it. You have a Republican majority in the Senate to contend with on that."

"Nick, the deficit is killing this country. How do you propose to get rid of it?"

"By cutting costs. You know that's where I stand."

"But we're going to have to compromise."

"Not me. That's not what I was elected to do. I'll vote to shut Washington down if it comes to that."

"You'd stop a continuing appropriations resolution?"

"Absolutely. If it doesn't better than balance the budget. And there's a majority with me on that one too."

The President stood up and walked across the room. "We've got six months to change your mind."

"You won't."

"Then it's going to be a tense October." He scanned the book-shelves as if looking for a title.

He spoke without turning. "This room was once Edith Kermit Roosevelt's private library. My wife's a fan of hers, though how she can admire one of you Republicans is beyond me. She's tried to re-store it. I doubt it looks much like it did in the Roosevelts' day."

"The TV set and fax machine are a little jarring," Nick said. He pushed himself to the edge of his chair.

"What's your point, Nick?" the President asked without turning.

"My point?"

"The point of your drug bill." He continued to scan the shelves. "It'll never pass the Senate."

Nick stood up. "Probably not. But it's going to focus attention on the issue." He ticked off items on his fingers. "It's going to be sent to committee. We're going to hold hearings there. Then we'll vote it onto the floor. And it'll be debated by the full Senate. The public will learn about alternatives to this wasteful war on drugs."

"And then the Senate'll vote it down." The President turned around. "Which committee?"

"Judiciary. Mine."

"You think you have the support there?"

"I know I do. I have a majority."

"Who, for instance? Ted Diefendorfer?"

"Yes," Nick said. "Among others."

The President tucked his chin in and drawled from the side of the mouth. "Bilge Pump Diefendorfer. I hope you caught him sober. Who else?"

"Calder. Pereira. Others."

"How do you know? They promised you? That's worth about a barrel of cow dung."

"They more than promised. They've cheered me on and guaran-teed their support."

"Then they're setting you up."

"Maybe so. But the issue will be spotlighted."

The President came back across the room and sat down.

"How old are you, Nick?"

"Almost fifty-four."

"How long have you been in the Senate?"

"Nine years."

"You like it?"

"Compared to what?"

"Oh, I don't know. Fishing?" He waited a moment and then laughed. "It's just I never figured you for a politician, Nick."

"It's a hereditary disorder."

"Yeah, I always forget your granddad. But you don't, do you? Down there in his cabin?"

"I'm grateful for what he gave me, yes. But I had ambitions of my own."

"Had?"

"Have." Nick glanced at the doorway. It was empty. "Is this off the record?"

"Of course, Nick. Why else would I be meeting you here, over the store, on a Saturday morning?"

"Okay, I admit it's getting tougher all the time. My next campaign's gonna cost ten million, we figure. Everyone thinks I'd rather fish than legislate. And my sense is that the tide is turning—the country's moving left."

"So maybe you don't really give a shit anymore?"

"I wouldn't say that! I mean the time is right to push this legislation."

"Easy, Nick."

Nick leaned back in his chair and took a deep breath.

The President looked at him again. "Tell me honestly. Don't you think you're letting your daughter—"

"Am I letting Lore's death influence me?" Nick stood up and went to the window. "Of course I am. And a lot of other things. But give me some credit. It's not just emotional."

"First you drop out for a year. Then you come up with this. It's hard to read it any other way but emotional. How far have you actually gone?"

"We're taking more polls. We've put out feelers to the House. We've talked—"

"To who?"

Nick rubbed the back of his head. "House leaders. Lobbyists. Drug experts. Medical people. I'm going to be speaking around the country."

"Have you heard from or been in touch with anyone in the . . . uh . . . drug business?"

"You mean like dealers?"

"I mean criminals at any level."

"No. Though we intend to call some of them in to testify. With immunity, of course."

The President glanced at the doorway. Somewhere a clock began to chime the hour.

Nick counted to himself.

The President looked back at Nick. "There was an incident last night," he said.

Nick felt the blood leave his face.

"It looks like a street thing, some kind of shoot-out."

"What happened?"

"Emery Frankfurt's number-two man got caught in the crossfire."

Nick swallowed. "John Holden?"

"He's in the ICU at Walter Reed."

"Jesus!"

"He was shot in front of his apartment on Q Street."

Nick shook his head.

"Did you . . . Do you know Holden?"

"I've never laid eyes on him."

"He's his own man. Tells you what he thinks."

Nick came back to his seat. "I'm so sorry about this, Mr. President. But I'm not sure I see . . ."

The President leaned closer to Nick and lowered his voice. "Holden shares some of your views. He's been distressed about the mission of the Drug Control Department. He was moving in his own direction."

Nick shook his head.

"He never contacted you?"

"Never."

"We think he was for legalization, and the mob didn't like it. We suspect they hit him."

Nick stood up and walked back to the window. He looked at the ship's rigging again and wondered who could have had the patience to weave such tiny webs. "I appreciate your concern, Mr. President. But I find any connection between me and Holden a little far-fetched."

"Well, my Drug Czar doesn't."

"Mr. President!" an insistent voice spoke from the doorway. Turner had come back with two men Nick didn't recognize.

The President stood up and let his breath out audibly. "Excuse me, Senator," he said and went to the doorway. He pulled one of the men aside and disappeared from Nick's view.

The other stranger stood in the doorway. "The President will be back in a moment, Senator."

Nick nodded. He looked at his watch. He had been there about twenty minutes.

The President reappeared and crossed the room toward him. Nick tried to read his face, but it was expressionless.

"Forgive me, Nick." He came within arm's reach and picked at a piece of lint on the shoulder of Nick's sweater. "Holden's gone. He never came out of the coma."

"Jesus!"

"Look, I've got to excuse myself now." He took Nick by the elbow and turned him back to the window. "But I want you to do something for me."

Nick looked at his face. All trace of warmth was gone from it.

"I want you to talk with Secretary Frankfurt. Right away."

"Well, I'd love to, but—"

"Do this for me, Nick. You know him. The two of you go way back, don't you?"

"To childhood, practically. But he's impossible to see these days."

"Mr. President," a voice called from the hallway.

"Where are you headed from here, Nick?"

"To my office, I guess."

"Call Emery as soon as you get there. He's expecting your call."

"All right, Mr. President."

"You two can work together. You talk to him, don't you?"

"Sure. When I can."

He put his hand on Nick's shoulder, turned him away from the window, and began to move him across the room. "I know I can count on you."

"Of course, Mr. President."

"And Nick, I want you to stay in touch. Feel free to call me." He flicked a hand toward the door. "They'll give you a number. You can reach me at any time. I want you to"—he paddled the air with his hand—"keep in contact." The warmth came back into his eyes. "Will you do that?"

Nick looked at him and nodded.

"After all, I have to know which way the country is moving, so I can lead it, right? And give Josie my love when you talk to her." He turned away and was gone.

"Your car is on its way, Senator," Turner said.

"My car? I don't use a car, Admiral."

"You do now. Come with me, please."

Nick followed Turner the length of the corridor, down the broad stairway, and out to the front of the North Portico. A black Lincoln limousine stood waiting there. The air had softened in the brilliant April sunshine. The darkened window of the car reflected Nick's and Turner's images, grotesquely wide—distortions in a funhouse mirror.

3

The Secretary

After a couple of shaky stabs with his key, Nick unlocked the door that led directly into his office in the Russell Building and went quickly to the chair behind his cluttered desk. He picked up the handset of his private telephone. As he reached for the button next to his wife's name there was a knock on the door to his outer offices. Dave Segal, his administrative assistant, peered in, his eyes blinking behind the thick lenses of his glasses.

"Yes, Dave?"

"You hear about Holden?"

"Yeah."

"Another victim of the war on drugs. It helps our cause."

"Don't be cynical, Dave."

Segal pushed the door open wider and flapped a sheaf of computer printouts. "I got the latest polls."

"How'd you know I was here?"

"Your new driver phoned in to alert us. She sounds efficient." He stepped through the door, scuttled past a row of chairs, and stood in front of Nick's desk, shifting his weight from one foot to the other. He was tieless, and his lightweight tan sports jacket was, like the dark suits he wore on weekdays, a size too large, presumably to hide his weight. Except for a dark fringe of hair, his head was bald and shiny. As he spoke, he thrust his face forward vulturelike.

"Look, Dave—"

"Just give me a minute. A lot is happening." His voice was high and insistent.

"I really can't now, Dave. I wasn't even planning to be in Washington today."

"What did the White House want?"

Nick leaned back in his chair and regarded Segal, who continued to peer back over the papers in his hands. "You know something—I really couldn't tell you."

"Did you see the President?"

Nick nodded.

"And?"

"He doesn't like our drug bill."

"That's no surprise."

Nick shrugged. "He wants me to see Emery."

"What for?"

Nick picked up a pencil and tapped it against the edge of his desk. "I guess to pressure me."

Segal backed up and draped his lumpy figure over two of the chairs. "How's he going to pressure you?"

"I can't imagine." He flipped the pencil back onto the desk. "But I'm sure we'll see."

"There aren't going to be any unpleasant surprises, are there?"

"What's that supposed to mean, Dave?"

"I mean something I don't know about your relationship with Emery. You never talk about it."

"There isn't all that much to talk about."

"Come on! He was part of your family."

"Yeah, but he's, uh, fourteen years older than I am. I was a child when he first showed up. He was maybe eighteen. That's a heck of a gap, especially for a kid."

"You must have looked up to him. That could give him some kind of an edge."

"Oh, sure I did. I worshipped him. Sometimes I wished he was my father. But he wasn't around that much."

"Why not?"

"My grandfather had him running one of his businesses in

Wheelersville—the family drugstore. Then Emery made his fortune with a chain of drugstores of his own and kind of disappeared."

"I thought you were close."

"I wish we were. I see him at big family gatherings like Christmas. But he plays in a different league."

"Well, if you think of anything he might use, you better tell me."

"I will. But there's nothing. Anyway, he wouldn't do that . . . bring the family into this, for God's sake." He slapped the desktop and noticed that the red light on his telephone console was flashing. "Who's in the office today, Dave?"

"I've got a full crew out there. Abby Stevens is here too." He gestured toward the outer office. "We have a draft of your drug speech ready."

"I'll just be making a comment when I introduce the bill. The speech will go into the *Record*."

Segal stood up again. "And I have these new polls. Where we compare the words 'legalization' with 'decriminalization.' They're going to make you happy."

Nick put up his hand and leaned back in his chair. "I'll tell you what's concerning me." He flapped his hand. "Sit down, Dave. What's worrying me—Is our majority firm? Or are they gonna fold when the pressure comes."

"In Judiciary?"

"Well, in the subcommittee, to put first things first."

"Absolutely. No sweat. We're solid, four to one. We're not going to get the one. But the other four—"

"Because we've got to have the subcommittee."

"I talked to Calder early this week. He's fine. He's reliable. And I talked to Diefendorfer yesterday. It was all fair winds and full sails. And Pereira's with him. You're the fourth. It's a lock. Besides, they want to see you catch the lightning on this issue."

"What about the full committee?"

"I'm working on it. I'm starting to twist arms."

"Let's go easy on that."

"On what?"

"On twisting arms. I want this to be as clean as possible. The object is just to debate this thing."

"Sure, Nick."

"Keep in mind that this bill is never going to pass the Senate."

"I disagree."

"So there's no point in making a lot of enemies." Nick looked at his phone. "I better take this call."

Segal flapped the sheaf of papers in his hand. "You've got to see these polls. Turn on your terminal."

"Not now."

"This is important."

"Give me the gist."

"The gist is that even people against legalization are in favor of investing more in educating people on drugs. That's the opening wedge of our bill."

"Has Abby seen these figures yet?"

"No." Segal waved his hand dismissively. "Plus, where we substitute the word 'decriminalization' for 'legalization,' we get a major shift in our favor."

"Hmmm." Nick looked at the flashing light on his phone and made a gesture as if to reject it. He leaned back in his chair. "Let me ask a dumb question, Dave. Why are some people so strongly against legalization?"

"Americans are against sin. And what did Jesse Jackson once say: 'You don't win a war by surrendering'?"

"The Japanese did. They proved that surrender is waging war by other means."

"That's too deep for me. I'm a tactician, not a philosopher."

Nick looked at the flashing red light again. "I've got a red call here. I better take it."

As Segal retreated, Nick pushed the button on his intercom. "What's happening, Abby?"

His executive secretary's voice came coolly over the line. "Secretary Frankfurt called. His office wants you to get back to him soonest. He's at home."

"Good. I'm just going to phone my wife first."

"She called, too."

"Yes?" He held his breath, the image of the dummy in his mind.

"She just wanted to see if by chance you were going to be in town this evening."

He let his breath out slowly. "We'll call the Secretary as soon as I've talked to Josie."

"The phones are going crazy, and it's Saturday. Also, that Mr. Rizzo called."

Nick nodded to himself. "That figures. If he calls again, I'll talk to him."

"I can handle him."

"I know, but I better talk to him." He picked up his private handset again and pushed the button for his wife.

The phone rang three times before she answered, "Yes."

"Josie?"

"Where on earth are you calling from?"

"My office."

"And how is the fishing there, Senator?"

"I had to come back suddenly, for reasons I'll tell you later."

"When *is* 'later'?"

"How are you?"

"I've been worse. I've been better."

"How's Matty?"

"He's fine."

"What's he been up to?"

"He bought a Morgan dollar yesterday."

"Good. What year?"

"I forget. Nick, I was wondering if you were free this evening."

"Well, I have to be in town for a TV appearance tomorrow. What did you have in mind?"

"A date."

"With?"

"With the Russian ambassador. With *you*, Nick."

"I'm sorry. Yes."

"Jessica is giving one of her evenings."

"I thought they spent their weekends in Virginia."

"Someone came to town on short notice. One of Tom's ambassador friends."

"Sounds fairly deadly."

"Actually not. It's her 'A' list."

"How big is that?"

"Thirty intimate friends. And a columnist or two. But suit yourself, Nick. I can always snag an escort."

"No, I'd like to go."

"It's just for dinner. No strings."

"Come on, Josie."

"Sorry."

"Don't worry about it. Where's Matty now?"

"He's upstairs with a friend."

"Which one?"

"Mike Doran. They're going to the movies later."

"With who?"

"Mike's mother. Or if she can't make it, Clara can always take them. Nick, forgive me for saying this. But why the sudden intense interest? Is there something I should know about?"

He closed his eyes and forced his voice to relax. "Nothing whatever. I'll call you later about tonight."

"Not necessary. If I don't hear from you, I'll expect you at the house for a drink at six."

"Sounds good. Bye, Josie."

"It's black tie. Don't forget."

"Right."

"Goodbye, fox."

He hung up, swiveled the leather chair around so that he could look out the window, and let his mind drift. In the distance, through the barely budding trees in the park, he could see pedestrians crowding around the fountain in front of Union Station. He raised his eyes to the station itself, and then to cathedrals of clouds towering above. It would still be too cool and windy down at the camp. It was just as well he'd had to come back to town.

He yawned, stretched, and watched a jetliner inching its way across the backdrop of clouds. Why was the President so eager for him to meet with Emery? What did Emery have in mind? Well, it would be good to see Emery. It had been too long. The jet disappeared behind the left edge of the window. He looked back toward the horizon and imagined the Rapidan flowing somewhere beyond it. Once again he could feel the dead weight on his line and see the dummy rising out of the murk. Had he really hooked that thing this morning? Or was it a dream? Wait, the Rapidan was to the south, and he was looking north now. Why did he always make that mistake?

He closed his eyes, pushed his glasses up onto his forehead, squeezed the bridge of his nose between his thumb and index finger, and watched the negative image of the window scene until it faded to darkness. It would be a relief to get home to Wheelersville for Carnival Day in June. It would be a time to start mending things with Matty. They would fish together again. The sulphurs might be coming off the streams by then. He could feel himself relax at the thought.

The buzzer on his intercom sounded sharply.

He leaned forward in his chair, spun it slowly around, and depressed the button.

"Yes, Abby?"

"Secretary Frankfurt's on two."

"Thanks."

He picked up the handset. "Emery!"

"Nick, my boy!"

"It's been too long."

"Yes! Where have you been?"

"I heard the news about John Holden."

"Devastating."

"Is there anything I can do?"

"We must talk. Are you free for lunch?"

"Sure," Nick said. "Terrific. It'll be good to catch up."

"Meet me at the White House Mess. At one of the clock."

There was a tap on the door to Nick's outer office. It opened enough to reveal Abby's face. Nick waved her in. She opened the door and entered, her heavy necklace and bracelets jingling.

"Look, Emery," Nick said. "We should meet in private."

"Where, then?"

"How about my hideaway?"

"Your sanctum sanctorum. Fair enough. What's on the menu?"

"I'll have one of my people pick up a couple of burgers."

"Come, Nick. If we're going to eat, we may as well treat ourselves. What do you fancy?"

"Doesn't matter. Something light."

"I'll order something from La Colline. Let me surprise you. This will be fun."

"Fine, Emery. But you're going to have to bring it yourself, because there's no way it can be delivered."

"I'll order from here, and pick it up on the way in. What about a wine? How say you to a 1987 Corton-Charlemagne? Or better still, a Montrachet?"

"You know that's not something I know much about, Em."

"You're undercivilized, Nick. I've always said it."

"I'll see you around one. Leave your car on the Senate side. I'm in the basement. Take a left beyond the elevators. I'm SB-Five. Just knock three times."

"My goodness! Should I come armed?"

"Yeah, with lunch."

"Looking forward."

"Me too." Nick hung up and looked at Abby, who was standing

behind one of the chairs facing his desk, tapping a file folder against the top of the backrest. She was tall and full-figured. Her graying blond hair was pulled back into a ponytail, emphasizing her high cheekbones and large gray eyes.

Nick shook his head. "It's hard to believe he's one of the tough guys in Washington."

"Meaning?"

"You know: 'What shall we eat? What shall we drink?' Sit down, Abby."

She circled the chair and alighted as if about to take off again. "Come on, Nick," she said. "There's no contradiction between taste and tough-mindedness."

"You're right. It's just hard to believe he started out as a pill salesman."

"I apologize for breaking in on you. But I've got to run and I want to bring you up to date."

Nick checked his watch. He had some time. He leaned back in his chair again. "You know where I came here from?"

Abby shrugged. "You know I do. Your fishing camp. And it's greatly in evidence from the look and smell of you."

"Wrong. I was at the White House. Got flown in on Marine One."

"To see Himself?"

"Over a cup of coffee."

"What for, if I may ask?"

"I'm not really sure. We talked about a lot of things, and it was cordial. But when I left I still didn't have a clue why he'd wanted to see me."

"Maybe he forgot."

"Unlikely."

"I've heard that when Reagan called people in for meetings, he'd sometimes forget what he wanted to see them about. Had to buzz Don Regan to remind him. Probably just one of those stories."

"This President doesn't forget what he wants to see you about. He just wasn't tipping his hand."

She slid back in her chair, as if picking up Nick's cue to relax. "You don't look entirely presentable," she said.

He nodded. "I know." He looked at his watch again. "I'm not going to have time for a shower. Guess I'll have to use the sink." He stood up and peeled off his sweater. He stooped and opened the bottom drawer of his desk, took out an electric shaver, switched it on, and began to shave. "So what have you got, Abby?"

"Just a long list of phone calls and some letters that need your real signature. You'll find the phone calls in your computer, in the usual file. But I made a printout for you." She touched the folder on her lap. "Are you coming in Monday?"

"I'm going to have to get down to the camp again before I leave. To pick up the wagon and my gear. Maybe tomorrow evening. I'll fish Monday morning."

"Alone?"

He looked at her. Her face was blank, her gray eyes cool. "Yes," he said.

She shook her head.

"Look, Abby. You've been with me how long now?"

She shrugged. "Since Harrisburg. Ten years?"

"In all that time, have I ever not fished alone?"

"It just seems lonely."

"It's a sport you pretty much do alone."

She stood up, put the folder on his desk, and went to the door.

"Listen," Nick said. "Give Jimmy what's-his-name a call. The park ranger."

"Prentice."

"Right. Ask him to check the cabin, see that the guys who picked me up put my gear back. I left a dirty mess kit by the sink. I'm worried it'll attract mice."

"All right."

"See you Monday afternoon?" he said.

She opened the door, and then turned back to him. "Good luck with the director of the Office of Drug Control Policy."

"It's the Department of Drug Control now. That's why his title's Secretary. You know that."

"You better be on your toes with him."

"Oh, come on. I know Emery."

She went out, closing the door behind her.

At ten to one Nick left his office and set off down the empty corridor. His footsteps echoed around him. As always when he thought of Emery Frankfurt, he pictured a tall silver-haired man cradling a shotgun in his arms. This made no sense, because the reality behind the image dated from Nick's childhood, when Emery would have been still in his late teens. Nick tried to remember the slim golden-haired youth who used to shoot clay pigeons with his grandfather, Big Stash, every Saturday morning in the autumn of . . .

When would it have been? After World War II. 1949? 1950? Nick would have been six or seven, and Emery nineteen or twenty.

He stepped into the elevator and pressed the button for the basement.

Emery would call out, "Pull, Stash," rotate his torso fluidly, raise the shotgun, and shatter the skeet every time. Nick had felt a little uncomfortable hearing Emery call his grandfather Stash. Emery was too young for that. But Nick's grandfather never seemed to mind. To him, Emery Frankfurt could do nothing wrong.

He stepped off the elevator and turned into the passageway that led to the Senate subway.

Then he thought of the fight. All he could remember about it was waking up to the sound of muffled shouting and slamming doors. But it had been some kind of turning point, because afterward his father seemed to fade from his life, and Emery was there in his place, a cross between a stepfather and a brother. The fight was painful to think about. He had to force himself to focus on the words he had overheard.

The subway car started up smoothly.

It must have happened around 1950, when Nick was seven, because he had always associated it with the arrival in the mail of the Samuel Gompers first-day cover, which had made his grandfather, Big Stash, harrumph with contempt that they would put "that Limey labor leader" on an American commemorative stamp. Nick could remember the dark shapes of his stuffed animals surrounding him like sentinels as he strained in the dark to make out the angry but tantalizingly incomprehensible words that had been shouted back and forth. It had certainly happened before 1953, because Nick's father, Little Stash, would have turned thirty that October, and he was not there for his birthday. That was something Nick's mother talked about that year. His father would have been only thirty, and he had gone away. His mother had too, a year or so later. Both had died shortly after, his father of pneumonia, though his drinking hadn't helped, his mother of cancer. So Nick had never found out exactly what the fight had been about. Eventually it had gotten to be one of those things he always meant to ask about but never remembered to when there was an opportunity.

He dismounted the subway car, climbed the ramp next to the escalators, and turned left just beyond the elevators.

There was no sound in the yellow maze that led to his hideaway. The entire Capitol seemed implausibly empty of life.

When he reached the entrance of SB-5, he took his keys from his pocket and opened the door. Since the room lacked windows, it was pitch-dark inside. He reached for the wall switch to the left of the door, snapped on the overhead light, and stepped into the room. It was wedge-shaped, its wider end to the left and its back wall concave, to accommodate some architectural feature of the original Capitol Building that Nick had never bothered to figure out. The place had been vacuumed and neatened, but it still smelled faintly of tobacco smoke from a meeting he had held there several nights before.

He pushed the door shut, looked up at the blank video monitor above the entrance, and snapped on the security-system switch that was on the wall panel next to the light switch. A wide-angle view of the empty hallway outside appeared on the screen.

He stepped to his desk, which was just to the left of the entrance, and turned on the three-power lamp to the second level. He surveyed the room. The bright blue upholstery against the gray wall-to-wall carpet and the ivory walls lent the room a slightly formal, ceremonial cast. His face in the mirror over the sofa looked haggard despite his having shaved.

He stepped to the long coffee table in front of the sofa, gathered up file folders, magazines, a glass ashtray, and a silver cigarette lighter, and arranged them neatly on his desk. He picked up the chair behind the desk and set it next to the coffee table, facing the couch. He moved the coffee table six inches to the right, so that it was a comfortable distance from the low armchair that stood to the right at the narrow end of the room. He looked around again, then went to a cupboard, got out a glass tumbler and a bottle of Courvoisier and poured himself a half inch of the amber liquid. He sipped it and shuddered as the heat hit his stomach. He returned to the narrow end of the room, pulled open a door in the corner beyond the couch, and entered the cramped bathroom that had been installed there by some enterprising predecessor. He set the glass of brandy down on the edge of the sink, splashed cold water on his face, wiped himself dry with a towel from a wall rack, took up the brandy glass again, flicked it through the stream of cold water to dilute its contents, stepped out, and closed the door.

The hallway on the video monitor was still empty. He leaned against the edge of his desk, took another swallow of brandy, and looked at his watch. It was ten past one. Was Emery having trouble finding him?

He drained his glass, keeping his eye on the monitor. The sound of footsteps from the loudspeaker came first, then two figures swept into view, one of them dressed in a white suit that shimmered on the screen. Both of them were carrying what looked like heavy objects.

There was a single light tap on the door.

"Who is it?" Nick called.

"Emery, of course!"

Suppressing the urge to ask who was with him, Nick pulled open the door. The white-suited figure strode forward, set down a large cube-shaped metal case he was carrying, and spread wide his arms. Nick stepped into the embrace and returned it, pressing his face against Emery's. The familiar smell of cologne made him feel at ease for an instant. Then he stepped back and looked at the dark-suited man who was standing in back of Emery, holding two metal cases like the one Emery had set down.

"What's going on, Emery?"

Emery's eyes regarded him seriously, though his mouth was smiling. He flicked his hand. "This is Raymond."

Nick nodded.

The dark-suited man nodded and said, "Hello, Senator." He stepped forward, and set the cases down next to the coffee table Nick had cleared. "Stand back and watch, Nick," Emery said. He passed his hand through the air as if waving a wand.

His companion removed the lid from one of the cases, reached into it, and with a crisp snap unfurled into the air a white tablecloth, which he guided down onto the table. Beside the table went all three cases, and out came dishes, tureens, platters, silverware, glasses, napkins, and an ice bucket filled with glistening chips. A metal dish cover was whisked away from a steaming platter; a cork was popped from a green perspiring bottle.

Emery stepped back and spread his arms again. "Behold!" he said, snapping his fingers over the dishes as he intoned: (Snap.) "Cold lobster soufflé." (Snap.) "Salade Mimosa." (Snap.) "A 1986 Montrachet." (Snap.) "Poached pears in chocolate cups." (Snap.) "Accompanied by a 1990 Taittinger comtes de Champagne." (Snap.) He pointed at Nick. "*You* no doubt will supply us with a brandy of dubious vintage."

"Christ, Emery," Nick said. "This is what you call something light?"

"As the French say, '*L'appétit vient en mangeant.*'" He turned to Raymond, who was stowing the cases in the corner beyond Nick's desk. "We'll be about two hours. Come back a little after three. Your pass will get you in." He removed a wine bottle from its bucket and began to pour. "So, Nick. Sit down."

Nick sat. "It's wonderful to see you again, Emery."

"Try the wine, Nick."

Nick sipped the wine, held it in his mouth, swallowed, smiled, and shrugged.

"Hopeless," Emery said. "You didn't even aerate it." He regarded Nick with a frown. "You look a mess."

"Between meeting you and the President, I haven't even had a chance to shower."

Emery lifted the platter of lobster and spooned a helping onto Nick's plate, then one onto his own. With the gravy boat he doused each portion with thick sauce.

"Now tell me if that isn't light."

Nick tasted a forkful. "It's good, Em. I admit it."

Emery took a sip of his wine, drew it through his front teeth, lifted his chin meditatively, and finally swallowed. "Give me your impressions of the President, Nick."

Nick thought a moment, shrugged. "I dunno. It's hard not to see him as the same familiar person. What do you think?"

"Entre nous, a lightweight. But I'm his humble servant—we all are. What about this bill of yours?"

"Oh, is that why we're having lunch, Mr. Secretary? I mean it's a pleasure to see you. But face it, you don't usually have time for this sort of thing."

Emery regarded him for moment with his troubled sooty eyes. He sighed and brought his head forward. "You're right, Nick. It was rude of me not to get straight to the point."

"Why did the President have me flown in from the camp?"

Emery frowned. "He did that?"

"Had his men pick me right off the stream. Landed me right on the White House lawn."

"Only family and heads of state."

"Come on, Em. You know all about this."

"Actually not *all*. Why don't you tell me what he talked about. Then perhaps I can interpret for you."

Nick separated a piece of soufflé with his fork and nudged it across his plate. "He talked about the Holden shooting. He hadn't gotten word of his death yet."

"Yes. Go on."

"He talked about my drug bill, obviously."

"Holden's death and your bill." Emery waved his fork in the air. "Well, there you have it."

"You don't mean the people who killed Holden are going to come after me?"

Emery put up his hand. "Wait. We don't know who killed Holden yet. Ostensibly he stumbled into a firefight."

"The President doesn't believe that. Neither do I."

"Hmm. It *could* have been an accident. But I tend to doubt it."

"So you think I'm in danger."

"There is a certain symmetry here. John was fed up with the war on drugs. Or so he indicated to me privately. You are about to introduce this legalization bill."

"Decriminalization."

"Whatever. In any case, we must take steps to protect you."

"Like this car and driver you've arranged for me."

"The car is bulletproof. The driver is a bodyguard and . . . quite resourceful, I'm told."

Nick smiled. "She's kind of small."

"Ah. Most deceptive." He poured them each more wine.

"Emery, I appreciate the gesture, but I don't want a car and driver. It's not my style."

"It's extremely important that you accept them, at least for the time being."

"How am I going to justify—"

"We have very good reason to believe that you're in danger."

Nick stood up, fetched the bottle of brandy and the empty glass from his desk, and poured himself some.

"You'll spoil your palate, Nick."

"Screw my palate." He took a mouthful and paced the length of his office, running his hand through his hair.

"There's no need to be nervous, Nick. We're very efficient."

Nick stopped and looked at him. Emery speared a leaf of salad, and raised a finger until he had finished chewing. "We'll also be discreet."

"It's not me I'm worried about. I doubt if anyone would be stupid enough to attack a U.S. Senator."

"Attack, no. But there are other unpleasant things they can do to you."

"Or my family."

"Exactly." Emery poured himself some more wine. He gestured with the bottle to Nick. Nick shook his head.

"Let me ask you this," Emery said.

Nick sat down again.

"And think very hard before you answer. Have you had any hint of a threat from anyone?"

Nick sipped his brandy.

"Or has anything unusual happened?" Emery added.

Nick put his glass down. He stood up again, went behind his desk, opened the bottom drawer, and brought out a pack of cigarettes."

"I'd forgotten you smoked, Nick."

"I haven't in a couple of years."

Emery raised his eyebrows.

Nick lit a cigarette and waved the match out. "The goddamnedest thing happened this morning, Em."

"Yes?"

The first lungful of smoke made Nick cough explosively. He put his hand on the table and waited until the dizziness passed. "Whew! Sorry." He cleared his throat. "Anyway, I was fishing at the Woman's Pool—"

"Ah, yes."

"From the rock on the camp-side shore. Just below the waterfall?"

"I remember. Where the big fish are."

"Yeah. I was casting a terrestrial there."

"The inner thigh. Your lovely fantasy."

"Right. I bounced a hopper against the wall and then began to pull in line fast when the fly had sunk in the current. The details are important."

"I'm listening."

"On the second or third cast, just when I began to retrieve the line—about maybe two or three feet from the wall, but in the current—I hooked what I thought was a fish. It was dead weight, but years ago I got fooled by that and lost what had to have been a lunker."

"Go on."

"When I finally retrieved the thing—downstream, in the shallow water below that little beach—it turned out to be a doll."

"A doll?"

"Yeah, like a ventriloquist's dummy. Charlie McCarthy, I think."

"How big?"

"The size of a small child."

"My God!"

"It was dressed in a black suit, red bow tie, shiny black shoes, and had a monocle stuck in its eye. It was weird."

"Surreal."

"It was new too."

"How so?"

"I mean brand-new. Not some piece of garbage that happened to be in the river."

"Yes, but it was pure coincidence that you hooked it. How could anyone have meant it for you?"

"Well, if someone knew the currents and the way I always fish that pool."

"That's not exactly common knowledge. And they would still have had to be watching you."

"Someone could have been, from above the waterfall. Or they could have had a lot of dolls, and kept throwing them in until I hooked one."

"That's a little paranoid, isn't it?"

"You just finished giving me a lot of reasons to be paranoid."

"It *is* disturbing. It also occurs to me that if you hadn't hooked the thing, it would have become visible in the shallow water at the tail of the pool, no?"

"Probably."

"You would have spotted it then, wouldn't you?"

"Damn right."

"So there was only one doll. Are you taking it as a threat to Matthew?"

"Do you blame me, after Lore?"

Emery lowered his head and took the last bite of his soufflé. "No. I can't say that I do."

Nick dragged on his cigarette and stubbed it out in the remains of his soufflé.

Emery said, "What did you do with the thing? I'd like to have our lab look it over."

"I stuck it under some dead leaves at the upstream end of the pool. I wanted to go on fishing. It had fishing weights in the pockets of its jacket. And a piece of cloth with writing on it that was mostly washed away."

"I'll see that it's picked up this evening."

"I'm going down tomorrow or Monday to get my gear. I could bring it back with me."

"No, I want it right away. We'll examine every thread."

"I'll tell you, it scared the shit out of me. For a moment I thought it *was* Matty."

"Let's have our dessert." Emery stood up, cleared the soufflé plates, and slid them roughly into a case. He set the poached pears in front of Nick and himself, drew a champagne bottle from the ice bucket, and began to pry up the wire loop at the neck. "This Taittinger should hit the spot." He untwisted the wire loop.

Nick found himself admiring Emery's sure-handedness.

"Let me ask you something, Nick. This doll . . . dummy." He looked at Nick. "Do you suppose your new friend could have had anything to do with it?"

"What new friend?"

"You know." Emery moved his hand from the wire to his face. He put his thumb against the tip of his nose and pressed it sideways.

Nick lowered his brandy glass. "What are you getting at?"

Emery gave a final twist to the wire and pulled it free. He began to work the cork back and forth. "This fellow who keeps calling you."

The cork came free with a pop. Emery quickly set it aside and wrapped a napkin around the bottle to catch the foam. He filled two glasses in front of him, and handed one to Nick. "Try that."

"Emery, how in hell do you know about him?"

"We've just been following his tracks."

"But how did you know he's been in touch with me?"

"It turned up in the wash."

"Who's the 'client' he keeps referring to?"

"We haven't a clue. They're too careful there. We were hoping you might know. Try the champagne."

"I haven't the faintest idea." He sipped his champagne.

"Good, no? Not too dry?"

Nick stared at his glass, then slowly nodded his head. "You think this Rizzo might be connected to Holden's death?"

"Bingo!"

"And I'm your lead to him?"

Emery ducked his head to the side and shrugged. "It's not an unreasonable notion. He's been in touch with you. He wants to get his client together with you. Have some dessert, Nick."

"I can't say I appreciate being wiretapped, Emery."

"You're not. Rizzo is."

"So it's you who arranged my meeting with the President this morning."

"Oh, come now. He was delighted at the prospect of seeing you. You're old friends."

"Yeah. And he's worried about my drug bill." Nick cut off a small piece of pear.

"Well, there you are. And what exactly does he think of your drug bill?"

Nick shrugged. "He talked about 'other priorities.' But he seemed to want to open a line to me."

"How so?"

"He told me to call him anytime I needed help."

"Really!"

"Even gave me a number he said I could always reach him at."

Emery lifted his eyebrows. "Be careful, Nick. I wouldn't trust him entirely."

"Why not?"

"He's cagey. For instance, he's extremely hard-line on drugs. Did he tell you that?"

"Not at all."

"He is. Privately he favors the Singapore solution. Death penalty for pushers. Anyway, he'd veto your bill."

"If it ever passed the Congress."

"You don't for a moment think it will, do you?"

"Not really."

"Then what's the point?"

"Debate. Drugs were legal before 1914, you know."

"I'm aware of that. People shot up in the privacy of their homes. Or drank their little pick-me-ups at five. And died discreetly wrapped up in straitjackets at the local nuthouse."

"Maybe it was better than crack addicts tearing apart public emergency rooms."

"Maybe. Maybe not."

"There's evidence that banning things makes them more attractive."

"Come on, Nick. Junkies take drugs because they need their fix. The state can't condone taking poison."

"That's sort of ironic, coming from you."

Emery lifted his champagne glass to the light and studied it. "In what way ironic?"

Nick touched the end of the spoon that he had left stuck in his pear. He pressed it down until the pear made a tiny sucking sound. "I mean you were once so anti-state. You were Big Stash's boy."

Emery closed his hand and looked at his fingernails. "Well, we can't just dismantle government. Even Reagan saw that."

"On drugs we have to retreat."

Emery raised his eyes to meet Nick's. "For Lore's sake?"

"No, Emery. For the sake of the drug cartels. For the sake of financial empires we can't beat without beating ourselves."

"You're talking nonsense. A fix of crack cocaine costs two dollars. What difference is legalization going to make to that?"

"Two dollars times thirty is sixty bucks a day. Times seven is two car radios and three muggings. And maybe a murder."

"Well, we're wasting our words. You'll never get it out of committee, Senator."

"We have the votes. We'll be calling on you to testify shortly."

"I look forward to that."

"Incidentally, we're getting a surprising amount of support around the country. In the boondocks, even."

"What makes you think so?"

"We've taken polls."

Emery laughed. "I'd like to see them."

"You can. I'll have Segal fax you a printout."

"Have him send it by modem over Internet. Saves paper and it'll stay on the computer, out of the way of prying eyes."

"Fine. I'll see to it."

"Good. Now let's get back to Rizzo. What do you suggest, Nick?"

"I don't know. What did the President really have in mind, getting you and me together?"

Emery finished his champagne, and pursed his lips. "I suppose he thought you might provide a logical way for us to get to Rizzo."

"*He* thought?"

"All right. *We* thought."

"*You* thought. What did you think?"

"Oh, that you might simply meet with Rizzo's client, for instance."

"I don't know that I want to do that. You said yourself it might be dangerous."

"There are always risks. But we could minimize them."

"What would be the point?"

Emery leaned back and unbuttoned his jacket. He laughed. "Why, Nick, you might recruit him."

Nick shook his head. "Recruit him? For what?"

"To deal. As a source of funds. We used to finance projects that way at the Company."

Nick stared at him. "You've got to be kidding."

Emery smiled and then slapped his hands on his knees. "Of course I'm kidding. How about a cigar? And some coffee?"

"I'll pass," Nick said. "I'd like to know anything you find out about Rizzo."

"We'll keep you informed."

"I've always wondered where Lore was getting her supply."

"You actually think Rizzo might have been involved?"

"Not directly, of course. But it wouldn't be too hard for him to know she was using. Wheelersville isn't exactly the drug capital of America. He might even be able to get a lead on Frankie Tonelli."

"Lore's boyfriend. You still suspect him?"

"Not exactly suspect. There's just stuff that doesn't add up."

"I see. Well, all the more reason for you to meet with Rizzo and his client."

"Maybe so."

"Think about it."

"How would it work?"

"Let's work up a plan. Wheelersville might even be the place to do it."

"That would depend on them, wouldn't it?"

"Not at all. You'd be calling the shots. You'd want it to be away from Washington. So would they, I should think. When are you planning to be there next?"

"It looks like early June now. Carnival Day. I'd hoped to get there during the Easter recess, but . . . " He waved his hand. "I've got a fund-raiser to speak at in Harrisburg on Thursday, June sixth, I think it is. So I'll get home for sure then."

"Good. That gives us time to plan."

"Well, let me think about it."

"Wheel'ville would be ideal."

"Speaking of Wheelersville and drugs, Em. My office is working up a profile of drug use before the Harrison Act."

"Yes?"

"I was just wondering if you might have access to old records."

Emery frowned. "Why would I? Kwikrite was started decades after Harrison."

"Still . . ."

"Anyway, even if you could look at those records, they wouldn't prove much. Opiates were sold over the counter in the nineteenth century. Or given straight out of the doctor's bag."

"There was nothing on paper?"

Emery rested his hands on the table. "Even if there was, it wouldn't prove anything. A druggist could write anything he wanted to."

"What do you mean?"

"Oh, I don't know." He looked away. "When I worked at Schlafer's we used to cover our tracks in little ways. It was standard operating procedure."

"Why? What tracks would you have to cover?"

Emery smiled. "We had to deal with the local element from time to time. One of the crime families worked out of Harrisburg. They would shake down the liquor stores in the area and an occasional drugstore."

"You're joking!"

"It was really nothing—small change. We'd give a bagman a few grams of morphine, for example. An apple for the cop on the beat. But then we had to cover our tracks."

"So the mob always had a finger in Wheel'ville. I'd like to see those records."

Emery shook his head. "You couldn't tell a thing from them." He stared at Nick for a moment, then stood up. He slipped off his suit jacket, revealing a harness holding a small holstered pistol.

"Is that necessary, Emery?"

"It hasn't been so far." He hung his jacket over the back of a nearby chair, removed a thermos bottle from a case, and unscrewed the cap and stopper. He poured coffee into the cup. "Speaking of the old ladies in their tower houses: Will you be seeing your grandmother in June?"

"Sure. I'll be taking Matty to see her."

"You'll convey my fondest."

"I will."

"You better shout it in her ear. I don't want any more misunderstandings."

"You've seen her recently?"

"Several times of late. Her mind comes and goes."

"I know. She must be lonely."

"I don't think so. She has her staff and her companion. She sees surviving friends. At least she says so. One doesn't know what to believe—she speaks of seeing your mother."

"Really? Is she hallucinating?"

Emery spread his fingers in the air and shrugged. He pulled a cigar tube from the breast pocket of his jacket and brandished it at Nick. "Not too close in here?"

"Never stopped anyone before."

Emery sat down. "Nick, I have to say this." He unscrewed the top of the tube and shook the cigar out. "I sometimes worry about your own preoccupation with the past." He stretched his legs, removed a cluster of keys from his trouser pocket, isolated a silver tool, and clipped the end from the cigar. "Ever think of that as a form of addiction?"

"Well, I understand what you're saying."

Emery struck a match and revolved the cigar in the flame. "I would hate to think that you were just erecting a monument to Lore with this drug bill."

"I've thought quite a lot about that myself."

"She was really little more than a junkie at the end. Look, I've got to be blunt."

"That seems awfully harsh, Emery. I have no proof of that."

"I thought you'd lost contact with her."

"That's true, in part. But—"

"Well, then. Don't romanticize her." He blew out the match, closed his eyes, and drew on his cigar.

"I just have a hard time accepting that picture of my daughter," Nick said.

Emery picked a flake of tobacco from his lower lip. "I do too, Nick. But we must face facts." He rose and slipped his jacket on again. "I must go. Someone will fetch the dishes, if you'll just be good enough to stay behind a moment and let them in.

"No problem. Thanks for the spread. It was really good to see you. I wish—"

"Yes, it was fun, wasn't it?" He lifted his chin and worked a crease into the knot of his tie. "Don't forget to send my office those voter profiles, Nick. I'll have someone get back to you about the drugstore records."

He stopped at the door. "And Nick. Give some serious thought to meeting with Rizzo." He closed his eyes and nodded. "We might even consider doing a little sting."

Nick stared at Emery.

The door closed.

Blue cigar smoke hung in the air.

4.

Lore

Back in his office, Nick sat behind his desk and poured himself more brandy. He looked at the photo on his desk of Lore as a little girl. Her round face beamed out at him, the beauty just beginning to show through the baby pudge, the eyes glowing warmly, the lower lip tucked beneath the gapped upper teeth that braces would later force together. Lore grinning spontaneously before she learned how to fake a smile. Lore before the trouble began.

Nick swiveled his chair to face the window. The clouds had thickened, and the day had turned gray and threatening. When *had* Lore's trouble begun? Was there any purpose in thinking about it anymore? Probably not, but there was always the hope that some new scrap of memory might turn up to take the pain away.

Nick swallowed the rest of his brandy and poured another inch into his glass. He put the bottle back in the drawer and kicked it shut with a bang.

He rolled his chair over to the computer at the left end of his desk. He flipped the power switch on the side of the system unit and pushed the button on the monitor. When the word-processing menu appeared on the screen, he called up the file "LORDEATH.NTS."

The document appeared, and he began to scroll down it.

The machine hummed in the silent office.

There was a knock on the door.

He started at the sound. "Yes?" he called out too loudly, revolving his chair. His voice sounded hoarse. He cleared his throat and called out again, "Who is it?"

The door opened a crack. It was Abby. "Hi," she said softly.

"Oh. Come in."

She opened the door wider and walked in. She had on her glasses. Her hair was still in a ponytail.

"I thought you'd gone home," he said.

"Well, I had. But I forgot something. Then I heard a bang in here."

Nick frowned and looked down. "Guess it was my desk drawer."

Her eyes went to the brandy glass on the desktop.

"Would you like a drink?" he asked.

"No, thanks." She sat down in one of the chairs that faced his desk. She looked beyond him at the window. "It's going to rain."

He kept looking at her. "Yeah. It looks that way."

The computer hummed.

"How did lunch with the Secretary go?" she said.

"Good. Interesting."

"That's unusual."

He looked at her. "What do you mean?"

"He can be . . ." She smoothed her skirt and crossed her legs. Her jewelry jingled. "I've heard he can be difficult."

Nick looked back out the window. "It was fine." He turned to face her again, leaned back in his chair, picked up his glass, and held it at eye level.

"They say one shouldn't drink alone, Nick," she said.

"They're probably right. But when I'm alone and I drink, I'm not so alone."

"You're thinking about your daughter again, aren't you?"

He studied her. "Yes." He reached down, opened the drawer, and poured himself more brandy. "Everyone seems to think I'm pushing this drug bill only because of her."

"Did Emery . . . Did Secretary Frankfurt suggest that?"

"Yes. The President, too."

She nodded. "You can hardly blame them."

"I was just thinking. What it all boils down to is she changed."

"You mean Lore?"

"Yes."

"How?"

"I don't know. Her grades went bad. Except in history and art, which were always her strong subjects. So it was suggested she take some time off to do a special project."

"You mean she was kicked out of school?"

"Not exactly. She was assigned this project. But it seemed the same thing as getting expelled."

"What was the project?"

"A history of the Schlafer family in Wheelersville."

"She was about fifteen, wasn't she?"

"That's what I was trying to figure out when you came in." He lifted his glass toward the computer screen. "She was fifteen or sixteen."

"That seems young for taking on family ghosts. Did she get anywhere with it?"

"I don't know. I think she was working on it. She had a job at a drugstore in Wheelersville. It used to belong to us but we sold it to the Eckert family about ten years ago. I don't know how far Lore got with her project. We weren't talking much at the end."

"Nick, you were communicating with her through me. Don't you remember?"

"Yes. I'd forgotten."

She looked at him and shook her head.

"I'm beat, Abby. I've been up since six."

"You're like this when you're rested too."

He shrugged. "Anyway, she lived with us in Washington for a while. But then she took money out of our bank account without telling us. I blew up at her and threw her out."

"I remember. You suspected drugs."

"I thought that was part of it. I have no real proof. She went to live with the couple who run the farm—Tom and Dorothy Tate. They've been with us since before Lore was born."

"I know, Nick."

"Then she stayed with her great-grandmother Schlafer for a while, who was old but pretty sharp. Sometimes. And Matty spent a month with them in the summer. He and Lore were close. Despite the seven-year difference in their ages."

"I made his travel arrangements, you'll recall."

Nick looked at Abby. "Of course. You know all this. Why am I telling you this?"

She shrugged. "You've never said a word about it before. Maybe you need to talk."

"There was a boyfriend too. Frankie. Frankie Tonelli."

"You didn't like him."

"I hardly knew him. But he was in his twenties, and I thought that was too old for her. And . . . How do I say this?" He sighed. "He was from the wrong part of town."

"Do you think he helped her get drugs?"

"I don't know. The police checked that out . . . afterward. They think he was clean. But I doubt if he discouraged her."

"Do you mean he gave her the . . . connection?"

"Maybe. Something like that."

He took off his glasses, massaged the bridge of his nose, and put the glasses on again. "Near the end . . ." His voice wavered. He swallowed and took another sip of his drink. "The last Christmas before she died." He turned his head to look at the computer monitor. "Two years ago. My grandfather, Big Stash, had died that spring at ninety-two. She was extremely fond of him."

"Another blow?"

"Yes. But let me make this point. We weren't going to make Christmas a big deal that year, because of our estrangement. We hadn't spent Thanksgiving together. But Lore surprised us by agreeing to come, and she showed up early to help prepare. We did the whole ritual. The hot chocolate at sundown. The singing of the carols; opening our presents; eating a traditional German supper of cold cuts, herring salad, and beer; and then going to a late church service.

"The four of us were together for the ceremony: Lore and Matty, Josie and me. Later the others came, including my grandmother and Emery Frankfurt. The boyfriend came by much later. Lore looked wonderful. Clean, dressed-up, and bright-eyed."

"You mean 'clean' sober?"

"I mean just clean." He lifted his eyes as if searching his memory. "Fresh. Sparkling. She even smelled good when she hugged and kissed me. She hadn't shown affection like that in a long time." He looked back at Abby. "And she pitched in. Helped set the table. Joined in the singing. Insisted on reading the verses from St. Luke: 'And it came to pass in those days, that there went out a decree from Caesar Augustus, that all the world should be taxed.' "

Abby raised her eyebrows and nodded.

"She had a present for me. A beautiful fresh mint copy of a rare stamp. When I opened the envelope and saw it, she said, 'Number one forty-four at last.' I was amazed that she knew I wanted it. It had a beautifully clear cancellation. It must have been really hard to find. It must have cost her most of her savings."

He shook his head. "Anyway, when I hugged her and thanked her, she held on to me tight and said, 'We have to talk soon. There are things I have to tell you.' But then something went wrong—at some point in the evening she turned surly. And then, I never saw her again." He took his glasses off and rubbed his eyes again. He grasped the glasses by the earpieces and tapped the frames against the surface of the desk.

"I think I would like to have a drink," Abby said.

Nick looked at her. She was still sitting. She had not uncrossed her legs. He leaned back and took a glass tumbler from the bottom drawer of his desk. "Brandy? Or would you like a beer?"

"A beer will be fine."

He stood up unsteadily and went to the bookcase on the wall to the right of his desk. He stooped, opened the door of a miniature refrigerator, removed a bottle of beer, and twisted its cap off. He carried it around the desk and handed it to her along with the glass.

She smiled and took the bottle from him. "I don't need a glass." She gestured toward the row of chairs beside her. "Sit down here a minute. I'd like to say something to you. It'll be easier if you're not back there behind your desk."

He frowned, put the glass back on his desk, and sat down two chairs away from her. He closed his eyes and shook his head. "I'm tired. Too little sleep and too much brandy."

"Listen, Nick."

He held his hand against his forehead as if shading his eyes and looked over at her. She had taken her glasses off and loosened her hair so that it fell in soft curves along her temples. Her gray eyes regarded him steadily. She uncrossed her legs, cupped the bottle with both hands, and rested it on her knees. Her nails were medium length and coated with clear polish. Her hands were slender but strong-looking, their backs sharply ridged with tendons.

"Nick," she said. "Lore is dead. Something went wrong for her. Maybe she did get messed up with drugs like a lot of kids. But she's gone." Her eyes held him. "Nick, some lives just go wrong. There's no accounting for it. It wasn't your fault." She grasped his wrist. Her face seemed to enlarge and soften. He tried to look away, but her warmth enveloped him.

"I'm not so sure about that," he said. He closed his eyes and turned his head slightly.

When he opened his eyes again, he saw that she had left her chair, set the bottle down on the floor and was crouching before him. "Nick, you've been brooding and grieving for over a year now. Hitting the bottle. It's time you came out of it. I thought I was seeing signs. But . . ." She gestured at the glass on his desk."

"I'll be okay," he said.

Her hands slid into his. "You have to work this out. You have to free yourself of it."

He stood up, stepped around her, gently pulled his hands away, and moved back behind his desk. He stood there. "Lore and I . . . We were once so close . . ." His voice caught. "When she was little, I was the world to her."

"Yes."

He turned away and looked out the window. The rain had eased a little, but the sky was still an iron gray. He heard her stand up and approach his desk.

"What do you feel when you think of her now?" she asked. Her voice came from directly in back of him.

He shook his head. "When I think of her now I always remember the first time I caught her lying to us. When she came home from school and said everything was fine, and then we learned that it wasn't. It makes me . . . dizzy. As if there was a person there I never knew."

"Dizzy?"

He thought a moment. "Yes, sort of like falling."

"That could be panic you're describing."

"Why would I feel that?"

"Maybe the incident triggered some sort of fear in you."

He turned around. She was leaning with her haunches against the desk. "Fear of what?" he asked.

She shrugged. "Maybe some loss of control."

He turned back to his desk and picked up a hemisphere-shaped magnifying glass and began to slap it gently against the palm of his left hand. "When she was still living in Washington, I was going over our bank records one evening and I found a twelve-hundred-dollar discrepancy. Cash withdrawals. Three of them for four hundred dollars each."

"And?"

"Normally we keep the ATM slips, but I couldn't find any to match those three withdrawals. I checked my wallet to see if my bank card was missing. It wasn't. Then I went upstairs to ask Josie if she knew about it. She didn't, and her card wasn't missing. So I finally climbed the stairs to Lore's room. It was on the third floor. Her door was locked, which was unusual."

He set the magnifying glass down and turned to look out the window again.

"When I knocked and called out her name I could hear someone moving inside. But there was no response. I rattled the doorknob and called louder, but the only answer I got was this . . . sighing sound. I was getting angry, and I threatened to break the door in if she didn't open it."

The rain fell harder, splatting against the air-conditioner frame outside.

"Go on," Abby said.

"The door opened then, and the boyfriend was standing there, Tonelli, blocking my way into the room. I didn't even know he was in the house. I didn't know he was in Washington even. I said, 'I want to talk to my daughter,' and when he didn't move, I pushed him aside. Gently but firmly. I could see Lore then, slumped across her bed, with her head at a funny angle and her eyes closed. She was smiling in a funny way. It was like seeing a stranger."

He shivered involuntarily.

"I went near her and said her name. She just sighed in response. Then I took her by the wrist and tried to pull her upright. She groaned and fell limply on her side. I said, 'Lore, goddammit!' She made a sound like growling and twisted her body, and then she spread her knees apart so her skirt slid up and exposed her . . . crotch. She had no underpants on."

He turned around and looked at Abby.

She was still leaning against the desk. Her head was lowered. In response to his silence, she looked up at him and nodded.

"You're not shocked by this?" he said.

"Come on, Nick. Do you think you're the first guy who ever saw his daughter naked and drunk or . . . drugged?"

"She was . . . ready . . . for sex. She said, 'Do me again, Frankie.'"

Abby closed her eyes and nodded. "That must have been rough."

"I was furious."

"Yes, of course."

"But Tonelli was pushing me away, yelling at me to get out. Lore pushed herself up and slurred something like 'Wass happening?' I let myself be pushed out of the room in my own house. The door closed in my face. I went downstairs and"—he shook his head—"and had a drink. I got drunk."

"I can understand why."

"Things got even worse after that. I ended up throwing her out. And that's when she moved back to Wheelersville." He picked up the magnifying glass again and banged it against the desktop.

"So, what do you think she was on?" Abby asked.

"I haven't the faintest idea. Something pretty powerful, wouldn't you guess?"

"Not at all. She was sexually aroused. Heroin or cocaine don't do that. Those drugs take you out of reality and provide their own high. I'll bet you it was nothing stronger than grass. Besides, she couldn't sustain a serious habit on the money she took from you. Unless she had another source of income. Or he did."

"They didn't have much money. But later, after I saw her at that last Christmas, she stole some stamps from me. From a safe at the farm. About a hundred and twenty-five thousand dollars' worth to be exact."

Abby stood up and walked back around to the front of the desk. "And you figure that went to drugs?"

He shrugged. "It's one explanation."

"Is there an easy market for rare stamps?"

"No. But anyone with a brain in his head would pay ten thousand or so for stamps like that. Put them away until it becomes a little less obvious they were stolen."

She pursed her lips and shook her head. "Doesn't really make sense. It takes more time and steady money to build a serious habit."

"The autopsy showed she was full of heroin."

"That by itself doesn't prove she was an addict. Do you have any other evidence?"

"Just that one incident in her room. And her general strung-out condition."

"Not all that much," Abby said. She sat down and lit a cigarette.

"She could have been getting stuff from the drugstore she worked at."

"Have you checked that out?"

"Police did. No evidence. But still."

"Well, let's worry about you now."

"And my trying to decriminalize drugs as a way of making Lore innocent?"

"You said that, Nick. Not me."

"Yeah. And you're the only one who isn't saying it."

She leaned forward on her chair, waving smoke away from her face. "That may be so. But you can't worry about that. It's what *you* believe that matters, and you better get that straight, kiddo, because you're going to have a fight on your hands with this bill."

He looked at her and nodded his head so slightly that the movement looked like a tremor. "I know that."

"And you better get the rest of it straight."

"What do you mean by that, Abby?"

She looked down and brushed imaginary ashes from her lap. "This isn't for me to say, Nick. But you have to separate your feelings from what actually happened. You can't change the past."

"But I can learn to understand it."

"If you can see that it wasn't your fault."

"Whose was it then?"

She shook her head.

"Believe me, if I had a single thing to go on, I'd . . . follow it to hell and back."

She held his stare. "Yes, of course you would. If anyone hurt a person I loved, I think I would kill."

He continued to look at her. "Yeah. So we're not so civilized when you come down to it." He averted his eyes. "Do you want another beer?"

"No, I have to run." She looked around as if she had forgotten where she was. She picked up her purse. "You have the folder of phone calls I left with you?"

He saw it on his desktop. "Yes."

"I'll see you Monday afternoon then?" She started toward the door.

"Probably. We have to start planning this trip to Harrisburg in June. I'm counting on you to be there."

"Of course."

"I've got to find someone to keep an eye on Matty. Sort of a bodyguard, y'know."

"A bodyguard?"

"Just to keep an eye on him. We still have Clara, but she would be useless if . . . Any ideas?"

"Sure. We could use Donald Fox."

"Who's he?"

"He does odd jobs for Segal. He's very able."

Nick shook his head. "What's he look like?"

"Square jaw. Short, curly reddish hair."

"Oh, yeah. Okay. Good."

"I'm not entirely helpless myself, you know."

"Well, of course not. But still—"

"I always carry a weapon, for instance."

"A weapon?"

"A pistol."

"What kind?"

"A Smith and Wesson thirty-eight Bodyguard. With Black Talon bullets."

"Christ, Abby. Those are the ones that open up like shrapnel."

"Damn right!"

"Tear someone apart." He shook his head. "How . . . ?"

"My brother."

"Of course. The FBI agent. But why those bullets?"

"You know. Woman alone in Washington. He wanted me to have the best. It makes me feel good."

Nick nodded. "Still, for Matty . . ."

"I'll talk to Donald Fox."

"Good. Oh, and did you call the fishing camp about cleaning up the mess I left?"

"Yes. But I'll follow up."

"Abby?"

She stopped with her hand on the doorknob and looked at him.

"Thanks for lending an ear."

"I hope it helped."

"It did."

She smiled stiffly. "Good. Let me ask you something, Nick."

"What?"

"How do you stay so oblivious to people's feelings?"

He shook his head. "Did I miss something again?"

"Never mind."

He shrugged. "I guess it's the secret of my success."

"Yes. That must be it." She went out and closed the door.

He turned, walked slowly back behind his desk, and stared at the closed door. He sat down, rotated his seat to the left and rolled the chair back to the computer. He scrolled the document down until he came to the year 1996. He read the entries:

Mar. 22nd: Lore b'day—17.
Apr. 14th: Call from police. Lore found dead.
Helicopter home.
Apr. 16th: Autopsy heroin. Cause of death? Or
blood loss? Impossible to say.

He remembered the official voice of apology and regret. Josie's hysterical scream in the darkness of their Georgetown bedroom. The frantic helicopter flight. The scene in the morgue of Belcher's funeral home. Even Tonelli was weeping.

And then to have to face the house and Lore's room. The image of the wall above Lore's bed came back to him. It had looked as if someone had dipped a brush in red paint and viciously shaken it. And the letters in blood: "RED HO . . ."

He drank the last of his brandy and turned back to the desk. He felt weak but cold sober. It was a quarter to five. He picked up the phone and punched the button next to Josie's name. There were two rings and then Josie's voice came on. "Hello."

"Hi. It's me. I've been sitting here drinking and brooding."

"Oh, Nick."

"I need a shower and a half-hour nap. Okay if we skip the drink?"

"Of course."

"Why don't I pick you up in Georgetown at about seven-thirty?"

"Will we take the Mercedes?"

"No. I have a car and driver."

"Really? Fine. Bring an umbrella. It's raining."

"See you then. How's Matty?"

"Still out with his friend. He'll probably sleep over."

"Did he call?"

"Yes. He's having fun."

"Great. See you around seven-thirty."

"Good."

As he hung up, his eye fell on the file folder Abby had left on his desk. He opened it and looked at the printout of phone calls to be returned. Halfway down was Rizzo's name and number with an exclamation point next to them.

Nick retrieved the handset and punched the numbers. There was only a single ring before a voice answered.

"Yes." It was Rizzo.

"Mr. Rizzo?" Nick asked, to be certain.

"Yes?"

"It's Nick Schlafer, Mr. Rizzo."

"Senator."

"Right. I see you called again."

"Yes, I did. Thank you for getting back."

"What do you want?"

"I think it's time we talked. My client and you."

"What would the subject be?"

"I'd prefer not to discuss that over the telephone."

"Well, could you define a general area? Like you, I'm a fairly busy man."

"A general area?" Rizzo paused. "There are a couple of general areas. How about 'recreation' is one. And say 'home security' is the other? Home is where most accidents happen, y'know?" There was the barest trace of animation in his voice.

"I see you're a man of wit, Mr. Rizzo."

"Senator, I try to satisfy my clients."

"Yeah, well, I'm considering meeting with you."

"That's very good news. My client will be pleased." The voice had gone toneless again.

"Is there a number I can get you at later?"

"You can always reach me at this number. Night and day. It might not be me, but I'll be back to you within minutes."

"Let's leave it at that for now. I may call you soon."

"I hope you will, Senator."

Nick pressed the button for a dial tone, then pressed the button for Emery Frankfurt's home phone. It rang four times and then was answered by a woman with the trace of some East Asian accent.

"Is Secretary Frankfurt there? It's Senator Schlafer."

"I'm sorry, Senator. The Secretary has gone out for the evening."

"Is there any way I can reach him? It's fairly important."

"I'm afraid not. But he'll be in touch with me shortly. Can I give him a message?"

"Uh, tell him . . . No, I'll get back to him later."

"All right, Senator."

Nick hung up and gazed at the phone for a moment. He turned off his computer and listened to the motor until it ran down. When it clicked to a dead stop he got up and headed for the door.

5.

The Dinner Party

The driver had close-cropped feathery black hair, long eye-lashes, and smooth tawny skin. Except for the faint shadow of a mustache, Nick might even have taken her for a child.

Josie whispered, "Is this your permanent one?"

"I think so," Nick said. He spoke at a normal level, counting on the glass divider to mute his voice. "Her name's Leila."

They rode in silence. Rain beat against the windows.

"She's very attractive," Josie said, still whispering. "I'm having pangs of jealousy."

Nick shrugged helplessly.

"What are you thinking?" Josie asked.

"I'm glad Matty's having a good time."

"Oh, yes. And he has a whole new list of coins he's longing for."

"I wonder who's going to be at Jessica's this evening."

"I couldn't get up the nerve to ask her about the guest list. Thirty people. She did mention the Senator Bodines—"

"With their hound dogs?"

"Wise guy. And the prize catch of the evening is Carl Wertheim. Or would have been, until word of your interview got out."

"Who's he?"

"Carl Wertheim? You're so out of it. He's a writer. *Vanity Fair* just did a story on him."

"Never heard of him. What's he written?"

"No books yet. But based on a couple of thinly disguised political fables in *The New Yorker,* he's very hot stuff. One of New York's leading social observers, as the col-yums put it. Even my editor is after him."

"Young guy, huh?"

"Not so young. He's been a New York character for years. Talks great book, as they say. Now he's down here on some large foundation grant to study our ways."

"We better watch it."

"No doubt he'll have trenchant things to say about your legislation. He's very bright."

Nick stretched his legs into the space where the jump seats were folded.

"You look astonishingly fresh for a man who's been boozing all day. I always liked you in a tux."

"Thanks. You look good too. What's it going to be this evening? Sharks or pandas?"

"Pandas, I'm sure. Jessica looks after her guests, especially her 'A' list. Pandas it will be, with an occasional baring of teeth."

"You're late!" Jessica Phelps sang out as she swooped into the hallway to claim Nick and Josie from the butler. He had relieved them of their dripping rain gear, escorted them upstairs, and taken their drink orders.

"And you promised, Josie! You promised to be on time!" She hugged Josie hard and kissed each side of her face, actually touching her cheeks with her lips.

"It's this guy's fault," Josie said, cocking her thumb at Nick.

"And Nick!" Jessica cried. She grasped him by the shoulders with her arms extended, her blue eyes sparkling, then pressed herself against him so that he could feel her breasts and thighs and smell her perfume. "You've made my evening," she said. She turned him to her side with one arm and caught Josie by the waist with the other. The three of them stood facing the high-ceilinged library where the guests were gathered.

"Look, Nick," she went on. "They're already waiting for your speech."

In the leather-bound room, whose dark colors were highlighted by sprigs of lilac and giant freckled lilies whose name Nick could never remember, people had stopped talking and were looking toward the entrance expectantly. Only a small group in the far corner continued animatedly.

"But you must meet some of them first," Jessica said. She hugged the two of them to her side, then propelled them forward. "Come."

The room smelled of the lilacs. Nick wished he had the scotch and water he'd ordered.

"Senator and Mrs. Bodine," Jessica said. "You must certainly know these dear people, Senator Nick Schlafer and his wife, Josie Wittvogel. Nick, Josie, this is Rick and Liz—"

"Course we do," cut in Liz Bodine, stepping forward and offering her right hand to Nick and her left to Josie. "Why, I am so delighted to see the two of you together again. Can we take this as an announcement?"

"Now, Liz," Jessica said.

"I know, I know. I'll shut my mouth. I was just so upset about your daughter's tragedy," she added, addressing Josie. "You know, you won't forget her as long as you live. Not as long as you go on living."

Nick turned warily to greet F. J. Bodine, who had taken a half step toward him and then paused with his left foot tipped forward on its toe and his right hand spread against his narrow chest, as if he were about to sing an aria. His wide froggy mouth was drawn down at the corners in an expression that was either baleful or smirking, Nick couldn't tell. He gazed up at Nick through half-closed eyes, then began to shake his oversized head.

"Sir, you have certainly started a sh—a storm." He completed his step forward and grasped Nick's right hand. His face was florid with what Nick took to be booze. "You have certainly tipped over the outhouse!"

"Well, Frederick," Nick said, pumping the Senator's hand, "I'm sure I can count on your support."

Frowning and taking a deep breath, Bodine came to full attention. A waiter arrived with a tray holding Nick's and Josie's drinks. Nick took his gratefully, still watching Bodine.

"Sir! You can count on me to oppose you with my dying breath!" He dropped his shoulders, placed his empty glass on the waiter's tray, and took the drink meant for Josie. "But we won't let that come between us, will we?" He raised the glass.

"Now, gentlemen," Jessica said, taking the drink from Bodine and handing it to Josie. "Let's save this political talk for later." She addressed the waiter. "Will you get Senator Bodine a bourbon, please." She took Nick and Josie by their arms and guided them on toward two older couples who had stopped talking and stood waiting. One of them Nick recognized as Supreme Court Justice Abe Kaplan and his lawyer wife. Why couldn't he think of her name?

As Jessica introduced them and they fussed over Josie, Nick glanced at the group in the corner. He could see now that their attention was on Emery Frankfurt, who stood with his back against the bookshelves, holding a glass of champagne in his left hand and gesturing with his right as if conducting an orchestra. The large sooty shadows under his eyes matched the darker streaks in his silver hair, the fringes of which overlapped his suit collar. Instead of a cummerbund he wore a crimson waistcoat. His bow tie was crimson too. He looked like an artist, not a Cabinet officer. He was holding his audience rapt. Nick felt a flash of possessive pride in Emery's elegance and poise. Big Stash had built well.

"So, young man," a voice came from next to him. "You're looking to retire from politics, I see."

"That's a little premature, Mr. Justice." Nick looked at the little man in front of him who was gazing up quizzically. "That will be up to the voters."

"That's just what I mean."

"We'll see." Nick looked beyond Justice Kaplan. "Let's see if we can hear what the Drug Czar is saying." He edged toward Emery's group. As he approached, Emery, still holding forth, let his eyes catch Nick's. The rest of the group turned to regard Nick curiously. Emery was silent for a moment, then continued. "In this case, capital punishment wouldn't be intended to deter."

His audience turned back to him.

"Its fell purpose would quite bluntly be to eliminate both the dealer and the user. The Chinese found it effective."

Nick stood alone watching.

"Mr. Secretary," barked a short, slight man in Emery's group. "Let me tell you a story."

People moved slightly away from the man. Emery regarded him with a frown.

The man looked around to be certain he had the floor, and then focused on Emery. "Let me tell you what's happening in the country on this drug issue. I've been filming videotape for a news story my station is doing, and believe me, the mood in the country is changing. People have had it with the war on drugs."

"I'd dispute that," Emery said, looking down and rattling the ice in his glass.

"One illustration, Mr. Secretary. I happened to be in court recently. A small traffic dispute. Little town in Virginia. Conservative part of the country. A man went up before the judge with his lawyer. This man was a middle-aged black fellow. Well dressed. His lawyer was a young white woman. The judge says to her, 'Bring me up to date on your client. Unfortunately, we've met here before.'

"The lawyer says, 'Your Honor, my client continues to hold down two jobs—daytime and evenings. He continues to support his family in comfort. His two sons are attending college, paying full tuition. His daughter will graduate high school next spring. Your Honor, my client regularly reports to his probation officer.'

"At this point, the judge starts shaking his head sadly and says, 'And yet he has once again tested positive for cocaine.'

"'Yes, your Honor,' the lawyer says.

"'Which just goes to show the insidiousness of this disease,' the judge says.

"'Or the absurdity of the laws prohibiting that disease,' the lawyer says."

Emery looked up from his glass. "A very isolated case."

"But significant," the TV man responded. "You can bet the people in that courtroom were for legalization."

Jessica came up to Nick with Josie in tow. When she spoke the Schlafers' names to Emery, he nodded slowly and looked at his audience. "Well, well, the man of the hour."

Nick raised his glass to Emery. "I hope we'll get a chance to visit this evening, Mr. Secretary."

Emery flashed Nick a smile. "I don't know that I can afford to be seen with you, Senator."

The crowd laughed politely.

Nick took a deep drink. There was too much scotch in the mix. Good.

• • •

"There is no drug problem in America, I say." It was Senator Bodine on the other side of the table.

Nick glanced around. Except for Jessica on his left, Justice Kaplan's wife on his right—what *was* her name? Violet, non-shrinking Violet!—and Bodine opposite him, he knew no one at the table. Yet everyone was waiting for him to respond to Senator Bodine. The only people who weren't looking at him expectantly were a gray-haired black man who had begun spooning his soup two places to Nick's right, and the woman to the black man's right, who was urgently confiding something to him.

Bodine asked loudly, "Did you hear me, Senator?"

Nick looked at Jessica just as she was turning away from the bearded man on her left. "Madame Hostess," Nick said. "Am I supposed to hold a forum?" He spoke loud enough for the table to hear.

Jessica looked around the table and laughed. "It does look that way, doesn't it, Senator?"

"Well, I'm off duty now," Nick said to the table. "So I think I'll pass."

The table began to buzz with conversation. Jessica put her hand on Nick's wrist.

Nick spoke to her softly. "I'd rather talk to you." He sipped from the drink he had brought to the table, his second. He could feel it now. Jessica had left her hand on his arm. He could hear the whisper of her garments as she shifted herself closer to him.

He said, "I didn't see Tom."

She tilted her head back to scan the other tables, then looked back at him. "I put him far away." She lowered her eyelashes. "I put him with Josie so they would leave us to each other."

Nick said, "But not alone, unfortunately." Tiny flames glowed in her eyes—reflections of one of the candled chandeliers overhead.

Bodine said loudly, "Do you want to know why there's no drug problem, Senator?"

The table fell silent once more against the background of chatter in the large room. Even the black man and his dinner partner were looking at Nick now.

"I guess you're about to tell me," Nick said. He could feel Jessica lightly tap her foot against his leg. He wondered why.

"I will tell you." Bodine put his wineglass down. His face was redder now and his dark eyes liquid. He was drunk, Nick thought.

"The druggies will kill themselves off, just like all the pederasts with AIDS are doing."

Nick could see several people lower their heads and begin to spoon their consommé. "That's certainly one way of looking at it," he said.

"And I say, 'Let 'em!' That's why there's no drug problem."

Jessica's fingers pressed Nick's wrist. She leaned close to him. "Don't take his bait," she murmured.

"But what about crime?" the woman to Bodine's right said shrilly. She was sleekly overweight, but her voice was still too big for her body. "What about all the innocent victims of drug crimes?"

Nick asked Jessica, "Who's she?"

"You must know her, Nick. Helen Miller, the gossip columnist."

"I'm afraid not," Nick said.

"There's no crime in my community," Bodine said. "We ran the junkies and their dealers out of town."

A tall man approached the table and squatted next to the black man.

Nick addressed Bodine. "Your community is the entire state of North Carolina, I believe."

"Is that so? Well, let me tell you something, Senator Schlafer." He looked around the table to see if everyone was listening. "You're gonna embarrass the Congress with this legislation you're proposing, and you're gonna regret it!" He hit the edge of the table softly with his open hand. "You're vulnerable and you're gonna regret it."

"But Senator Bodine," the bearded man to Jessica's left said. "If you think drug addiction is self-policing, you ought to be in favor of Senator Schlafer's legislation."

Bodine regarded the man with narrowed eyes. Waiters began to clear the soup dishes. Bodine put his right hand against his chest. "You can count on me to oppose him with my dying breath!"

"I'm interested in your legislation, Senator Schlafer." It was the bearded man. He was addressing everyone at the table.

"Nick, do you know Carl Wertheim?" Jessica asked.

"Only by reputation."

The writer closed his eyes and dipped his head forward ceremonially. He glanced at Nick out of the corner of his eye and continued to address the table. "Has it ever occurred to you that coca and marijuana and the poppy are the Third World's justified response to Yankee imperialism?"

Jessica turned to Nick and widened her eyes.

A voice came from Nick's right. "Try telling that to a peon pickin' the marijuana weed for six dollars a day, sir." It was the black man.

Jessica asked, "Is that what they're paid, Congressman Leslie?"

"More or less," said Leslie.

Nick said, "Of course. The drug business is a near monopoly."

Wertheim said, "Which doesn't really contradict my point about the Third World's revenge."

Nick looked at Bodine, who was swaying like a cobra preparing to strike.

Wertheim went on, looking into the distance beyond the table. "The economist Ludwig von Mises opposed intervening in drug traffic on the grounds that it interfered with market forces and hence the freedom of the individual. The illicit drug business has been described—not entirely in jest—as the best means ever devised by the United States for exporting the capitalist ethic to potentially revolutionary Third World peasants."

Nick followed Wertheim's gaze and saw the table reflected in a large wall mirror. The scene it framed—shadows studded with points of light—reminded him of an Impressionist painting. He turned back to Wertheim. "It's not really the free market I'm concerned with," he said. He was suddenly aware of a sweet scent he associated with childhood. It smelled like a Christmas tree burning. He looked down and saw that a candle near his plate had set fire to a few needles of an evergreen centerpiece.

"What *are* you concerned with, Senator?" the black congressman asked sharply. The man squatting next to him suddenly stood up.

Nick dipped his fingers into his water glass and snuffed out the tiny flame.

The Congressman went on. "I'll tell you what you're *not* concerned about. The underclass. The poor people in the ghetto caught in the cycle of poverty and drug dependence."

"Right on!" said Helen Miller and shrieked her manic laugh.

"You're not concerned about the children that this drug plague is killing."

Jessica moved closer to Nick to make room for a waiter offering a platter of what looked to Nick like poached salmon.

"The Senator's own daughter—" Violet Kaplan began.

"Come into the ghetto and look for yourself before you start legalizing poison," Congressman Leslie went on. "You rich people . . .

your children have someplace else to go. They play with drugs, experiment, and then they say, 'Well, I've done this and I'm tired of it. Now I think I'll go to law school and maybe run for President or something. Run for the Senate and make drugs available to everybody!' But the poor people, the children of the ghetto, have no place else to go but to stay with drugs and die."

Several people at the table applauded.

"The Senator's daughter . . ." Violet Kaplan said.

Nick touched her arm. "Never mind," he said softly. He turned back to Leslie. "It's prohibition that drove drugs into the ghetto," Nick said. "Before Harrison, drugs were a middle-class thing."

Leslie raised his hand and slowly made a fist. "You're legislatin' genocide, sir!"

Nick stared at him. He felt Jessica touch his arm again. He turned to her. The waiter was trying to serve him.

Jessica said, "Why don't we change the subject."

As the waiters began to pour coffee, Congressman Leslie abruptly folded his napkin, excused himself to Jessica, and left the table. He was accompanied by the man who had been squatting beside him earlier.

Violet Kaplan turned to Nick. "That gentleman did not care for you," she said.

"I'm sure it wasn't personal."

"Still, he didn't care for you at all. He couldn't wait to get away."

Other guests were getting up from the table. Jessica leaned against Nick. "Don't go yet."

"I wasn't planning to."

"Let me order you a cognac."

"I still have my scotch.'

She toasted him with her half-filled wineglass, held it against the hollow of her bare shoulder, and smiled.

Nick smiled back. He held her gaze for a few seconds, then let his eyes drift down to her wineglass, and on to the swell of her breasts, pale against the bodice of her black gown.

She said, "How is Josie?"

"You mean how are we?"

She lowered her eyes and sipped her wine. "Okay."

Nick shrugged. "I don't know. We're on hold, I guess."

"I loved her book. Well, 'loved' is the wrong word. I mean I was mesmerized by the horror. That poor woman."

"You certainly have nothing in common with her, Jessica."

"So, you're living in the Watergate now?"

"How would you know that?"

"I think I'm not going to tell you. Didn't you want me to know?"

"That's not the point."

She laughed and poked his shoulder with her finger. "I'm teasing, Nick. You're so uptight."

"Hmm."

"Do you have a cigarette for me?"

"That's one habit I kicked. More or less."

She bit her lower lip. "Shall we try something stronger?" She cocked her head minutely, as if indicating some back room.

Nick looked away. Most of the dinner guests were now near the door at the far end of the room.

"Don't worry about them," she said. "They'll be well looked after."

A small string orchestra in the next room began to play "A Hard Day's Night."

"It's been a hard day's day, Jessica."

"Tell me about it." She leaned toward him. "I would never leave Tom, you know." She looked at her glass. "However . . ."

"However," Nick repeated.

"However."

Carl Wertheim, who had been standing behind his chair and talking with Helen Miller and Congressman Leslie's dinner companion, took his seat again.

Nick nodded to him. "So what do you think of our little town?"

"It's just that, isn't it? You expect it to be headlines, but it's a company town whose business happens to be world leadership."

"Or world followship," Jessica said.

Wertheim said, "I'm very interested in your drug legislation, Senator. Do you understand its implications?"

"I've got a feeling you're about to tell me."

"I apologize for seeming to patronize. But I'm fascinated with the subject. I've given it a lot of thought." As he spoke, he looked around to include the few people standing nearby. Jessica leaned back in her chair as if to free the space between Wertheim and Nick.

Wertheim said, "I define addiction as the human need to escape the tyranny of time." He looked at Nick, waiting for a response. Nick nodded. In the distance over Wertheim's shoulder, he could see Emery and Josie approaching the table, arm in arm.

"There is always the temptation to escape time," Wertheim said. "'The woods are lovely, dark, and deep.'"

Jessica said, "'But I have promises to keep.'"

Wertheim asked, "Have you read *Naked Lunch*?"

"William S. Burroughs Junior," Jessica said.

"He understood that junk was more than just junk."

Nick said, "I'm not sure I see where this is going." He looked up. Emery and Josie were now standing in back of Wertheim. The writer, following Nick's gaze, turned to look at them, stood up, then turned back to Nick. "I'm opposed to your position, Senator. Society needs its outlaws. We are the creative ones."

"'We'?" Nick asked.

"All artists are outlaws. Besides," Wertheim added, nodding at Emery, "we wouldn't want to put the Secretary out of work."

Emery laughed. The strings were playing "Lucy in the Sky with Diamonds."

Nick leaned toward Jessica. "Do me a serious favor," he said softly.

"Anything."

"Where can I talk to someone alone?"

"With a bed?"

"No." He laughed.

"Tom's study. You can get to it by going through the kitchen, if you don't want anyone to know you're there."

"Perfect."

They both stood up. As they moved around the table, Wertheim took Jessica's arm.

Josie said, "Look what I found, Nick." She hugged Emery's arm.

Emery said, "You should take better care of this lovely woman, Nick."

Nick waited as Jessica and Wertheim moved away.

"I need a word with you, Emery. In private."

"Fair enough," Emery said.

"Am I excluded?" Josie asked.

"Of course not," Emery said.

Josie looked at Nick. She said, "I'll join you later. After I go to the ladies' room."

"We'll be in the study off the library," Nick said.

"I like the waistcoat, Emery."

"Century Association."

"It's for artists, isn't it?"

"And those with an interest."

Nick took a brandy snifter from the shelf, found a bottle of Remy Martin VSOP in the cabinet below, and poured himself a half inch.

"Can I fix you something, Em?"

Emery stood in front of a leather armchair in the corner of the room and shook out the match with which he had just lit his cigar.

"I've had enough. I imagine you have too."

Nick swirled the amber liquid and moved to join Emery. "There are times it keeps me going."

Emery said, "Maybe." He examined the ash of his cigar. "What's on your mind? I don't mean to be rude, but we shouldn't be seen as the friends we are. Especially when the President gets here. Nothing personal. It just sends confusing signals."

"I understand. When can we talk?"

"What about?"

"I wondered if you had anything for me from your lab."

Emery shook his head. "My lab?"

"About that thing I pulled out of the river this morning."

"Ah, your dummy. No, not yet."

"Did they find it?"

"I should think so, if it was where you said you put it. I'll have news for you early in the week."

Nick sipped his cognac. The heat took his breath away. He coughed. "Well, I've been thinking about your trap."

"Trap?"

"Your sting. The business you mentioned at lunch. With this fellow Rizzo."

"Yes?"

"I want to meet with Rizzo's client. See what he wants."

"How do you propose to do that?"

"That's what I'm asking you. What did you have in mind?"

Emery sat down in the leather chair and crossed his legs. He regarded Nick and shrugged. "Why don't you tell me what you have in mind."

Nick sat down opposite him. He picked up a box of matches in a silver case and examined the design. He shook it. "Rizzo keeps saying his client wants to see me. That's all I know. So what does he want? Since one of the main points of my legislation is to put people like that out of business—"

"'People like that'?"

"You have to hear this character."

"I've had to make do with transcripts of him."

"Well, he's out of a bad movie. Hoarse, high-pitched voice. He talked about 'accidents happening.' "

Emery nodded.

"So I have to think they don't like my bill. Now what can they do to stop it?"

Emery arched his eyebrows and widened his eyes.

Nick said, "You told me you could minimize the risks."

"Yes, but not eliminate them entirely."

"But if they wanted to, uh, get me, why bother to set up a meeting first? They know where they can find me. They knew enough to plant that dummy, didn't they?"

"Or someone did."

"Don't you see, Em? They've already done their threatening. There must be another reason for a meeting."

"You've got this all figured out, haven't you?"

"I'm tired of being on the defensive." Nick stood up, looked around the room, and got himself a cigarette from a box on the shelf by the liquor cabinet. "I figure they want me to do something. And to do something, I have to be . . ." He sat down again and lit the cigarette with a match from the silver box. "You know, unencumbered."

"Alive, Nick."

"Right."

"So?"

"So what?"

Emery held his cigar up and studied its tip. "What do we gain from this little lark?"

Nick stared at Emery. "Well, we learn who the client is, for one thing."

"Yes?"

"We learn what he wants, and maybe get some evidence of it. Isn't that what you meant by a sting?"

"Hmm."

"And maybe we get a lead to John Holden's killer, if he really was assassinated. Isn't that what you had in mind?"

"I really don't know what I had in mind."

"Damn it, Emery. This was your idea. You were hot to go."

Emery slowly shifted his focus from the cigar to Nick. "Yes, I was, but you're the one who has to be the bait, Nick."

Nick got up and went to the liquor cabinet again. He poured himself another splash. He banged the stopper into the bottle with the butt of his hand.

"So it's crazy, huh?"

Emery nodded absentmindedly. "Probably it is. You could get me a short brandy, Nick. Short."

Nick pulled the stopper again and poured cognac into another glass. The sound of the orchestra stopped. There was a low murmur of voices.

Emery asked, "Where would you propose to do this?"

Nick handed Emery the drink.

"I don't know. Where do you do a sting?"

Emery passed the snifter back and forth under his nose. "Ideally, you do it where the stinger has most control." He sipped his drink. "But where the target is going to feel comfortable too. As I said earlier today, someplace in Wheelersville would be ideal."

Nick sat down. "I want to do it down at the fishing camp."

"Too risky. It's uncontrollable space. I'd want it in a single room."

The violins sounded "Hail to the Chief." Emery made spirals with his right hand and extended it in a gesture of welcome. "The Chief has arrived."

"We both know every inch of the camp, even in the dark. Especially in the dark."

"You want me to wire the trees, I suppose."

"You could use directional mikes outside. Wire just the cabin."

"It would take time to set up."

"How much time?"

"Weeks. We can't just rush down there. We'd have to infiltrate the area cautiously. Get people used to our being around."

"Okay. Let's start now."

"I'll look into it. We'll have to stay in close touch." Emery set down his drink and removed a small leather folder and gold pen from inside his jacket. He opened the folder, wrote some numbers on a small pad of paper, tore off a sheet, and handed it to Nick. "You can always reach me at that number. Commit it to memory and flush the paper."

Nick slipped the paper into the side pocket of his jacket. "The more I think about this the better I like it, Emery."

"You must be drunk."

Nick raised his glass. "All the better."

"You make one dumb move, you know, and they *will* kill you." Emery's eyes lifted to look beyond Nick. "Josie! At last." He stood up.

Nick leaned forward. "Just give me a safety switch. That's all I ask."

Emery looked down at him. "A safety switch?"

"Some way I can bail out. Signal you if I'm in trouble."

"Are you gentlemen almost finished? Jessica is pining for you, Nick. And the President is here, as you must have heard."

"We're coming now," Emery said. He stopped beside Nick's chair. "Let me explore this."

"I want to do it, Emery."

"We'll speak soon. Come, Josie. Let's pay our respects."

Nick stood up and turned to follow them. He saw Senator Bodine standing in the doorway. He was swaying, an empty glass in his hand.

Bodine said, "Let's you'n me have one for the road." He advanced on Nick.

"We should be hailing the Chief, Senator."

"Aw, there's a line through two rooms to greet that sumbitch. Siddown, brother." With surprising agility, he guided Nick back to the chair where Emery had been sitting. He took Nick's glass from him and sniffed its contents. "You'll have another cog-nack, and I'll have me some more of this gooood mash." He did a little dip of joy in front of the liquor cabinet and rubbed his hands together. "I wanna apprise you of what I think of your legislation, Senator."

"I think we've been over that ground, comrade."

"Comrade, huh?" He handed Nick his refilled glass and lowered himself into the chair that Nick had occupied. "You trying to provoke me?"

"What's on your mind, Senator? It's late."

"Now don't you be getting inhospitable. We got a lot to talk about. I go home, and the good people of Carolina start asking about this colleague of mine . . ."

Josie reappeared in the doorway. She caught Nick's eye and beckoned him with a tilt of her head.

". . . this comrade," Bodine went on. He followed Nick's eye and turned to see Josie. "Mizz Schlafer!" He stood up. "If you'll spare him, I'm going to take about ninety seconds of the Senator's time."

"Don't mind me," Josie said. She sat on a small red leather couch at the far end of the room and picked up a magazine from the glass table in front of it. "I can't hear you."

"Can I get you a drink, ma'am?"

Josie lifted her half-filled wineglass and shook her head. Bodine turned back to Nick and sat down again. He lowered his voice. "You serious about this drug deal, man?"

Nick glanced at Josie. Her face was hidden by her magazine. He looked back at Bodine. "You know I am. If you don't, just watch me on the tube tomorrow morning."

"Yeah, I will. Then maybe you and me can do some business."

Nick stared at Bodine, who seemed to be holding back laughter at his amazement. Beyond his shoulder, Nick could see Josie lower her magazine far enough to reveal a childish pout. The shoe of her crossed leg had slipped off her foot and fallen sideways onto the coffee table, and she was trying to work it into an upright position with her long, nearly prehensile toes.

Nick looked back at Bodine. "Business?"

"Yeah. You ain't gonna have such an easy time with this bill of yours. The people might be for it, but it's not such a sure thing in the Congress." He smiled broadly. "You could even *lose*." He drew the word out.

"I'm very much aware of that. In fact—"

"But then, that wouldn't have to be the end of it."

"How so?"

"Well, there's more than one way to skin this polecat. I'm on the budget committee, y'know. We have a lot of little tricks in our bag. Specially at the end of the fiscal year."

"What would be in it for you?"

"Who knows what you could do for me. And then there's all the tobacco growers in my constituency. You know, the cigarette companies have not been at all kind to the growers. Not at all. They're my people, and they could use something else to farm."

Nick nodded. A movement caught his eye. He looked over at Josie. She had flung her knees apart and lifted back the hem of her skirt. Garters held up her old-fashioned silk stockings. She had no panties on. The white of her gown made her pubic hair seem blacker. Her tongue touched her upper lip in a parody of a *Playboy* centerfold.

Nick fought to shift his eyes back to Bodine. He nodded vigorously, hoping the gesture would fit whatever the man was saying. "I'm listening, Senator," he said.

He tried to hear Bodine's words but couldn't pick up the thread. He looked back at Josie. She had lowered her skirt and slapped the magazine over her face. She was quivering with laughter.

Nick added, "I'll keep what you've said in mind."

Bodine nodded. "You just do that." He turned to look at Josie. She was sitting upright now, and biting her lips. Bodine stood and addressed her. "I told you it would just take a minute, mizz."

Nick remained sitting.

Bodine turned back to him and frowned. "I'm gonna be attacking you hard, Senator. But don't pay it no mind. Just remember this little talk of ours."

"Fair enough," Nick said, getting up. As he stepped forward, Bodine took him by the arm with one hand and reached for Josie with the other.

"Now let's go tickle the ears of that rat-ass Chief Executive."

"That was quite a stunt."

"Yes."

"I had trouble standing up. Bodine was wondering about me, I think." Nick looked to see whether his driver was watching them, but the rearview mirror reflected nothing but the flash of passing streetlights. He slid closer to Josie. She shifted pliantly to make room for him.

"The garters were the best part. Lord, the age of garters must have been great."

"Tsk."

He breathed hard. "Tell me something. Did you have them on when we left for the party?"

"What, the garters?"

"No, your underwear."

"My panties, Nick? Ah, that would be telling, wouldn't it?"

He leaned and found her lips with his. Her mouth was warmly wet. She pressed her knees against him. They were shaking. He reached to grasp them with his hands, slid himself away from her, and lifted her legs. They came up lightly onto the seat, and fell apart. He pulled her toward him, lifted her dress, and slid his hands along her thighs until he could feel her garters. Her skin there was soft and warm. He lowered his head and touched his cheek against her inner thigh. It was wet. The sweet-acid smell that rose from her excited him more. He licked her flesh. She lurched, grazing his forehead with her damp mound, then reached her hand and pushed him away.

"Don't touch me there, Nick," she said, trying to catch her breath. "I'll go right off." Her fingers hooked the waistband of his trousers and tugged softly. "Do me, Nick. Do me."

He pushed himself awkwardly against her, cupped her neck with his left hand, and kissed her again. Her mouth seemed drier.

"What's wrong?" she asked.

"What?" he breathed.

"What turned you off?"

"Nothing. What do you mean?"

"I don't know."

He sat back and shook his head. "We better wait."

She tucked her legs under her and leaned toward him. "What happened, Nick?" Her breath had turned sour.

"I don't know."

She retreated to her corner and hugged herself. He looked at the rearview mirror. He still could not see the driver.

"I'm sorry, Josie."

She put her hand on his.

"There's a bar in here, I think." He groped and found a button on the back of the driver's seat. When he pressed it, a small door swung down revealing by soft light a cluster of bottles and glasses. He splashed cognac into a glass.

"You want something?" he said.

"No."

He leaned back. "I don't know what happened just now."

"It was Lore again."

"No."

"I know. It's also why you didn't come by this afternoon. You were sitting there in your office sipping your brandy and brooding about Lore."

"Yes, I was. But not just now."

"You won't accept it, will you?"

"I accept that she's gone. It's the circumstances I'm still having a problem with."

"You still blame Frankie Tonelli."

"I don't *blame* him. I'd just like to be convinced he wasn't getting her drugs."

"Just because of his name."

"It isn't that so much. I . . . I have to blame somebody." He moved away from her and leaned into his corner.

"You know, Nick, I have reason to feel guilty too."

"Why?"

"For being away, on my book-promotion tour, when Lore needed me."

"That hardly counts."

The tires of the car hissed against the wet roadway.

"It rained hard," he said. "It'll be clear tomorrow, and cool."

"But just now," she said, "when you were going to . . . it wasn't anger that stopped you."

"Oh, come on, Lore. Let's drop it."

"Lore?"

"What?"

"You just said 'Lore,' Nick."

"I didn't."

"You did. So my case rests."

"Give me a break, Josie. We were talking about her. She was on my mind."

"I'm not going to give up, Nick. I want us back together."

"I've been feeling a lot better, actually. Ever since I decided to go ahead with this legislation."

"How about us?"

Nick grunted and sipped his brandy. "Don't push me, huh?"

The car swung to the left and climbed a hill. Josie braced herself.

"You didn't have to come with me this evening," she said.

"I wanted to, and I'm glad I did."

The car slowed, turned sharply into a driveway, and stopped.
Josie said, "This is where I get off."

They both sat silent.

"What were you and Emery talking about?"

"Business."

"Okay, I'll butt out."

"I'll tell you if anything comes of it."

"Whatever it was, it upset you."

He thought a moment. "Emery upset me."

"Well, you probably tend to upset him. You probably remind him of your father."

Nick poured himself more brandy. "I still admire the hell out of him. I was watching him at the party tonight, and I felt proud, as if he belonged to me."

"Will you come in with me?"

"He could still turn out to be a great man."

She was silent.

"You don't agree," he said.

She shrugged. "Let's not go into it."

"You looked like you were enjoying him tonight."

"I was."

"What did *you* talk to him about?"

"I asked him about James Angleton, and about who killed Mary Meyer, the ex-wife of Angleton's CIA colleague Cord Meyer."

"The girlfriend of JFK's who was killed on the C and O Canal towpath."

"Yes. I'd love to get to the bottom of that story."

"What did he say?"

"Nothing. He got very quiet. Then he did a funny thing."

"Tell me."

"He asked me if I was still mad at him. I asked him why on earth I would ever have been mad at him. He said, 'Because I wouldn't give you an interview for your book.' "

"I didn't know you'd asked him for one," Nick said.

"That's the funny thing. I never did. I called him to confirm a detail he'd once told me about the woman I wrote about."

"I remember."

"But that was it. A three-minute conversation. It never occurred to me that he had more to say about her."

"I don't get it."

"Neither did I. Then tonight, when I guess I was looking puzzled, he said, 'I never slept with her, you know.' "

"Did he?"

"Until that moment, it had never occurred to me that he might have."

"But now we have to wonder."

"We certainly do. I'm glad the book is done with."

"Have you got an idea for a new one yet?"

"Nothing solid."

"I never think of Emery with a woman."

"I suspect there's a side of him you don't know."

"I know him pretty damn well. And I think of him as a confirmed bachelor."

She stared out the window for a moment, then retrieved her pocketbook from the floor.

"Will you spend the night?" she asked.

"I don't think so."

"It would be great for Matty to have you there in the morning."

"Josie."

"You've become almost a stranger to him. A year is a long time in a ten-year-old's life."

"That's not fair. He's seen me."

"For an occasional movie or meal. With Senate business on your mind."

"That's why I'm taking him to Wheelersville with me in June."

"He'll barely remember it."

"Come on! He's been there often."

"But not recently and not with you. I still don't understand why you had to move out on us."

"Maybe I don't either. We should sell the house. It isn't safe anymore in Georgetown."

"Oh, Nick darling. I don't care where we live, so long as . . ."

"Don't, Josie. Give me time."

"Just trying."

"Anyway, I've got a TV show first thing in the morning."

She pushed open the car door.

"Let me walk you," he said.

"No, it's okay. It's stopped raining."

She got out. Nick slid over to her side of the seat. She leaned back in and kissed him on the mouth. "How can I . . . get through to you?"

"What do you mean?"

She looked at him and shook her head slowly. "I just feel you're not there."

"I don't know what you mean."

"I never know where you are. I'm not going to wait forever, Nick."

"Maybe it won't take forever."

She turned, stumbled on the uneven paving stones, and caught her balance. Nick watched her walk to the front door of the house. She let herself in without waving to him. He watched until the light in the transom went out. He imagined her hanging up her raincoat and going into the kitchen to see if the cat had enough dry food and water.

He pulled the car door shut and pressed a button beside him to lower the glass between himself and the driver.

"I guess we'll go to the Watergate now, uh, Leila. Take the Rock Creek Parkway."

The car did not move. The driver seemed to be waiting.

"Is there a problem?" Nick asked.

"Excuse me, sir. Do you think if I didn't know the streets of Washington, D.C., I would be driving for you?" The voice was a soft tenor.

"I'm sorry. No offense. But I hope you have other ways to pass your time."

"Why is that, sir?"

"Because I really don't have all that much need for a driver."

"I do other things too."

"Such as?"

"I'm your bodyguard."

Nick grunted. "Well, I don't expect there'll be too much call for that. I lead a nonviolent life."

Leila sat looking at the mirror.

Nick could see that she was smiling warmly. "Shall we go now?" he said.

Leila grinned at him in the mirror. "You and the lady."

"My wife."

"You make an attractive couple. Pardon me for saying this."

Nick regarded the face in the mirror. "You're supposed to keep your eyes on the road."

"But some things I cannot help seeing." She lowered her eyes from the mirror.

In the dim interior light, Nick could see the soft outline of her profile. Her mouth hung slightly open.

"Why don't we get a move on," Nick said.

The car backed out of the driveway.

Nick was on the verge of sleep when the telephone rang. He rolled over, picked up the cordless handset, and pressed the talk button. "Yes?"

"Nick!" a man's voice said too loudly. "Ted Diefendorfer here."

"Jesus!"

"What's the matter?"

"It's the middle of the night. Hold it a sec." He pushed himself up and sat on the edge of the bed. "What's up?"

"We're in irons, mate. It's time to heave to." He was practically shouting.

"Talk English, Ted."

"I can't support your bill."

"We haven't begun hearings. I haven't even introduced it yet."

"I can't support you. I'm going to vote to table."

Nick reached for the lamp on the night table, switched on the light, and looked at the clock. "It's two-thirty in the morning."

"I had to let you know, Nick." The voice was softer now.

"I thought I had your word."

"It's gale force winds. I can't do it, Nick. They're breaking my back."

"Who is, Ted?"

Silence.

"You sound a little fuzzy, Dief."

"I've had a couple."

"Why don't we talk about it in the morning?"

"It'll be the same story in the morning."

Nick rubbed his eyes. "You're joining the minority, you know. I still have the votes."

"Not for long."

"Then I'm sorry, Ted. Good night."

"Hold on, Nick. I have to ask you something."

"Go ahead."

"Where do you stand on the budget?"

"Why?"

"We'd like your support."

"Let me get this straight, Ted. You're calling me up in the middle of the night to tell me you're reneging on a solemn promise—a done deal. And you're asking me to support something you know I'm dead opposed to?"

"It's foul weather, Nick." There was a barely audible crack in his voice. "We can't ride it out."

"Good night, Ted." He moved the phone away from his ear and held it in the air.

"Wait, Nick!"

He disconnected by pushing the talk button again and put the handset back on its stand.

PART TWO

Friday, June 6th

6

Home

"And so I say to you, my friends . . ."

Nick's voice echoed harshly. He grasped the lectern with his left hand and passed his right thumbnail across his forehead.

"And so I say to you . . ." Did Segal write this?

He looked around the huge ballroom. Uniformed waiters and busboys stood along the back and side walls. Most of the banqueters at the tables looked up at him, their faces waxy pale in the low light.

He began again: "And so I say to you, my friends . . ." He tried to soften the harshness of his broadcast voice. "My friends and fellow Pennsylvanians."

He made a fist with his left hand and thrust it beyond the microphone.

"I have not forgotten the mandate you gave me by supporting me."

Silverware jangled somewhere in the room.

He thumbed through his script to the last page and found the initials T.D. at the bottom. He could not place them. *Who was T.D.?*

He lifted the speech and dropped it on the tabletop to the left of the lectern. From the corner of his eye, he could see Max Silvers, the state party chairman, regarding him doubtfully.

He looked out over the audience. "Friends, what I have to say to you tonight is simple."

At the table just below him, Abby was nodding and smiling. To her left, Matty slouched on his elbow and poked at the tablecloth with his fork. To Matty's right was a young man with a square jaw and short, curly reddish hair. *Matty's new bodyguard, Donald Fox.*

"I was going to read you a speech about abortion and family values and industrial pollution.

"I was going to talk to you about priorities: trade barriers and the deficit and lower taxes and the other issues I based my campaign on three years ago . . . the issues you elected me to represent you on.

"I haven't forgotten or neglected those issues. But you know what's on my mind tonight."

He turned to his left. Silvers was frowning and shaking his head.

"My friends and neighbors, what is on my mind tonight, and I'm sure on yours as well, is the bill that I introduced in the Senate this past April to decriminalize illicit drugs."

At a table somewhere beyond Matty, Nick could see a man slowly clasp his hands and shake them in a gesture of triumph.

"Now, we have all heard the arguments on both sides of this . . . profoundly troubling issue. I'm not going to bore you with a lengthy review of them tonight. I've been talking about them on television and in speeches around the country during the past few weeks.

"But let me say this."

He lifted his hands and placed them flat on the lectern.

"I personally do not advocate the use of any drug—opiate, narcotic, amphetamine, barbiturate, or hallucinogen. I am not in favor of the indiscriminate use of drugs."

He leaned forward. "But the laws against drugs do not work. Let me quote you something that was once written about drug addiction: 'The sufferer is tremulous and loses his self-command, he is subject to fits of agitation and depression. He loses color and has a haggard appearance. As with other such agents, a renewed dose of the poison gives temporary relief, but at the cost of future misery.'

"That was written by eminent scientists some hundred years ago—about the Bohemian cult of coffee drinking.

"About caffeine, the 'poison' that one quarter of you in this room are absorbing at this very moment.

"Along with those other drugs—alcohol and nicotine."

He grasped the edges of the lectern.

"No, my point is not that drugs are tolerable, although I do ask why some drugs should be less tolerable than others. I do ask why those who are addicted to alcohol are judged to be sick people while heroin addicts are classified as criminals. That doesn't make sense to me.

"But I do not say that drugs are not dangerous.

"Drugs *are* dangerous. All drugs. Alcohol and tobacco too.

"But we live in a dangerous world, my friends.

"A week ago, on Memorial Day, we honored the men and women who sacrificed their lives for this country in wartime. In the wake of that occasion it is fitting to recall just how dangerous the world is.

"The world is filled with instruments of destruction. For over half a century now, we have possessed weapons powerful enough to destroy our planet.

"Yet it might well be argued that those very weapons have helped us to stay at peace. By knowing the danger of those weapons, we have avoided using them.

"Could the same be true of dangerous drugs?

"My friends, let me appeal to your sense of reason.

"By acknowledging the existence of nuclear weapons and by working out a system of inspecting and policing them, we have taken vital steps toward preventing their use.

"So, paradoxically, the very danger they pose has made us safer.

"But by trying to stamp out drugs we have put ourselves at greater risk from them. We have created a black market for them. We have brought into being a criminal class to deal in them. We have told lies to our children about them, lending drugs an allure that the truth would quickly dispel.

"So I say: Let us bring drugs out into the open now."

In the back of the room, one person began to clap.

"Let us grant the danger of drugs by showing respect for them. The root of respect means 'to see.' Let us acknowledge those who are incurably sick from drugs by letting them come out into the open to seek help. Let us admit in public that drugs like marijuana are not as harmful as heroin and crack cocaine.

"My friends, by recognizing the real danger of drugs, the legislation I have introduced will make our society a safer place for all of us to live in, but especially for our children."

Now there was scattered applause.

"With your support, I will press forward in passing my bill to decriminalize the drugs that are making our society corrupt and our people sick.

"The so-called war against drugs has by now cost America upwards of six hundred billion dollars, if we factor in the expense of running our prison systems. It is time to put those enormous sums of money to better use. It is time to stop waging war against the drug problem and begin to cure it."

At the table below, everyone was looking up at Nick except Matty, who continued to poke the tablecloth with his fork.

Nick released the lectern, extended his hands to the audience, and then brought them to his chest.

He waited. The room was quiet except for the clinking of dishware.

"I would like to insert a personal note here. As many of you are aware, someone very close to me died a little more than a year ago. My beloved daughter, Lore Schlafer. She was full of heroin when she died. My guess is she got hooked somehow and owed money or found out something about drug traffickers and they killed her.

"Now some people—friends and people I respect, and others—are saying that I've introduced this drug legislation out of guilt over my daughter's death."

He looked around the room.

"They say I'm building a monument to Lore . . ."

He raised his voice. "You know what, folks? They're right!"

He looked around the room again.

"When I think of Lore—yes, she was white and privileged—I think also of some poor black child in the ghetto of New York City forced to deal drugs at the age of nine. I think of a Mexican child in a street of Los Angeles—tormented, hopeless, and drug-ridden. I think of children everywhere across this land. Sick children—the prey of evil men armed with the weapon of illegal narcotics.

"My friends, let us disarm these gutless profiteers. Let us take their weapons away from them. Let us free the children and lead them to the light.

"I thank you."

Someone let out a cheer. The applause spread. People here and there stood up, although most remained seated. Silvers was now beside Nick, grasping his hand.

"Good speech, Senator," someone nearby said.

The clapping failed to sustain itself and began to die. Silvers raised Nick's arm in triumph, grinning broadly at the audience. Someone else was grasping Nick's other arm. "You were great on TV." The applause stopped, the overhead lights came up, the ballroom buzzed with talk.

Nick followed Silvers's bulky figure from the podium and returned to his seat, which was to the left of Silvers's. They both sat down. Nick reached for the scotch on the rocks he had left there. It was watery by now. Silvers's left arm came up around him and tightened forcefully; his jowly face loomed.

"We'll get you a fresh one of those later," he said.

A new speaker was at the microphone. "Thank you, Senator Schlafer. I know that was heartfelt."

It was the Speaker of the State House of Representatives, Nick recalled. Monaghan. Frank Monaghan.

"Folks, let me tell you an anecdote," Monaghan began. The microphone popped each consonant. "I think it will bring out what the Republican Party means to this state."

Silvers kept his arm around Nick's shoulders. "I understand it's not going so good, your bill."

Monaghan said, "I was walking along Walnut Street the other morning. By Strawberry Market."

"I think it's going to serve its purpose," Nick said. "Get the issue debated." The lights in the ballroom had not dimmed again. Some of the diners were standing.

"I hear your committee support is slipping," Silvers said.

"Not so," Nick said. At the table below them, Matty had thrown back his head and was staring at the ceiling. Donald Fox was whispering to him.

"We still have a majority in the subcommittee," Nick added. "It's held for two months now. And others are still undecided."

There was applause for something Monaghan had said.

"That's not how we read it," Silvers said. "We'll have a nightcap in the lounge. A couple of people will be joining us."

A few of the guests were leaving the ballroom. Nick twisted to look up at the podium. Silvers loosened his arm hold.

"Folks, I think that tells you something about this great state of Pennsylvania. Thank you very much. And I want to thank . . ."

Nick said, "We'll have to make it some other time, Max."

More people were standing and clapping weakly. Monaghan stepped down and stopped behind Nick's chair. Nick stood and turned to him.

"We were counting on you, Nick," Silvers said. "Some people wrote sizable checks to meet you tonight."

"Sorry, Max."

"The party leaders feel out of touch with you."

"We'll have to do it later." Nick shook Monaghan's hand. Others on the dais were crowding toward them.

"Marvelous speech, Senator," the Governor called out. She raised her open hand and pushed her way toward Nick. People stepped aside. Nick reached his hand upwards. She gripped Nick's hand firmly and pulled him. Her face came closer, tanned and smiling. "You're going to be tough to beat," she said. She looked at him intently, smiled, released him, and moved away. Nick looked back over his shoulder. Matty was yawning. He looked at Nick and rolled his eyes upward.

Silvers said, "She can smell your blood in the water."

Nick steered the camper off Front Street onto the cloverleaf to Route 83. Matty's head turned to follow something they had passed.

"How did you like tonight?" Nick said.

"I don't know. Kind of boring."

"Hey, thanks."

"Not you. You know."

Traffic on the bridge was light.

"Do you know what river this is?"

"Duh. The Susquehanna. Can we come back to Harrisburg tomorrow? There must be coin stores here."

"I don't think there'll be time. We have a lot to do." Nick swung into the left lane and passed a pickup truck.

"What do we have to do?"

"First, we're going to get up early and go fishing. That's why you're heading straight for bed when we get home."

"Where are we going to fish?"

"I thought we'd try the Yellow Breeches at Allenberry Inn. It's big water, easy for you to wade and cast. The Letort's too tough."

The sign for the Park Hill exit came into view. Nick slowed and steered right. He swung onto the exit ramp, going slow until he could see the headlights behind him.

"How come we're going this way?"

"I want to see how they've fixed up the town for tomorrow. Carnival Day."

"But it's dark."

"We'll get the idea."

"How come we're not using your driver?"

"She's in Washington. You like the limo better?"

"Sort of."

"I feel freer in the camper."

"So?"

"We'd look kind of silly going fishing in a limo with a driver, wouldn't we?"

"I guess. Are Abby and Don Fox gonna spend the night?"

"Yes." Nick checked the rearview mirror. "You like Don Fox?"

"Yeah. He's cool."

The road curved left past a car dealership. They were on Central Avenue. There were booths with canopies set up along the sidewalk. Brightly colored streamers hung above the street.

Nick looked at Matty. He could not make out his expression. "After the fair, I thought we'd pay a call on your great-grandmother."

Matty nodded. "Fine."

"The town looks nice, huh?"

"Yeah."

Nick slowed and peered to his left. He saw Eckert's drugstore, its glass front reflecting the streetlights.

"How old is she?" Matty asked.

"Over ninety."

"I can't believe she's *your* grandma. It's like she's mine."

"Yeah, she's amazing." Nick slowed and turned left off Central onto Commerce Street. He watched for the headlights to follow him.

"Where are my grandparents again?"

"Your grandpa's dead. Your grandma lives in Baltimore."

"No, not Mom's parents. Yours."

As the town thinned, Nick sped up.

"My dad and mom are dead a long time. Long before you were born. I've told you that."

"I just never thought about it before."

Nick swung left at Tisdale Road.

"How is Emery related to us?"

"He's not."

"I used to think he was your father."

"God, Matty, he's not *that* much older than me."

Nick turned into the long driveway. The headlights played off the canopy of cottonwood leaves. He lowered his window. The cool night air carried the smell of cut alfalfa.

"What made you think of Emery now?"

"I don't know. Being here."

Nick steered onto the oval to the left of the house and stopped by an old maple. The car following them stopped just beyond the entrance to the oval. As Nick turned off the headlights, he noticed a tall ladder leaning against the gutter of the back wing. A flashlight bobbed in front of them. Nick climbed out.

"Hiya, Tom," Nick called.

"Evening, Senator."

The beam of the flashlight went to the ground. Nick could see Tom's stocky form.

"How's Dorothy?" Nick asked.

"She's not complaining."

Car doors banged sharply in the dark behind them.

"How's the fishing?" Nick went around to the back of the camper and raised the tailgate. Footsteps sounded on the gravel driveway.

"Gettin' good sulphur hatches," Tom said. He played the flashlight on the legs of the approaching figures, taking care not to blind them.

"Tom, you know Abby," Nick said.

"Good to see you," Tom said.

"Hi," Abby said. "This is Don Fox."

"Abby'll be using the guest house," Nick said. "Don'll be in the main house." He pulled out a small suitcase and handed it to Matty. Tom removed a larger one. Nick carried his briefcase and notebook computer.

"I thought we'd try the Yellow Breeches in the morning."

"Water's kind of swollen from the rains. But she'll do."

They all set off toward the house. The light came on in the front hall. The lawn looked freshly mowed.

"Alfalfa's in?" Nick asked.

"Almost. How you doing, Matty? Been a while. We've missed you."

"I'm good."

They climbed the steps of the portico. The front door was opened by a tall woman in jeans. At her feet stood a dark-brown cat.

"Hey, it's Fur!" Matty cried. He raced up the steps and scooped the cat into his arms.

"Hi, Dorothy," Nick said.

"Good evening, Senator. Look, Matty. The cat remembers you. And it's been a year at least."

Nick opened the door on the left side of the hallway and turned on the light. He could see the red light blinking on his answering machine. He put his briefcase and computer on his desk. Matty had followed him into the room, still holding the cat. The others exchanged greetings in the hall.

"Upstairs and into your pajamas, young man."

"You come."

"I'll be up when you're ready. And brush your teeth."

"You want company?" Dorothy asked Matty from the door.

"That's okay," Matty said, setting the cat down. He picked up his bag and climbed the stairs at the end of the hall. The cat trotted after him.

Nick went to the door and watched them until they turned at the landing and disappeared. "Dorothy, let's put Don in the room at the end of the hall. Check that there are enough blankets."

"I'll be fine, Senator. It's warm."

"We'll be getting up early to go fishing, Don," Nick said. "We'll use the camper. You take the Camry."

Fox smiled. "Don't worry. You won't even be aware of me."

"Get a good night's sleep. Tom, I noticed that ladder."

"I was cleaning the gutters. I'll move it in the morning."

Dorothy looked at Nick. "You'll move it tonight, Tom," she said.

"I'll see to it," Tom said. He moved to the front door. "I'll take you to your room, Miss Abby."

"I appreciate it," Nick said. "Dorothy, we'll fix breakfast for ourselves."

"Welcome home, Senator," she said.

"Good to be home." He went back into his study. The front door closed. Dorothy's and Don Fox's footsteps sounded down the hall. Nick pressed the playback button on the answering machine.

"Dave Segal at ten Friday evening. Call me tonight as late as you want. Important but no emergency."

The machine beeped.

"It's Josie. Call me, huh?"

Nick took his suitcase and climbed the stairs. He found Matty sitting on the edge of his bed in his pajamas. He was reading an old coin magazine. His clothes lay folded on his desk chair. His jacket hung over the back. The cat was stretched out at the foot of the bed.

"Teeth brushed?"

Matty nodded absently.

"Into bed!"

Matty tossed the magazine onto his desk and climbed into bed. He switched off the lamp. "Sit with me."

Nick turned off the overhead light and sat down on the foot of Matty's bed. Matty rolled onto his back and sighed.

"Hi," Nick said.

"Hi."

Light came from the partly open closet. A thumping and a squeak sounded from outside the windows.

"What's that?" Matty asked.

"Tom's moving that ladder."

"Oh."

"You going to sleep?"

"Yes, but stay for a minute."

Nick moved farther onto the bed and leaned against the wall. Matty's feet moved against Nick's legs. Nick felt for the boy's ankle and held it. The cat climbed onto Nick's lap and flopped down purring.

"Dad?"

"Yeah?"

"If drugs were legal, wouldn't that be like the government was saying it's all right for people to take them?"

Nick turned to look at him. The silhouettes of his stuffed animals lined the wall beyond his pillow.

"That's a good question. It's one of the reasons people don't want to legalize drugs. What I want is not to legalize drugs but to make it so people aren't punished for using them. We could have something like the Surgeon General's warning on cigarette packs: 'You won't be punished for taking drugs but we're warning you that they're harmful.' "

"Oh."

"Would that do it for you?"

"No. They should make cigarettes against the law. And liquor."

"Well, they tried that and it didn't work."

"Oh." He sighed. "But if it's okay to sell drugs, won't there be advertising? Like liquor?"

"Laws can be passed against doing that."

"Oh."

Nick listened to Matty's slow breathing.

He leaned forward, set the cat on the bed, and stood up.

"Stay."

Nick sat back down on the edge of the bed. "What's spooking you, Matt?"

"I don't know. This house."

"You'll get used to it again."

"I haven't been here since Lore . . ."

"We were here for the funeral, Matty."

"Yeah, but I didn't have to sleep here."

Nick patted the boy's leg. "I'm going to be with you more now."

"Good."

Nick tried to make out Matty's expression, but his face was shadowed. "Can I ask you something about Lore?"

"What?"

"Do you think she . . . uh, did . . . used drugs?"

There was no response.

"You know, Matty, she would have loved you for being loyal. But you can help her more now by trusting me."

"I don't know."

"I should have asked you sooner about this. It's just that—"

"It's okay, Dad."

"Anyway, I'm sorry."

"She smoked grass," Matty said. "That was all. At least when I was with her."

"Do you think you would have known, y'know, if she had used something stronger?"

"Yes."

Nick waited. Then: "What do you think went wrong . . . ?"

"I don't know. She was fine."

"She got so thin and . . . strung out."

"She worked hard. She didn't get much sleep. She was nervous all the time."

"What about?"

From the movement of the bedclothes, Nick sensed a shrug.

"Things," Matty said. "But she was really fine. We had"—a catch in his voice—"fun." He pulled the covers over his face.

Nick held himself still and waited.

"I can go to sleep now," Matty said.

"How about if I sit across the hall?"

"Okay." Sleepily. "Leave the door open so I can see the light."

Nick walked slowly to the door and across the hall. He turned the knob of the door opposite Matty's room and pushed. The door stuck for a moment, then sprang open. Nick could smell fresh paint, but from what he could see by the hall light the room had not been changed.

He felt for the desk lamp and switched it on. He looked at the bed. The wall above it was white. He sat down on the metal chair.

"Dad?" Matty called.

"I'm right here," Nick said. He picked up a heart-shaped picture frame. Lore with Matty on her lap. They must have been about fifteen and eight.

A telephone began to ring in another part of the house.

He picked up the receiver of the phone on Lore's desk, put it to his ear, and listened for the dial tone. When he heard it, he punched in Josie's number. She answered after a single ring.

"Hello."

"Hi."

"Where are you?"

"At the farm."

"How did it go?"

"Silvers thinks I'm in trouble."

"Election trouble?"

"Everything trouble. Election. The bill."

"What's he know?"

"A lot. I wouldn't have been elected without him. He controls a lot of money."

"Well, I'm sure he'll come around. How's Matty?"

"Asleep. I'm across the hall."

"Oh, Nick."

"It's okay."

He pulled open the bottom left drawer. It was empty. He rested his foot on it.

"When are you coming back to Washington?"

"I don't know. Depends if Segal has any speeches planned for me."

"What about Matty?"

"He'll be back early Sunday evening."

"Don't forget he still has a week of school."

"I know. If I don't bring him, Abby will."

He pulled open the top left drawer. It looked the same as he had last seen it, stuffed with letters and notes in Lore's handwriting. He had read every one of them. "We're going fishing in the morning."

"Don't wear him out."

"Don't worry. He's in great shape. A little spooked by the house."

"He's still having nightmares about Lore. He's only starting to get over her."

Nick pulled the handle of the top right drawer. It wouldn't move. He pulled it harder. It was locked.

"Nick?"

He pulled the lower drawer. It slid open easily. Lore's answering machine was in it, disconnected.

"I'm here," Nick said. He picked up the desk lamp and lowered it to the level of the top drawer. In the crack between the drawer and the desktop he could see the tongue of the lock shot home.

"What are you doing?" Josie asked.

"I'm trying to figure out how Lore's desk drawer got locked."

"She must have locked it."

"No, it was open after she . . . I went through it with the police. I'm sure there was a key."

He put the lamp back on the desk and picked up a crystal dish. In it were paper clips, rubber bands, and a postage stamp.

Josie said, "Well, I'll bet there's a logical explanation."

He removed the pencils from a black porcelain mug with a slogan printed on it, "Life's a bitch. Then you die." Some loose change lay at the bottom. He put the mug back on the desk and replaced the pencils.

"The key's missing. I'm going to break it open."

"You'll wake Matty up."

"You're right. I'll do it tomorrow." He gave the drawer another useless yank and leaned back. "What have you been up to? Have you got a book idea yet?"

"Not really. Things in publishing move slowly. I'm finally meeting my editor next week."

Nick yawned. "I'm beat. We're getting up at six."

"Are you going to see Helene?"

"We're dropping by tomorrow afternoon."

"Send my love."

"Which reminds me. I have to pick up a prescription for her at Eckert's. How am I going to remember?"

"Write a note to yourself and put it on the dashboard."

"Yes. Good. Thanks."

"Stay in touch, huh?"

"It helps when I get away. From Washington, I mean."

"I understand."

"I'll call you soon."

He hung up and sat for a moment looking at the locked drawer.

He stood up, snapped off the lamp, and went to Matty's door. He listened to his steady breathing. He switched off the hallway light. There was no response. He glanced down the hall. The door to the room where Don Fox was sleeping stood slightly ajar. Soft light shone from inside. Nick moved quietly along the hall and down the stairs.

In his study, he listened to a new message on his machine. Segal again. He pushed the button next to Segal's name on the phone console.

"Yeah," Segal growled.

"Dave, it's Nick."

"Silvers is hot."

"Screw him."

"Why couldn't you have had a drink with them? Stroke him a little?"

"What does it matter? He hates the bill. He hated my speech tonight. Who wrote it, by the way? Who's T.D?"

"Third draft. I hear you threw it away."

"It was pompous bullshit."

"Well, you haven't heard the last from Silvers. He wants to see you this weekend."

"I'm off this weekend."

"We'll see."

"How's it going?"

"We're holding on in the subcommittee. It's four to three, depending on if Diefendorfer's really gone."

"He is. He won't budge."

"I'm talking to Calder tomorrow. It may come down to him."

"Well, Calder is with us."

"Calder isn't anywhere until he checks out his bank balance."

"That's not nice, Dave."

"We're not getting any more players in the Senate either."

"It doesn't really matter. So long as we get it onto the floor. I'll give Calder a call in the next day or two—stiffen his spine a little."

"You better ram a poker up it."

"Do you have any speech dates for me? Or do I come back to Washington on Sunday?"

"I'm working on it. Call me in the morning."

"I'm fishing in the morning. And it's Carnival Day."

"The fishing Senator."

"Sleep tight, Segal."

"Take your beeper with you."

"Don't call me. I'll call you."

The line clicked. Nick put the receiver back.

He got up, went to the liquor cabinet, and stood there. He shook his head, turned off the light, and went into the hall. He stopped next to the entrance to the dining room. The chairs were pulled away from the table as if people had just finished eating.

It was here that he had last seen Lore happy. When she had given him the stamp that last Christmas. After that evening he had never seen her again—alive.

"RED HO." What did it mean?

He shook his head again, moved down the hall, and climbed the stairs. Matty had thrown off his covers but was sleeping soundly. The cat lay curled up behind his knees.

In the master bedroom he unpacked his suitcase, laid out old clothes for the morning, and undressed. He found a pad of yellow adhesive notes on the night table and wrote himself a reminder to pick up the prescription for Helene.

He set the clock radio for six. Five hours—if he could get to sleep. He switched off the night lamp. The sheets smelled sweetly clean. He punched the pillow and turned onto his right side.

The curtains stirred. A tree frog buzzed.

The telephone rang. He groped and found the receiver.

"Nick!"

"How did you find me, Emery?"

"Why didn't you take your driver?"

He pushed himself up and put his feet on the floor. "What's happened?"

"Nothing. I just want you to be careful."

"Is there anything new on Holden?"

"Nothing."

"What about the dummy?"

"Not much. A report came in. Seems it's a store-bought toy."

"What about the writing in the pocket?"

"An inspection slip."

Nick combed his fingers through his hair.

"Have you heard anything from your friend Mr. Rizzo?"

"Not since April," Nick said. "Just before the dinner where we talked."

"We can do it anytime now."

"At the fishing camp?"

"We're just about set up. The trees have ears."

"Well, I don't know."

"Cold feet, Nick?"

"I just want to see the point of it more clearly."

"Well, whenever you want."

"Okay."

"Stay in touch, Nick. You have that number I gave you?"

"Yes."

"Commit it to memory."

"I will," Nick said.

"Good."

"Emery?"

"Yes, Nick."

"I have to say there's one good thing about this drug bill of mine."

"What's that?"

"It's given me a chance to . . . to be in touch with you more. That means a lot to me."

"Well, Nick. The feeling is mutual. We'll speak, then." The line went dead.

Nick put the handset back. He stood up and went to the window nearest the bed. The night air was cooler. He could hear the wind in the trees.

7

The Autograph Book

Nick parked the camper with its windshield facing the river. Sunlight was beginning to shred through the woods on the opposite shore and fall in patches on the fast-moving water.

When he had opened the tailgate, he handed Matty a pair of waders. The smack of tennis balls sounded from in back of them. Nick glanced around and saw the gray Camry parked beyond the courts, at the foot of the hill leading up to the inn. Don Fox leaned against the front fender.

Matty put one foot into the waders.

"Don't forget, those will go up to your chest," Nick said. "If you've got a handkerchief or something in your jeans pockets that you want to use out on the stream, you better get it out now and put it in your shirt pocket."

Matty dug his hands into his pockets, made two fists, tugged them out and exposed his palms. One held a rubber band, a wrapped stick of gum, and a small Swiss Army knife. The other held some coins, a balled piece of tissue, and a small key with a loop handle. No handkerchief.

"What's the key for?" Nick asked.

Matty shrugged and pushed the objects back into his pockets.

When they had rigged their rods, they approached the river. The rush of the current enveloped them, cutting off the sounds of the early-morning tennis players.

Nick leaned his rod against a tree and stepped into the water with Matty. They waded until the water was up to Matty's thighs. Nick stood to the boy's right rear and signaled him to begin casting. Holding the rod in his left hand, Matty unfurled the light green line and laid his fly ten feet from the far shore. The fly danced through spangles of sunlight until the drag of the line took hold. Matty lifted his rod tip slowly and cast again.

Nick stepped back and to his right. He looked at the back of Matty's head. The baby fat was going, the contours of the adult beginning to emerge. Behind his right ear was the dark patch of skin that had once vaguely troubled Nick. Just a birthmark, the doctors had assured him.

The boy looked back and grinned. Nick pointed at himself and then upstream. Matty nodded. Nick turned and made his way back to shore so that he could walk on dry ground.

Upstream, on the still water above the dam, he could see the circular ripples made by rising trout. His breathing quickened. It was harder fishing quiet water because the trout could see the flies better, but it was his favorite all the same.

He laid his rod on the stone wall that bordered the river above the dam and lowered himself into the water. In the middle of the stream the water came up to his chest—too deep for Matty.

The sunlight hit his back, warming his shoulders. The rubber of his waders clung to his legs. Small light-colored flies skittered off the water. Fish were breaking the surface on three sides of him.

He cast above a rise-form and watched his fly drift over the feeding trout.

The fly began to drag. He lifted the rod tip to cast again. On the lawn above the stone wall a girl no more than fifteen or sixteen was sitting on a deck chair, sunning herself and watching him. She wore a full dark skirt and a light cotton blouse.

He cast upstream again, trying to see himself through the girl's eyes.

An old gray-haired man.

The water bulged near the fly. He snapped his forearm back. A fish was on.

A good one. The reel clicked.

He raised the rod, locked his eyes onto the bent tip and the quivering line that ran straight down into the water. The line moved in a wide arc toward the shore away from the girl. He turned away from her himself, feeling her silence at his back. He wondered if he was taking too long to play the fish.

The fish gave up and came to his net. Grasping it through the wet mesh with his left hand, he raised it high for Matty to see.

The river below the dam was empty.

Matty was gone.

He unhooked the fish, released it, and pushed his way through the water to the shore. He climbed the wall and strode sloshing past the tennis courts. The Camry was still there, but Fox was nowhere in sight. Nick leaned his rod against the camper and hurried to the water's edge.

No Matty. Not even as far as he could see downstream.

A blue van was climbing the road beyond the tennis courts.

His shoulders and chest were clammy with sweat. He trotted along the lawn downstream until he came to the next break in the trees. He stumbled to the bank and splashed into the river.

Away off downstream, near the far shore, he could see Matty's small figure. His arm was raised. He was playing a fish.

Nick stumbled slowly downstream, lifting his arms for balance.

Matty netted his fish, turned upstream, and held his catch high for his father to see.

Nick smiled and waved.

Nick pulled out of the driveway onto Boiling Springs Road. "That little key in your pocket. Mind if I ask what it's for?"

Matty looked away. "Nothing. It's just a key."

Nick braked and eased the camper across an intersection. He checked the rearview mirror and saw the Camry following in the distance.

Matty asked, "Why does Don Fox have to follow us?"

"He's just looking out for me."

"Are you in some kind of trouble?"

"Of course not. It's just a precaution you take if you're a public figure. To be extra safe."

"I wish I could have kept that fish."

"You'll catch him again when he's bigger."

They had to slow for a tractor that was crawling in front of them.

"How long have you had it?" Nick asked.

"What?"

"That key."

Matty shrugged and turned his head away.

"Look, Matty. I know you don't like prying, but I—"

"She made me promise not to tell."

"Lore?"

Matty was silent for a moment. "Yes."

"And you kept her secret. That's good. She'd be proud of you."

The tractor swung off the road.

"Some secrets should be forever," Nick said. "But I think this one should be told now. At least to me."

"Why didn't you turn there?"

"We'll never get into town that way. Too much going on with the carnival. I'm going to come in from the north and park on the outskirts." He removed the yellow note that he had stuck on the dashboard earlier in the morning to remind himself to pick up the prescription for Helene. He crumpled it and stuck it in his shirt pocket.

"Are we going to walk far?"

"No. There'll be lots to see. Rides too."

"Really?"

"Interested?"

"Not really."

"I noticed last night that the key to Lore's desk drawer is missing."

Matty shrugged again.

"Matty, I think whatever is in that drawer might help Lore now."

"How can anything help her now?"

"You know. Maybe help *us* . . . understand what happened to her."

"It's just a book, like."

"Well, could you think about letting me remove it and take a look at it?"

"Yeah. I'll think about it."

• • •

Nick found a place to park on Machinery Street next to a deserted building with SHENANDOAH FLORAL MFG CO painted in large yellow letters across its facade. He and Matty walked back along Machinery and turned on Arch Street toward the center of town. Balloons bobbed in the air everywhere. Music jangled from different directions. Children ran and shouted. The sun burned down directly overhead.

They walked up Arch across the old railroad tracks and past the open garage where the hearses from Belcher's Funeral Home were parked. It was in Belcher's morgue that Nick had first seen Lore after she died. He pushed the memory from his mind.

People began to wave at Nick. As they approached Central Avenue, the crowds thickened. A police cruiser was parked near the corner on the sidewalk with its barlight flashing. As they walked around it, Nick saw that Chief Don Ebright was sitting at the wheel looking straight ahead. Nick reached through the open side window and tipped Ebright's hat down over his eyes. The chief snatched at it, jerked his head around irritably, saw Nick, and broke into a grin.

"Hey, Senator Nick!"

"I'd have been a hold-up man, I would'a had you there."

Ebright climbed out of the car, readjusted his cap, and pushed his glasses against the bridge of his nose. At over six feet, he was as tall as Nick, but with his bottle-thick lenses and big rear end, he cut an odd figure for a policeman.

Ebright looked down at Matty. "Whatcha up to, Matty?"

"We went fishing."

"Oh, yeah?" Ebright turned to Nick. "Tough life."

"We're just here for the weekend, Chief."

"Where did you fish?"

"Yellow Breeches. In front of Allenberry. Took a couple of pretty good ones."

"Dad, I noticed that antique store last night." Matty pointed east on Central Avenue. "They might have some coins."

"We'll stop in later," Nick said.

"Let him go look," Ebright said.

Nick looked at him.

Ebright nodded. "He'll be okay in this crowd," he said softly.

"Okay, Matty. But stay there. I'll pick you up before we stop at the drugstore."

Matty ran off across Arch Street.

Nick looked around for Fox but couldn't see him. Must be in the crowd. "How's it going?" he said to Ebright.

Ebright took his cap off and ran his fingers through his crewcut. "I'm still following up on a couple of things."

Nick lowered his voice. "Tonelli?"

Ebright shook his head. "Stone wall. How about you?"

"Nothing worth talking about."

"Any clue on what that red whatsis might be?"

"Nope. Nothing."

A man came toward them from Central Avenue. He wore a checked shirt and a knit tie, loosely knotted. Nick did not know him, though he looked familiar.

Ebright said, "Come around anytime you feel like it. If I'm not in my office, they'll know where to raise me."

"Thanks," Nick said.

"Hiya, Senator, Chief," the man said. He stuck out his hand. Nick took it, smiling at him. The man tilted his head to one side and moved his large square jaw close to Nick's face. "So are we going to have a drug concession here next year?" His voice was husky. Bits of spittle flew from his lips as he spoke.

Nick tried to pull his hand free. The man held it fast.

"We could have a lot of booths. One for coke." He pumped Nick's hand. "One for heroin. One for crack. One for ice. One for marijuana."

"Bug off, Hess," Ebright said. He took the man's arm and pushed it firmly. Nick got his hand away.

The man grunted. "Meanwhile," he said, still with his face close to Nick's, "the policeman here has less to do, right?" He gave each syllable equal emphasis.

"Nice to meet you," Nick said, touching the man's shoulder. "There are a lot of people who agree with you, and their views will be heard."

"Oh, yeah?" Hess said. "If you get a chance later, come around to my store down Central. Art supplies. We can have our photograph taken together. For my kids."

"Maybe. See you, Chief," Nick said, moving away.

Ebright touched the visor of his cap.

Nick turned and made his way up Central in the direction Matty had gone. People smiled and nodded at him as he pressed through the crowds.

In the store he found Matty looking at a picture frame filled with coins.

"Buffalo nickels," Matty said. "Thirty of them." His voice was flat.

"Quite a find," the store owner said.

"You want to buy it, Matty?" Nick said.

"I don't know, I think I'll wait," Matty said. "Do you have anything else?"

Got some silver dollars last week, but I sold 'em right away."

"Okay," Matty said. "We can go, Dad."

As they crossed Central, Matty explained. "The nickels were polished. Smoothed down. Every one of them spoiled."

Nick pulled open the door of Eckert's drugstore. The interior was preserved from another age, with antique bottles lined along the dark wood shelves and a marble soda-fountain counter flanked by shining metal spigots. Tall wire-backed stools stood in front of it.

An old woman sat near the front window gazing out placidly at the passing throngs. A pair of crutches leaned next to her. The woman turned slowly to look at Nick and Matty.

"I'm Nick Schlafer."

"I know who you are," she said. "Hello there, Matty."

"Hi," Matty said.

"How are you, Mizz Eckert?"

"Miss Eckert. I am just fine. You've come to get Mrs. Schlafer's prescription."

"Right," Nick said.

"It's waiting for you on the counter over there." She pointed across the room. "Would you mind getting it yourself?"

"Not at all." Nick crossed to the counter perpendicular to the soda fountain and found a small plastic pill container.

"That's it," Miss Eckert said.

Nick took the container, put it in his jacket pocket, and looked around the room.

"I put it on Mrs. Schlafer's bill."

"Oh. Right," Nick said. "I was just wondering, do you still keep the old pharmacy records? Prescriptions and such?"

"If it's about your daughter"—she glanced at Matty—"the police have already checked those."

"No," Nick cut her off. "Actually, I was interested in much further back. The, uh, 1940s, 1950s."

"Those records are in the cellar. There must be a hundred years' worth. I have to clean them out one of these days. I thought you got the ones you wanted."

Nick looked at her. "Me?"

"Yes. Well, your family. Somebody came and got them a while back."

Nick shook his head. "I wasn't aware of that."

"They took a couple of years' worth away. I'd have to check."

"I'd be curious to know."

"Certainly." She looked out the window and then back at Nick. "But not today, if you don't mind. I'm all alone here today. I gave the kids the day off."

"How about tomorrow?"

"Tomorrow will be fine." She looked at Matty. "Young man, would you like an atomic fireball?"

"No, thank you," Matty said. "It'll burn my mouth."

"Well, pick something out that won't." She pointed toward a shelf next to the soda fountain. "There's cinnamon, peppermint, butterscotch, and I don't know what all. Help yourself. It's good to see you again."

"Thank you," Matty said. He walked over to a row of glass containers and began to browse.

Nick and Matty walked along East Carver Street.

"Is she mad at you, Miss Eckert?"

"I don't think so," Nick said. "She's just a little gruff. She speaks her mind. That's unusual these days. Here we are." They turned onto a front walk. "What's wrong?"

"It always seems so spooky," Matty said, looking up at a mass of porches, bay windows, and balconies, topped by an elaborate square tower.

Nick stopped and looked up. "It was the very latest thing when it was built. Like having a Porsche in your driveway."

"When was that?"

"Oh, about a hundred years ago."

"They didn't have sports cars then, Dad."

A woman in a starched white uniform opened the front door.

Nick gave her the container of pills.

"She's tired today, Senator. You mustn't stay too long. How are you, Matty?"

"Good."

She led them down a wide hallway and through a passage to the right. They came to a solarium filled with plants and wicker furniture. The room was hot and smelled of damp earth and talcum powder. An old lady sat in a high-backed chair, staring blindly into space. Her hair was elaborately coifed and dyed absurdly blond. She was smoking a cigarette. An ashtray full of bent and broken butts lay on a table beside her.

"Miss Helene, the Senator is here."

"Sit here, Nick." She waved at the empty space next to her. "You're not to mention my smoking. Is that you, Matty?"

"Yes, Greatgram."

"I want a kiss."

Matty went to her and brushed her papery cheek with his closed mouth.

"Hello, Matty. How are you?" She wheezed and coughed.

"I'm fine," Matty said.

She caught her breath. "What are you interested in these days? Would you like to read a book?"

"No, thank you. I'd like to look at those coins."

"Of course. Hilda, take the boy up to see those old coins of my husband's in the study."

"Yes, Miss Helene."

"Come back down when you're finished and we'll have some tea. But take your time."

Matty and the nurse went off.

"Sit down, Nick. It's about time you showed up here."

Nick pulled a wicker chair near the old lady and sat down.

"Light me a cigarette."

Nick took a filter tip from a pack on the table, lit it with a match, and handed it to her.

From the pocket of the housecoat she was wearing she removed a cigarette holder and deftly stuck the cigarette in it. "Now tell me a joke."

"Three Japanese divinity students sit for their oral exams."

"I've heard it. Funny, but far too long."

"My repertory is limited."

"Never mind." She stubbed out the cigarette Nick had just given her. "Tell me about Josie. Would you like a drink?" Her hand groped beside her chair.

"No, thanks. There's not much to tell. She's looking for a new book idea."

"I hope it's better than the one about that awful woman, Jeannette what's-her-name. Disgusting. Are the two of you back together?"

"How did you know we were apart?"

"I know what I know. Do you think we just sit here in Wheelersville tending our window boxes?"

"Josie and I talk every day. But no, we're not back together."

"What's the matter with you, Nick?"

"I don't know that anything is."

"It's your mother's fault. Your mother pushed you around."

"I don't know."

"Give me a cigarette."

"Grandmother . . ."

"Now, you promised, Nick."

Nick lit her another cigarette.

"Do you still sleep with Josie?"

"Grandma, I think—"

"Answer me, Nick. I'm as close to a disinterested friend as you'll ever find."

"I sleep with her occasionally."

"It's your mother. Your mother was too seductive."

"I'm not sure that's true."

"How would you know? You mustn't be afraid of asserting yourself, Nick. You can be tender *and* assertive. Women like to be swept away."

"Uh-huh."

"Why, I'm embarrassing you." She stared at him, as if she could see him. "You must not confuse anger with passion. That's your problem. Your anger interferes with your feelings."

"Dear Grandmother. Is it possible to have a normal conversation with you?" He took a cigarette out of the pack and toyed with it.

"No more than it's possible for you to show your feelings. Do you want a drink now?"

Nick sighed. "No, I'd better not."

"Ah, well. It's probably all *my* fault," she said.

"What is?"

"I pushed your father around. I didn't mean to, but he was no match for Stationer, and I tried to make your father stand up to him."

"I guess nobody was a match for Big Stash."

"Oh, I don't know about that."

"I take it back," Nick said. "You were a match for him."

"My mother was a strong woman. She gave her strength to me. Your father, God rest him, was weak." She stubbed out her cigarette. "I'm tired."

"Shall I go?"

"No, no. I mean I'm tired of living. Ninety-three is too long."

"Stop complaining, Helene. You look fine to me."

"I look like the witch of the crypt. But I have my memories. That's the compensation of old age. The past seems as real as the present. More real. I see your mother sometimes."

"Why don't you write down your memories?"

"I'm too blind."

"Dictate them, then. Hire someone and tell them the family history."

"I was telling it to Lore, Nick."

Nick looked at the cigarette in his hand. He brought it to his mouth and then stopped himself.

"You didn't think Lore was that focused, did you?" Helene said.

"I seem to be learning otherwise."

"Lore was made of good stuff. The strength goes on and on through the generations. The Vienna witch doctor was right. I'm only sorry she didn't keep living here with me."

"I've been thinking about Lore a lot. It isn't easy, you know."

"Poor Nick." She stared vacantly into the distance. "I don't know if I forgive you for throwing her out."

"You're one to talk."

"She moved out on her own, I'll have you know. I don't want to think about it now."

He looked at her. Tears were brimming in her eyes.

Nick sighed. "Well, Matty's all right."

"I hope so. I hope he's one of the strong ones. Like Stationer. Not like your father."

Her hand groped for the cigarettes. Nick pushed the pack within her reach. "There's one thing I want to know," he said.

"Only one thing?"

"The argument that night. What were they fighting about?"

"What argument? What night?"

"When I was a child, there was a big fight between my father and Emery. The house was full of people. It's hard for me to remember, but there was a lot of shouting. And then Dad just seemed to disappear. I can't remember him after that."

"When was this? How old were you?"

"About ten. Matty's age."

"That would be about nineteen fifty-two, three. Big Stash's fiftieth birthday! It must have been about the drugstore."

"What about it?"

"Your father didn't want to expand. He thought the family had enough. But Emery was full of grand ideas—he wanted to franchise, go public. And of course he was right. As always."

"Was my father trained as a druggist?"

"He even went to pharmacy school for a year. You've forgotten?"

"No, I don't think I ever knew that."

"Your father's idea of the world was a Norman Rockwell painting. He wanted to wear his white jacket and mix magic elixirs. From the look in his eyes sometimes, I'd say he mixed a few for himself." She sighed and wheezed. "Anyway, he was happy enough. Until Emery began expanding the business."

"And then Dad went away and we came to live with you."

"You were already living with us. It's hard to explain. Anyway, it's all in my diaries. You'll read them when I'm gone."

"Emery really took my father's place, I guess."

Her blank eyes seemed to search for Nick. "Yes, I suppose he did. God, he was a handsome boy. And your grandfather loved him. Stash worshipped Emery."

"We all did."

"Yes, he was your hero. It was monkey see, monkey do."

"You know, now that I think of it, I don't even know where he came from."

"From town. He lived with his mother. She worked for the phone company in Harrisburg. I don't know what became of the father—if he was ever in the picture. Why this sudden interest?"

"I don't know."

Voices sounded down the hall.

"About your mother, Nick," the old lady said. "I must tell you: she's been in touch with me."

"I'm glad, Grandmother."

"I mean it, Nick."

Matty and Hilda appeared in the doorway. A young man with long hair was with them.

"Hi, Matty," Nick said.

"We'll have tea now," Helene said.

"It's time for your medicine and nap," Hilda said.

"They'll stay for tea."

Nick looked at Hilda. She shook her head.

"We're going to push on, Grandmother."

"You must have something in your stomachs."

Nick stood up. "We had a late lunch. We're going to fish the evening hatch and then have dinner in town."

"Adrian will take you upstairs now, Miss Helene," Hilda said.

The young man approached Helene.

"Did you like the coins, Matty?" Helene asked.

"They're cool," Matty said.

"They'll be yours someday," Helene said. "Soon, I hope."

Nick pressed the playback button on his answering machine.

"It's Abby. I'm in Harrisburg. It's a little past seven Friday evening. Uh . . . I'd love to pick up Matty first thing in the morning. Don Fox and I will take him to Harrisburg for the day. That leaves you free to deal with this firestorm. Call me as late as you want."

"What firestorm?" Nick muttered. He looked across the room at the cabinet where he kept the brandy. The machine beeped. "It's Segal. Why the fuck didn't you call?"

Nick felt for the beeper in his pocket and realized he hadn't put it on that morning.

Segal's voice went on: "All hell is breaking loose. They want to meet with you first thing in the morning. You have to do it. Call me."

Nick took his hat off and sailed it onto the leather couch by the window. He rubbed the back of his neck. It was sticky with insect repellent and sweat. He sat down at his desk, picked up the phone, and punched Segal's number.

"Yeah?"

"It's Nick."

"Where the hell have you been?"

"What's the panic?"

"Silvers has been on my ass all day. He's threatening to make trouble. I've set up a breakfast meeting at the Penn Plaza in Park Hill tomorrow. Eight o'clock."

"I can manage that," Nick said.

"He wants to torpedo the bill."

"Let him try."

"Call Abby."

"I will. Cool down, Dave. I can handle Silvers."

"Maybe."

"Any new poll results?"

"They just came in. They look very good, but I haven't broken them down yet."

"Don't forget to send them to Emery Frankfurt."

"I always do. By modem."

"Okay. I better get some sleep before I face Silvers," Nick said.

"There's something else. I'm getting a lot of questions about your position on the budget."

"Well, you know what that is."

"I hear the President isn't getting anywhere with the Senate leadership."

"I'm not surprised."

"It may come down to a stopgap resolution. Members want your support."

"Well, they ain't getting it."

"Okay," Segal said. "Just keeping you up to date."

"I'll talk to you after the breakfast." He hung up, searched the desktop for his notebook, found it, and called Abby's number in Harrisburg.

She answered sleepily.

"Sorry to wake you. I got your message. You got yourself a deal."

"Okay. Good. What time?"

"I have to leave the house by seven-thirty."

"We'll be there around seven."

"He'd love to go coin hunting."

"We've got the whole day planned, including that."

"Good. Uh, do me a favor, Abby. When you see Fox alone, tell him I couldn't find him this morning."

"What do you mean, Nick?"

"When Matty and I were fishing. I could see the Camry, but he wasn't around."

"Probably went to the bathroom or something."

"Well, tell him to pee on his own time. I'd tell him myself, but I haven't had a chance to talk to him alone."

"Will do."

After checking in with Josie, Nick went upstairs. He found Matty sitting at a computer in his pajamas.

"Come on to bed, Matty. You're going coin hunting in Harrisburg first thing in the morning."

"With you?"

"No, with Abby and Don."

"How much can I spend?" He climbed into bed.

"How much do you have in your account?"

"Do I have to spend my own money? Hi, Fur."

"Of course," Nick said.

The cat stalked gingerly to the foot of the bed and flopped down.

"How 'bout you chip in?"

Nick sighed. "Okay, I'll match you up to twenty-five dollars."

"All *right!* What are you going to do?"

"I've got a meeting. And other stuff. Did you floss your teeth?"

"No."

"Okay, we'll skip tonight." Nick turned off Matty's bedside light. "Don't tell Mom."

"Promise."

"Matty, I'm going to take that key. All right?"

Matty sighed. "Yes."

Nick found Matty's jeans hung over the chair by his desk. He groped in the right-hand pocket until he found the key.

"Leave the door open so I can see the light," Matty said.

"I will."

Nick sat at Lore's desk, turned the key, and slid the drawer open.

Matty was right. There was only a small booklike object lying at the bottom.

Nick lifted it out and examined it. It was a red leather album about the size of a large postcard and three-quarters of an inch thick, with gilt-edged pages. The word "Autographs" was stamped in gold leaf on the front cover, and the book was held shut by a leather strap attached to a clasp with a keyhole in it. The strap could be easily cut, Nick thought, but when he pushed the button on the clasp, the strap sprang free.

He opened the album and turned the endpaper. The next page was imprinted with the words "Graduation Photograph" and held a snapshot of Lore squinting in sunlight, tall and thin, about twelve.

Her name was penned underneath in childish lettering—"Hannelore Wittvogel Schlafer."

Nick turned more pages—"School History," "Class Officers," "My Teachers," "My Favorites," each space below the various categories neatly inked in. Each page was a different color, some shiny, some matte. He stopped at a yellow page that had writing on it upside down. He turned the book over and read:

> When up you take this little book,
> And on this page you frown,
> Think of the girl who spoiled your book,
> By writing upside down.
>
> Helene Rupp Schlafer,
your Great Grandmother
5 June, 1989

On the following pages there were more inscriptions and signatures. "Thou art thy mother's glass, and she in thee calls back the lovely April of her prime—surpassed. Mom."

Then on a shiny green page: "To my sexy sister. Signed"—and then in a childish scrawl: "Matthew Schlafer"

Why had Lore never asked him to sign? Nick wondered. Farther along, he found written sideways on a blue page:

> I have a gentle cock
> Croweth me day;
> He doth me risen early
> My matins for to say.
>
> I have a gentle cock
> Comen he is of great;
> His comb is of red coral
> His tail is of jet.
>
> His eyen are of crystal
> Locken all in amber;
> And every night he percheth him
> In my lady's chamber.
>
> Anonymous 13th Century English poet
Cock-a-doodle-do, Francis Tonelli
August 1994

Nick shook his head. This was an unfamiliar Frankie. He closed the autograph book, turned off the light, checked to see that Matty was asleep, and went back downstairs to his study. He took a brandy bottle and a glass from the cabinet, went to his desk, poured two inches, and laid Lore's book on the blotter in front of him.

He took a mouthful of brandy. It burned as it went down.

He opened the autograph book again. Past the poem Tonelli had copied in, there were blank pages of various colors, more inscriptions, then on a yellow page, an exultant cry from Lore that stopped his breath: "This is the first day of the rest of my life!"

On the following pages were diagrams. Nick could make little sense of them. One, in black ink on a bright green page, looked like a tree with long curling vines hanging from its branches; when Nick looked closer, he saw that the vines were strings of numbers. Another spelled out in block letters the words "EAST BERLIN." A third showed a sketch that looked like a cigarette holder. Could that refer to Helene?

He turned to the end of the book. Fastened to the inside of the back board was a clear glassine envelope holding several postage stamps. Nick immediately recognized one that Lore had taken from his collection—a margin block of six four-dollar Columbians, crimson lake, issued in 1893, depicting Queen Isabella and Columbus, mint, unhinged, very fine, worth over $100,000. But overlapping it was another he hadn't even realized was missing, a heavily canceled copy of the 1942 Win the War issue, dull violet, worth almost nothing—pennies at most.

He took another sip of brandy and turned back to the beginning of the diagrams. The first one was a simple rendering of a square house with windows and an exterior staircase going up to a door on the second floor. Next to it was cross-hatching that formed what looked like a tower with a disk at the top. Above the house and the tower was what seemed to be a bridge with a curve beneath its span. It was as if the house were nestled by a river under a bridge. On the door were printed the numbers 4711.

The page of the sketch was red.

A red house?

Nick tried to think of a red house by a river. A house on the Yellow Breeches or the Conodoguinet, maybe? Offhand he couldn't remember any, at least not any with bridges over them. There was a bridge crossing the Yellow Breeches on the campus of Messiah College, but there was no building near it that he could recall.

A red house under one of the bridges crossing the Susquehanna? He could explore after the breakfast meeting tomorrow, but with five or six bridges in the Harrisburg area alone it would be like looking for a needle in a bale of hay.

Nick shut the book, pushed the strap back into the lock, and put the book in the drawer with the answering machine. The red light was blinking.

When had another message had time to come in? When he was upstairs?

He pushed the replay button. The machine beeped. "We're still waiting to hear from you, Senator."

It was Rizzo's hoarse voice.

Nick turned his desk lamp off and sat in the dark, sipping brandy.

8

The Red House

Nick followed the hostess down the aisle between the banks of tables. Her short ponytail switched as she walked. He could see Max Silvers sitting at the corner table, a cloud of pipe smoke drifting around him. To his left was State House Speaker Frank Monaghan, laughing loudly. To Monaghan's left, with his back to Nick, was a small, vaguely familiar figure whom Nick did not recognize at first.

When Nick reached the table, the men stood. The third man was Lester Calder of North Dakota, a member of the Senate Judiciary Committee as well as of the subcommittee that was considering Nick's drug bill.

"Sorry to be late, gentlemen," Nick said.

"You're not," Silvers said. "We were early."

They all sat down.

"A pleasant surprise to see you here, Senator," Nick said to Calder.

"No problem," Calder said. "It's an easy stop on the way home to Fargo."

"An unpleasant surprise for you, Nick," Silvers said. "We're not going to beat around the bush."

A waitress stood by with her pad.

"What'll you have, Nick?" said Monaghan. "The Bloody Mary here will wake you right up." He lifted his glass. His weathered face was already flushed.

Nick looked around the table. The two other men were drinking coffee. "I'll stick with coffee."

"You're from Wheelersville, are you not?" Monaghan asked.

"More or less," said Nick.

"Then you surely must know Belcher's Funeral Home on Central Avenue. A handsome wood building?"

"I know it all too well," Nick said. "Two handsome wood buildings, to be precise."

Silvers frowned, raised his hand and made a warning gesture to Monaghan.

"Well," said Monaghan. "Didja hear what happened there last week?"

"No," said Nick.

The waitress poured Nick coffee.

Monaghan sipped his drink and looked around the table to be sure he had everyone's attention. "Well now, they had a run on cadavers last Thursday evening, and two of Henry Belcher's morticians had to work late into the night." He sipped his drink. The men at the table regarded him curiously.

"When they had finished at last and were locking up the back door—the one where the corpses make their entrance—what should they find lying there but another carcass. Stark naked, he was."

Silvers sucked on his pipe and narrowed his eyes.

"Well, b'gosh, they unlocked the back door, lifted him up, dragged him into the morgue, and laid him out on one of the preparation tables."

"You're kidding," Nick said.

"Listen now, lad," Monaghan said, putting his hand on Nick's arm. He took a deep pull of his drink. "Belcher's two boyos scratched their heads and circled the table, trying to figure out what had killed him. But they could find nothing wrong with the stiff. 'We'll have to turn him over,' says one."

Monaghan finished his Bloody Mary, put down the glass, and tapped its rim with his finger to signal the waitress for another.

He went on. "Again, they perused the remains until one of them spied a stopper in his bunghole."

"Christ, Monaghan!" Nick said. "I first heard that one a hundred years ago."

"What?" said Calder, who was struggling to keep from laughing.

"A cork," said Monaghan. "A cork in his rectum."

"Oh," said Calder. He took a package of sugar from a bowl in the center of the table.

"Aw, you've heard it?" Monaghan said to Nick.

"Several times," Nick said.

"No, go on," Calder said.

Monaghan turned to Calder. "Well, they pulled the cork, and out of that dead man's fundament came the most lovely sound."

"Enough, Frank," Silvers said.

Monaghan threw back his head and began to sing: "'Oh, Danny Boy, the pipes, the pipes are ca-aa-lling.'" His silver tenor voice lifted thrillingly over the dining room. Customers stopped eating and turned their heads to look at Monaghan.

Silvers rapped the bowl of his pipe in an ashtray. "For God's sake, Frank."

Calder was quivering with laughter. He tore a strip off the sugar pack and poured its contents onto his bread plate.

The waitress returned to take their orders.

Nick asked for toast and half a cantaloupe.

"I'll just have another cup of coffee," Calder said. "I have to catch a plane."

"You've heard the joke, gentlemen?" Monaghan asked.

"A dozen times," said Silvers. "A dozen different versions."

"Go on, go on," Calder said. He dipped a teaspoon into the pile of sugar and brought it to his mouth. He caught Nick staring at him. "I have a sweet tooth." He slipped the spoon into his mouth.

"Is that healthy?" Nick asked.

"When my doctor tells me my blood sugar is too high, I'll kick the habit." He turned back to Monaghan. "Go on."

"'We better call Henry Belcher,' the first mortician says."

Silvers turned to Nick and said, "We've got some disappointing news for you."

"I guessed as much from the company present," Nick said.

Monaghan plowed on. "'It's the middle of the night,' Henry Belcher says. 'I was sound asleep.'"

"Can it, Monaghan," Silvers said.

"No, let him finish," Calder said.

"So down to the morgue he goes and they pull the cork out for him," said Monaghan.

"I don't get why you're so concerned with my bill," Nick said to Silvers.

"I'll tell you why I'm concerned, Senator."

Monaghan was shouting. "'Why am I pissed off?' says Belcher. 'I'm pissed off because you woke me up in the middle of the night and dragged me down here just to hear some asshole singing "Danny Boy"!'"

Calder and Monaghan dissolved in laughter.

Monaghan croaked: "Get it? 'Some asshole singing "Danny Boy"!'"

"Enough," Silvers shouted, his jowls quivering.

Monaghan retreated to his drink.

"So what's the news, Senator?" Nick said.

"He's withdrawing his support of your bill," Silvers said, indicating Calder. "That's the news."

"I'd like to hear it from him, if you don't mind."

The waitress arrived with their orders and served them.

When she had gone, Calder said, "I can't vote with you, Nick. I'm sorry."

"So where does that leave us?" Nick said.

"It leaves you in the minority, Nick," Silvers cut in. "It's four to three, or maybe even five to two."

"What happened, Lester?"

"I can't support you, Nick." He averted his eyes.

"I thought you were solid."

"I'm under too much pressure."

"He saw the light," Silvers said.

"Light, hell! I felt the heat," Calder said.

"From who?" Nick asked. "From what?"

Calder looked at his watch. "I have to catch my plane." He stood up.

Nick got up and began to move around the table to Calder.

Calder put up his hand. "I can't talk about it, Nick."

"Sit down, Nick," Silvers said, standing up. He shook Calder's hand. Calder turned and walked away. Nick and Silvers sat down again. Monaghan studied his Bloody Mary.

"Win some, lose some," Silvers said. He relit his pipe.

"Maybe," Nick said.

"It's dead, Nick. Forget it. Now you can drop this cockamamie thing and get back in the loop. I'll tell you this much. I've been hearing directly from the chairman of House Appropriations and he was talking about the supply depot's contract with the Navy. Ten thousand people could lose their jobs while you're out fighting for their right to put cocaine up their noses."

"I'd just like to know where all this pressure is coming from," Nick said.

"Nobody liked your bill, Nick. From the White House on down."

"There's a Democrat in the White House," Nick said.

"Well, you managed to create a nonpartisan issue out of this one. Now, let's forget it. We've got money to raise."

Monaghan chuckled to himself. "Some asshole singing 'Danny Boy'!"

Nick chewed his toast in silence.

Nick headed for the bank of telephones opposite the entrance to the dining room. He punched in the numbers of Segal's office phone and then his credit card.

Segal answered immediately. "Yeah?"

"We're dying in the subcommittee, Dave."

"What happened?"

"Calder was wetting his pants at the breakfast. Somebody got to him in a big way. He was so nervous he was spooning sugar into his mouth."

"Somebody hit him in the wallet, probably," Segal said.

"I'd like to know who."

"Where are you now?"

"I'm still at the Penn Plaza. Look. I think they're all overreacting, and I wonder why. What kind of pressure can we put on Diefendorfer?"

"He just called. I'm supposed to get back to him."

"Have him call me here." Nick read aloud the number. "How can we twist his arm?"

"He's starting to line up votes on the budget. Maybe that's your bargaining chip. Oh, there's a message for you to call Senator Bodine."

"What's *he* want? I don't want to talk to him. He hates the drug bill."

"Maybe he's had a vision. Call me back after you've talked to Diefendorfer." Nick hung up and watched the traffic in the lobby.

The phone rang.

"Nick Schlafer here."

"Greetings, mate. It's Dief."

"Let me ask you something, Ted. Which of the many favors you owe me do I have to call you on to get back your vote on this drug bill?"

"I can't deal, Nick. The word came from the top."

"From the President?"

"Close to. I've got no room to jibe."

"What about the budget?" Nick asked.

"I can't give you my vote, Nick. Anything else."

"Maybe we'll talk later." He replaced the handset.

Heading south for home, Nick realized that he had forgotten to pick up the morning papers. He swung the camper into the second cloverleaf he came to and picked up Hampton Ferry Road. To avoid the residue of Carnival Day, he turned north at the outskirts of town and parked the camper where he had the day before, next to the abandoned factory. Once again he walked up Arch Street, across the railroad tracks past Belcher's hearses. The weather was warm and muggy, the sky bleakly overcast. Most of the concession stands had been dismantled already. Traffic along the streets had returned to normal. Half a block from Central Avenue, he passed an old man in a black suit, walking a small black mutt. The man tipped his hat to Nick.

When he got to Central, he turned right to go to the stationery store. At the end of the block he saw Eckert's drugstore across the street. Hadn't he told the old lady he would drop by today? About those records she thought he had taken? He waited for the light to change, crossed the street, and entered. She was at her perch by the window, but there were two customers at the soda fountain and a young man in a white pharmacist's coat serving them from behind the marble counter.

"Hullo. I was expecting you," Miss Eckert said.

"Would this be a good time to see about those missing records?" Nick asked.

"Good as any, I guess. Come along."

She took only one of her crutches and with surprising agility led Nick to a door at the back of the store and down a flight of rickety wooden stairs. At the foot she took a flashlight from a shelf and snapped it on. The basement was lit by a single bare overhead bulb.

"I mean to clean this all out someday. We keep our records on the computer now, of course." She played the beam of the light around the room.

Nick looked up at a vast wall of shoeboxes piled on shelves. Stepping closer, he saw that each box was marked with a year. The dates ran consecutively up and down and to the right.

"Those are copies of prescriptions," Miss Eckert said, steadying the beam. "As you can see, they're filed by date. They go back to the 1890s, about two boxes to a year. The ones that were taken come from there." She played the beam on a gap off to the right.

Nick looked to the left. "The years before 1914. I'm interested in those too. Maybe I could send some of my staff to go through them? They're working on a profile of drug use before the Harrison Act was passed."

"Suit yourself. They could clean them out for me."

"Maybe we could make a deal." Nick took the flashlight from her and went to the right side of the wall. He played the light against the gap in the boxes. "From the early 1950s. Looks like about four boxes."

"I'm surprised you didn't know about it. I'm almost certain it was one of your people who came by and got them. Course it was a while ago."

"When?"

"Oh, a couple of summers ago. Why, I think it was when Lore was with us, as a matter of fact."

Nick lowered the beam to the floor and moved back to where Miss Eckert was standing. "Can you recall who it was who came for them?"

She shook her head. "I don't have the foggiest. I don't think I was even in the store. But . . . well, it's a mystery. I'm sorry."

"One of those things," Nick said.

"There would be copies on file over to Harrisburg. I think the law was the same then."

"Good point. Thank you." He handed the light back to her and started up the stairs.

The old woman followed him. "Come to think of it, I might have a receipt for those records somewhere in my desk."

"That would help."

When they reached the top of the stairs, Miss Eckert went over to a small rolltop desk to her left. She pulled some papers from one of the cubbyholes, uncurled them, and began to look through them. "Here!" she said. "I knew it." She handed Nick a letter-sized sheet of paper.

He took it from her and scanned it. The letterhead of his Harrisburg office was on it, although in a form he didn't recognize. A request for the records from 1950 and 1951 was written over his name. But the signature was an indecipherable scrawl.

He shook his head and handed the paper back to her. "It's certainly my office. I must have forgotten."

"Well, I was sure of it."

"Thank you for your trouble, Miss Eckert. If we decide to go through those boxes, I'll give you plenty of warning."

"Anytime." She led him to the front door. "You know, Senator, when you asked about the records yesterday, I thought you had something else in mind."

Nick waited for her to go on.

"I thought you were going to ask about your daughter."

"My understanding was that the police spoke to you at the time," Nick said.

"Oh, they did. But I keep hearing talk."

"Really?" Nick said. "What kind of talk?"

"That she might have gotten stuff here. Drugs."

"Well, I'd be less than candid if I—"

"She was not messing around with drugs, Senator. She was a good girl. A little headstrong, maybe, but good. I don't know what was going on between the two of you, but that was a young woman who was finding her way."

Nick reached out and touched her shoulder. "Bless you for that."

"Don't you forget it. Good afternoon, Senator."

Outside, Nick walked back on Central to Arch. At the corner he stopped and looked down the street. The old man in the black suit had stopped in front of a building near the railroad crossing. The dog was nosing the ground underneath a staircase attached to the side of the building. Nick's eye climbed the stairs. They went halfway up the brick exterior and connected to a balcony that ran partway along the second story to a boarded-up door. A window beyond the balcony was also boarded up, as were a door and window below and the windows and doors at the front end of the building. To judge from all the blinded windows, the building had long since been abandoned. Nick couldn't even remember the last time he had seen it occupied.

But the balustrade along the staircase and balcony was freshly painted white. At the head of the stairs, at the near end of the balcony, there was a new white door with glass panes in its upper half. To the door's left, a small window with two large panes and white framing had been cut into the old boarding. The glass of both the door and window looked freshly washed. Below the balcony, where the dog was now leaving his mark, a modern garage door had been installed with framing that was painted white in a jaunty ticktacktoe pattern. It looked to Nick as if someone had carved up-to-date living space out of the old abandoned warehouse and done so with an eye to appearances. But why hadn't the rest of the building been renovated?

Nick crossed Central and walked down Arch Street. As the area to the right of the old building came into view, he saw that standing nearby was a three-sided metal tower with a TV dish antenna attached at the top.

It was like Lore's sketch.

It was a red house!

But where was the bridge?

Nick thought of the curving span in the sketch and saw the connection.

It was an arch.

Arch Street.

It was a red house on Arch Street!

He hurried farther down the street. The cross street in front of the old building was Quarter Lane. The old man was standing on a patch of gravel in front of the building and trying to pull his dog from beneath the staircase.

"Hi," Nick called as he crossed the street. The old man turned to him.

"Didn't mean to startle you," Nick said.

The man stared. The mutt pulled at the leash.

"Do you know anything about this building?" Nick said.

The old man looked back at it. "Nosir!" He turned to Nick again. "Just that it used to belong to the cable company. Before that I don't know."

"Cable?"

"TV cable, y'know. Least that's what people said."

"Right," said Nick. In fact, coils of insulated wire hung from the wall of the building. "But it looks like somebody lives here now."

"I don't know. The midget used to live there with his mother, but they made them move."

"They?"

The dog moved off in the direction of the antenna. The old man let it drag him. He pointed across the street in back of Nick. "Ask them. They'll probably know."

Nick turned and looked where the man had pointed. An old railway passenger car stood beside the tracks. A sign on it read WHEELERSVILLE AREA CHAMBER OF COMMERCE.

"Thanks," Nick said.

The old man raised his hand and followed his dog up Quarter Lane.

Nick stood on the gravel between the building and the street and looked up at the door at the head of the staircase. It was secured with a brass padlock. Sunlight glinted on it. He thought he could see the tiny wheels that would make it a combination lock.

He took a step toward the Chamber of Commerce railway car, and stopped. Maybe it would be smarter not to advertise his curiosity for a while. He turned and crossed the tracks to his right. He stopped and looked back at the red building, shading his eyes against the sun. The windows on the track side of the building were all boarded up too.

He headed back to where his camper was parked.

"I'm damned if I know what that building was ever used for," Ebright said. "It's been sitting there so long I guess nobody sees it anymore."

"It seems to have been renovated," Nick said. "At least partly. Some fellow I talked to said a midget used to live there with his mother. But somebody made them move."

"Sure, but that was a long long time ago, if it's true. And I doubt it is. They also say a cable-TV company used it for a while too. That's why the tower. But it's all just talk."

"Why does the trim look newly painted?"

Ebright shrugged. "Beats me. Could have been done without anyone noticing." He knit his hands behind his neck and leaned back in his chair. "There's a woman at the Historical Society who might know who owns it now." He leaned forward again and reached for his phone.

Nick put his hand over the sketch he had made for Ebright. "Don, I'd just as soon we kept this between us for now."

Ebright removed his hand from the phone and looked at Nick. The light of his desk lamp reflected in the thick lenses of his glasses. "What do you want me to do then?"

Nick folded the paper in half. "Forget it. How's your eyesight these days, Chief?"

"Just fine, you S.O.B.," Ebright snapped. He lifted the wires from behind his ears and held his glasses in front of him.

"No trouble threading a fishhook?" Nick said.

"None at all. Or tying up a fly either."

"Care to prove that to me?"

Ebright put his glasses back on and slapped his desk. "You're on. This evening, as soon as I get off work."

"Good. And then, after dark, maybe we'll make a little trip downtown."

The glasses flashed. "Meaning what?"

"I'd like to take a look in that building."

Ebright shook his head. "I'd need a search warrant for that, Senator."

"Fine. Get one."

"On what grounds? 'Clear and present danger'? 'Concealing evidence of a crime'?"

"Maybe that last one," Nick said.

"Pretty flimsy." Ebright pointed at the folded sketch in Nick's hand. "How about this? That sketch there could be a 'Dying Declaration.' The district magistrate might buy that."

"But I don't want anyone to know I'm interested," Nick said.

"Why not?"

Nick unfolded his sketch, flattened it on the desk, and looked at it. "Because I don't know what I'm looking for."

Ebright stood up. " 'Scuse me a minute. I'm gonna get your daughter's file."

"Forget it. There's nothing there."

"How do you know?"

Nick sighed. "How do I know? Every comma of that file is in my head."

Ebright sat down and touched Nick's arm. "I understand that.

But maybe we're missing something in the pattern."

"Forget it, Don. I've been over and over the pattern. There's nothing more to connect Lore to the red house. Only the bloody lettering on the wall. And maybe Frankie Tonelli."

"He's clean, Nick."

"He's clean as far as her death is concerned."

"His alibi is airtight."

"But that's about all we know about him."

Ebright ran his fingers though his hair. "Well, his people aren't exactly talkative. And I can't be pushing them around. I have to live here."

"I understand that, Don. But on this red house thing: now I've found this drawing in her book." He tapped the sketch.

"It's not a whole hell of a lot to go on."

"But it's something. It's a piece of the thread."

"I would still have to have a warrant to go in there."

"If you have a warrant, who do you serve it to?"

"To whoever owns the building."

"That's great!"

"Or we can leave it on the premises."

"How do you get in?"

"With bolt cutters."

"Wonderful. Maybe you should get searchlights and a bullhorn too."

"What would you suggest?"

Nick slapped the sketch. "That the numbers on Lore's drawing are the combination to the padlock."

"How would Lore have gotten the combination?"

"That's one of the big questions, isn't it?"

"I can't do it, Nick. I can't let you go in."

"Then let's forget I even brought it up."

Ebright stood up again and turned to face the window behind his desk. In the distance, the traffic moved along the turnpike. "What do you think is in this building, Nick?"

"Well, I'll tell you this, Chief. I don't expect to find her killer cowering inside. And anything short of finding her killer red-handed would mean giving our suspicions away."

Ebright turned back to Nick. "Explain that to me."

"Come on, Don. It's obvious."

"Then state the obvious. That's what police work is."

Nick looked out the window again. "We've suspected that Lore was somehow connected with drugs."

"She was a druggie."

Nick bit his lip. "No. All we really know is that she had heroin in her body when she died. And that she used grass from time to time. In fact, I'm beginning to think she wasn't an addict after all."

"What's your point?"

"Okay." Nick hooked his index fingers. "One, she dies full of heroin. It might have killed her. We don't know. Maybe she injected it herself, as you guys seem to think. Or maybe someone wanted it to look like she did. Two, she leaves behind an elaborate set of clues, one of which seems to point to that building on Arch Street."

"Which you're not about to break into."

"Three, her dying act is to write words referring to it in her own blood."

"Maybe."

"If we connect these three points we can see the shape of something."

"Such as?"

"Such as something was and probably still is going on in that building that Lore shouldn't have found out about."

Ebright shook his head. "But why kill her?"

"Because it was something big."

"Something big in little Wheelersville?"

"Part of something big. Why not?" Nick said. "Just look at a map. You've got major routes coming in from two, four, seven . . . about ten different directions. Harrisburg is a hub, and Wheel'ville is just out of the way enough to be a perfect hiding place."

"For drugs?"

"Possibly. Or drug money. Or just information. Which comes in through that antenna tower next to the red building. I think Lore was onto something."

"You're talking interstate."

"Well, I'm going to talk to someone in Washington. Right away. Tonight. Meanwhile . . ."

"Not without a search warrant. I can't risk my job."

Nick stood up. "I understand that."

Ebright looked up at him. "Wouldn't that be the point of any legislation that came out of your drug debate? To knock out the kind of activity you think might have gone on in this red house?"

"It is, or was. Between us, it isn't exactly catching fire."

"I'm not surprised. But also between us, I'm beginning to think legalization is the only way. A lot of people I know feel that way. Though I could lose my job for telling you."

"They won't hear it from me. We'll both forget I was even here." He went to the door.

"We fishing, Senator?"

"I guess not this evening. Maybe tomorrow."

"Stay away from that building, Nick. This isn't like when we were kids."

Nick opened the office door and turned back. "You know I wouldn't do a thing like that, Chief. Trust me." He closed the glass-paneled door.

He parked the camper on East Carver Street, just down the block from his grandmother's house. He turned off the headlights and ignition and sat in the dark for a minute.

He climbed out, locked the car door, and walked west. The night air was cool. The sound of his footsteps echoed.

When he got to the corner of Carver and Arch, he turned right and slowed his pace.

Brandy buzzed in his head.

Dutch courage.

At Central Avenue he stopped at the corner next to the drugstore. The town seemed deserted. And it was Saturday night. Far up the street a pair of headlights came into view.

He looked at his watch by the streetlight. Ten-fifteen. Reasonable hour to be out. He crossed the street. When he was halfway down the block, a car passed slowly behind him. He forced himself to keep up a brisk pace.

Abreast of the funeral home garage he slowed.

No sign of life anywhere.

The red building loomed up to his right. A light bulb he hadn't noticed before shone from a fixture on the wall above the staircase. The window and door were dark; so was the rest of the facade.

He stopped at the foot of the staircase and tried to steady his breathing.

He grasped the railing, easing his weight onto the first step. It was firm.

He climbed the stairs slowly and mounted the landing. It too was solid.

He looked around. In the distance, he could see lighted windows at the backs of the buildings along Central and beyond, but the area around him was dark and quiet.

He turned to the door and knocked softly with his knuckle on one of the glass panes.

He waited.

Silence.

From the right inside pocket of his sports jacket, he removed the sketch he had made for Ebright. The light by the staircase allowed him to make out the numbers he had written, 4711, but the padlock was obscured by the shadow of the door frame. He took a penlight from his pocket, stepped closer to the door, and aimed the beam at the lock.

There was a set of four dials at the bottom.

Holding the penlight in his right hand, he grasped the body of the padlock with his left and rotated the disks with his thumb. They turned easily, as if they had been recently oiled. He set the combination at 4711 and gave the body a tug.

The shackle came free.

He lifted the padlock from the staple, swung the hasp away from the door, and replaced the padlock. Turning the knob, he pushed the door. It opened without protest.

He stepped over the threshold, pushed the door shut behind him, and stood listening. Faint light fell on a partition in front of him that was covered with small framed pictures. To his right was a wall fronted by a coat rack hung with garments and a stand filled with umbrellas. A short corridor led off to his left.

At the end of it, he stood once more and listened.

No sound.

He stepped beyond the partition and swung the penlight around.

There was a tiny flash of movement off to his left.

He took an involuntary step back and aimed the light toward the flash. He saw that it had been caused by the swinging pendulum of a glass-domed anniversary clock. It rested on a large desk near the west end of the building. Figurines of what looked like bronze and jade stood next to the clock.

He moved closer to the desk. Cobwebs stuck to his face.

The clock had black roman numerals. It read 10:32.

Had someone wound it recently?

Then why the cobwebs?

Beside the desk stood a large globe on a stand. Its lacquered oceans and continents were labeled in antique script. On the wall behind the desk hung five or six small paintings with ornate gilded frames. A brace of dead birds; a river scene; a bowl of fruit that made him think of Cézanne. In fact, it could be a Cézanne, from the look of it.

The paintings were surrounded by glass bookshelves lined with leather-bound volumes with intermittent gaps where more small objects stood. Delicately carved birds. A galleon cast in silver. Three standing picture frames, all empty. Above the shelves the wall rose to the exposed rafters that ran along the underside of the roof. The spaces between the rafters were filled with white stuccoed plasterboard.

He turned to his right and played the light beam across the ceiling and down the far wall. It revealed a four-poster bed with a white spread on it. The bed was mounted on a platform high enough for a room to fit underneath. A ladder went up to the platform. An open door to the room beneath revealed the porcelain and chrome of bathroom fixtures. Off to the right, the light passed over a sofa and chairs facing a wide glass coffee table and a large-screen television set. Beyond the television, on the far side of the room, stood a dining table with silver candlesticks and a bowl of dried flowers on it. Beyond the table rose a wall formed by a tall china cabinet with cut-glass doors. Inside it were shelves holding crystal and china. In the corner to the right, beyond the partition that defined the entranceway, Nick could make out what looked like a kitchen area. A large refrigerator stood at its entrance. Beyond was a sink, a stove, and a butcher-block counter.

He moved to the center of the room and swung the light beam 180 degrees from the kitchen alcove to the desk area and back again.

The room stopped short. It did not extend the full length of the building.

He aimed the light at the desk area again. The distance from the entranceway to the wall where the paintings hung seemed to match the length of the exterior staircase he had climbed to get into the building. Since the staircase took up only half the length of the building there had to be space beyond the cabinet that formed the east wall.

He moved beyond the dining table and shone the light along the glass-fronted cabinet. It rose from the floor almost to where the ceiling would have been were the roof not exposed. Along its top stood foot-high carved wooden chess figures: knights, bishops, rooks, a king, a queen. The cabinet ran from the wall to Nick's left all the way to the side of the refrigerator that defined the entrance to the kitchen. The refrigerator was brown, presumably to blend with the woodwork of the cabinet. It looked new, with an external ice dispenser and a cold-water outlet.

He stepped closer to the cabinet, turned a key to one of the glass doors, and pulled the door open. He removed one of the plates that were leaning inside and with the back end of the penlight tapped against the rear wall. It was solid. He put the plate back, closed the door, moved closer to the refrigerator, and repeated the procedure. Still solid. He moved slowly to his left again, looking for a break in the cabinet or some other sign of a passageway.

There was no way to get through.

He walked back to the leather couch at the center of the room and sat down. To the right of the couch stood a mobile bar adorned with half a dozen crystal decanters filled with fluids amber, crimson, and clear.

He turned the penlight off and breathed in the darkness.

Who lived here? Why didn't the old man with the dog have any idea? Why didn't Ebright know?

A low electric hum started up. Was it the refrigerator? No; its pitch was rising too rapidly. It rose and rose until its whine began to fill the darkness.

He stood up and turned his head back and forth, but he could not place where the sound was coming from. It seemed to scream all around him. It hurt his eardrums and made the back of his scalp tingle.

It went still higher and began to throb.

He moved back to the partition, went around it and along the passageway, and found the front-door handle. The building had come alive and was screaming at him.

He pushed open the door and was about to step outside onto the balcony when he saw the flashing barlight of a patrol car moving toward him down Arch Street.

He pulled the door shut again and watched through the glass. The patrol car slowed as it approached, then moved on, its colored lights pulsing.

Had someone seen him enter the building?

He waited until he could no longer see the reflection of the barlight, opened the door again, and stepped out onto the landing. When he closed the door, the sound of the electric hum was remarkably softened.

He went down the staircase and stepped beyond the corner of the building onto Arch Street. The patrol car was gone. The night was still.

He turned and began to walk up Arch Street toward Central.

Halfway back to Central he turned to look once more at the building.

At the far right end, beyond where the balcony extended, he could just make out the boarded-up window.

It dawned on him that the reason he could see the window was that strips of light were defining its outline. Where the facade had been a shadow earlier, it was now clearly defined by light shining from within it.

He had not been alone inside the building.

He felt for Matty's shoulder and shook it gently. The boy stretched and smacked his lips. At the foot of the bed, Fur stretched himself.

"Matty," Nick whispered. "Matty."

"Wha?" Matty forced his eyes open and stared at Nick.

"It's me," Nick said. "You awake?"

"Mmmmmmmh."

"Sorry to wake you, Matty. It's important."

"What?"

"You have a good day?"

"Yes."

"Did you find any coins?"

"Yeah, a few."

"Good ones?"

"Pretty good." He yawned.

"Matty, you have to tell me something. About that key. About Lore."

Matty stared at Nick.

"When did she give it to you?"

"She didn't. She gave me the little book."

"When?"

"Before she—"

"How long before?"

"A week or so. When I was out here on my February vacation."

"Are you sure, Matty?"

"Yes. Because she never let me look at it before."

"Why?"

"She had a list of boys she liked. I used to tease her. She'd get mad. Suddenly she wanted me to have it. She was acting kind of crazy."

"Did she say why she wanted you to have it?"

"She told me to put it in my closet. Then if anything ever happened to her, I should put it in that drawer and take the key and not say anything to anybody." He pushed himself up onto his elbow. "I did it when we were here for the funeral."

"What did she tell you to do with the key?"

"What I did. Always keep it in my pocket."

Nick reached out and combed his fingers through Matty's hair. "You did right. Did you ask her why you should do all that?"

"Yeah, but she got mad. She said, 'Just do it.' "

"But why the desk?"

"She said she wanted it to be found there."

"That's right." Nick pressed Matty's shoulder. "Go back to sleep now. We'll talk more in the morning."

Matty fell back and dug his head into his pillow. "What are we going to do tomorrow?"

"I think we're going to drive back to Washington. But we'll do something along the way—have some fun. Go to sleep. I love you."

"Sit with me."

"I'll sit across the way. Okay?"

"Okay. Leave the door open."

"So you can see the light."

Nick crossed the hall. The door to Fox's room stood ajar, but no light shone through. Nick sat down at Lore's desk.

He pulled open the drawer that had held the autograph book. He slid it free of its frame and turned it over. A paper clip fell out and clicked on the wooden floor. He looked at all sides of the drawer, but there was nothing unusual there.

He set the drawer down on top of the desk, reached inside the empty frame, and felt the underside of the desktop.

He felt rough wood and then the edge of a piece of paper that was stuck there.

Downstairs, the telephone rang, and stopped after a single ring. The machine hadn't answered. Abby must have.

He lowered himself to a sitting position on the floor in front of the desk and craned his neck to look into the drawer gap. It was too dark to see. He groped for the desk lamp, picked it up, and held it below the drawer frame.

He saw that a yellow page from the autograph book had been taped there.

He returned the lamp to the desktop, sat on the chair again, and worked at the tape with his thumbnail. It came easily away. He carefully peeled it free and brought it out into the light.

On it was a sketch of what looked like two cannons facing each other. At the bottom, in block letters, was written: "You have to ask the right question!" He folded it once and slipped it into his jacket pocket.

He fit the drawer back into its space, pushed it shut, and turned off the lamp.

After checking to be sure that Matty was asleep, he went downstairs.

Abby met him in the doorway of his office. Her long hair hung loose. She was wearing a full dressing gown. "I couldn't sleep. Don Ebright just phoned. He wants you to call him at home as soon as you can. No matter how late."

"Okay. Is Fox upstairs?"

"Of course."

"Did you talk to him about—"

"Yes. He's sticking to Matty like adhesive."

"Thanks."

"No problem. Don't forget to call Segal."

"I won't."

She made no move to let him pass.

"Thanks for today," he said.

She shrugged and smiled. "He's a good kid. We had fun."

"He and Don Fox hit it off?"

She nodded. "Oh, yes."

"Good. I'm grateful to you for finding him, Abby."

She looked at him with her eyes flashing. "Christ, Nick, you don't have to thank me."

"I guess I better call Ebright."

"His number's on your desk. You want a drink?"

"No, I don't think so."

She put her hands on his shoulders and kissed him on the cheek. "G'night, then." She moved around him and went down the hall.

He dialed Ebright's number.

"Don? It's Nick."

"Alive and well."

"Never better."

"And what did you find in your red house?"

"Find?"

"Come on. The beam of your flashlight was bouncing all over."

"Is that right? Were you downtown this evening?"

"So the lock combination worked?"

"Maybe," Nick said.

"Now, how did your daughter get it?"

"That's a question, isn't it?"

"Anyhow, I got a lead on the building."

"The red house?"

"Yeah."

"I hope you were discreet in asking questions."

"Totally," Ebright said. "I had a friend in real estate call."

"And?"

"Some outfit in Scranton. The IK Corporation."

"Can't tell much from that, but I'd guess it was a fake, a shell, wouldn't you?"

"Well, Scranton is a mob town."

"I appreciate your help, Don."

"Anything I can do."

"There *is* something, come to think of it."

"Yeah?"

"Would you know someone who could check prescription records on file in Harrisburg? Discreetly?"

"I might. They've probably been computerized."

"That'll make it easy then. From, say, 1951 through 1953. I need the records for prescriptions filled by Schlafer's drugstore."

"By and for who?"

"Let's try Schlafer, for starters."

"Okay, Nick. Prescriptions written by or for Schlafer. I'll give it a try."

"Good. I'll stay in touch."

"Be careful."

He dialed Segal.

"Where the fuck you been?"

"What's happening?"

"You talk to Diefendorfer?"

"Yes. It's no dice for now. He says the pressure is coming from 'close to' the Oval Office and it's heavy. I don't get it. The President didn't seem that much opposed."

"So what do we do now?"

"Just wait. Something may turn up. Eventually they're going to need votes on the budget. Maybe we can put something together when the time comes."

"I'll smell around."

"Listen, Dave. Did you say you sent those new poll results to Emery Frankfurt? I'm about to call him."

"I did. Wasn't easy either."

"How come?"

"A computer glitch. When I called them on Internet, someone else was transmitting a file, and it fed back into our system."

"What sort of file?"

"Just lists of numbers. Like a diagram. I saved it. I'm a nosy body."

"Did you ask your friend there what it might be?"

"I'm not sure that would be such a good idea."

"Oh? Why not?"

"I don't think he'd appreciate our intercepting his mail, whatever it is."

"Who is this guy?"

"His name's Merced. But keep it to yourself. He's a little paranoid about being in touch with us. He wanted to set up code names, but I said bullshit."

"It takes all kinds. Stay alert, Dave. I'm coming back tomorrow, it looks like. I'll be in touch."

"Good, boss."

Nick hung up. He opened the drawer with the answering machine in it and took out Lore's autograph book. He slipped the clasp, opened the book to the back, took the yellow page with the cannons on it from his pocket, and placed it between the last page and the binding. He pulled three inches of Scotch tape from a dispenser on his desk and secured the new page to the back of the last one.

He browsed through the clues: the red house, East Berlin, the bright green page with the numbered family tree, a half dozen blank pages, and the page with the cannons.

"You have to ask the right question." That was what he would tell Lore to help her solve the Easter treasure hunts he made up for her when she was little.

He opened the center drawer of his desk and took out a pair of brass tongs. He opened the flap of the glassine envelope, slid the tongs inside, and gently removed the stamps. There were four of them in all. Three were nineteenth-century issues: a ten-cent Washington, black, imperforate with bluish paper, the fourth regular stamp ever issued by the United States; a one-cent Franklin pair, Type III, and the magnificent four-dollar Columbian block of six. And there was one twentieth-century issue: the three-cent Win the War, early 1940s.

The nineteenth-century stamps were fresh and brilliant in color, superb copies. Using the tongs, he placed them along the back of his left hand and wrist and held them under the halogen lamp on his desk. The stamps were black, blue, and crimson lake. They glowed as rich as freshly minted money. He knew by heart the names of the companies that had produced them: Rawdon, Wright, Hatch & Edson; Toppan, Carpenter, Casilear & Company; the American Bank Note Company. Their work was weighty with officialdom, yet there was delicate beauty in the ornamentation of shields, rosettes, and scrollwork, and in the grave demeanor of the portraits. The World War II stamp was dull violet, heavily canceled, in poor condition, worth virtually nothing.

What was it doing in such exalted company?

It was helping to send a message.

But what was the message?

With the tongs, he put the stamps back in the envelope, closed the book, slipped home its clasp, stood up, and turned to the closet behind his desk. Inside, he turned the dial of a wall safe, swung open a small door, and locked the book away.

Turning back to his desk, he dug out his wallet and found the slip of paper that Emery had given him, then tapped in the numbers.

A man's voice answered after half a ring. "Delta one-niner."

"This is Senator Schlafer."

The line clicked and seemed to go dead.

Then a voice exploded: "Nick, my boy. What's up?"

"Emery, I'm ready. I'm ready to do our sting."

"When shall it be?"

"I'm coming back to Washington in the morning. How about tomorrow night?"

"We can handle that. Can you arrange it with your friends?"

"We'll soon see."

"How is your research going?"

"Emery, do you remember the . . . uh . . . writing that Lore scrawled on the wall?"

"Yes, of course. 'Red' something."

"I think I've tracked down what she was referring to."

"Indeed! That's good, Nick. How?"

"It's a long story, but I think she was going to write 'red house,' and I believe I've found it."

"Where?"

"Right in the heart of Wheel'ville. On Arch Street and Quarter Lane. Across from the garage where Belcher keeps his hearses."

"And what's inside the building?"

"I'm not sure. It's strange. Furniture. Paintings. And something else, but I haven't figured out what it is."

"Can I be of any help on this?"

"I'll let you know, Em. Thanks."

"Meanwhile, activate your friends. I think you'll appreciate what we've arranged for you."

"I'll alert you as soon as I've confirmed."

"Sleep well, Nick."

"You too, Em."

The line clicked off.

He walked slowly to the liquor cabinet, stood in front of it for a moment, and changed his mind. He went back to his desk, sat down, and took a deep breath.

He picked up the receiver of the phone and slowly punched the numbers for Salvatore Rizzo.

9

The Trap

He wanted a drink. It was just as well that he'd left the flask in the camper. He had to keep his head clear. Besides, it would be a shame to break the hushed spell of nightfall. The air had cooled quickly at sundown. Wisps of mist had begun to come off the water at the bend where the current slowed. Upstream, the huge boulders of the woman's thighs had turned black in the failing light, and he could just make out the froth of white water at her crotch. High above her far knee, he could see a quarter moon floating beyond the tops of the hemlocks.

He watched and listened hard for a fish to rise. It was too cool for hatches now. But big brown trout were known to come to the surface at dusk. A half hour earlier, while tying on a lighter-colored fly, he had heard a splash like a rock hitting the water. He had turned in time to see the ragged rise-form still drifting in the current near the opposite wall. He had nearly slipped in his hurry to get his lure onto the water. But a dozen casts of a light-colored caddis imitation had produced no action.

Now he sat by the stream on his grandfather's bench. The urge for a drink came over him in waves. But he had better be sober for what lay ahead this evening.

The cool night air made him rub his hands together. He switched on the tiny gooseneck light that he kept clipped to his vest for tying on flies after dark, and looked at his watch. It was 9:12. They would be here in a little less than an hour. Once again he slid his hand inside his shirt and felt for the tiny mike that they had taped to the hollow of his left shoulder. Amazing. It took up no more space than a Band-Aid.

He groped for his fishing rod, stood up stiffly, and set off on the path that led back to the cabin. His waders slapped and squealed as he stepped to avoid the snaking roots. His little lamp bobbed and caused the shadows of the tree trunks along his path to ghost across the forest floor. He looked for the glow from the cabin in the distance, but the woods were black. He felt alone. It was hard to believe that there were people all around him.

He was surprised that Rizzo and his client had been willing to meet at such a civilized time. He had been sure they would want to get together in the small hours of the morning. But Rizzo had agreed to everything. The fishing camp? Good. Tonight at ten? Fine. Just Rizzo and his client; nobody else? Okay. Done.

It was almost too easy.

But what was there to worry about? There were guards watching the camp's two entrances to make certain that only the two men showed up. The guards had metal detectors to check for weapons. They would abort the meeting if anything went wrong, or intercept anyone who tried to take Nick away with them—an unlikely development. But you couldn't be too careful, Emery said.

Of course whoever came could bypass the guards. They could approach the cabin through the woods instead of by the road, especially if they knew the area, which Nick was convinced they did, assuming they were responsible for the dummy he had hooked back in the spring. But he could signal for help just by pressing hard on the tiny microphone taped to his shoulder.

Once again he reached inside his shirt and traced the delicate wire from the middle of his chest to his shoulder. The device would also emit a signal if anyone tore it loose. So would all the other bugs Emery's people had planted.

He could just make out the faint light of the cabin in the distance. He turned off the lamp on his vest and quickened his clumsy pace.

Emery's men had also agreed to his demand for an emergency signal. They had placed a tiny toggle switch on the living-room wall.

It was connected to the cabin's electrical circuit. If the switch was thrown or any of the cabin's various appliances were turned on or off, all the lights would go out and Emery's men would know that he was in trouble. They would come running with their weapons ready. There were few appliances: a couple of lamps, a small black-and-white TV set, a fan, a space heater, a toaster, and an old upright vacuum cleaner.

He had also asked that a separate assault team be hidden in the trees around the cabin, but Emery had insisted that two men hiding just across the stream would provide enough support in an emergency. Even that might be overkill, but it made him feel more secure.

He came to the end of the path and stopped to look at the cabin. Only a few lights were on—the yellow one on the porch that was supposed not to attract insects, a couple of lamps in the living room, and the overhead light in the kitchen. It was hard to believe the place had been turned into a recording studio. Nine twenty-eight. Half an hour to go.

He climbed the steps to the porch, took off his hat, vest, and waders, and piled them with the rest of his gear on the porch's wooden picnic table. He found a pair of his running shoes on the floor and took them inside. As he sat on the bench inside the porch door and double-knotted the long laces, he scanned the L-shaped room. The place looked untouched, as it had for so many years now. He must remember not to throw any light switches absentmindedly. Luckily, they were placed in out-of-the-way places. He could remember his grandfather cursing the inconvenience when they had first been installed.

In the kitchen he turned on a gas burner to heat water for instant coffee and looked through the cupboards for a box of crackers. Behind a door in the corner, he came upon the espresso machine that Josie had insisted on having. It had looked so out of place in the rustic kitchen that he had built a cabinet with a ventilated door to hide it. Lore had helped him work on it, reluctantly at first; then she had gotten into it: a surprise for Mom.

When had that been? The last time Lore had come to the camp with him. She was . . . sixteen. Two years ago this month. The summer before the trouble began. The machine had never been used.

He found the jar of instant coffee in the cabinet by the sink where he had put it the last time he had been there and scooped a tablespoon and a quarter into a mug.

They had never found a single clue to connect Lore to her murderer, if there was a murderer, as Nick continued to believe. The Tonelli boy had been the first to find her. Nick had wanted him arrested as a suspect, but Tonelli had produced witnesses who had been with him when, according to the medical examiner, Lore must have died. And though they were not among the most reliable citizens of Wheel'ville—they were a couple of drivers and the night receptionist at Belcher's, where Tonelli still worked as a handyman—their testimony was acceptable enough for the police to eliminate him as a suspect. Ironically, he had been on duty that night, cleaning the very room in which Lore's autopsy would be performed a few days later.

The water in the kettle was boiling. He filled the mug and stirred in the residue of brown powder on the surface. He turned to the refrigerator with the thought of looking for a carton of milk, then wondered whether opening the door and triggering the light inside would shut off all the lights. Probably not, but why risk it? Might as well drink the coffee black.

Back in the living room, he paused to make sure the various couches and chairs were arranged within the camera's field of vision. It had been placed in the ceiling of the open stairwell at the crook of the L. They had disguised the lens as a smoke detector. They had told him not to worry as long as he talked to Rizzo's client somewhere in the room. The camera would find them.

Out on the porch, he looked in the direction of the road and saw nothing but blackness. The night was still. He cleared an area on the cluttered picnic table and put down his mug of coffee. He reached for the kerosene lantern that hung by its wire handle from a nail on the wall, swung it gently back and forth until he could hear the liquid sloshing inside, and set it on the table next to the coffee. With his left hand, he depressed the lever that lifted the glass chimney, and with his right hand he turned the metal disk that raised the wick until an eighth inch of whiteness showed. He rubbed away the excess char with his finger. He could smell the kerosene.

With a book of matches from his shirt pocket he lit the wick and adjusted it until the flame steadied and the lantern glowed warmly, lighting up the entire wing of the porch. He lifted the lantern by its handle and picked his coffee up with his free hand. Gently he elbowed the screen door open, and went down the steps. When the door slammed loosely shut behind him, its sound echoed in the woods.

Out by the bear's throne, he could hear the stream. He set the lantern down on the rock table and lowered himself stiffly into the seat. The cool night air made the coffee steam.

Fifteen minutes to ten.

He sipped his coffee. It was still hot enough to scald his lips.

The investigation into Lore's death had gone nowhere. Though Nick had insisted it was murder, no one could come up with a motive. When Nick suggested drugs, the police questioned that she had been a serious enough addict to get into trouble over them. Although she had been full of heroin at her death, there was perplexingly little evidence that she had ever bought anything more than marijuana. She had no needle marks on her to indicate regular heroin use. She didn't owe anybody. Why would drug dealers kill her? It didn't add up.

Nothing else did either that might have suggested homicide. There was no indication of forced entry. No rape or robbery. No signs of struggle. No clues except the five bloody letters on the wall, which proved nothing. It had to be suicide, the police said.

Another complication was the impossibility of establishing what had caused her death. The blood from her wounds had soaked into her mattress, so that whether she had lost enough to kill her could not be established. At the same time, the fluid in her lungs—pulmonary edema—indicated an overdose of heroin. But no determination could be made if it was severe enough to cause death from hypoxia. Either way, she could have committed suicide, and in the absence of any other evidence, the police were content to leave it at that. But Nick couldn't buy it. If there was no forced entry, then Lore must have let her killer in.

He looked at his watch. Seven minutes to ten. The woods were still black for as far as his eyes could see. He lowered the wick of the lantern so that it would be easier to detect the light of an approaching car.

Whenever he forced himself to think about that last night, he found the most terrible part was not in discovering what had been done to Lore but the moment just before, when they had been about to pull the sheet back to show him. What led up to that moment seemed unreal—random images from a third-rate movie he had been forced to play a part in: the multicolored lights of the police cars flashing in front of the funeral home; the tall uniformed men crowded in the parlor with bared heads that made them look as if they were attending a fallen comrade's wake. He had been weak in the knees as they led him into the back room. The sweet smell of embalming fluid had almost made him sick. He had to force himself to look down at the examining table where his daughter lay, all covered up with a sheet. The coroner stood on the far side of her, watching Nick's face to see if he was ready. Then he had leaned over and slowly peeled the sheet away.

Nick held his breath and looked. What he saw was a ghost—Lore drained of blood. Her mouth was parted in amazement. Her eyes, sunk in caves, stared out as if in shock. Her breasts lay skewed off center on the two sides of her rib cage. It struck Nick that this was the first time he had ever seen them. Her arms rested on either side of her hips. The fingers of her left hand were still stained with the blood she had used to write the beginning of her message on the wall—RED HO—if it was really her message. Nick moved his gaze up along her left arm to look for the needle mark where, they had told him, she had injected the potentially lethal dose of heroin. But her arm was still too crusted with the blood from the gaping gash in her wrist.

He shifted his eyes to the wound on her other wrist. Who else but she could have cut her wrists diagonally like that, at just the correct angles for self-inflicted wounds? A knowledgeable killer could have done it if he had subdued Lore first or attacked her after she had drugged herself. That was what Nick believed had happened.

But it was just as plausible that she had drugged herself, then cut her own wrists. Then with her remaining strength she had written her message on the wall to explain her suicide. That was what the police believed.

Between her arms rose the mound of her belly. It wasn't flat or sunken because, he now knew, inside it lay a four-and-a-half-month-old female child.

Not Tonelli's, the DNA had told them.

Whose then?

That had cinched it for the police. Lore was pregnant. She had killed herself by ODing and cutting her wrists.

He drank the last of his coffee and looked at his watch again. It was 10:02. A whisper of wind stirred in the treetops. A bobwhite whistled its two-note song nearby. He looked toward the stream to see if there was any sign of the men hiding on the other side. Of course there wasn't. He would be almost happy for some company now, but the woods remained silent.

He pushed his hand against the stone table and began stiffly to rise.

He felt something brush lightly against his shoulder.

A branch, he thought half consciously.

He leaned to pick up the lantern. As he straightened up, something covered his mouth and pulled his head back hard enough to hurt his neck. He tried to cry out but he couldn't breathe. All he could see was the branches above his head. As he struggled to loose himself, powerful arms embraced him from the front and a thigh pressed up against his groin, driving him back against the solid body that was holding him from behind. It occurred to him that he was about to be raped.

The hand on his mouth slid up to cover his eyes, and he could breathe again. But before he could cry out, he heard a tearing sound and felt sticky material being pressed against his lips and cheeks. It tasted rubbery and sealed his mouth, but he could breathe through his nose. The hand went away from his eyes and he was no longer being hugged, only held lightly at his elbows by someone in back of him. As he tipped his head forward, a bright light shone in his eyes and he heard a high-pitched electronic squeal that went higher like the rising sound of a siren until it passed out of the range of his hearing and made his head ache, then came down again and steadied.

He was waiting for Emery's men now.

"I think I got it," a man's voice behind the light said.

"Okay," said the man who was holding him. "I'm going to take it now." His fingers went up Nick's arm and groped at his shirt collar, then slid down his chest and probed lightly back and forth until they found the tiny wire and tore it firmly away. The squealing sound stopped, the light went away from Nick's eyes, and he was released. He still could not see.

"You can take the tape off your mouth," a shadow in the lamplight said.

Nick found the edge with his fingernails and pulled the tape painfully away. He gulped for air. He could now see the two figures standing in front of him. One of them held what looked like some sort of assault rifle. Their faces were dark.

Nick gasped, "You made a mistake removing that microphone."

"Don't worry about it, Senator."

The man with the gun picked up the kerosene lantern and looked at it. "How do you turn this thing off?"

"Turn the little wheel," Nick said.

The other man reached for it. He had a ski mask on. He raised the lantern to the level of his eyes, looked at it, and then handed it to Nick. "Isn't that kind of risky around here?"

Nick shrugged. "I never thought about it." He looked toward the woods. There was still no sign of light.

"Forget it, Senator. No one's coming."

The screen door on the porch slammed. "You can bring him in now," a third man called out. "It's all clear."

The man with the gun gestured with it toward the house. He too had a ski mask on, and a cap with a pompom. He was short and very fat.

"Move," he said. His voice was high-pitched. He tapped Nick's shoulder with the gun."

"That isn't necessary, buddy," Nick said.

The fat man tapped Nick with the gun again. Nick braced himself and drove his right shoulder at the man, raising his left arm to deflect the weapon. The fat man absorbed Nick's charge with his stomach and stepped forward effortlessly, knocking Nick to the ground. He stood over Nick, not bothering to aim the gun at him again.

Nick clambered up, pushing his eyeglasses back into position, and faced the man.

"So you're the enforcer, huh?"

The man gestured with the gun toward the porch. "You got a problem with that, Senator?" He grasped Nick's shoulder with his left hand.

Nick tried to shake himself loose. "Yes, I do." He tried to steady his voice. "I don't like bullies."

The fat man gripped Nick's shoulder tighter and propelled him toward the porch.

Nick pulled himself free and backed away. "I think maybe my daughter ran into someone like you."

The man moved toward Nick and then stopped as if he'd walked into a wall.

"Hey, mister. I don't know what you're talking about, whatever happened to your daughter. I don't mess with women." His torso deflated. "Now let's go back inside."

Nick stumbled forward on his own. He still could not catch his breath. The man on the porch held the door open for them. Inside, two more men, both wearing ski masks, were standing by the stairwell.

"Take a seat, Senator," the fat man said.

Nick set the lantern down on the bench by the door. Its flame burned brightly. He crossed the room and headed for a rocking chair that faced the couch.

"No. In the corner, on the couch."

Nick sat at the end of the couch where he had planned to put Rizzo's client. He could see now that the men by the stairwell had covered the dummy smoke detector with black tape.

"Just relax there, Senator," one of the other men said. Nick spread his hands in a gesture of helplessness and leaned back. The fat man waddled toward Nick and then stopped in the middle of the room. "We got the camera and all the bugs," he said. "Is there anything else you wanna tell us about?"

Nick shrugged. The man nodded and moved across the room to the front door off to Nick's right. The other four men crowded out the back door onto the porch. Suddenly Nick was alone again. The only sign of life was a cigarette glowing in the dark beyond the porch. Nick waited. The house gave off a single ticking sound, its woodwork adjusting to some obscure change of temperature.

The front door creaked, and a man Nick recognized as Rizzo was standing there. He wore sharply creased slacks and a light windbreaker over a blue dress shirt and red tie. He stared at Nick indifferently.

Nick forced himself to nod a greeting. Rizzo, ignoring him, looked around the room, then turned to face the door. He put his hands in the side pockets of his jacket. It occurred to Nick that he might be gripping a gun.

They both waited.

Nick looked across the room at the kerosene lantern. The flame was still burning steadily. He heard footsteps on the front stairs.

A small figure bounded into the room and stood facing Rizzo. He had on jeans, a red-and-black-checked woolen lumberjack shirt that was not tucked in, and ragged sneakers. He carried a scuffed vinyl attaché case. His face was red from exertion, but his eyes looked not unfriendly behind eyeglasses with clear plastic frames. He regarded Rizzo with amusement.

"Rizzo," he said in an unnaturally deep and resonant voice. "Look at you." He extended his hand. "You look like a hood. Shame on you. You scare people." He turned toward Nick, still gesturing at Rizzo. "He looks like a mafioso."

Nick looked at Rizzo. His haughty expression hadn't changed.

"Don't mind him," the smaller man said, advancing lightly toward Nick. He held out his hand. "I'm the client. My name is Leonard Meyers Scordia. You can call me Lenny."

Nick took his hand. It felt fragile.

"Sorry about the rough stuff, but you know . . ." He shrugged, looked around, then stepped to a bentwood rocking chair opposite Nick and sat down.

"Okay, Senator." He rubbed his hands together, then looked around at Rizzo. "Why don't you go watch the door, Sal."

Rizzo stalked to the front door and leaned against its frame.

"Good," said Lenny, turning back to Nick. "So, Senator." He bounced his heels on the floor and looked around the room. "This is nice. Cozy." He looked at Nick.

Nick said nothing.

"What would you have to pay for something like this, if you don't mind my asking?"

Nick stared and shook his head.

"I'm being nosy. It's a failing of mine."

"Your single blemish, no doubt."

Lenny's face froze for an instant, then broke into a smile. "You're right, Senator. You've been assaulted. You need time to recover. My apologies."

"I'm fine," Nick said. "You people don't bother me."

"No, no. Relax. Tell me when you're ready to talk."

"I just take issue with the way you asked for this meeting."

Lenny cocked his head and frowned. "I don't get you."

"The note you planted outside. 'Why don't we meet?' And the dummy in the stream. I resent it."

Lenny rocked forward and held up his hand. "Wait. Wait. Wait. The note, yes, that maybe was not so nice. That's Rizzo's way. I can't always control him. I apologize for that, though it was hard to get through to you. But the thing in the stream? I don't know from that."

"A Charlie McCarthy doll."

"It wasn't us, believe me." He looked around again. "Anyway, you got a nice place here. You're here alone a lot, or so I'm told."

"How do you happen to know that?"

"I make it a point to know as much as I can about the people I'm going to do business with."

"This is business, Mr. Scordia?"

"Lenny, Lenny. Please. Well, I'm sorry about the rough stuff. They didn't hurt you, did they?"

"Not really. They just surprised me. Your fat man flexed his muscles a little."

"Tell me, did we locate everything? All the gadgets?"

"I guess you did," Nick said.

"I don't like it any more than you do, the goombah stuff. I'm really trying to do something about it."

Nick looked at Rizzo and then in the direction of the porch. He raised his eyebrows.

"I know, I know," Lenny said. "Rome wasn't sacked in a day. And you know something? That *Godfather* movie didn't help."

"I don't think I follow."

Lenny stood up, circled behind the rocking chair, and balanced himself against it. "Have you read Nozick?"

"Nozick?"

"Robert Nozick. A philosopher. Went from being a New Left guy in the early sixties to a Harvard professor in the seventies."

Nick shrugged. "Never heard of him."

"In his book *Anarchy, State, and Utopia,* Nozick explains how the minimal political state—what classical liberal philosophers called 'the night-watchman state'—how it evolved from a state of nature."

Nick slowly shook his head. "This is a little heavy, Scordia."

"Lenny."

"I'm not a political scientist."

Lenny came around the chair. "You'll see what I'm getting at." He sat down and extended the palms of his hands toward Nick as if offering him something. "Nozick tells us that nothing more extensive than that minimal 'night-watchman state' can be justified. Justified philosophically, that is. See what I mean?"

"Sort of."

"A state that protects us from anarchy and does nothing more is as close as we can get to utopia, Nozick writes. Anarchy, state, and utopia, get it?"

Nick nodded.

Lenny sat back and sighed. "It's a pleasure to talk to an intelligent man." He leaned forward again and lowered his voice. "You think it's fun being with these guys all day?"

"I still don't understand."

"I didn't make my point yet. My point is, a lot of people wanted to go back to that minimal state. They had it with the welfare state, what Nozick calls 'redistributive justice.' It's why people voted for Reagan."

"Is that all you're saying?"

Scordia threw his hands up. "Is that all I'm saying!" He pressed his glasses to the bridge of his nose and smiled at Nick. "You're right. Forgive me. I spend too much time reading. What I'm trying to say is that what we do—"

"Who's 'we'?"

"You know." Scordia pressed his finger to the tip of his nose and pushed it to one side. "People secretly admire us because we're running like a minimal state. We give justice. We protect from anarchy. See?"

Nick stared at him. "You don't expect me to—"

"No, no. Listen. People secretly admire us too because of *The Godfather.* Or you could say they liked the film because it was about justice. Swift justice. Hard to get these days."

"It was a good story," Nick said.

"But it was wrong, wrong." Lenny stood up and leaned toward Nick. "It made the whole thing romantic. It showed people going to the don to ask for protection. What it did not show was the don going to the people and telling them they had to have protection." He pounded his right fist into the flat of his other hand. "Whether they want it or not. Which is what it's really like. Not so romantic."

Nick nodded again.

"The 'night-watchman state' is imposed against the people's will," Scordia said, raising his voice. "This is *not* utopia! This is dystopia." He sat down and nodded his head thoughtfully. Then he looked at Nick again. "I get carried away on this subject." He rubbed his hands together and looked around the room. "Let's have something to eat. Sal, tell the boys it's time to eat."

Rizzo nodded and went out the door. Nick could hear low voices murmuring out front.

"You'll have something too, Senator. We got plenty."

"I'll pass, if you don't mind. I had supper."

"Okay. But I didn't. I'm a little hungry. I'll eat and then we'll talk."

"Suit yourself, Mr.—"

"Lenny."

Nick uncrossed his legs.

"Would you mind if I stand up a minute? My leg's asleep."

"Please, Senator. You're not a prisoner here. I'm *your* guest."

Nick stood up stiffly, and gingerly shifted his weight. He heard voices approaching the house out front. There were more footsteps on the steps, and then Rizzo and a new man appeared. The new man was small and out of breath. He had on a ski mask and was carrying a large wicker picnic hamper. Rizzo directed him to set it down on the coffee table between Nick and Scordia.

"There you go," Rizzo said. "Everything's there, including the beer and wine."

"Thank you, Sal."

Rizzo took three steps back and stood with his arms folded and his right leg thrust forward. With a slightest gesture of his head, he signaled the new man to his side. They watched as Lenny began to rummage in the hamper, removing a foil-wrapped tube, a wickered jug of Chianti, a glass, and a folded white-and-red-checked napkin, which he shook out and tucked ceremoniously into his collar. He peeled away foil and greasy wax paper from the tube, exposing a foot-long roll sliced lengthwise and bursting with lettuce, tomatoes, peppers, and cold cuts. Indicating the wine bottle, he made an upward spiraling gesture with his finger pointed down. Rizzo snapped his fingers at the new man, who stepped forward, removed a corkscrew from his jacket pocket, and went to work on the bottle.

"You sure, Senator? We got plenty."

"Thanks. I'm sure."

The small man tugged the cork free and filled Lenny's glass.

"Glass of wine?" Lenny asked.

"No, really." Nick sat down again, tapped his stomach and shook his head.

Lenny searched in the hamper, removed a glass jar, uncapped it, and poured its oily contents along the length of his sandwich. "Okay. It's all yours, Sal. *Mangia.*"

Rizzo snapped his fingers again. His companion lifted the hamper and the wine bottle and carried them to the table in the dining alcove beyond the front door. Rizzo joined him there. Lenny picked up a section of the sandwich and tore off a large bite. He chewed thoughtfully, then sipped his wine.

"Good," he said, his mouth still half full. He wiped his face with his napkin. Nick forced a smile and looked away. The flame of the kerosene lantern was beginning to flicker. The room was quiet, except for the sound of munching.

"Okay," Lenny finally said, wiping his face and hands with the napkin. He smiled and opened his arms. "Perhaps you're wondering why I've called you all together here today?"

Nick said nothing.

Lenny laughed. "You gotta forgive me, Senator. I like to play the fool, like the characters in Russian novels say. Or whoever translated them. I want to talk to you about your drug legislation."

"I had a feeling that might be it," Nick said.

"Of course."

"But I'll tell you right now, *Mister* Scordia—you're not going to intimidate me."

Lenny rocked back and planted his feet so that the chair could not come forward. Over at the dining table, Rizzo and his fat companion lowered their sandwiches. The fat man, who had raised his ski mask to eat, watched with his mouth half open.

Nick went on. "Anything happens to me, it will only help my bill." He leaned forward. "You're not going to stop this thing." He caught himself about to pound his fist on the table, then opened his hand and let it fall gently.

Lenny frowned and kept nodding at Nick.

Nick saw that the lantern flame had gone out. The house ticked again.

Lenny lifted his gaze to a point above Nick's head and drummed his fingers on the arm of his chair. Rizzo and the fat man watched him alertly.

"Well, I think maybe we can help you, Senator," Lenny said.

Nick looked at him and frowned. "I don't understand."

"With your drug bill. We can help you get it passed."

"What?"

Lenny removed his glasses and looked at them. "We could give you ten guys, maybe a dozen who would support your bill in a floor fight. Senators. Some congressmen too."

Nick leaned back. "I wouldn't be party to that."

"Party to what?"

"To intimidating people. Whatever you do."

"My goodness, Senator. We got nothing like that in mind. Just a few legitimate pressure points. Same as you would do if you knew what we know." He put his glasses on again and looked at Nick. "A lotta people are on your side who can't go public."

"I'd want to find that out for myself."

"The House Majority Leader, for instance. He'd like for you to get in touch with him."

Nick shook his head. "I didn't know."

Lenny frowned. "The House Banking Committee is very concerned about all the drug money in the Federal Reserve system."

Nick nodded.

"Some members of Ways and Means think exposure might tear the system apart. They're beginning to think that decriminalization may be the only way to protect it."

"My office can take care of those contacts," Nick said.

"There's something else we can give you."

"What's that?"

"Security. I would say you could use it."

"Security?"

"Protection."

Nick laughed dryly. "Protection from your goons?"

"Hey, we didn't do anything to you. We just came for a meeting." He swept one hand around the room. "You and your people set all this up."

Nick nodded. "We had our reasons."

"No offense. We're used to it."

"So I see."

Lenny smiled.

Nick said, "So why are we here?"

"Like I told you. We can help you."

"But what's in it for you?"

"We know about drugs. We would like to get into the 'biz-i-ness.'"

Nick let out a laugh. "My impression was you already were."

"Aw, we're getting killed. Slaughtered. The Latinos, the Asians, the Schvarzers. Everybody's killing us."

"Come on now. You people are up to your ears in Miami."

"Not my family. My family wants to go legitimate."

"You couldn't. Under my plan the government would control all distribution."

"The government can't be selling stuff on street corners. It's going to go into the drug business. I know that business."

"You and who else, Mr. Scordia?"

Lenny edged forward in his seat. "I'm independent. You might have noticed the rest of my name?"

"Yes. Spell the middle part for me."

"M-e-y-e-r-s."

"Doesn't sound Italian."

"I was adopted."

"I didn't think Italians took orders from outsiders."

"Are you kidding? Look at who worked for Meyer Lansky. Look at the old Cleveland Syndicate. I'm family now. But I'm in a special position to go legitimate." He nodded. "With your help."

"And you can just do that?"

"What?"

"Go into the legitimate drug business? Without any opposition? I would think some of your people might object."

Lenny let his head bob. "There are objections. There's friction. But it's something we can handle, I think."

"Well, there's nothing I can do for you . . . Lenny."

"Sure there is. Just push ahead with your legislation. The rest will happen."

"My bill isn't doing all that well."

"That's okay," Lenny said.

"In fact, right now it looks as if it's going to be tabled in sub-committee."

Lenny nodded thoughtfully. "If that route is closed, then you gotta take another."

Nick laughed dryly. "I really don't know of any other."

Lenny pushed the chair back and let it rock a couple of times. He brought it to a stop. "Have you heard from the Senator from North Carolina?"

Nick studied Lenny. "Bodine? He's called my office."

"Talk to him." He began to rock again. "Meantime, there might be other ways I could help you."

"Suppose I don't want your help?"

"Hey, I'm not pushing you. Remember what I said about *The Godfather*? You gotta want our help."

"Well, I don't think I do."

"Okay. But keep in mind, a lot of people aren't gonna be so happy with what you're doing. You might be hearing from some-body."

"Like John Holden did?"

"I don't get you."

"Who shot John Holden, the assistant to the Drug Czar?"

Lenny shrugged. "I wouldn't know about that. I thought he was a mushroom. A bystander."

"It's thought he might have been set up."

"Not by us he wasn't. But maybe we could help you there too."

"I'd be curious to know, but it's not really in my hands."

"I see," Lenny said. He looked at Nick. "Well, maybe we could help you with your daughter."

Nick forced himself to meet Lenny's gaze.

"I understand you had a tragedy," Lenny said.

Nick let his breath out slowly.

"I understand the police are stuck."

Nick held himself still.

"We got some friends out there in the Harrisburg area."

Nick said nothing.

"Could we maybe do something for you out there?"

Nick looked at him. "I don't think so."

Lenny rocked back and took a breath. "Well, that's about it then. Unless you got something else."

Nick shook his head.

Lenny looked around at Rizzo. "How about some coffee before we hit the road? You got some coffee in the kitchen, Senator?"

"Instant," Nick said.

Rizzo and the fat man were standing.

"Make us some coffee, Sal," Lenny said.

Rizzo and his partner set off for the kitchen.

"There's a jar by the sink," Nick said.

Rizzo disappeared into the kitchen without acknowledging Nick's instruction. The fat man lumbered after him.

"Rizzo's not so happy," Lenny said to Nick. "He thinks it's beneath him to run errands. General Grant had a simple-minded captain that he would test his orders on. If the captain understood them, anybody could. I'm training Rizzo to be my Grant's Captain, but he isn't doing too good."

Nick nodded.

"Hey, Salvatore," Lenny called out. "Have 'em put a little milk in mine." He turned to Nick. "There's some milk in the refrigerator?"

"There should be," Nick said. "But there's something your men might have missed. The cabin's electrical system is rigged. If you turn anything off or on, all the lights will go out. It's a signal."

Lenny looked around the room and laughed. "That's pretty good. But we must have caught it." He got up, went to the porch door, and opened it halfway. He spoke to one of the ski-masked men. The man stepped into the room, and Lenny came back to Nick.

"You're right, Senator. They missed it. We won't throw any switches. I guess the stove is gas."

"It is," Nick said. "But what about the refrigerator light?"

Lenny turned to the man. "That's a good question, huh?"

"Separate circuit," the man said in a muffled voice.

Lenny walked back to his chair and sat down again. He rocked for a moment. "What happens if the lights go out?"

"Let's not find out," Nick said. "It was a worst-case step."

"Worst case, huh?" Lenny laughed again.

Rizzo reappeared from the kitchen.

Lenny asked, "You find the stuff?"

"We found an espresso machine, Lenny."

"No shit!" Lenny said. "Why didn't you tell us, Senator?"

Nick stood up. "Wait a minute. He can't turn it on!"

"Oh, that's right," Lenny said.

"What the fuck?" Rizzo said.

The man by the porch door strode toward the kitchen.

Nick glanced at the lamp hanging over the dining-room table.

The lights went out.

Nick blinked and stared into blackness. The floating after-image of the lamp glided across the room and faded. He breathed in deeply and smelled garlic and peppers. "Get down," he yelled, feeling his way with his shins along the coffee table. "Everybody get down on the floor. Get near the wall, if you can." He came to the end of the table, and stepped tentatively forward. Nothing stood in his way. "It's a signal to attack," he called out, his voice absurdly loud. "It means I'm in trouble."

"Nobody's out there." A voice from the direction of the porch. There were thumps and the scraping sound of furniture being moved.

Nick dropped to his hands and knees and crawled forward until his face scraped a hard surface. It was the cedar chest where towels and extra blankets were stored. He called out, "It's a signal for another team, across the river." He tried unsuccessfully to get his voice to a normal level. "They're armed, and they're supposed to shoot." He crawled to the left of the chest and stretched himself out next to the wall. He could smell mothballs.

"Whatta you think, Sal?" It was Lenny from somewhere on the other side of the wicker hamper.

"I'm sure we got everybody." Rizzo from the dining area. "We'll look around, but I swear the place is clear."

The porch door slammed. Footsteps thumped on the ground out back and faded away.

Nick rested his head on his arm. This was like a children's game.

"What's next, Senator?" Lenny said. "There's nobody within five miles of this place."

"Let's wait a little longer," Nick said.

"Come on, Lenny," said Rizzo. "We're acting like a bunch of jerks."

Footsteps pounded rapidly on the porch steps. The screen door screeched and slammed. Nick pressed himself to the wall. The back door groaned.

"Nothing happening around here, Lenny," a voice said. "We been all over."

"Okay. Try the lights," Lenny said.

Nick raised his head. A bright beam shone near the back door. Nick turned and spoke into the darkness. "The switch is in the stairwell, behind the lower corner of the map." The light bobbed across the room. A switch clicked, but the room remained dark.

"No dice, Lenny."

Nick said, "I can light the kerosene lantern. There's also a gaslight in the kitchen, on the same line as the stove."

"Go ahead," Lenny said. "Nobody's coming."

Nick pushed himself to his knees.

A shattering explosion of breaking glass filled the room. The sound went on and on, as if the bottom had been removed from a cupboard full of dishware, except the sound was more delicate and was combined with a confusion of other noises—hissing and splintering and ripping, and then, at the end of it, there was the thud of a piece of furniture falling over.

Halfway through it, Nick realized that one of the windows behind the couch where he had been sitting had burst inward. He thought that someone had heaved a stone through it.

It was quiet now.

"Son of a bitch!" someone said.

Nick, kneeling, could see the flashlight move quickly to the front door and disappear through it. Many footsteps sounded on the ground outside.

"Is everybody okay?" Lenny called out.

Nick groped his way to where he had put the kerosene lantern. "I'm going to light the lantern," he said loudly. He found the book of matches in his pocket, and lit the wick. When he lowered the chimney, half the room became visible.

"Bring that thing over here."

Nick carried the lantern across the room. The rocking chair that Lenny had been sitting in was lying on its back. Lenny and the man in the wool cap were kneeling beside it. When Nick raised the lamp he could see glints of light reflecting from the couch. The window behind was punched out, with only shards of glass and splinters of wood remaining around the edges and the cool night air was blowing in.

"Put the light down here, Senator," Lenny said.

The backrest of the rocker was in splinters and its wicker covering torn and gaping.

"What the hell did that?" Nick asked.

Lenny looked at the fat man, who had pushed his ski mask up to his forehead.

"Assault rifle," he said in his high voice. "One quick burst." He took the lantern and moved slowly toward the kitchen until he was about ten feet away from the chair. He set it down. Next to it, the braided rug was shredded and the floorboards fragmented. He lowered his head to the floor with his face turned toward the broken window.

"Jesus," Nick said. A wave of dizziness came over him and cold sweat broke out on his face and hands.

"A weapon in a tree, most likely," the fat man added. "Timed to go off. Or triggered by remote control."

Nick groped his way back to the couch and sat down. He felt light-headed. He leaned his upper body forward and pushed his head between his knees.

"Aimed right at me," Lenny said. "What's the matter, Senator?"

Nick looked up. The dizziness was passing. A flashlight blinded him. "I was supposed to be sitting in the rocking chair," he said. He lifted his left wrist and turned his watch to the light. It was 10:43.

Footsteps sounded again on the front steps. Another flashlight came through the front door.

"We can't find anything," a voice said.

"Did you look up in the trees?" Lenny asked.

"I shined the light up around where it came from. We couldn't see anyone."

"You won't find anyone," the fat man wheezed. "Let's get out of here, Lenny."

"You're right," Lenny said. "Let's go."

The man moved to the front door and disappeared.

"I'd offer you a lift, Senator," Lenny said. "But it might not look too good if somebody saw us together."

Nick stayed sitting on the couch and blotted his face with a handkerchief. "What did you do with the people who were supposed to be guarding me?"

Lenny came over to the couch and looked down at Nick. He pressed his finger to the bridge of his glasses. "They're all locked in the van. We took the batteries out. They're behind the left front wheel."

The light reappeared at the front door. "We found it, Lenny. An AR with some kind of mechanism attached to it."

"Did you get it down?"

"No, but I got a good enough look at it. There's either a timer or a radio receiver on it. Let's get out of here."

"Okay," Lenny said. "Get everybody ready." He turned back to Nick. "Who knew about this deal?"

Nick shook his head. "Just the people who set it up. Maybe five men. At my end. I can't speak for yours."

"You got a point," Lenny said.

"It was me that was supposed to be in the rocking chair."

"Not after the lights went out, you wouldn't be."

"Whoever set a timer couldn't know that the lights were going to go out," Nick said.

"But someone with a radio transmitter might know. Which is why you gotta take a look at that gun."

"Let's go, Lenny." It was Rizzo at the front door.

"Hold on, Sal."

Nick asked, "But what would be the point of setting it off after the lights went out?"

"You got me. Maybe they knew I was in the chair. Maybe it didn't matter. Maybe they just wanted to shake us up. Or even get us to go after you."

"Could this possibly have something to do with the friction you were talking about? Among your people?"

Lenny nodded thoughtfully. "It's possible. Anything's possible. But I don't like it. I'm gonna say goodbye. If I was you, I'd get out of here too."

"I've got the camper."

"You got a telephone?"

"There's a cellular one in my camper. We never installed telephones in the cabin."

Lenny retrieved his battered briefcase from the coffee table and reached into it. "Take this for if you want to get in touch, Senator." He handed Nick a card. "Keep it to yourself. There's an eight-hundred number on it. Save the taxpayers' money." He extended his hand.

Nick shook it. It was as clammy as his own.

"Pleasure, Senator. Sorry it had to end this way."

Nick took a breath. "There *is* something you might be able to help me with. Out there in the Harrisburg area."

"There," Lenny said. "You see?"

Nick cleared his throat. "I'm curious about a building."

"A building."

"Yes, in the middle of Wheelersville. It's a red brick building by the railroad tracks. On Arch Street and Quarter Lane. I think something's going on there."

"We'll have it checked out. How do you know about it?"

"My daughter, really."

"You were close with her?"

"Not really. At the end we were on the outs."

Lenny shrugged. "It happens. We'll look into your building."

"Be careful. It's important not to alert whoever it belongs to."

Lenny nodded. "Don't worry."

"I suspect it's owned by . . . people you would know," Nick said.

"Oh? What makes you think that?"

"My daughter had a friend, a young man. Frankie Tonelli."

"You think because he's Italian . . . ?"

"Well, he's been very hard to check out."

"We'll find out about him *and* the building."

"How long will that take?"

Lenny shrugged. "That depends. If it's as you say—ours—we'll know in a couple days. Otherwise, it could be a while. Could be delicate. Just stay in touch with Rizzo here." He smiled. "My captain."

"I'm always available, Senator," Rizzo said from the door.

"Yes," Nick said.

Lenny stepped back, holding his briefcase against his chest. "I'm gone." He backed to the door, gave a little wave, and disappeared. His footsteps on the ground outside faded quickly.

Nick stood and listened. All he could hear was the rush of wind in the distance. His scalp prickled. He lifted the lantern and turned the wick down until the flame died out.

Better not use a light. Somebody could still be out there watching for him.

He moved cautiously to the front door and went down the steps. The moonlight glinted on the camper across the clearing.

He stopped at the edge of the clearing. The night was cool and hushed. It seemed to be holding its breath, waiting for him to step into the open.

He took a step back and set off to his left. At the edge of the house it was darker. He raised his hands to protect himself from the branches and groped his way forward until his feet could feel the depression of the path in the pine needles.

About ten feet along it, he found the fork to the right that would take him through the woods to the camper. He moved more quickly now.

When he came to the dirt road that led away to the left of the house, he turned to his right and approached the camper. The cabin was a looming shadow. To his relief, he found that he had left the driver's window open. He reached through, pressed the switch to disable the overhead light, opened the door quietly, and climbed into the driver's seat. The interior smelled of plastic. In the dark he found the glove compartment, snapped it open, and took out his flask of brandy. He unscrewed the cap and tipped it back. The warmth spread in his stomach. He took another deep draft, screwed the cap back on, and stuck the flask on the ledge above the dashboard. He felt for the phone next to his seat and lifted it. He pulled out the antenna, flipped open the mouthpiece, and pressed the power button. A beep sounded and the number pad lit up. He began to tap in the number that Emery had had him memorize. He got halfway through it and found that his mind had gone blank. He started over again but got no further.

Luckily, the paper with the number written on it was still in his wallet. But his wallet was in the pocket of his waders, on the porch.

He would have to go back to the house.

He took the phone, climbed out of the camper, and found the path through the woods. He moved slowly, trying to make as little noise as possible. When he reached the corner of the house, he decided to circle it and approach the porch from the side. He felt his way through the darkness. He remembered the way from night games played in his childhood.

When he reached the porch, he pulled the screen door open. Groping for the table, he found his waders and removed the slip of paper from his wallet. He pressed the power button again. By the dim light of the dial, he read the numbers off the paper in his hand, punched them in, and pressed the send button.

A man's voice answered after half a ring. "Delta one-niner."

"Senator Schlafer here."

The line clicked and seemed to go dead. Nick looked out toward the stream and tried to control his breathing.

"Nick! Thank God. You're all right!" Emery's voice boomed out clearly.

"I'm all right, Emery." He kept his voice low. "No thanks to your people."

"What on earth happened?"

"I don't know. Emery, I'm on a cellular phone."

"Isn't it digital?"

"Yes. But I'm still afraid someone'll unscramble what we say." He felt for the edge of the bench, pushed his waders aside, and sat down. "Have you heard anything from your people?"

"Nothing whatsoever. I'm completely cut off."

"It was a total screw-up."

"But you're fine. That's what matters. Where are you calling from?"

"I'm . . ." He slid along the bench until his legs were under the table.

Whoever's responsible for that rifle could be listening in.

He looked off to his left in the direction of the road. He could see nothing. "Do you have any idea where your people are now, Emery?"

"They were under orders to get out of there as soon as your meeting was over. They should be on the road by now."

Nick slid back along the bench and stood up. "I'll be in touch as soon as I can."

"Call me soon, Nick. I can't understand what went wrong."

"I suspect there's a wild card in the deck."

"What do you mean?"

"I can't explain now," Nick said. "I'll be in touch, Em." He disconnected the line. He found his windbreaker on the table and slipped it on. He opened the door to the living room and looked in. He could see only the shadows of the furniture.

He stepped across the threshold cautiously and stood listening. There was no sound.

He made his way across the rug, remembering to steer clear of where the gunfire had hit, though he didn't know why he thought that necessary.

He heard a sound. It was the tinkle of glass breaking. It came from the front of the room.

Of course. It had to be a shard from the broken window. He could see the dark silhouette of the curtains wafting. He would have to telephone down and have the window replaced.

Outside, he turned the key in the front door, pocketed it, and trotted across the clearing. Back in the driver's seat of the camper, he returned the phone to its holder.

He sat for a moment and tried to clear his head.

What was going on? What was the point of the shooting? Was Lenny the target? Or him? Was it his drug bill? But it was nearly dead by now.

Of course, whoever rigged the rifle might not know that. And why go to the trouble of the rifle?

The possibilities seemed to branch out infinitely.

The best thing now would be to get out of here, be careful, and wait for whatever might happen next. Play it cool. There were too many puzzles, and the pieces were too scattered.

He turned the ignition key. The motor kicked over instantly.

When he switched on the lights, he caught sight of something next to him. It was a small figure slumped in the seat. He could see that it had long yellow hair.

He reached for it and lifted it gently. By the dim light of the dashboard he saw its eyes blink open. It was a child-sized doll.

He let out an involuntary shout and shook the thing violently.

Its head flopped to one side. Its neck had been cut through, leaving only a hinge of plastic. He threw it into the well in front of the seat. It let out a thin mechanical cry. "Mamaaa."

He shifted into reverse and backed the camper into the middle of the clearing. He pushed the gear forward to drive, yanked the steering wheel to the right, and gunned the gas pedal. The spitting gravel hissed. The flask slid along the dashboard and bounced onto his lap.

The camper swerved and steadied. Its headlights picked up the rutted road ahead. In the distance, off to the left through the trees he could see the dark rectangular shape of the van. When he reached the broader road, he considered turning left and releasing the men locked inside. Instead he swung the wheel to the right and pressed the pedal to the floor.

PART THREE

Friday, October 10th

10

The Fix

"Nick, it's time you stopped playing cat and mouse with us," Emery said.

"It's not with you, Emery," Nick answered. He clamped the handset of the phone between his ear and his shoulder and swiveled his chair around until he could see out the window. The leaves in the park had begun to turn yellow, but he still could not see Union Station through the foliage.

"It's been . . . July, August, September, October—four months," Emery went on.

"July and August don't count," Nick cut in. "I was hardly in town and you weren't either."

"That's right. But many of my people were. It's October now, and they still don't have a clue to what happened down there."

"Emery, I've told them what I know. They're the ones who have to come up with some answers."

"That's what they're trying to do. They want to sit down with you. Go over everything from beginning to end."

"I've steered them to the hard evidence. The gun in the tree and the doll in my camper. Frankly, I'm not too impressed with your people. They're fuck-ups, Emery."

"That's not entirely fair. They're up against—"

"I guess I am reluctant to meet with them."

"Then how do you expect any answers?"

"What about the gun and the doll?"

"Both dead ends. They don't tell us a thing. But there are indications the answers may lie with the people you met. There are signs of, uh, conflict—even warfare—there. I still don't have the slightest sense of what went on at your meeting."

"What happened to all the tapes and videos?"

Nick heard a sigh on the line. "Nick, you know the machinery was compromised. They didn't get a thing except a long night in the van."

"Emery, if you and I could get together alone—"

"That's difficult now, Nick."

"I could go over the meeting in detail."

"Have you heard from them again?"

"Uh, not really."

There was a knock at the door to the inner office. Nick swung around to face his desk.

"Be careful, Nick. Very careful. They're highly skilled and dangerous, as we've learned to our regret. Don't trust them. You'll be in over your head."

"I know." The door opened to reveal Segal.

"I'm concerned about you," Emery said. "Are you using your driver?"

"Sure, when I'm in town." Nick waved Segal in.

"Why not everywhere?"

"It's awkward to drive a stretch limo into Camp Hoover."

"She's good, Nick. She comes highly recommended."

"By whom?"

"My people."

"There you are."

"Perhaps I could fit you in for a sit-down next week."

"You and I alone."

"Fair enough. Right after the budget vote."

"Great, Em. You'll call?"

"I'll be in touch."

Nick replaced the handset and slumped in his chair. He looked at Segal. "Sit down, Dave. What's on your mind?"

"The budget. It better be on yours too."

"Screw the budget."

"What's the problem, boss?"

"The problem with what?"

"With everything."

"What makes you think I have a problem?"

Segal pointed at Nick's desk. "You haven't reacted to any of those memos. You haven't been here."

Nick shook his head. "I've been here every day since Labor Day."

"You've been here, but you haven't been here."

Nick stood up, went to the window, and looked out. "It's hard to explain. I don't want to involve you. I guess you could say I'm stuck."

"How so?" Segal said.

"Let's see." He turned to face Segal. "I'm caught between two . . . entities, call them A and B, and I don't trust either of them."

"I guess one of them is the Drug Secretary."

"Yeah, that's right. But it's not him I have a problem with. It's his people."

"That's interesting. Who is B?"

Nick shook his head. "That's tricky, Dave." He sat down again at his desk. "At this point, I really can't say."

"Okay," Segal said. "Can't you just sit tight? Do nothing?"

"Maybe. No, not really."

"Then you have to probe."

"What do you mean?"

"Probe." He raised his two index fingers and jabbed them in opposite directions. "Test them. Find out who you trust more."

Nick picked up a pencil and tapped its eraser against the desktop. "Yes."

"Okay, good. Now, if you don't mind discussing more mundane matters, have you looked at that file folder yet?" He gestured at Nick's desk.

Nick pulled an unmarked manila folder toward him. "This?"

"Yes."

"I'll get to it. What else?"

"Bodine keeps calling. He wants to see you."

"We've met twice this month. He talks in circles. I can't follow him."

"He says he's got something for you now."

"I'll bet." Nick jotted a note. "Okay. I'll call him."

"Also, Rizzo called again."

Nick nodded and tossed the pencil onto the desk. "Dave, give me ten minutes to make a couple of calls. I'm gonna probe, as you put it. Then come back with Abby."

Segal stood up. "Good. When in doubt, start lashing out." He went to the door.

"Ten minutes," Nick said. He took his address book from his jacket pocket, picked up the phone, and tapped out Salvatore Rizzo's number. He felt a hollowness in his stomach as the phone rang.

"Yeah?" The voice was surly.

"Rizzo? It's Nick Schlafer."

"Hiya, Senator." A few degrees warmer.

"Have you got any more news for me?"

"Yes."

"Good. What is it?"

"The boss is ready to talk to you."

"At last."

"When can you meet him?"

"Anytime."

"He wants to meet with you out there. You gonna be out there?"

"Wheelersville?"

"That's right. He wants to walk around with you and show you some things."

"How about next weekend?"

"The sooner the better. How about *this* weekend?"

"It's kind of short notice. But I guess I could do it."

"Call again after noon. I'll give you the details then."

"After noon. Fine."

"And Senator, have you talked to Senator Bodine yet?"

"Sure. Several times. But he hasn't said anything."

"The boss thinks you should talk to the Senator again now."

"I'll call him this afternoon."

The line disconnected. Nick moved to replace the handset, stopped his hand in midair, pushed the button to get a dial tone, and punched Josie's number. There were four rings. He was about to give up when the phone answered.

"Hullo?" Josie said.

"Hi."

"Nick?"

"Yes."

"Sorry. Let me catch my breath."

"Is anything wrong?"

"No. No. I was just going out. I thought it might be you."

"I'm calling to see if I can take Matty out to Wheelersville tonight."

"I don't believe it!"

"Come on, Josie."

"Nick, he hasn't seen you since—"

"I know. Since I visited him up at summer camp in August."

"I thought you were going to work on getting closer to him."

"Josie, he was away for July and August. And I've been down at the fishing camp practically every weekend since Labor Day."

"Well, I don't think you should take him down there."

"I know. I understand. Though I'm beginning to think it's perfectly safe there."

"Really?"

"Absolutely, Josie. It's as if that incredible evening never happened."

"Still . . ."

"Josie, I don't intend to take him down there. I'm planning a long weekend on the farm. My plans aren't set yet, but the budget vote won't happen before Tuesday."

"Are we actually going to get a budget?"

"We'll get something."

"Matty'll be thrilled, Nick." Her voice had softened. "Don't forget he has school on Monday."

"I won't. I'll let you know definitely this afternoon." He hung up and reached for the file folder Segal had referred to. He opened it. Inside was a single sheet of paper covered with a dozen or so numbers arranged like the branches of an elimination tournament. Nick read the top one. "BFH 981." It didn't mean anything to him.

He reached and buzzed the intercom.

"You ready for us?" Abby said.

"Yeah, for just a couple of minutes. I want to get down to the steam room."

"Sure."

He looked at the sheet of paper in front of him again. It had no title or legend. Just the oddly arranged numbers. He closed the file and slid it back to where he had found it.

Abby appeared at the doorway, her jewelry jangling. "Dave'll be here in a minute," she said.

Nick stood up and moved around his desk to the conference table. "I may have a problem this weekend." He waved Abby to a chair.

She sat down at the far corner of the table and placed a stack of papers in front of her. "Can I be of any help?"

"Are you busy?"

"Not with anything I can't get out of."

Segal came into the room. "What's happening?"

Nick put up his hand to silence him. "I may go home for the weekend. Tonight. I'd like to take Matty, but I'll have to get away some of the time. Sit down, Dave."

Abby said, "Would you like me to come along?"

"Yes. You and Don Fox."

"No problem."

"It's not set yet. I'll know by early this afternoon, I think." He took the folder from his desk and sat down at the head of the table. He touched the file. "I looked at this file, Dave. I don't get it."

Segal looked over at Abby.

Nick looked at Segal and nodded. "You can talk."

Segal gestured at the file. "That came on the screen when I was sending the latest poll results to Emery Frankfurt's office. I'm always getting feedback like that when I get on line with them. I think I mentioned it to you once."

"You downloaded this?"

"Yes."

"What in hell is it?"

Segal shrugged. "Beats me."

Nick looked at him. "Your friend there. What did you say his name was?"

"Merced. Julio Merced."

"You ask him about it?"

Segal leaned back, removed his glasses, and shut his eyes tightly. "I told you, I don't think that would be such a good idea."

"Why on earth not?" Nick asked.

Segal replaced his glasses. "It could just stir things up. Aside from it being none of our business, it might not have anything to do with Merced."

"So what?" Nick said.

Segal shook his head. "The creation of the Department of Drug Control was supposed to have ended the infighting between the DEA, the ATF, and so on. But from talking to people over there, I don't get the feeling that's happened. I think the rivalries have just intensified. I think the place is full of cabals."

"That's ridiculous!" Abby said.

Nick and Segal looked at her.

"I just mean . . . it doesn't make sense."

No one spoke.

"Well, your numbers are a mystery, Dave." He folded the sheet, slipped it into his inside jacket pocket, and looked at his watch. He stood up. "I'm going to get myself a steam bath and a massage."

"I need time with you this afternoon," Segal said. "There are votes coming up. There's word that a budget deal has been struck."

"So I hear. There's talk of a Continuing Resolution."

"The vote could be as soon as Tuesday. I'm getting a lot of pressure for you to support it."

"Well, I'm not about to."

"It would be a huge bargaining chip."

"For what?"

Segal shrugged.

"They should know better," Nick said. "You'll get more time with me this afternoon, I promise. I should be back around noon."

Nick sat on the slatted bench with his elbows resting on his knees and his eyes closed. He was streaming sweat, rivulets of liquid running down his face, neck, and torso. He longed for the relief of the plunge into cool water. The steam burned dryly in his throat.

"Hey, there, Senator Schlafer! Imagine finding you here!"

Nick lifted his face from his hands and opened his eyes. He saw Bodine standing in front of him, his wide pale body slick with sweat. He had a fluffy white towel wrapped around his middle. His mouth was stretched into its froggy grin.

"Hello, Senator," Nick said, lowering his face again.

"You feeling a little uptight?" Bodine said in his chirrupy voice. "That why you're sweatin' it out here?"

"I'm fine, Senator. I come here for a rubdown once a month or so."

"Mind if I join you?"

Nick looked up again. "Be my guest."

Bodine had removed his towel, folded it in two, and laid it on the bench. He sat down on it and took a deep breath. He said, "Your drug thing just about dead?"

Nick did not look at him. "What is it now? October. You've been asking me that question for four months now."

"Yes, I have."

"You know it's dead."

They sat in silence.

Bodine spoke in a low voice. "I understand the budget boys may have theirselves a deal over at the White House."

"So I'm given to understand," Nick answered. "They've agreed to disagree. The President is going to settle for a stopgap budget. I'm not surprised."

"Well, then maybe it's time for you and me to talk a little."

"What's on your mind?"

"Not here," Bodine said, looking around.

"Fair enough. How about your office Monday?"

"How 'bout your hideaway in a couple hours? That'll give you time to have your swim and get your massage."

Nick looked at him.

Bodine stopped smiling. "This'll interest you."

Nick lifted his left arm to look at his watch, and remembered he had left it in his locker. "My hideaway—at noon, then." He stood up, touched Bodine's shoulder, and headed for the pool.

Bodine was standing by the entrance to SB-5. Nick unlocked the door and followed him in. "Make yourself comfortable, Senator. Drink?"

Bodine moved behind the coffee table and lowered himself slowly into the corner of the couch. He stretched his arms back, yawned, and looked at his watch. "A drink? Naw, it's too early. Unless you're having one."

"No," Nick said. "I'll pass. It may be a long afternoon." He sat at the other end of the couch, about four feet from Bodine. "What's on your mind, Senator?"

Bodine narrowed his eyes and gave Nick an appraising look. "What's on my mind is that drug deal of yours."

"As I recall, you were rather strenuously against it."

"Yes, I was. Am. That's my position. The State of North Carolina does not want its citizens injecting dope into their veins."

"You did manage to convey that view."

"Well, that's good. Now, whatever did happen to your bill?"

"Dead. As I keep telling you."

Bodine lifted his eyebrows. "Why?"

"It was shot to death in the judiciary subcommittee."

"Didn't you count heads before you started, man?"

"Sure."

"And?"

"We had a majority. In the full committee, and in the subcommittee. We did our homework."

"So?" Bodine fixed Nick with his black eyes.

Nick held the gaze with an effort, shrugged, and dropped his eyes.

"C'mon, man!" Bodine said, an octave higher. "Did you bang heads together?"

"Of course. We twisted arms. We called in favors."

"And?"

"I even persuaded one or two people that it was a good idea. Something the American people need. That there's support out there."

"Yeah, so what went wrong?"

Nick shook his head. "Members changed their minds."

"Why?"

"Pressure."

"From where?"

"From the top, I'm assuming. People got very nervous. Calder was crapping in his pants."

Bodine smiled broadly. "It's exactly what I told you. You were wrong from the start to do it as a bill. There's no way anybody's gonna have the balls to associate themselves with drug legalization."

"Why are we here?"

"I think I got a way for us to get it done."

"What?"

"This drug deal of yours."

"Decriminalize drugs?"

"Not anything so sweeping. But a beginning. Guerrilla politics."

Nick shook his head. "I'm lost."

"The budget deal," Bodine said. "The Continuing Resolution. It can pass now. That is, the President's not gonna veto it now."

"So?"

"Well, we'll slip your plan in."

"You can't do that."

"You're right, we can't. But then again, maybe we can."

"You mean amend the stopgap budget to decriminalize drugs? That's crazy. That would amount to new legislation." Nick looked up toward the ceiling and recited, "The initiation of a program not funded in the prior year's appropriation." He brought his eyes back to Bodine's. "That's not allowed."

"My committee can do it. Appropriations can. And you know it."

"Where's the precedent?"

"Oh, well, there's plenty of that. We stopped funds to rebuild North Vietnam. We barred aid to Iran, funding for abortions. Ten years ago there was a ban on inflight smoking. I remember that one pretty good."

"But drugs!"

"It wouldn't be such a big deal." He put up his hand for silence. "It's simple. All we got to do is revise the tobacco appropriation. Designate part of the allotment for marijuana and whatever. Coca. Can you grow coca in a North American climate?"

"Sure. Everything grew here once. Before the Harrison Act."

"We'll designate it for medical use, say. There's already a provision for medical experimentation on the books. Terminal cancer patients, people with glaucoma, MS, AIDS, and the like."

"The DEA opposes that."

"Yeah, but the courts have questioned the legality of their opposition. It's still up in the air."

"But even on the committee, how are you going to get the votes?"

"You know how. All I need is the senior members, House and Senate. And you are lookin' at one of 'em."

"How are you going to convince the others?"

"Now, don't be asking what you don't need to know."

Nick shook his head. "But the CR is only for three months. That's not enough time." He smiled. "The crop would hardly be up."

"There'll be another CR. And another. That's the way we do business now. By the time there's a real budget, poppies will be waving their orange heads all over the South."

Nick stood up and moved to the middle of the room. He turned and looked at Bodine. "What I really don't understand is, what's in this for you?"

Bodine smiled crookedly. "Now that is a good question, Senator." He looked at the ceiling. "I told you, I'm unalterably opposed to drug legalization." He lowered his eyes to meet Nick's. "However, we must take the interests of all our constituents into account when we legislate. And there are powerful forces in the sovereign State of North Carolina that are unhappy about what is happening in this country of ours to the rights of the cigarette smoker."

"The tobacco companies," Nick said.

"You pronounced the words, sir. Not I. These folks are looking for new products and new markets. Though I remain a dedicated foe of drugs, these people bring powerful pressures to bear."

"I see," Nick said.

Bodine stood. " 'Course, we'd expect your support on the budget."

"I can't do that, Rick."

"Come on, man!" Bodine's voice went up its octave.

Nick turned away and moved behind his desk. "I've gone public with my opposition to the budget. I'd look like a damn fool."

"But this is the Continuing Resolution, man!" His voice swooped up and down. "Everybody compromises." He spread his arms. "You'd make some sort of statement. We gotta keep the guv'-ment going."

Nick squared the blotter on his desk. "Actually, I'd like my name kept out of it." He tapped the desktop with his fingers. "I'll vote to support. But keep my name out of the drug amendment."

"The tobacco appropriation, you mean." Bodine moved around the coffee table and went to the door.

"It'll have a better chance without it being connected to me."

Bodine laughed. "It's not a matter of chance. It's just fixing up a little language. No names need come up. No one can even be held responsible."

"That's how we like it, isn't it?" Nick said, opening the door for him. "Zero responsibility."

"How else would we get reelected?" Bodine said.

"Let me ask you one more thing," Nick said.

"What's that, Senator?"

"Certain people have been urging me to get together with you. I was wondering . . ."

Bodine's smile widened. He moved out the door. "Can't imagine what you're talking about." He waved his hand at Nick. "You won't be hearing from me."

Nick pushed the door shut and went to his desk. He pulled the bottom drawer open and lifted out the bottle of brandy. He looked at his watch. He put the bottle back.

He removed his wallet, found a slip of paper with numbers written on it, picked up the telephone handset, and tapped the numbers.

"Yeah?"

"Rizzo? It's Nick Schlafer."

"Right, Senator. The boss just called in. The word is you should head home. Your meeting is Sunday morning."

"*Sunday* morning?"

"Yeah. It's quieter then for what he wants to show you."

"Where do I meet him?"

"You should be in front of the drugstore on Central Avenue at nine Sunday morning."

"Eckert's?"

"That's it." The line went dead.

Nick flashed the dial tone and tapped more numbers. "Josie? Hi. I'm going to Wheel'ville. But I don't have to leave until tomorrow. Why don't I pick Matty up about ten in the morning?"

"He'll be delighted."

"We'll make it leisurely. Have lunch on the road."

"Sounds good."

"See you around ten."

He tapped more numbers. "Abby, we're heading out tomorrow morning. Okay?"

"You're on. I've cleared with Fox. Do you want your driver?"

"No, we'll take the camper. I'm going to get a bite of lunch at the Capitol now. Tell Segal I'll be back in an hour. On second thought, is he there?"

"Just a sec."

Nick took his glasses off and rubbed his eyes.

"Segal here."

"Dave, I'm switching my vote on the budget resolution."

"Jesuuuuuus!"

"It's supposed to be a secret, but it'll be all over the Hill by dinnertime." He replaced his glasses.

"What the fuck? I coulda got something for it."

"Don't worry, I got plenty."

"I can't believe this! What's happening around here?"

"I'll explain when I see you this afternoon. Now I'm going to lunch." He hung up and pushed the telephone back. Standing and turning to leave, he looked at his image in the mirror on the wall in back of his desk. His eyes looked sunken.

"The art of the possible," he said to his reflection.

He ran his fingers through his hair and turned to leave.

II

Bodies

Dead leaves swirled in the street. Nick pulled the collar of his jacket tighter so that he could feel the lining at his throat. He dug his hands into his pockets and looked up and down the street.

A vaguely familiar figure approached. "Hiya," he said.

"How are you?" Nick said.

The man came too close to him, tipping back his head and thrusting out his oversized jaw. "Meanwhile, I see your drug bill is dead." The man ducked his head to one side as if he were trying to get a better view of Nick. "People knew better, right?" His voice was hoarse and high. The flecks of spittle flew.

"I remember you," Nick said. "You had a concession at the carnival." He hunched his shoulders against the cold wind, and stuck out his hand.

The man ignored the extended hand. "How about some coffee?" he said.

Nick put his hand back in his coat pocket. "That would be good. But I'm meeting someone."

"Oh, yeah? Well, we can talk right here. You'll be interested in my situation."

A black Lincoln stretch limo with dark opaque windows crept slowly toward them from the west end of town. Except for its Pennsylvania plates, it looked exactly like the car that had been assigned to Nick. It slowed, passed Nick and the man with him, and came to a stop twenty yards beyond them.

The back door swung open. No one got out.

Nick walked to the car and looked in. Lenny Meyers Scordia sat alone in the back seat. He wore a dark suit and tie, a dark brown fedora, and a dark brown overcoat. He held a large unlit cigar in his right hand. The dark glass prevented Nick from seeing the car's driver, or if there was anyone in the seat beside him.

"Can you break away from that fellow and take a ride?" Lenny said.

Nick looked back. "You'll have to excuse me," he called.

The man waved him away. "We'll talk later," he said. "I'll catch up with you." He turned and started off down the street.

Nick climbed into the limo and sat back next to Lenny. He pulled the door closed.

"We'll drive around town and come in the same way again," Lenny said loudly for the driver's benefit. He looked at Nick and gestured with the cigar. "Then we'll take a little walk."

The limo moved slowly along Central Avenue.

"People will think this is a car going to the funeral home," Lenny said.

"You passed it."

"I mean, where the hearses go. The back. You'll see."

At the end of Central, the car swung left.

"It's not the greatest day for a walk," Lenny said, "but there's nobody around. That's why Sunday's a good time. Where's your son? His name is Matthew?"

"Yes. Matty."

"You bring him out here with you?"

Nick looked at Lenny.

"You're nervous about him," Lenny said. "I don't blame you. I was just asking." He smiled.

"He's at the house."

"You take him fishing this morning?"

"Too cold."

They rode in silence. Wind slammed against the windows. The car rocked as it moved. They turned another corner.

"There's your building," Lenny said.

Nick saw the red house coming up on the left.

"We'll circle around," Lenny said. They passed the building. "That's the back of the funeral home."

"I know," Nick said.

"We'll go around."

A few blocks farther, they turned left again. Nick saw that they were approaching the west end of Central.

They turned onto Central. When they reached Eckert's again, they slowed and stopped. The man was gone. Lenny twisted his head back to look out the rear window. "All clear now. Let's take a stroll."

Nick opened the door and climbed out. The cold air made him gulp. Lenny followed him, then turned back. He looked at a watch on his left wrist. "We'll meet you right here in about an hour," he called to the driver. He slammed the door. The limo moved away.

The wind gusted and Lenny held the brim of his hat. "We'll walk down Arch Street." He looked at the hazy sky. The sun was a pale disk.

They crossed Central. Lenny stopped on the opposite corner and used the building as a windbreak to light his cigar with a small plastic torch. "It's too bad . . . you've been in the dark about . . . all this so long." He gestured at the surroundings.

"I've been waiting," Nick said.

"What we found out didn't come easy." He put the lighter back in his coat pocket.

"What did you find?" Nick asked.

"I'll show you." They went down Arch Street. "We checked with every family in the country. Nobody knows."

"Knows what?"

"Who's operating here."

"Is someone?"

"Nobody knows."

The red house came into full view. Lenny stopped walking. Nick went a few steps farther, then turned to face his companion.

Lenny spread his arms wide. "The railroad was first built in 1872. It was a branch line of the Cumberland Valley Railroad. It lost money."

"I know," Nick said. "The first Schlafer—my ancestor—was an investor."

"Yes, I know that." Lenny removed a particle of tobacco from his lower lip. "How come your people came so late? I would have thought they were original settlers."

"No, he was a forty-eighter. From the Rhine Palatinate."

"A disappointed liberal. I suppose he could afford the loss that the railroad cost him?"

"It seems so." Nick stood beside Lenny and looked at the red house. "This is it."

"Yes."

"It looks abandoned," Nick said.

"Until you take a closer look at it," Lenny answered. "Then you notice a couple of new windows. And the paint on the garage door. I asked a half a dozen people about it—you know, people on the street—and they all shrugged and said it was just an old abandoned building."

"Was that a good idea?" Nick asked.

"What?"

"Letting people know you're interested in it. I decided not to ask. Except for one guy I could trust."

"Oh, it's one thing for you, a big-shot U.S. Senator, to go around asking. It's another thing for me, a little Jewish guy, to be making a few inquiries."

"Then this isn't your first look here?"

"Of course not. Would I waste your time?" He took a step forward and stopped again to relight his cigar. "When General Charles de Gaulle went . . . to visit President Dwight David Eisenhower . . . at his farm in Gettysburg, the two of them . . . walked the battleground together." He waved his cigar. "The French general knew as much about it as the American general who lived there. Have you been to Gettysburg?"

"No."

"Not even campaigning? You surprise me, Senator."

"Oh, I've campaigned in the area. But I never visited the battleground itself."

"You have to go. Take your son. They have an electronic map there, on the floor of a building. You sit in a grandstand and they reenact the three days of the battle, using these little lights. Red ones for the campfires at night. Very moving. Tears actually came to my eyes."

"Really?"

"Yes, but I cry easily. I cry at the movies. I cry over television ads. I blame the modernist movement—it took the sentiment out of art, so we're left to cry at junk. The garage door goes up and down."

"What?"

Lenny pointed at the building with his cigar. "The garage door. It's automatic. Up and down. But we can't find the button."

"Wouldn't it be a remote? In a car?"

"Sure, but there's also gotta be a way to work them on site. A lock or a button. There's no way to open it from the outside or from the apartment above. There's no way to get in."

"What about the room at the end?"

Lenny raised his hand and pushed it forward in the air. "We'll get to that. Let's go to the left here."

They turned onto Quarter Lane, away from the red house. "It's interesting," Lenny said. "We associate Gettysburg with two presidents, Lincoln and Eisenhower. Lincoln delivered his big address there. What did Eisenhower do? He bought a farm there to retire to. Just like that, he stuck himself in the middle of American history. He was no dummy."

"I think his ancestors came from Pennsylvania," Nick said. "They were Mennonites. Anyway, he had a right. He won another great war to preserve the union."

"I suppose so, in a way. It's a pleasure to talk with an intelligent man. Your parents . . . are they still alive?"

"No."

"You're a young man. They died recently?"

"No. A long time ago."

"Hmm." Lenny stopped and turned around. "Now take a look. Describe for me what you see. Describe everything."

Nick turned around and looked for a moment. "I see the red building and the tower beside it. The railroad tracks to the left, the buildings along Arch Street to the right."

"Go on. This was my own bright idea. My people got stuck." Lenny extended his left arm with his fingers spread. "Empty your mind and look. You'll understand what I'm saying. Each person sees everything. Some people understand it better. Einstein. Freud. But the *picture* is the same for each of us. That's hard to grasp."

"I don't think I follow you."

"It's not important. Just go on telling me what you see."

"Across the street, to the left, there's a garage."

"Yes."

"In it are the hearses for the funeral home."

"That's it. That's it."

"The license-plate numbers look familiar," Nick said.

"What?"

Nick compared the license-plate numbers of the two hearses parked in Belcher's garage. They were in sequence, BFH 981 and BFH 982. "The license-plate numbers. I've seen them before."

"Where?" Lenny asked.

Nick shook his head. "I must have seen them here before."

"Well, forget the license plates for now. You've got all the information you need."

Nick shook his head. "I don't get it."

"I'll explain." Lenny looked at his watch. "Where can we get a cup of coffee and talk in private?"

"There's a place just around the corner," Nick said. "I think it's open on Sundays."

They turned the next corner and walked to the entrance of a flat brick building. Inside was a dance floor with a bar on the right and booths lining the other three walls. The place was dark and empty except for a bartender and a young waitress.

"I'll be right back," Lenny said. "You could order me some tea and toast." He looked around and moved off toward a doorway at the near end of the bar.

Nick went to the far corner on the other side of the room and took a seat in a booth. The waitress took his order for coffee, tea, and toast. From his breast pocket Nick removed the sheet of paper with the numbers written on it that Segal had accidentally intercepted. He unfolded it. Sure enough, five of the numbers in the upper left-hand corner began with BFH. They included the two license-plate numbers he had just noticed, BFH 981 and BFH 982. He underlined them with a pencil.

When he saw Lenny coming, he put the piece of paper back in his pocket. Lenny slid into the booth opposite Nick. His coat was still on. "It's cold in here," he said. "I guess they're saving money. Did you order?"

Nick nodded.

Lenny held his cigar up and examined the tip. It had gone out again. He placed it in a small tin ashtray next to the lamp. "So, Senator. Have you put the pieces together yet?"

"No."

"I don't blame you. I was only guessing myself till I checked it out."

"What do you mean?"

Lenny leaned forward and began to trace vague lines on the black tabletop. "See, once we began watching the funeral home, we noticed that they were processing more cadavers than the local population would produce."

"How could you know that?"

"The morgue at Belcher's serves the whole county along with a couple of other homes. The county goes west from the river. Population is about seventy, eighty thousand. Belcher's should get four to five stiffs a week—that's what the others do. There might be a little bulge on Saturday night, when people are most liable to die unnaturally, if you get me. But Belcher is taking in three-four every Saturday. That's a few too many."

"How do you know they are?"

"We've been keeping close track."

"Where . . ." Nick fell silent. The waitress arrived with their order.

"I'll need some milk for my tea, if you don't mind," Lenny said.

She nodded and hurried off.

"The English put a little milk in their tea and have a lower rate of esophageal cancer than the Japanese, who drink theirs straight."

Nick nodded. "I didn't know that."

"We don't know anything about those extra bodies except they're coming into Wheelersville in refrigerated trailers. Police don't like to inspect cold-storage trucks too carefully 'cause it can start spoilage. That can mean lawsuits."

"I don't believe this," Nick said.

"It gets better."

The waitress came back with the milk. "You boys okay now?"

"We're fine," Nick said.

She scribbled and put the green check on the tabletop. "Think it'll snow?"

"No," Lenny said. "Air's too dry. It might in here, though."

The waitress rolled her eyes and left.

Lenny leaned forward. "The hearses pick up the off-loaded bodies from an outfit called Produce Specialists, just east of town on Hampton Ferry Road."

"What happens then?"

"They come back to the funeral home and get taken in on gurneys. One after the other."

"Don't people notice?"

"It's not that obvious. It's like the red house. You only see something odd if you pay close attention."

"So what happens to the bodies?"

"We don't know that yet. We're going to find out, though. Probably tonight."

"How?"

"We finally planted a guy in the morgue. A kid who just graduated from a training school in Harrisburg. It's another little detail that took time."

"They'll be onto him," Nick said. "It's too much of a coincidence."

"Not at all. You target bright guys who live in the area. We're very good at it." He munched on his toast.

"Just what do you expect to find out?"

Lenny leaned back and glanced toward the bar. He came halfway forward again and sipped his tea. He put his cup down and shrugged. "I don't want to say. It would only be a guess."

"Fair enough."

"I would imagine there's powder or cash sewn up in those bodies. It's a pretty standard practice. Nobody wants to be cutting open stiffs if they can help it."

"What do you mean, powder?"

"White stuff. Snow. Smack."

"Coke or heroin?"

"Maybe a little of both. Maybe everything."

"And then what?" Nick asked. "Where does it go from the morgue?"

"To that sealed-off room in your red building, we think. But we can't figure out how."

"Some sort of underground passage?"

"Sure. But we haven't found it yet."

"You think the guy you planted will?"

"That's the idea."

Nick shook his head and sipped his coffee. It was cold and bitter. "I don't get it."

"What?"

"Why Wheelersville?"

"Why not? It's perfect—close to a major transportation hub, far enough off the beaten track to make you wonder, 'Why here?' "

"And you can't figure out who owns it?"

"Sure. The IK Corporation in Scranton. It pays the taxes. But it's a dummy. We can't get to the bottom of who's behind it."

"Can't you trace their checks?"

"The taxes are paid out of an escrow account."

"Who set it up?" Nick asked.

"Nobody knows or nobody's talking. You got any notions?"

Nick looked at him hard. "Yes."

"What?"

"The kid, Frankie Tonelli." Nick kept his voice low. "Do you remember I mentioned him?"

"What about him?"

"He works at Belcher's."

"I know that."

"I always thought he was Lore's drug connection."

Lenny ran his tongue along the inside of his lower lip. "You're wrong," he finally said.

"How do you know?"

Lenny shook his head. "There's nothing there."

"Come on!"

Lenny looked Nick in the eye. "Nothing."

"How can you be so sure?"

Lenny looked down and tapped his teaspoon against the rim of his cup. "I said there's nothing there. Leave it alone."

Nick waited.

Lenny looked up again. "You got any other ideas?"

"Of what?"

"Of who's behind this."

Nick met Lenny's stare and fought to hold it. "No. I don't."

Lenny gazed back without blinking. "What about the gun in the tree?"

Nick shook his head. "A dead end, Secretary Frankfurt says."

"I heard it never went to the lab." Lenny threw his hands in the air. "Poof! It disappeared."

Nick touched his face and kneaded the flesh around his mouth with his thumb and fingers. "How can that be?"

"Why don't you ask Secretary Frankfurt?"

"Well, I . . . He suggests that the gun may have been put there by *your* enemies."

Lenny stiffened. "I wouldn't push that one too hard."

"You can be certain the Secretary is pushing it."

"Well, then, I think maybe he's not in complete control of his people. There's something a little strange about Holden's shooting too."

"You mean Holden was shot by someone inside the Drug Control Department? And that the same people may have gone after me?"

Lenny tipped his head back, still holding Nick's eyes. He raised his hands again and let them fall apart. "I'm just looking for straws."

"I understand. But I don't have any for you."

"Don't be so sure. You might." He leaned forward. "Relax, Senator. Think."

"About what?"

"About what you told me at your fishing camp. How did you know about the building?"

"Lore. My daughter."

"Right," Lenny said. "Tell me more about it. You want your coffee warmed up?"

"No." Nick sat back and took a breath. Despite the coolness of the room he felt trickles of sweat under his arms. "When she died, she was trying to write something on the wall with her blood. She got as far as RED HO . . ."

"How did you know the second word was going to be 'house'?"

"I didn't. It was just a possibility."

"So how did you find the building?"

Nick looked down at his coffee. The edge of the cup was chipped. "One night last spring I found some diagrams that she left behind. One was of a house with a bridge over it. It was drawn on red paper in her autograph book. I didn't understand the bridge until I happened to be standing near Arch Street. Then it hit me. Coincidence."

"Maybe coincidence. Maybe not. Where did you find the autograph book?"

"In her desk drawer. There were other clues in it."

"Wait a minute. Save that part. When did you find the book?"

"May, uh, June of this year. In a locked drawer in her desk. My son had the key in his pocket."

Lenny put a scrap of toast down. "This is very interesting. How long after she died?"

"A year and a couple of months."

"So how come nobody noticed the locked drawer before? It was the room she died in, no?"

"Yes."

"It wasn't gone over by the police?"

"The drawer wasn't locked when she died. I guess the police did overlook a piece of paper taped on the underside of her desk inside one of the drawer slots. But the autograph book wasn't there."

"Why not?"

"Because she gave it to her brother to keep. With instructions to lock it in the drawer later if anything happened to her."

"So someone would find it later. Someone in the family."

"Yes. I guess."

"This doesn't sound like such a *pazza*—such a crazy kid—to me."

"I know. That's slowly been dawning on me."

"She knew someone was after her."

"Exactly. Because she knew something about the red house. The numbers of the padlock combination were written on the sketch. That's how I got into the apartment."

Lenny ate the last piece of his toast. "Who would have been after her?"

"I assumed she didn't want the police to find the book. To protect her drug connection."

"No. No. That's your point of view. You're blowing up the drug thing too much."

"How do you know that?"

"From what you've told me, I doubt she was even a big user. She had discovered what was going on in the red house. Through some drug connection, maybe, but it was a separate thing. Maybe she thought she was in danger from somebody she knew. Somebody who knew your house. Who could get into her room."

"Somebody did get into her room. Her killer."

"She could have let the killer in," Lenny said. "I mean somebody who might know enough to look in her desk. That's why she didn't leave it there."

"Maybe. But that's only one of a couple of ways of looking at it."

"Tell me some others."

Nick thought. "I can't offhand. But it feels like we're working backward from what we know, as if what we know is the only thing possible to know. I'm not a detective-story fan. Makes life too rational."

Lenny frowned. "Maybe so. I enjoy them. Tell me about the other clues she wrote in her book."

"A piece of paper with 'EAST BERLIN' written on it. And there were some stamps from my collection that I thought she'd stolen to buy drugs."

"But she hadn't, had she?"

"I guess not."

"How did she get the combination to the padlock?"

"That's a mystery," Nick said.

"Is there anyone she might have talked to about it?"

"Yeah. That's what I've been driving at. Frankie Tonelli."

Lenny shrugged. He drew an imaginary diagram on the table-top. "You and your wife were living in Washington. Your daughter was here in Wheelersville?"

"She'd been kicked out of school, more or less. But she kept working on a project she'd started in school. A history of our family."

"Was she staying at the farm?"

"Yes. Some of the time."

"Who was with her there?"

"The couple that run the place. The Tates. They're good people, but they don't know too much."

"What about when you were here?"

"What do you mean?"

Lenny lifted his hands from the table and sat back. "Excuse me for prying, but you said—at the fishing camp—that you were on the outs with your daughter."

"That's correct."

"Was she out of touch with her mother too?"

"They may have spoken. My wife generally took my side."

"I'm wondering, did your daughter ever stay in the house when you were there?"

"I wasn't out here much at that time." Nick looked out across the dance floor. "But you're right. She was not at the farm when I was."

Lenny spoke softly and deliberately. "Then where was she staying?"

"With her great-grandmother. My father's mother. Helene Schlafer."

"Were she and your daughter close?"

"Yes. I believe they got close then."

"You believe? Senator, these are members of your own immediate next-of-kin family."

Nick looked at him. "Yes, they were close."

"Where did your grandmother live?"

"Right here in town. On East Carver Street. She still does."

"She's alive?"

"In her nineties."

"Is she . . . ?" Lenny touched his head.

"She has her moments. She can be pretty sharp."

"Would she remember details from the time your daughter was living with her?"

"She might."

"Have you seen her recently?"

"We talked in June. Right around the time I found Lore's book."

"Did you ask her about that?"

"It didn't occur to me. I might have found the book after I saw her. Now that you mention it, one of Lore's clues—a sketch of a cigarette holder—may even point to my grandmother."

"I think you better talk to her now."

"Yes. I will. This afternoon if she's up to it."

Lenny tapped the table. "That's it, then. Until after tonight."

"How will you reach me?" Nick asked.

"Don't worry." He stood up and put his hat on.

Nick slid out of the booth and stood. He looked at Lenny, who was wrestling his coat back on. "I guess I owe you."

Lenny peered at him over the top of his glasses. "Don't worry about it. It's my pleasure to be of any help."

"I'm in your debt," Nick said.

"No. It'll all work out. Just keep pushing your legislation."

"My legislation is all but dead."

"No, it's not. You're making progress."

"Well, it's out of my hands now," Nick said.

"But it's in *good* hands. We'll talk tonight." He pulled back the flap of his coat to reach for his wallet.

"No," Nick said. "This is mine."

Lenny smiled.

Nick took a ten-dollar bill from his pocket and put it on the table. The two of them headed across the dance floor.

Nick stopped. "I'll say goodbye here. I have to make a call."

Nick found a pay phone on the wall by the rest rooms. He dialed the farm. Abby answered.

"It's Nick. It looks like I'm not going to make it back this afternoon."

"So busy?"

"Yes. I promised Matty I'd do something with him."

"That's okay. He's fine. There's a movie he wants to see. We'll take him."

"I don't know yet whether we'll head back tonight or early to-morrow."

"Whatever suits. We'll be fine."

"Be careful."

"Don't worry. We get along great. He's a wonderful kid."

"Just be careful."

"Light me one. My eyes are terrible today."

Nick tapped a cigarette from the pack on the coffee table in front of him, struck a match to it, and handed it to Helene.

"How are things with Josie?" she said.

"I'm glad I found an excuse to visit with you again," Nick be-gan.

"I can imagine. It's been only four months." The final word caught in her throat and melted into a fit of coughing.

"But I don't want to talk about my marriage today."

"A pity."

"I want to talk about Lore."

"What will you have to drink?" She was looking up, beyond Nick.

Nick turned his head and was surprised to see Hilda standing at the door. "No alcohol," he said. "Whatever you're having."

"We'll both have tea, Hilda."

"Yes, ma'am."

Helene seemed to watch Hilda's departure.

"I said I want to talk about Lore, Grandmother."

"I know."

"About the time she was staying with you here."

The old woman continued to stare toward the door.

Nick tried to soften his voice. "After she left school."

The cigarette smoldered in her fingers. Her hand was trembling. "What about Lore?" she said.

"That history of the family she was writing? Do you remem-ber?"

Helene stubbed out the cigarette, though she had smoked only a quarter of it. It broke in two places. "What is this all about?" Her hand went unerringly to the cigarette pack and pushed it toward Nick. "And don't be vague. I want details."

Nick lit another cigarette and drew on it deeply. Helene reached over and took it from him.

"I don't know where to begin," he said.

"Begin at the beginning."

"I've picked up a trail of clues that Lore left behind."

"Clues to what?"

"One of them leads to a red building downtown. On Arch Street and Quarter Lane."

"Aah!"

"It might be part of a . . . a drug operation."

"In Wheelersville? How curious! Have you discussed all this with Emery?"

"Well . . . yes. Emery knows about the building. My interest in it."

"And what did he say?"

Nick waved smoke away from his face. "Not much. But why bring Emery into this?"

"You mentioned drugs. That's his specialty now, isn't it?" She looked toward the door. "Yes, Hilda, come in."

Hilda placed a tray on the table. "Shall I pour, ma'am?"

"No, I'll do it. The Senator will help me, if necessary."

Hilda stood by with her hands clasped and shook her head dubiously.

"You can go," Helene said. "We're two perfectly capable people." She leaned forward, grasped the teapot firmly, and poured. "There we are. Now tell me, Nick, have you asked anyone in town about this red house?"

Nick stirred a teaspoonful of sugar into his tea. "I mentioned it to the police chief. I'm leery of asking more people about it."

"You're investigating on your own?"

"Not entirely." He sipped his tea and set the cup and saucer down. "I've had some help."

"Whose?"

"A kind of expert."

"What kind of expert?"

Nick stirred his tea. "Someone who knows about these things."

"I bet it's a gangster!"

"Helene!"

"Someone from organized crime!"

"Look, Helene—"

"I'm right! I can tell. Good God, Nick! What's the matter with you? You could be risking your whole career."

Nick dropped a thin slice of lemon into his tea and tamped it with a spoon. "Well, it's an extreme situation."

"Does Emery know him?"

Nick stirred his tea slowly. "Yes, he does, as a matter of fact. He helped set up our first meeting."

"Good God!"

"But Emery doesn't know all the details."

"Why not? Don't you trust him?"

"Of course I do."

"You must. Emery has been very good for you."

"I'm just not sure I trust the people around Emery completely."

"I see," Helene said. "Nick, you must understand one thing. I'm forever grateful to Emery. He worked magic on Big Stash. You can't imagine how lonely your grandfather was. He was surrounded by people, but they were all afraid of him. And then along came Emery. He was just a boy, a golden boy, but he had no fear."

"Yes."

"You thought he was God. You followed him around like a duckling." She gazed into space. "Emery was the spark, the catalyst. He made the young people happy, your mother and father, who were a few years older. For a while at least, they were happy."

"Until the fight."

She held up her left hand as if to quiet him. "Even as a young man Emery understood how lonely it was to have power. And he could make my husband laugh. Emery the court jester, with his cap and bells."

"I remember he stopped being around so much when I was about fourteen."

"Yes, he began to travel for his drug store franchises."

"I missed him."

"Oh, I missed him too. But you know, he never stopped coming around, from time to time. Even in Big Stash's old age."

"Yes."

"He never forgot us, Nick."

"Yes."

"And you must never forget that. I'll always be grateful."

"But—"

"But what?"

"What am I missing here? You seem to be holding yourself back from saying something . . ."

"Well, Emery's charm had certain drawbacks, that's all. Everything came so easily to him. People were jealous of him. And of course"—she tipped her head from side to side—"he has a fondness for women."

"That I wasn't aware of."

"That's your obtuseness again, Nick. Emery has always inspired a passionate response in women."

Nick spread the fingers of his left hand. "Is that a problem?"

"My goodness, no." She leaned forward to sip her tea and then paused. "Except perhaps in one or two cases." Her cup rattled in the saucer as she set it back down. "There was a young lady in town who got a crush on Emery. She wouldn't take no for an answer."

"When was that?"

"Oh, a few years after Emery came to us." She picked up her teacup again. "She got hysterical and made all sorts of wild accusations. She claimed that she was pregnant. She accused Emery of . . . of forcing himself on her." She laughed. "One could just imagine that. I mean, she was a mere child!"

"What came of it?"

"Oh, Stash took care of it. She was set up very nicely."

"That sounds like blackmail."

"It was easier to pay. No fuss. No scandal. Emery was young—his whole future was in front of him."

"You're not saying there was any truth to her accusations, are you?"

"Of course not. Emery was beyond reproach. It was the curse of being a god. Now tell me more about this trail of clues you've been following."

Nick drew his head back.

"You can confide in me of all people." She sipped her tea. "Those are cucumber sandwiches. And shortbread. You always liked shortbread."

Nick took a piece of shortbread. "One of the clues led me to the red house, as I said."

"Yes."

"Another pointed to you, I think."

"Me?"

"A cigarette holder."

"You're not to comment on my smoking."

"And one just said the words 'East Berlin.' "

"Aaaahhh!" There was sadness in her voice.

Nick looked at her. She was staring into the distance. "Does this mean anything to you?" he asked.

She furrowed her brows. "Doesn't it to you?"

"Just the obvious. What used to be Communist Berlin? The east side of the wall?"

She sighed. "Oh, dear. This is getting difficult." She shifted in her chair and fixed her vacant eyes on Nick for the first time. "Are you serious about pursuing these clues?"

"Yes, I am, Grandmother. I've got a lot at stake here. My peace of mind, for one thing."

Her small frame shifted restlessly.

"I'm committed," he added.

She continued to look at him. "You know," she said, "one great benefit of your seeming obliviousness to subtleties was that it made things so much less complicated. Well, now, here we go."

Nick shook his head. "Where to?"

"You must surely know that south of here, about a half hour's drive, there's a town called East Berlin. A pretty little Pennsylvania-Dutch farming community."

Nick smacked his forehead with the heel of his hand. "Of course. What's the matter with me?"

"That, I strongly suspect, is what Lore's so-called clue refers to." She kept her eyes on him.

Nick looked back. He did not speak for moment. Then, with a tiny shrug: "Do you have any idea what I'm supposed to find there?"

Helene turned away. She picked up her cup and lifted her gaze to the distance beyond the table. "You had a difficult childhood, Nick, what with various things—the family's prominence, your father's special problems, the difficulties in your parents' marriage. You've never asked very much about these things. Ever. In a way, I was grateful for that, but I knew the chickens would come home to roost eventually, and now they're gathering, aren't they?"

Nick was silent.

"We tried to make things easier for you as a child."

"Yes," Nick said, "and I appreciate it."

"You had better wait and see about that. We tried to protect you, as I've said. We didn't tell you much about your father's death. And of course, you didn't ask."

"Well, I knew he died of pneumonia or . . . some disease."

"And that was enough. But we didn't tell you about your mother either."

"Only that she died too. Of cancer."

"We never told you that, Nick."

"Somebody did. I remember asking and being told."

"No."

"Believe me, I wouldn't forget that."

"Then someone was being irresponsible. Someone who looked after you and meant well, no doubt. I'm sorry." She sighed. "That was wrong. Very wrong."

"Are you saying she didn't die?"

"Stash did not approve of her, as you may or may not know. So we let sleeping dogs lie."

"Just exactly when *did* my mother die?"

"I never said she did."

"You mean she's still alive?"

Helene turned to look at him again. She nodded imperceptibly.

"She's . . . she's in this town, East Berlin?"

The nod slowed to a tiny quaver.

"How long . . . has she been there?"

"About—" The word came out as a croak.

"Why am I just finding this out now?"

Helene cleared her throat. "She came back about two years ago. She had been living in the Midwest."

"What!"

"Yes."

"Were you in touch with her then?"

"Indirectly, yes."

"And when she came back, to East Berlin, she got in touch with you directly?"

"Yes."

"And with Lore?"

"Well, that's another story."

"Why didn't you tell me then?"

"You weren't around, Nick."

"Did Matty know?"

Helene shook her head. "Of course not. It was after the summer he was here."

"So Lore and she met? They knew each other?"

"Yes."

Nick touched his cheek, as if to stop a tic. "What about Josie?"

"It didn't occur to me to tell her without telling you."

"How could . . . ?"

Helene reached out and touched his arm. "I think you should go and see her, Nick. I think you should go and see her now."

Nick looked back at her blankly and then nodded his head slowly.

"It may be very important that you see her," Helene said.

"What do you mean by that?"

"I don't know that I mean anything by that. I don't know that I mean anything."

"I could drive there now." Nick looked off into space. "I can't believe I'm hearing about this now. I just don't understand."

Helene drew herself up. "You can't possibly realize how utterly impenetrable you can be. In a way it's been to your advantage. Always has."

"But some reporter . . . Some political opponent. Why wouldn't they have dug it up?"

Helene shrugged. "Why should they? There was no scandal. She was using a different name."

"What name?"

"Her maiden name. Showalter."

Nick stood up slowly. "I'll go there now."

"Hilda will give you directions." She reached for the bell on the table.

"It's Marian, isn't it?"

"Yes. Marian Showalter. And Nick . . ."

He looked at her. Her eyes seemed blank again. "Yes?" he said.

"Eventually, when you find out how angry you are about all this, don't do anything cruel or stupid."

"At the moment I don't know what I feel."

"Of course you don't. But you will, you will."

Nick nodded.

"Now hand me the little bell."

Nick picked up a small silver bell from the tabletop and gave it to Helene.

"You must forgive us, she said." She shook the bell gently until it began to ring.

12

East Berlin

The big green sign for East Berlin loomed up about ten miles north of Gettysburg. Nick looked off to his right. The sky had turned a deep slate gray, but he guessed there was maybe a half hour of dim light left.

He slowed and steered the camper onto the exit ramp, which circled to the right and put him onto 234 heading east. The empty roadway dipped and rose, still leafy trees lining its edges, wastes of spent cornfields stretching away on either side. There was no sign of life anywhere that he could see.

He checked the time on the dashboard clock. A little after six.

He opened the phone, turned it on, and tapped out the number for the farm.

After half a ring, Dorothy Tate answered.

"Dorothy, it's Nick. Is Matty there?"

"No, but he should be in any minute now, Senator. They said they'd be back between six and seven."

"Well, I said I'd be there for dinner, but I'm not going to make it. Tell them to go ahead without me. I should be back, oh, around nine or ten. We'll head back to Washington then, or first thing in the morning. Depending."

"I'll tell them."

"Everything okay?" As he crested a hill, he caught sight of a car in the rearview mirror.

"Just fine. There were a couple of calls on your office phone. I let the machine take 'em."

"I'm sure they'll keep. See you tonight."

At the next rise in the road, the car behind him seemed to have fallen farther back. Still, could it be following him?

East Berlin was a tidy cluster of brick buildings. He could see from the sign swinging outside a bed-and-breakfast at the center of town that the wind had risen. He drove slowly past the inn.

At the far end of town he bore to the right and followed the blacktop for a mile or so, counting farmhouses as he passed them. The fifth one on the right—the one he was looking for—stood against the horizon at the top of an upward-sloping meadow. A winding dirt road led up to it.

He steered onto the road slowly, climbed for fifty yards, and pulled the camper off to the right into the tall grass. He got out and looked up at the house. The wind combed the meadow's grass in waves and tossed the branches of a large tree that loomed above the house against the darkening sky.

He dug his hands into his coat pockets and started up the road.

He was halfway to the house when he heard the whisper of a car cruising by on the road below.

He looked back. Was it moving too slowly?

It was a black Lincoln stretch limo. The dark glass of the windows kept him from seeing the driver. His own car? Or Lenny's?

The limo moved slowly out of sight.

At the top of the dirt road, a flagstone path led to a low enclosed veranda. A storm door at the center stood partly open. Gusts of wind kept banging it against its frame. Nick pulled it open and pushed against the screen door inside. The interior was dimly lit and stuffy and cluttered with wicker furniture piled high with blankets and cushions.

He crossed the room to a door that seemed to lead into the main house.

"Who's there?" The voice was deep and came from in back of him.

He turned quickly. In the dying light he made out a large man in overalls stretched out on a glider. Nick realized he had passed within a foot of him. His lantern jaw was covered with gray stubble. He wore a baseball cap with a shade that obscured his eyes. He held an open can of beer in his hand—Yuengling, a local brand.

"Sorry," Nick said. "I guess I didn't see you."

"No. You did not."

"I'm Nick Schlafer. I'm looking for Marian, uh, Showalter. Is she home?"

"Go on inside." He flapped his large left hand. "She's out back."

Nick started back toward the entranceway.

"You can go through to the kitchen—she'll be coming in that way."

"Thanks."

Beyond a dark, musty parlor, Nick found the kitchen. The wooden floorboards were painted lime green. Dishes were piled in the sink. The faucet was dripping. There was a smell of mildew.

He went to the door at the back and looked out through its window.

The light had faded. But in the dusk he could still see that behind the house a meadow dipped gently down and then rose again to the edge of a forest about a quarter-mile away. Near the bottom of the meadow, beyond a fence that enclosed a lawn and a border of flower beds, the beam of a flashlight dipped and wavered in the gathering darkness.

When Nick pushed down on the door handle, the wind slammed the door in against him. He stepped aside, pushed open the screen door beyond, and went down three steps outside, letting the screen door slam sharply behind him.

The wind made his eyes tear. The flashlight beam in the meadow flickered and brightened, as if it had searched for and focused on him. There was a ragged yelp in the distance, and a rushing, pounding sound. A large dog, a rottweiler, exploded out of the darkness and hurdled the fence.

Nick involuntarily backed up one of the steps, willing himself to keep his arms unthreateningly lowered.

The dog skidded to a stop, fell back on its haunches, and bared its teeth.

The bobbing light beam approached the fence. Nick could just make out the silhouette of a woman behind it.

"It's all right, Dukey," she called.

The woman pushed open a gate in the fence. Nick could see that she was wearing a skirt that came down to just below her knees.

"Could you call your dog off?"

"He's okay. Who are you?"

She stopped in the middle of the lawn and played the flashlight on Nick's face. She seemed to start but said nothing. The light beam moved slowly down to the ground beside her.

She moved a few steps toward Nick and stopped. "Do me a favor. Reach inside the door and snap the light on." Her voice sounded hoarse.

Nick opened the screen door a crack and found the switch on the wall inside.

The woman stepped into the newly formed circle of light. She had black hair flecked with gray, pulled tight back against her skull. Her face was angular but handsome. She looked in her late sixties, and was slim and lithe. She wore a blue denim jacket over a black turtleneck. Her skirt was also denim. She had on black hose.

"You're Marian Showalter," Nick said.

"I am. I'll come inside." The dog whined.

She climbed the steps and went past Nick through the door. The dog followed her. She walked the length of the kitchen and disappeared.

Nick stepped inside and stood by the door. He had the beginnings of a headache.

After half a minute she returned. She had removed her jacket. She walked with her hands pressed against the sides of her scalp, her head tipped forward and her eyes closed. The dog followed her back and flopped down on a blanket in the corner, yawning hugely.

She stood a moment adjusting the knot at the back of her head. Then she lifted her head to look at Nick. Her dark eyes were liquid.

Nick stared at her.

"So." She frowned and brushed a hair from her forehead.

They stood regarding each other. The skin of her face was dark and weathered, but she did not look old.

Finally she looked away and took a deep breath. "Can I offer you a drink or something?" She turned to a wooden table and touched a bentwood chair beside it. "Please sit."

Nick moved to the chair and stood in back of it. "What are you going to have?"

She looked around the kitchen and shook her head. "A good stiff scotch."

"I guess I'll join you."

She fetched a bottle, a couple of tumblers, and a bucket of ice and set them on the table. She poured herself a drink, handed Nick the bottle, and sat in the other chair at the table.

She took a long swallow and stared into her glass. "I guess you could say I just fell off the wagon. So." She looked up and twitched a smile. "Where do we begin?"

Nick put the bottle on the table without letting go of it. "I don't know. I'm . . . I'm . . ."

She let out a barely audible cry, put her glass down, and moved to him with a couple of quick steps. She slipped her arms around him, put her head against his chest and pressed against him lightly, as if she felt uncertain about touching him.

He lifted his arms and let his hands hang in the air. His face felt numb. He put his hands tentatively on her shoulders.

In response, she tightened her hold on him. "Oh, Nick."

His throat ached. To his surprise, he felt a tear trickling below his left eye.

"Why are you here, Nick?" she said softly. With her head still lowered, she released him, turned away, and went back to her chair.

He ducked his head, lifted his glasses, and quickly wiped his eye with the back of his left hand.

When she turned to face him again, he tried to force a smile, but it didn't work. He looked away, and poured himself some scotch. "I'm here because of . . . Lore."

"Yes."

"I didn't know you were alive until today." He dropped two ice cubes into his glass and looked around.

"I'll get you some water," she said.

"No. I'll get it." He went to the sink, and splashed tap water in his drink. "Lore left a . . . book of clues. It was an old game we used to play when she was a child. One of them said, 'East Berlin.' " He took a sharp involuntary breath. "Helene finally told me what it meant."

Marian sat down and poured herself more scotch. "I moved back here about two and a half years ago." She tapped a nonfilter cigarette from a pack and lit it. "I'd always stayed in touch with Helene . . . more or less. So I let her know when I moved back here. She told me Lore was living with her, working on a project about the family. She asked me if she could tell Lore about me. At first I hesitated, then I thought, why not?" She shrugged. "Lore came to see me. We became friends. We'd have dinner together once a week or so. I work at a high school in Gettysburg. I keep the books. We'd meet after work and talk and talk. She began to get interested in all sorts of things." She waved smoke away from her face and poured herself some more scotch. "Then she stopped coming."

Nick went back to his chair and sat down. He put his hands on his head.

Marian looked at him. "Helene tried to tell you."

"Yes, I see that now." His headache began to throb.

"When I finally left you to be with your father, he was dying. Killing himself, actually. He needed me."

"How do you mean, killing himself?"

"Booze. Drugs. It didn't take that long. He had been living in a rooming house in Harrisburg. We moved to my family's farm in Upper Fremont Township."

"And then?"

"And then what?"

"Where did you go then?"

She shook her head. "I ran far away."

"Just like that?"

She lowered her head.

"And you never came back."

"I couldn't. But I always kept up with what you were doing."

"I don't understand why you never made contact again. Especially . . . after my father died."

She sat down again and put her hand against her forehead. "I couldn't come back. Big Stash wouldn't have let me near you."

"I thought you were dead!" His head was pounding.

"Of course you did. That's the way your grandfather wanted it. It always had to be his way." She was slurring her words.

"But why?"

"Because he hated the sight of me. He called me farm trash."

"Why? Why?" He pressed his head with the heels of his hands.

"Oh, my God, why? Because he thought I destroyed his precious son."

Nick leaned forward. "What I find it hard to understand is why nobody ever dug up the fact that you weren't dead."

"What I find it hard to understand is why didn't you?"

"It never occurred to me."

She shrugged. "So there."

"But anyone doing background research—"

"Stash put it out that I was dead. Period. So I was dead. Nobody ever questioned it. And I was living far away under a different name."

Nick shook his head, leaned back, and drank. "What was the fight about?"

"Fight?" She blinked and moved her head back as if trying to get him in focus. "Would you like something to eat?"

"Not really."

"I'll get some crackers. The booze is really hitting me." She got up, swayed, and steadied herself with a hand on the back of her chair. Moving with elaborate care, she brought crackers, a wedge of cheddar cheese, a knife.

"The fight when I was a child. The night of Big Stash's birthday party. My father was gone in the morning. I never saw him again."

She waved cigarette smoke away from her face. "That was between your dad and Emery Frankfurt. About the drugstore."

"What about the drugstore?"

"Emery's master plan." A deep cough rattled her chest. "Emery thought you could have a drugstore like"—she moved her hand in a circle—"like a supermarket."

"Kwikrite Drugs."

"That's it!" She tipped her glass back, set it down, and poured more liquor.

"And my father was against it?"

"Your father didn't want things to change."

"There must have been more to it than that." Something popped in his sinuses and made his headache ease.

She put her fingers to her mouth and widened her eyes. " 'Scuse me." She pushed her hand at him, her fingers splayed unnaturally. Her cigarette fell to the floor. Nick picked it up and handed it to her. She took it.

He heard heavy footsteps in the other room. The old man appeared in the door.

She waved her arm at him without looking up. "No. Leave us be."

The man looked at Nick. His eyes fell on the bottle.

She turned around to look at him. "I'll be all right in the morning. Just leave me alone now."

The man nodded and retreated.

She closed her eyes. "He's good to me."

She took a deep breath, guided her cigarette unsteadily to an ashtray, and stubbed it out. "Your father was so jealous of Emery. Jealous . . . because . . . because Emery was Big Stash's favorite." She nodded her head and closed her eyes. "And . . ." She lit another ciga-rette and pushed herself to her feet. "I have to go lie down now."

Nick stood up and steadied her. She slumped against him.

He walked her slowly into the room next door and guided her to a sofa against a wall to the left. He took the cigarette from her and put it out. He could hear the click of the dog's nails on the floor-boards, following them.

Out on the porch, he found a quilt. She sighed as he covered her. "Don't go," she mumbled. He kneeled and touched her forehead. It was hot and dry. "Listen . . . Marian."

"What?"

"Where did you go after my father died?"

"Ohio. A small town near Columbus."

"Why there?"

"I don't know. To get away."

"From what?"

"The mess. The mess we made."

"Who is 'we'?"

"I'm tired."

"Tell me!" His mouth was dry.

Her voice was almost a whisper. "Emery."

"Emery?"

"Yes."

"You and Emery?"

"Yes."

He stood up, looked around, and made out a wooden chair in the dim light. He brought it to the side of the couch and sat down. "Did Helene know?"

"Yes."

"But I—"

"Big Stash blamed me, not Emery. Just me. He never forgave me. Only Helene did."

"But Emery?"

"Stash forgave him."

"Why did you come back here?"

"I thought the past would be dead."

Nick got up from the chair. "What about Emery now?"

"Later. I have to sleep now." Marian closed her eyes.

"No. Please talk to me. You said that Lore was interested in other things besides her family project."

Marian nodded.

"What other things?"

"No," she groaned.

"Marian. What other things?"

"The red house."

"A building?"

"Yes. In Wheelersville. She called it the red house."

"Why was she so interested in this building?"

"I don't know."

He leaned closer. "Marian, listen to me. How do you know she was interested?"

"This was near the end."

"The end of what?"

"Just before she stopped meeting me. She started asking me what I knew about it."

"Why would she have thought you knew anything?"

"That's what I asked her."

"And?"

"She wouldn't explain. She said she'd discovered a secret room with a safe in it. She said it was dangerous."

"Dangerous how? To who?"

"Dangerous to all of us. Those were her exact words."

"All of us? Who is 'all of us'? It doesn't make any sense to me."

"I thought she meant our family. *Your* family. She was scared to be talking about it."

"Where was this?"

"In the restaurant. In Gettysburg where we used to meet."

"Why would Lore have left behind a clue leading here to East Berlin?"

Marian opened her eyes and stared. She rolled onto her side and pushed herself up until she was resting on her elbow.

Nick could see her eyes in the dim light.

"Does anyone know you came here?" she asked. She spoke clearly. "Were you followed?"

"I could have been. Why?"

"Go home quickly now."

"Why?"

"They have to know you're here."

"Who?"

"Where's your son?"

"Matty? At the farm. Who is 'they'?"

She fell back and brought her hands to her face. He grasped her by the shoulders and shook her. "What are you talking about?"

"Don't hurt me. You're hurting me."

"Tell me what you're talking about."

"The people in the red house. I have a terrible feeling."

Nick stared at his mother. He was still pressing down on her arms. "What people?"

She strained to lift her head. "Don't you understand? You've followed the same trail that Lore did."

Nick lifted his hands from her and gazed into the darkness of the room.

"Go," she moaned.

He stood up.

"Hurry."

He felt his way across the room.

Outside it had begun to rain. He remembered his jacket and went back to retrieve it from the kitchen. The house was quiet.

The ground between the flagstones was turning muddy. The swirling wind pelted Nick's face with rain.

When he reached the driveway, he began to run.

Beyond East Berlin he pushed the speed of the camper up to forty, then stepped hard on the brake. Though the rain had gotten heavier, the surface traction was still good. There was no one else on the road.

Dangerous, Lore had said. To all of us. What exactly did that mean?

He eased the camper up to fifty.

Who was behind the red house if not the mob?

Out of the dark, rain splattered the windshield.

If not the mob, then who? The police? The people who were supposed to be fighting drugs? A rogue operation inside a law-enforcement agency? A rogue operation inside the mob?

Dangerous to all of us.

No. It was too wild to think the police were behind it. There were too many other possibilities.

Like what? If not the mob, then who?

The road was dark behind him as far as he could see. His headache was gone.

Why didn't Lore talk openly with Marian? What was Lore frightened of? Or was Marian hiding something? She was drunk, but she was still in control enough to be holding something back. Yes.

As he slowed for the approach onto Route 15, he noticed the pinpricks of headlights several hundred yards behind him. He reached over his shoulder and depressed the lock button on the door.

On the highway he sped up. The headlights appeared in the distance. They were gaining on him.

He pushed the speedometer needle past sixty-five and dimmed his brights to cut down the glare. The rain flooded the windshield, but he could still see where he was on the road.

The headlights behind continued to get closer.

It would be risky to go any faster. The visibility was too poor to tell what was along the roadside.

The headlights moved to within two hundred feet of him. He pressed the power button on the phone and pushed O for the operator and send.

There was a single ring and then a voice said, "Operator. May I help you?"

"Yes, operator. I'm calling from a car phone on Route fifteen about ten, fifteen miles north of Gettysburg, moving north. I may be in trouble."

"What kind of trouble, sir? Are you disabled?"

"No."

"How can I help you, sir?"

"Uh, I'm not sure yet."

The beams were a hundred feet away.

"I'm wondering where the nearest State Police barracks are."

"North of Gettysburg on Route fifteen."

"Yeah."

"Let's see. There's . . ."

Colored lights came on above the headlights behind him and began to flash.

Nick looked in the rearview mirror. "Hold on a second."

"I'm right here, sir."

He braked the camper gingerly. The lights in back of him moved into the left lane and came up on him quickly. He glanced to his left and saw that it was a State Police cruiser with all its lights flashing.

"Check that, operator. I think I already have help."

He slowed, steered onto the shoulder, and pumped the brake to a stop.

"Sorry to bother you."

"Are you all right, sir?" she said.

"I'm fine, thank you." He disconnected the line.

The police car pulled to a stop behind him, its lights still flashing gaudily.

He reached for the glove compartment and took out the folder holding the camper's registration. He opened the door, climbed out, turned his jacket collar up, and stood waiting. A uniformed trooper got out of the cruiser and walked toward him.

"Something wrong?" Nick said.

A light shone briefly in his face. "Senator Schlafer?"

"Yes? Is something wrong?"

"No, sir. Nothing's wrong. I got a radio call. I'm supposed to escort you to Wheelersville."

Nick's mouth went dry. "Is . . . Do you have any idea why?"

"It's not an emergency, Senator. Somebody wants to talk to you. Headquarters said to find you and deliver you."

"Do you know who wants to see me?"

"No, sir."

"Well, I'll tell you what, officer. I've had a couple, and I shouldn't be driving. Can I hitch a ride with you?"

The light beam came up to his face again. Nick tried to hold himself steady.

"I can do better than that," the trooper said. "I'll drive your vehicle, if it's okay with you."

"It's fine, but who'll take your cruiser?"

"My partner." He turned and gave a hand signal.

Nick walked around the front of the camper, and got into the passenger seat. The trooper climbed behind the wheel. He stuck out his hand. Nick took it. "I'm Sebastian. They call me Sebe." He gunned the engine and pulled onto the highway.

"Some weather," Nick said.

"Yup."

The police car passed on the left and pulled in front of them. The rain continued to fall.

• • •

Nick jerked awake. The camper came to a stop. His neck was stiff and his eyes ached.

They were parked on Central Avenue near the center of Wheelersville. The police cruiser was behind them. The rain had lightened.

"This is it," Sebastian said. "You're supposed to wait over there." He pointed across the street at Eckert's drugstore.

"Where did the message come from?"

"The officer on night duty at headquarters."

They both got out. "Thanks for the lift," Nick said.

"No problem, Senator. You okay now?"

"Yes."

The trooper waved his hand and made for the cruiser. Nick stood by the camper. The air seemed warmer.

Nick watched as Sebastian opened the passenger door of the police car and climbed in. The car pulled away and turned down Arch Street.

He crossed the street to the drugstore, still watching. The cruiser went over the railroad tracks by the red house and turned right a block beyond. When its taillights had disappeared, Nick looked up Central to his left. A set of headlights came on in the distance and began to move toward him.

As they approached, he saw that they belonged to Lenny's black limousine. It pulled abreast of him and stopped. The door swung open.

Nick stooped and looked inside. In the dim light he could see Lenny sitting in the far corner.

"Hi, Senator. Let's take a ride."

It was warm inside. Nick unzipped his jacket. The limo moved slowly forward.

"So," said Lenny. "It's been an interesting day?"

"It's been a confusing one," Nick said. He massaged his neck. "I don't know how comfortable I am about having the State Police bring me here."

"Don't worry, Senator. I passed a message through a guy—a police buff who hangs out in a bar near the local barracks. Said it was a family situation. Nobody knows they delivered you to *me*."

"Okay."

"Did you learn anything?"

"Just that I'm pretty sure my daughter got into that building. What time is it?"

"Ten-thirty. I wanted to fill you in before I left."

"Did you find the passageway?"

"We confirmed the whole deal. They bring in the cadavers, put 'em on the tables, and open 'em up. They take out either bags of powder or wads of paper currency. Drugs or money."

"How do they get it to the red house?"

"There's a passageway, like we guessed."

"Where?"

"You stand at the foot of the examining table in the middle—there are three of them. You grab it by the sides and give it a little pull. It slides back and leaves a hole in the floor. There's a ladder down. It's not too nice, I understand."

"What do you mean?"

"Leads to the sewer. It stinks."

"Can the entrance be closed from below?"

"Very sharp, Senator. Yeah, it can. There must be a switch down below. Anyway, after someone goes down, the table slides back."

"You were there?"

"Our boy was there."

"He's pretty observant."

"You just gotta ask him the right questions."

"Is Belcher himself involved?"

"No, not directly. He knows something's going on, but he hasn't caught them yet."

"The boy didn't go down the ladder himself, did he?"

"No."

"Then we still don't know for sure where the passage leads."

Lenny looked out the window and spoke to the driver. "Turn here and take us back to the drugstore." He turned to Nick. "No, but it's a pretty safe bet. We'll know where it goes in no time."

"It has to go to the room I couldn't get into," Nick said. "Or to a staircase or ladder."

"That's what we think. The command center must be there. Communications. A chemical lab for fixing up the drugs. A place to hide the money before it gets cleaned. Laundered."

"And a safe."

"Probably."

"I'm pretty sure there's a safe there," Nick said.

"You are? Does that mean you know who the house belongs to?"

"No."

"Well, maybe we'll find out when we go in there."

"And just how are you going to manage that?" Nick asked.

Lenny shrugged. "No problem. They keep the key to the morgue under the back-door mat, believe it or not."

"Why would they do a thing like that?"

"Why not? There's nothing to hide except the entrance to the passageway, and you have to know how to get it open. There's an alarm too, but it's a piece of cake to disconnect. We want to send somebody in tonight."

"You know the alarm code?"

"Sure. Our kid got it. Six-zero-one-five."

"I don't want you to do it yet."

"Why not? We're almost there."

The limo slowed and stopped.

"I'd just prefer that you wait. I'll tell you when I think it's time."

Lenny regarded him from under the brim of his hat. "You worried about what we'll find, Senator?"

Nick leaned back against the seat. "I don't want to lose control of this process. But don't get me wrong—I'm very grateful for the way you've helped me."

Lenny looked away and studied the window next to him. "Say no more, Senator."

"There's been trust between us. But—"

Lenny looked back. "Say no more—I understand. You have my number."

Nick opened the door and got out. "I'll be in touch. Soon."

"Oh, Senator?"

Nick leaned back into the limo. "Yes?"

"Leave Frankie Tonelli out of it."

Nick remained silent.

"Leave him alone."

"All right. I guess I owe you that."

"And Senator, be careful."

"Thanks."

Nick closed the car door and crossed the street to his camper.

Nick let himself in the front door. He paused at the entrance to his study, took his jacket off, and tossed it over the back of the armchair just inside.

He listened. The house seemed to be waiting. He took a step toward the foot of the staircase.

Where was everybody?

He hurried to the stairs and took them three at a time. He had never felt more sober. At the head of the stairs he paused to catch his breath. Fur was sitting in front of Matty's door. He looked at Nick and meowed.

Matty's door was shut.

That was odd.

Nick lunged for the knob and threw the door open. He stared into the darkness.

He groped for the wall switch and turned on the light.

The bed was neatly made.

Matty was not in it.

13

The Safe

Nick stood in the middle of Matty's room and looked around. The cat brushed against his ankle.

The suitcase that had been at the foot of the bed was gone. The album of coins on the night table was gone.

He went to the closet and slid open one of the door panels. The clothes they had brought from Washington were gone. Someone had taken the trouble to pack.

That was some cause for hope.

He left the room and ran down the stairs. "Anybody here?" he shouted.

He turned on the dining-room light. The table was bare.

In his study, he looked around for a note or some other sign that someone had been there. The room was exactly as he had left it. There was a single brief message on his answering machine. He held his breath as the tape rewound. "It's Segal. Where the hell are you? Call me."

He picked up the phone and touched the button labeled "Caretaker." Dorothy answered on the first ring. "Yes?"

"Dorothy."

"Yes, Senator. Is anything wrong?"

"I don't know. I seem to have gotten my signals crossed."

"Yes?"

"Were you around when Matty left?"

"Of course. I hugged him goodbye."

"What time was that?"

"Oh, six-thirty. Seven. It was after sundown."

"What time did they get home?"

"Ten, fifteen minutes after you called. They packed and left about half an hour later. They said they'd been in touch with you."

"Yes. Of course. Matty didn't eat dinner?"

"They said they were going to stop on the road. Matty had someplace in mind. He was looking forward to it."

"Yeah, that makes sense."

"Is there a problem, Senator?"

"Uh. Probably not."

"I *was* a little puzzled because when you called this afternoon you didn't mention they'd be leaving before dinner."

Nick fought back a wave of dizziness. "I thought they were staying for dinner. I'd hoped to see them off."

"Well, they didn't seem too concerned one way or the other."

He took a deep breath. "That's good. Did they leave any messages for me?"

"Not that I know of. They just said Matty had school tomorrow and had to be back."

"Do you remember who said that?"

"Certainly. It was Abby."

"Was she driving when they left? I'm just curious, because—"

"The young man was driving."

"Donald Fox."

"Yes."

"Dorothy, would you mind asking Tom if they left a message with him."

"He's right here. I'll put him on."

Nick heard a muffling sound and unintelligible murmuring. He pressed the corners of his eyes with his thumb and finger and whispered to himself, "Dear God, dear God, dear God."

"Hiya, Senator."

"Hi, Tom. Abby and I got our signals crossed. I was just wondering if she or Fox left any message for me."

"None that I know of."

Nick took another deep breath. "Okay, I'll catch them in Washington. Sorry to have bothered you so late."

"No bother."

"Apologize to Dorothy for me."

"See you tomorrow, Senator."

"I may go back tonight myself. Don't count on seeing me."

"We'll look after things here."

"Good night."

" 'Night."

He disconnected by pressing the flash button, then tapped Josie's button.

She answered on the second ring, sleepily. "Hullo?"

"It's me."

"Nick!"

"Sorry to call so late. I just got in."

"Oh? Late doings?"

"Heavy politicking. What a day!"

"You sound a little fuzzy. So do I, probably."

"Yeah. I drank too much."

"How's Matty?"

"Uh, he's good. He's fine."

He looked at his watch. They had been on the road over five hours now. Too long. Too long.

"Nick? Are you there?"

"Yes. I'm wrung out. I don't think we're going to be back tomorrow."

"Oh, Nick, you promised he wouldn't miss school. What's going on?"

"A lot. I'll tell you about it later."

"Is something wrong."

"No. No. It's just that I'm embroiled in something out here. I'll stay in touch."

"Well . . . I love you, Nick."

"I may be able to send Matty back with Abby sometime tomorrow. Late in the morning, maybe. She'll take him right to school."

"Okay. Good."

"I love you."

He pressed the flash button again, and punched in Don Ebright's number. The phone rang three times before there was an answer. "Don," he said. "It's Nick Schlafer."

"Yo, Senator. What's up?"

Nick squeezed his eyes shut and swallowed again. "I'm in full panic, Don. Bear with me."

"What's the matter?"

"My son's not here."

"Whatta you mean?"

"I just got home and found out he left for Washington with the people who were looking after him."

"What's the problem?"

"They weren't supposed to leave till I got home. We were all supposed to go together tonight or tomorrow morning."

"You sure there wasn't some kind of mix-up?"

"Positive."

"Maybe they misunderstood you."

"Anything's possible. But they left over five hours ago, and he hasn't gotten home yet. I just talked to my wife."

"Who'd he leave with?"

"Abby, my assistant."

"You trust her, don't you?"

Nick thought a moment. "Well, yes. Of course. But why would she leave without telling me?"

"Anyone else with them?"

"My son's bodyguard."

"So what do you want me to do? I can sound the alarm. Call the State Police."

"I think you'd better do that."

"They'll put out a statewide alert."

"Yeah, but then if someone has taken him, we're forcing them into a corner."

"That's true, Nick."

"We know the vehicle and license number. Can't we just sort of quietly track them down?"

"No. It's all or nothing. And when they cross the state line, it's the Feds who are responsible."

"I don't think I want to do it yet. Does that make sense?"

"It does, it does. Just sit tight for a while. First, you don't know if it's even anything. They might have stopped somewhere."

"Why haven't they called then?"

"Maybe they haven't had a chance. Maybe they will."

"You're right, Don."

"Well, good. You got company?"

"No."

"You want me to come over?"

"I don't know. Just keep talking to me."

"Okay. Have you got any idea who might want to take Matty? Or why?"

"It could have been a couple of things. I've got to think about the timing." As Nick spoke, he stood up, opened the closet door behind his desk, and stepped inside. The stretched telephone cord jerked the base unit across the desktop a few inches.

"You want to tell me what you're thinking?" Ebright said.

Nick turned the dial of the wall safe at the back of the closet.

"Nick?"

"I'm here."

"I said, do you want to try your ideas out on me?"

"Not yet. The whole thing's kind of hazy." He pulled open the door of the safe and removed Lore's autograph book. He took it back to the desk and sat down again.

"Nick? Are you all right?"

"I don't know." He unlocked the clasp of the book and riffled the pages until he came to the green page with the family tree of numbers on it. He rotated the book ninety degrees. Sideways, the tree looked more like the brackets of a tournament.

"Well, here's the bottom line, Nick, if you want my opinion."

Nick took Segal's diagram from his pocket, unfolded it, and spread it beside Lore's book. His eye went from the top left-hand numbers on Segal's chart—the ones he had underlined in the restaurant that morning—to the top ones on Lore's diagram. They were identical: BFH 981 and BFH 982.

"Nick? Damn it, Nick, are you there?"

"I'm sorry, Don. I'm distracted." He compared a second set of numbers. The same. "Let's have your bottom line."

"That it's probably just a problem of missed signals."

"Right. I hope. Look, Don. I've got to do some thinking here."

"Don't fool around with it, Nick."

"You're right."

"No trips downtown."

"What's that supposed to mean?"

"I don't know," Ebright said. "You never did tell me what you found in that building."

"Okay, Don. I promise to let you know if things get any clearer."

"Incidentally, I had someone call Harrisburg about those prescription records."

"Oh, yeah?"

"There's nothing under Schlafer for those years."

"That's impossible!"

"Zilch. Neither by or for."

"But my father was the druggist then, supposedly. It doesn't make sense. But I can't think about it now."

"You'll be all right?"

"I'll be okay."

"Well, I'm right here if you need me.

"That's good to know. Thanks, Don."

He took a pencil from the center drawer and drew an inverted triangle in the blank space below the numbers on Segal's diagram. Beside the left-hand point he wrote the words "HEARSE PLATES." At the right-hand corner he wrote "LORE'S BOOK." At the bottom point he wrote "SEGAL'S DIAGRAM."

The numbers from the three sources were the same: the license plates, Lore's autograph book, and the diagram that Segal had inadvertently downloaded from Internet. But what connected them? Lore could have copied her numbers from the license plates in Belcher's garage. But what was the source of Segal's numbers?

Someone had been sending them to Segal's contact in the Drug Control Department.

But who? And why?

He wrote the word "DRUGS" in the center of the triangle and circled it so hard that the pencil-tip broke.

And now Matty was gone.

He picked up the telephone and pressed the button for Segal's home. The phone barely rang before there was an answer. "Yeah."

"Dave!"

"Where have you been?"

"Listen, Dave—"

"Why haven't you called? Big things are doing. The budget vote's probably on Tuesday, and—"

"I'll be there. Don't worry."

"People have been calling to congratulate you on your decision to support."

"It was supposed to be a secret," Nick said.

"Well, it isn't. Diefendorfer's bubbling over. He wants me to guarantee you'll make it back for the vote. It's real close—they're counting heads.

"I'll be in late tomorrow, probably. Or early Tuesday. Now let me ask you something."

"Yeah?"

"Do you happen to know where we got Donald Fox from? The guy who's looking out for Matty?"

"Abby found him somewhere. Why?"

Nick closed his eyes. "Nothing. Just curious. I'll see you sometime Monday. Or Tuesday."

He pushed the flash button, took a slip of paper from his wallet, and tapped out numbers.

"Delta one-niner."

"Is Secretary Frankfurt there? It's Senator Schlafer."

"Sorry." A toneless voice. "The Secretary is not available right now."

"When will he be?"

"Later. Would you like to leave a message?"

"Uh, no."

He flashed the dial tone, consulted his wallet again, and tapped more numbers. "Lenny Scordia, please."

There was silence on the line. He waited.

"Sorry, but he's on the road where we can't get through to him. You can try him later."

He replaced the receiver. It was important not to panic. He had to be able to think clearly.

There had been a series of threats, beginning with the note on the rock saying "Why don't we meet?" and now escalating to Matty.

He tried to steady his breathing.

He found another pencil, and scrawled on the piece of paper next to the triangular diagram:

> *Note on rock—April*
> *Dummy in stream—April*
> *Pressure on Judiciary members—April-Oct.*
> *Rifle in tree—June*
> *Doll in camper—June*
> *Matty—Oct.*

He stared at the list. At the top he wrote, "John Holden death—April." Above this he wrote, in capital letters, LORE.

Was there any pattern?

Not really. He had half consciously assumed that whatever had been happening to him over the past six months was a reaction to his drug legislation. That was true of the note on the rock, certainly, which had come from Rizzo, and the pressure on the committee members—if you counted that as a threat. But Lore's death had happened before the drug bill. And the legislation had died, while the other threats had grown stronger.

He crossed out two of the items. He was left with:

> *Dummy in stream—April*
> *Rifle in tree—June*
> *Doll in camper—June*
> *Matty—Oct.*

Was there anything about his behavior that might have provoked someone to mount these progressive threats?

The red house. He'd been circling closer and closer to it. The rifle in the tree and Matty's kidnap had both followed some breakthrough in his search. And East Berlin. Could that be connected?

Of course. Marian might have been the only person Lore had talked to. And someone could easily know that. Someone who didn't want him near the red house.

Or near the safe.

He looked at the diagrams he had drawn. It was a gamble, a wild gamble, but maybe if he got to the secret room, he could find something. He was crazy to try. He knew that. But it was better than sitting around and waiting.

The safe.

Flipping the pages of the autograph book to the end, he lifted the flap of the glassine envelope, inverted the book, and tapped it on the desk surface until the four stamps fell out. He put the autograph book to one side, took a pair of stamp tongs and a sheet of eight-by-eleven white paper from the center drawer, and laid the paper on the desktop. With the tongs, he placed the stamps on the sheet of paper and began to line them up in a horizontal row.

He arranged them by date: the ten-cent Washington pair, the one-cent Franklin pair, the four-dollar Columbian block, and finally the three-cent Win the War.

What was the cheap stamp doing there? Was Lore trying to tell him something? If so, why had she gone to such elaborate lengths to send her message? And where did Frankie Tonelli fit in?

He rolled his chair away from the desk, turned, and looked into the closet at the dial of the wall safe. The numbers went from zero to thirty-five. He stood up and pulled a green paperbound book from the top shelf on the wall to the right of his desk. It was the 1992 edition of *Scott's Specialized Catalogue of United States Stamps,* the latest edition he owned.

He sat down again, placed the book to the left of the sheet of paper that held the stamps, and opened it. Thumbing the pages toward the front, he found the listing for the ten-cent Washington. It was Scott number 4. Under the left-most stamp on the white sheet of paper, he wrote the numeral 4. He repeated the procedure for the other three stamps: 8, 244, and 905. He looked at the numbers he had recorded: 4, 8, 244, 905.

Moving the pencil tip lower on the paper, he copied the numbers again in a uniform sequence: 4 8 2 4 4 9 0 5.

He stared at them. With the pencil tip, he bracketed them into groups of two: 48——24——49——05.

Was it possible? He picked up the telephone and rang Segal.

"It's me again," he said.

"What now?"

"Is your head clear?"

"Sort of."

"Okay, tell me: the safe in the office. Do you know what kind it is?"

"The safe? It's a standard brand. A Mosler, I think."

"How many numbers are there in the combination?"

"Let me think. Left: that's one. Right: two. Left: three. Right. There are four numbers."

"How high do they go? How many digits?"

"What do you mean?"

"What's the range on the dial. One to . . . what?"

"One to . . . ninety-five, I think. Or ninety-nine. Two digits."

"Have you ever heard of safes having more?"

"No, but I'm no expert."

Nick tore off a corner of the paper that held the stamps. He copied the stamp numbers onto it: 48 24 49 05.

"That's it?" Segal said.

"Yes." He pressed the button for a dial tone and punched Don Ebright's number again.

"Don."

"Anything happen?"

"No, but I can't sit around here waiting anymore. And I need someone to sit here and answer the phone if Matty calls."

"No problem. I'll send someone right over."

"I'll tell the caretaker. The front door'll be open."

"Good."

"And Don, I need you to park in one of the lots in Quarter Lane and watch the back door of Belcher's morgue."

"Nick, you're crazy!"

"Sit with your lights out. If anyone goes in besides me, turn your headlights on to signal me."

"What about the other building?"

"The only way in is through the morgue. Can you be there in twenty minutes?"

"Right."

Nick stood up, put the stamps back into the envelope, and put the autograph book back in the safe. He slipped the paper with the numbers on it into his shirt pocket. He picked up the larger sheet of paper and tore it slowly in half.

He held the two halves in his right hand and studied them for a moment. He removed a matchbook from the middle desk drawer, lit the papers, held them aloft until they were all on fire, and dropped them into a wastebasket. When the flame had died, he took the pencil from the desk and stirred the ash into fragments. He put the matchbook into his shirt pocket.

He removed the penlight from the middle drawer, stuck it into his shirt pocket too, went to the armchair, and put his jacket back on.

He took another deep breath and went to the door.

He parked the camper in front of his grandmother's house on East Carver Street, turned off the lights and motor, and sat in the dark. There were no other cars on the street.

He opened the door and climbed out. The rain had stopped, and the temperature had turned sharply colder. He shivered. His breath came in gouts of steam.

He pushed the door of the camper shut, moved around to the sidewalk, and began walking west.

Did it matter if anyone saw him? Probably not.

He turned right on Arch Street. Where Arch crossed Central there was still no sign of anyone.

At the corner of Quarter Lane, he stopped and looked around. The air was still and metallic. The red house looked black behind the dim light of the bulb above the staircase. There were no cracks of light where the hidden room might be.

There were no signs of life anywhere.

He thrust his hands into his jacket pockets, hunched his shoulders, and set off up Quarter Lane away from the red house, as if out on a brisk evening stroll. There was no way to tell if Ebright was parked among the vehicles behind the morgue.

When he found himself between the garage where the hearses were stored and the back of Belcher's Funeral Home, he stopped and looked around again to be sure he was alone.

A light was on above the back door, but the windows were dark.

"Go!" he whispered to himself.

He looked behind to see if any lights were on in windows where someone might be watching him.

All the buildings in view were dark.

"Go, damn it! Go!"

He strode toward the back of the morgue. When he reached the back door, he stooped and lifted the mat. He felt cold cement until he found the key, as Lenny had said he would. He gently guided it into the keyhole in the doorknob.

He listened.

A truck motor accelerated somewhere in the distance.

He turn the key to the right and felt the latch give. He grasped the knob and pushed the door open.

The thin whistle of the alarm warning started up. He had thirty seconds.

He moved quickly inside and closed the door. A tiny red light was blinking on the opposite wall, next to where the door was hinged. He groped beneath his jacket for the penlight, flicked it on, and shone the small beam on the number pad next to the blinking light.

He punched the numbers Lenny had given him: 6 0 1 5.

The alarm beeped and stopped whistling.

He turned off the penlight and breathed in the still darkness.

Formaldehyde.

After a half minute he turned the penlight on again and moved the small beam to the left, away from the alarm pad. It moved across artificial knotty pine wall planks, across black-bordered framed certificates, to the end of the partition, where black space yawned.

He followed the beam into the darkness beyond the edge of the partition. Around the corner he saw glass bottles on shelves above a large white porcelain sink with pink-and-black rubber tubes sprouting from its gleaming faucets. Next to the sink was the first of the three examining tables that Lenny had described. It was empty, a stainless steel platform shaped to hold the human form, curled up at the edges to catch fluids, and sloped to carry them down to a gaping drain.

The room was cold.

He moved the light beam left to the next table. It was not empty. A small figure lay on it with its right arm unnaturally raised.

Nick dropped the penlight from his grasp and fell to his knees. A wave of nausea rose in his throat.

He put his hands on the cold tile floor and lowered his head.

He steadied his breathing and waited for the dizziness to pass. The sweat trickled icily down his face and armpits.

He picked up the light and pushed himself to his feet again.

A sheet covered the small body, except for the oddly raised arm.

He stepped to the side of the table, shifted the penlight to his left hand, and with his right hand drew the sheet slowly away from the head.

He lifted the light.

The hair was caked with dirt and dried blood. The face, half turned away, was battered beyond recognition.

The boy was wearing a white T-shirt and denim overalls.

Matty never wore overalls.

He stooped slightly and shone the light at the boy's right ear. He reached and lifted the flap. The skin felt leathery to his touch.

This child must have died at least two days earlier.

The crevice behind the ear was caked with grime. He scratched at it with his fingernail. The skin beneath was smooth and unblemished. There was no dark birthmark.

He leaned against the table, closed his eyes, and let his chin rest on his chest.

He looked up and drew the sheet up over the dead boy's face. Stepping to his left, he moved to the head of the table and grasped it firmly on both sides.

He braced his feet and pulled the table toward him. Nothing happened. He braced himself again and yanked harder. The table gave an inch. A humming noise started up. The floor began to move beneath his feet.

He stepped off to the side, catching his balance as he landed. He played the light beam along the floor and saw that the table had moved away from the wall, leaving a black opening in the floor just big enough for someone to fit through.

He squatted and duck-walked to the edge of the gap. A sweet stench hit his face and made him gag. He could hear a hollow sound of liquid trickling below.

He leaned forward and shone the light into the hole. It was framed by four stained cement walls that descended into the darkness beyond the reach of the light beam. Dark blotches ran down the walls. A rusty metal ladder with its top rung a foot below the opening was bolted to one side.

He swung his legs into the hole and braced himself on the floor until his feet found a lower rung. He moved his hands to the top rung and began his descent.

The trickling sound grew louder. Flaking rust scraped his hands. The stench got stronger. He breathed through his mouth.

When he could barely see the opening above him, he stopped and shone the beam downward. Below him the shaft opened out into what appeared to be a horizontal tunnel. The ladder ended just above a narrow cement ledge that dropped off into further darkness.

He climbed down until his feet reached the ledge. It was wide enough to stand on. To the right of the ladder, metal insulation tubing came out of the wall and ran down a foot or so to a switch box with two buttons on it.

He lifted his hand to the switch box, hesitated, then pressed the top button. It was stiff but finally gave under pressure. The metal hum sounded again above him.

His light could not reach the trapdoor, but he assumed it had slid shut.

Still facing the ladder and holding on to one of its rungs with his left hand, he stood on the ledge and shone the light around. To his left was a wall with white cement bulging from between its bricks. Opposite the wall, to his right, was a keyhole-shaped tunnel with a ceiling of smooth cement. The ledge on which he was standing seemed to continue along the left-hand side of the tunnel. An iron pipe along the wall served as a railing. Below the ledge ran a deep ditch at the bottom of which dark liquid seemed to be flowing.

The air was cold and damp, and the stench was worse.

He released his hold on the ladder, grasped the railing, and began to grope his way along the ledge. He could hear a rustle of movement up ahead. He shone the light down. Small red eyes glowed and moved on the far side of the ditch. Rats, most likely.

The tunnel seemed to be sloping gently down and to the right. The air was a little warmer. He stopped to get his bearings. The only sound he could hear was the sewer flowing below him.

He extended his right arm to give the light beam added reach. Though the tunnel continued, there was a break in the ledge just up ahead. Where the ledge came to an end there was an opening in the wall. The pipe railing stopped too.

A narrow passageway led off to the left at nearly a right angle to the tunnel. Its walls were stone and dirt, and its floor consisted of wide wooden planks. Warm air wafted from it.

The foul smell was gone.

He stepped from the ledge onto the planking, and stooped to get beneath the low overhang of the smaller tunnel. The floor sloped gently upward. Twenty-five feet into the tunnel he came to an archway crudely formed of three four-by-fours. Loose dirt had sifted down to form two mounds on either side of the passageway.

He banged one of the timbers with his fist to see how firm it was. It gave slightly.

He tried to move faster, but now the tunnel was narrowing. He came to another rickety-looking archway with mounds of fallen dirt piled on the planks beneath it. Just beyond, the flooring began to rise more steeply. Then it ended abruptly at another archway. A steep wooden stairway rose into a narrow cut in the low ceiling.

He pointed the beam of light upward, but all he could see was a hole that was barely wide enough to get through. He gripped the wooden ladder and began to climb into the darkness. Cobwebs brushed his face.

Why were there cobwebs if the passage had been used earlier today?

The air here smelled of damp soil. The opening narrowed to the width of his shoulders and slowed his progress. There wasn't enough room to get his arm past his body to shine the penlight. Had he gone the wrong way and come to a dead end?

Desperately he pushed with his legs. He lifted himself half a foot, and suddenly found room to raise his right arm. He shone the penlight around.

The passageway came to an end a few feet above his head. But there was an opening just in front of him. It led back five or six feet to what looked like the entrance to a wooden dumbwaiter. He clambered over the lip of the opening and snaked his body forward. He found that he could rise to his hands and knees. He heaved himself into the dumbwaiter, turned over into a sitting position, and rested against the back wall. He was bathed in sweat.

Hard to believe this was the way they regularly carried in the shipments.

The light beam had grown weaker, but he could see that there was room to stand in the compartment. He pushed himself stiffly to his feet and played the weak beam around him. An old-fashioned elevator lever was mounted on one wall about waist-high. He thrust it sideways. It slid with surprising smoothness across its arc. A low electric hum started up, rose rapidly in pitch until its whine filled the darkness. The compartment began to lift.

The whine rose to a scream, then to a throb. It made his head ache. The cage continued to rise slowly, creakingly. Clumps of dust fell around him. He turned the penlight off to preserve its waning power. The cage groaned, slowed, and shuddered to a halt. The throbbing scream of electricity went on in the darkness.

Had he activated an alarm? Had he walked into some kind of trap?

He turned the penlight on again. He could see by its weak beam that the wall of the cage opposite its entrance was sliding slowly down. Beyond it was another passageway, dimly lit by small recessed light bulbs. When the wall had descended to floor level, the whining noise diminished. He groped for the elevator lever and pulled it back to its starting position. The electronic hum died.

He stepped into the passageway. The floor was hard and felt like steel. The air smelled fresh and clean. He had crossed some threshold. He was facing another ladder, made of new and polished metal. It gleamed in the dim light. It rose eight feet to the ceiling of the passageway.

He mounted it tentatively and climbed. The sound of his shoes on the rungs rang softly. When his head reached the ceiling, he shone the dim light against what appeared to be a trapdoor. It must go into the room. He placed his right hand against it and pushed, but it refused to give. He moved the light around the edges until he found another switch box with two buttons on it. When he pressed one of them the electric whine started up again. The ladder beneath his feet began to rise. The trapdoor opened into darkness. He rose through the ceiling.

The movement stopped. He could see almost nothing. He took a step forward and found solid flooring under his feet. He banged the back end of the penlight against the butt of his left hand. The beam seemed to brighten slightly. It picked up a wide metal counter with a sink recessed into it. Pans and knives and surgical instruments lay around its edges, neatly arranged. Plastic bags of white powder lay along the counter in neat piles. The floor beneath his feet was concrete—or steel. The light beam faded again, but his eyes had begun to adjust to the darkness around him.

He knew beyond any doubt where he was. He was in the red house. He was standing in the center of the room that lay beyond the partition with the chess pieces on it.

He turned slowly. The table with the bags lay across the north end of the room, near the side of the building next to the railroad tracks.

He walked the west wall, the partition between the two rooms. Here, as on the other side, there was nothing but shelves. He moved along it to his left. In the corner he found a large refrigerator. It stood exactly opposite the one in the other room. To the right of it, below the bottom shelf, was a copying machine.

He made his way along the south wall. This would be where he had seen the light shining through the cracks when he had left the building last spring. He raised the failing penlight. As he expected, there was a boarded-up window in the wall. He turned the penlight off and waited. The cracks in the window boards remained dark. There was no sign of Ebright's headlights.

Below the window was a desk on which he could see the outline of a computer monitor. He moved the palm of his hand along the surface of the desk until he found what felt like a rocker switch. This must be to activate the automatic garage door.

He went left past the desk. He groped and felt a steel cabinet, taller than he was. He turned the penlight on again, aimed it a few inches from the cabinet's surface, and moved the faint beam in a widening circle. His hand struck a metal handle.

He stepped six inches to the right, shone the light above the handle, and found what he was looking for. A circular dial. With numbers engraved around its rim.

The light was too dim to read them. He felt for the matchbook he had put in his shirt pocket and removed it. He struck one, brought it to the dial, and moved it around. The numbers ran from 1 to 95. He took the slip of paper from his pocket and moved the flickering match near it. On the paper he read: "48 24 49 05."

The match began to burn his fingers. He shook it out, let it fall, tore off and struck another. He held the scrap of paper in the palm of his left hand and placed the burning match between his left thumb and index finger. He moved the paper and the flame close to the dial.

With the fingers of his right hand, he spun the dial quickly to the right a full revolution, and then turned it slowly until the number 48 was lined up with the hairline indicator. He rotated it back to the left to 24. The dial moved too easily. He could not feel any tumblers clicking into place.

He turned the dial to the right again to 49 and then left to 5. He shook the dying match-flame out. He gripped the metal handle, took a deep breath and jerked it firmly downward. It refused to give.

He struck another match and brought the flame back to the dial. Had he turned it incorrectly? Were you supposed to complete an extra revolution after one or another of the numbers? He spun the dial quickly two complete turns to the right, then slowed and brought the number 48 to the indicator. He reversed it a complete revolution and brought it around to 24. Right to 49, left to 5. A sharp jerk of the handle.

Nothing.

He shook the match out and found that he could still see his hand on the safe. He could see the dial as if in daylight. He was bathed in brightness. He turned his head slowly and found himself blinded by light. He raised his left hand to shade his eyes.

"Put both your hands up," a man's voice said from the direction of the light.

Nick raised his right hand to join the left.

"Open your hands. Let me see your bare palms."

He spread his fingers. The penlight fell from his right hand and clattered on the floor.

"What are you doing here, Senator?"

Nick shrugged. The light beam twitched. It was shining from the corner where the refrigerator was.

"I have a message for you," the voice said.

"From who? Who are you?"

"That doesn't matter. The message is: If you want your son back, go to your fishing camp. Wait there for more instructions."

"Where is he? What have you done with him?"

"The boy's okay. He's still on his way to Washington. If you want him to get there, go to the fishing camp and wait."

"Nothing better happen to him. How do I get out of here?"

"Okay." The man laughed dryly. "Here's what you do. Stand right where you are and count to a hundred. Then cross to where you see this light. It'll be gone. Open the refrigerator door and walk through into the other room. That's the way we usually come and go. It's easier than the way you went, believe me."

"You mean you just carry the stuff across the street?"

"No. There's an exit from the tunnel into the garage. Nobody goes the way you did, except once in a while."

"Why are you telling me this?"

"Who gives a rat's ass? They'll close this place down now. When you leave, go straight to the front door and get the hell out of here. And don't get curious along the way. You'll be watched."

Nick nodded. "I understand."

"And don't tell anyone you're going to the camp."

"But people are expecting to hear from me."

"You can make all the calls you want. Just don't say where you are. And don't try to bring anyone with you. We'll know if you do. Start counting now."

The light went out. Nick watched the afterimage float away. He blinked and tried to see in the blackness. He listened. He counted to himself. There was no sound in the room.

When he reached a hundred, he began to move across the room. The outline of the refrigerator came dimly into view. He found the handle of the main compartment and pulled the door open. A soft light came on at the edge and he could see that within it was a passageway.

He stooped, went through it, and moved into the darkness beyond. He raised his hands in front of him and went forward until he came to the partition that defined the kitchen. He moved to the right until he reached the corner and felt his way along the wall that separated the room from the hallway. When he got to the end, he turned left around it and went quickly to the front door.

Down below on the near side of Arch Street, a police cruiser was parked with its barlight flashing blue, red, yellow, and white. The back of Belcher's Funeral Home across the street was still dark.

He hurried down the wooden staircase and approached the cruiser. Don Ebright was sitting at the wheel, his face reflecting the barlight's various colors. A voice crackled from his radio.

Nick stood at the car window. Ebright stared up at him. Nick shook his head as imperceptibly as he could. "I have to go. I can't tell you where," he said softly.

Ebright nodded. "Okay. Get in. I'll run you up to your camper. I *know* where you're headed."

Nick walked around the cruiser, opened the passenger door, and climbed in.

The cruiser moved slowly back up Arch Street.

PART FOUR

Monday, October 13th

14

Fish

Nick placed the kettle on the edge of the grill so it would be out of the way of the licking flames. He sat back in the bear's throne and stirred his coffee with a teaspoon. The moon had set. The hemlocks, the shrubbery, and the cabin had turned black in the predawn darkness. He could hear the rush of the stream, but otherwise the air was still. Firelight played on the tree trunks beyond the barbecue. He shivered, yawned, and sipped his coffee. It was only a few degrees warmer than it had been in Wheelersville.

He set the mug down on the stone shelf to his right and picked up the cellular phone. As he began to punch numbers, an ember exploded in the fireplace, sending a shower of sparks onto the hemlock needles at his feet. He watched them die on the damp forest floor, then punched Josie's number.

"Hi," he said when the ringing was interrupted.

"Nick?" Josie said. "Where are you?" Her voice was muffled with sleep.

"Uh . . . at home."

"Wheelersville?"

"Yes. I just got up."

"What time is it?"

"Four, four-thirty."

"My God!"

"I couldn't sleep. Anyway, I have an early meeting in Harrisburg."

"Why on earth?"

"It's a touchy situation."

"Your voice sounds fainter than usual."

"I'm on a cellular phone. So I can move around the house."

"Are you all right, Nick?"

"Sure."

"Where's Matty?"

"Fast asleep. I guess we're not going to make it back this morning."

"What's going on, Nick?"

"Complications."

"I don't like this."

"Come on, Josie! School's not a problem. He's missed a day or two before, and he's having a great time here. Don Ebright's offered to take him fishing."

"Isn't the Senate in session?"

"You know nothing happens on Mondays. I'll have him back tomorrow morning."

"You sound tired."

"I'm fine. I'll call you this evening. Late."

"Wait, Nick."

"What?"

"Something's wrong, isn't it?"

"Josie, I'll call you tonight. I've gotta go."

He disconnected and tapped more numbers.

"Huh."

"Dave!"

"Wazzit? What time is it?"

"You don't want to know."

"Where are you?"

"At the fishing camp. Don't ask questions. Have there been any calls for me? Messages?"

"At this time of night? Are you coming in today?"

"I don't know."

"The budget resolution . . ."

"There won't be any vote today," Nick said.

"But you've got appointments."

"I don't know if I'll make it in."

"But—"

"Make excuses for me. I'll be there for the budget vote, Dave."

"This isn't going to help your image."

"Please. Just please tell people I'm in Wheelersville. Including Josie, if she calls in. Listen, sorry to wake you."

"It's okay," he said weakly.

Nick's teeth chattered from panic and fatigue.

He used the firelight to consult the slip of paper from his wallet and punched in Emery's number.

"Delta one-niner."

"Secretary Frankfurt, please."

"I'm sorry. Secretary Frankfurt is not available."

He disconnected and stared into the darkness. Finally he punched in more numbers.

"Sorry to wake you," he said when Lenny came on the line.

"Don't worry about it. You called last night, I understand. I was out of reach."

"They've taken my boy, Matty."

"Who?"

"My son!"

"No. Who took him?"

"I don't really know yet. I don't trust this phone."

"It's digitized."

"Still."

"When did they take your son?"

"He was gone when I got home last night. He's been gone nine hours."

"Why didn't you keep on trying me?"

"I panicked. I went to the underground passage."

"What?"

"We were right. There's a hidden room with a drug lab in it."

"Where are you now?"

"At the camp. They gave me instructions to come here."

"That's what I guessed. I got people already there."

"No! You'll scare them off. They'll hurt Matty."

"Nobody'll know. Call me as soon as you hear more. Just stay a little calm."

Nick pushed the power button and put the phone back on the rock shelf. He sat in the seat again and listened. His teeth were chattering. How would they come? The way Lenny's men had?

A twig snapped somewhere in the direction of the stream. He stood up, walked to the edge of the firelight, and stared into the darkness beyond.

Was something moving out there? An animal maybe?

He listened more intently until the stream seemed to be whispering inside his own head. He began to turn back toward his seat.

Something lightly brushed his left arm. He turned and felt it gently grasp his right wrist and begin to twist his arm uncomfortably backward. He moved to ease the pain and found himself having to lunge to keep the pressure off his arm.

Suddenly he was in the air, and then tumbling on the ground. There were cold hemlock needles on his face and in his mouth. His neck hurt from the fall. His eyeglasses were gone.

He sat up and tried to clear his mouth. A shadow was moving toward him. He put out his arms to protect himself.

The shadow extended its arms. No gun.

He tried to scramble up. The shadow stepped forward and took one of his hands. The grip was light but firm. Again he found himself trying to avoid any pain, and being thrown and falling. Something solid hit his shoulder. A tree trunk. He sat up and rubbed himself.

The shadow was coming at him again.

He struggled to a kneeling position and got his feet under him. The figure seized his right arm. He stumbled forward, grappled with his left arm, and locked his opponent in a choke hold. He yanked his right arm free and managed to grasp his own left wrist with his right hand. He staggered and pulled the choke hold tighter. He could feel a wool-covered skull pressing against his left cheek. He yelled and squeezed harder.

A sharp blow to his ribs took his breath away, but it only heightened his anger. He roared and squeezed and bore down with his weight. He could feel the slightness of his opponent. He could feel him collapsing under the weight. He hooked his left leg around his assailant's ankles and pitched himself forward. Together they went down in a heap, with Nick on top. In a rage, he squeezed still harder.

Suddenly he was on his back gasping for air. There was pressure against his throat. The figure loomed above him. He couldn't breathe. He was growing faint.

He closed his eyes. He lifted his arms helplessly, hoping to convey defeat.

The pressure eased.

He could breathe again. He opened his eyes. By the light of the fire he could see a dark ski mask. The figure sat back. Nick's arms were free. Reaching up with his right hand, he tried to grab at the mask. The figure slapped his hand away and lifted the mask for him. The facial skin was dark bronze in the firelight. Black eyes looked down at him. Silky black hair fell around an oval face.

"Who the hell are you?" Nick shouted.

"It's Leila."

"Leila?"

"Your driver."

The figure shook her head to arrange her long hair. Nick moved his right hand down and felt the softness of her hip. "What in hell are you doing here?"

She said nothing.

"How did you get here?"

"I drove the limousine."

"What the hell did you do to me? I almost passed out." He touched his throat, expecting it to hurt but finding no pain.

She moved her hands to Nick's shoulders and leaned closer to him. Her face filled Nick's vision. Then it darted down, and Nick's upper lip was between her teeth. He grunted and held still. His head was being pushed against the ground. He pulled back his right hand and made a fist to hit with. Suddenly his lips were released and her tongue was between his teeth. It thrust sharply and filled his mouth.

He tried to pull away, but she had his head pinned. Her skin smelled sweet. Her hair felt feathery against his face. With an effort, he freed his right hand and pushed her face away. He rolled her off him. Her body seemed almost delicate now.

"What's your real name?"

"It's what I told you. It's Leila."

"You're an Israeli?"

She laughed softly. "No. The opposite! I'm Palestinian. From a *qiryat* in occupied Palestine."

"Palestine?"

"Tubas. In the north, near Nablus."

Nick sat up and touched his throat again. "You could have killed me. I don't understand."

She shrugged.

"How did you get to this country?"

"I work for certain people."

"Who?"

She shook her head.

"Where did they find you?"

"They interrogated me in a Syrian refugee camp. They . . . how do you say it . . . recommended me."

"Why did they interrogate you?"

"I was known to have certain abilities."

"I can see that." He looked at his watch by the dying firelight. It was 5:10. "Why are you here?"

"I have a message for you," she said.

"Where's Matty?" His voice wavered.

"Go fishing," she said.

"Fishing?"

"Yes."

"I don't get it."

"You will catch a fish in the . . . the Woman's Pool."

"That's the message?"

"Yes."

"Who sent this message?"

She shook her head again.

"Okay. You delivered it. Now get the hell out of here." He stood up and brushed wet hemlock needles from his clothes. He began to walk in small circles, searching the ground.

"What are you doing?" Leila said.

"My glasses."

"They are there," she said, pointing at the ground about ten feet from the grill.

He went to pick them up.

"I'm going now."

"You fucking well better." He put his glasses on. He looked at her and spat in her direction. "Get the fuck out of here! Go."

She shrugged, turned away, and walked into the darkness.

When he could no longer hear her, he went to the bear's throne and found the phone where he had left it under the stone table. He walked to the edge of the stream with it. He was still shaking.

The water looked black in the night. He shivered. It felt like snow.

He stepped upstream, relieved himself at the water's edge, and moved downstream again until he found a rock to sit on. He took out his wallet and found Lenny's number.

An unfamiliar voice answered immediately. "Yeah?"

"Can I speak to Lenny? It's Nick Schlafer." There was silence. "Hello?"

No response. He studied the surface of the water.

"Senator!" The voice sounded fresh and awake.

Nick spoke as softly as he could. "They're setting me up."

"You better explain that."

"The messenger they sent was my driver."

"I know."

"How do you know?"

"Just tell me the message."

"She told me to go fishing."

"Where?"

"At a place we have here called the Woman's Pool."

"We're familiar with it."

"It'll probably put me in a sniper's gunsight."

"No, no," Lenny said. "They can't shoot you. If they thought they could kill you that way they wouldn't be going to all this trouble."

"Yeah, that's true. This woman could have killed me if she'd wanted to."

"See?"

"What's the point then?"

"An accident. Drowning, it sounds like."

"But standing on that rock I'm totally vulnerable. All they have to do is bash me on the head and throw me in the stream. It'll look like I fell off, cracked my head, and accidentally drowned. The water's deep and fast there."

"Could this girl do that?"

"Not if I was alerted. Anyway, she's gone."

"She may be hanging around. Could you handle her if you had to?"

"I don't know. She'll have help."

"Don't worry. Nobody else is coming. We got the place surrounded."

"Then why did you let her through?"

"Somebody had to be the messenger. She had no weapon. Nothing metallic."

"This doesn't make any sense."

"That she was your driver doesn't make any sense. The important thing now is to get your son back. Play out your hand."

"Yes."

"Okay, then. When are you going to the rock?"

"After daybreak. Around six-thirty. But what's the point if nobody but the girl is there?"

"It's just a guess that they're going to try to drown you. It could be something else. You have to spring the trap to see if we're right. We'll be watching. Just take care of yourself." The line clicked off.

He stood listening to the ripple of the stream, then turned and went back to the cabin, leaving the phone under the stone table. He walked unsteadily, as if on a heeling boat.

He went up the stairs, onto the porch. He found his brandy flask on the table where he kept his fishing gear. He turned the porch light off and moved cautiously around the corner to the mattress where he slept. He sat down on it, with his back to the wall and pulled his open sleeping bag over his legs.

He unscrewed the cap of the flask and took a deep draft. His hands were shaking. He stared into the darkness. He thought he could hear the sound of rain.

By gray light, he looked at his watch: 6:15. He tried to gather his drifting thoughts.

It was time to go to the Woman's Pool.

He stood up stiffly and walked around the corner of the porch to the table with his fishing gear. He stood beside the table and began the dressing ritual—socks, waders, vest, hat.

He selected a rod tube from the table, removed its contents, went outside, pieced the rod together, and rigged it with a sinking line and a heavy leader and tippet. Considering the coolness of the air, he picked a number-six streamer from his fly box—a brown muddler minnow—and tied it on.

Though the day was overcast, it was light enough to see now. The ground looked damp, the foliage was dripping, and the stream was swollen. It would be numbing to wade in. He was not wearing long underwear.

He leaned the rod against the cabin wall and went back inside. The soles of his boots squeaked against the smooth wood of the stairs.

He rummaged through the equipment on the table and found a coiled army web belt with a brass buckle. He went outside again and stood at the foot of the steps listening.

No sound.

Something felt wrong with his equipment, but he could not pinpoint what was bothering him. He felt springier when he walked, for a reason he couldn't identify. Maybe it had to do with the atmospheric pressure.

He uncoiled the belt and slid its brass tip through the four rubber loops that ringed the waist of his waders. He buckled and tightened it. That would keep the cold air out.

He set off toward the stream, slowed, veered to his left and found the path through the woods. He tried to clear his head. He should have had some coffee.

When he came to the flat place next to the Woman's Pool, he looked around. Wind was moving the treetops. There was no sign of life. He made his way carefully to the edge of the pool. The wind rippled its swollen surface.

He stepped down onto the crescent of beach, which was now submerged in a half a foot of water. He waded to the upstream end of it and inspected the water rushing past his ankles. The stream was up by at least a foot. To reach his underwater stepping-stone, he would have to slide his feet down the bank until the water reached nearly to his waist.

It would take a much stronger leap to reach the ledge by the woman's knee.

He stared into the water's depth and rehearsed the maneuver in his mind. His heart was beating too quickly.

Keeping his head down, he raised his eyes, and from underneath the brim of his hat he scanned what he could of the far shore. The woods seemed alive with people watching him.

He shifted his rod to his right hand, raised both arms, and stepped cautiously into the water. Something still felt different about his equipment. Maybe it was just his nerves.

He counted slowly down from five. When he got to one, he expelled his breath sharply and began his slip-slide down the bank. The stream rose rapidly up his waders to his crotch. The cold made his stomach clutch.

When the water was two inches from his waist, he flexed his right leg and extended his left foot forward. It found the slippery surface of the underwater stone. He raised his arms for balance and thrust his weight forward, at the same time bracing his left leg in preparation for his leap. Instead of gripping the submerged stone, his foot slid crazily across it.

He was sliding out of control.

His left shoulder slammed into the rock face and his head exploded with pain. Something scraped his scalp. He fell into a gurgling darkness. Coldness numbed the pain in his head, and he tumbled through wet blackness. The roaring all around him thinned into a bubbling whisper. You will drown now. The water will fill your waders and you will drown and drown.

Tumbling, he tried to lift his left arm, but pain and cold had deadened it. The whisper told him to get his waders off, but they were clinging to him and dragging him farther down into the blackness. He tried to kick his legs. A huge pain was growing in his chest and head. The whispering was flattening into a hiss. He thrashed in the blackness and found that he could swim.

His chest felt as if it was about to burst. He tried to find where the surface was. He was swallowing water. He was nowhere near air.

Something solid brushed against his thighs. He reached down with his right hand and felt rough surface rushing by. He tried to grab it and found his movement slowing.

The roughness scraped the length of his body. He pushed against it with his hand and felt air on his back.

He was at rest now, lying on a rocky bed. He tried to lift his head, but could not. He rolled his head to the side and felt air on his face.

With a tremendous effort he opened his eyes. Instead of blackness he saw a green haze. He tried to breathe, but choked. In desperation he worked his right arm underneath his chest, pushed up with it, and lifted his head. He began to cough up water. He felt air come into his lungs.

He rolled himself onto his back and found himself lying in six inches of water. He could barely hold his head up. His entire body was trembling. He was lying in the tail of the Woman's Pool, at the side, where it was shallow.

He closed his eyes again; pinpricks of ice stole over his body. He felt an urge to sleep. Water choked him again and he snapped awake. His head felt clearer.

He opened his eyes and looked down the length of his body. His waders lay pressed against his legs and torso. *Why hadn't they filled up with water?* It took what seemed like hours to think about it. He moved his right hand to his waist and felt the belt. The answer came to him. The belt had kept the water out.

But why had he slipped when he tried to leap onto the stone?

With another huge effort, he bent his right leg so that he could reach down with his hand, touch his foot, and feel the bottom of his boot. He touched bare rubber. The layer of felt that gave him traction was gone.

Something or someone had scraped it away.

With still another effort he lifted his head. A blurred figure was standing on the opposite shore. He squinted but could not see who it was. He had lost his glasses again. The figure was moving toward him. It had some sort of pole in its hands.

Nick squinted harder. The figure was a third of the way across the stream. It had long hair. It must be Leila. She was brandishing what looked like a length of pipe.

Without intending to, he began to shout. The woman kept coming. The water was halfway to her knees.

He tried to get up, but there was still no strength in him. He tried to brace himself with his left hand. Brace himself against what was to come. The pain in his shoulder prevented him.

She was halfway across the stream, in water up to her knees. She raised the pole with both hands, like a baseball batter approaching the plate.

He waited on his back, watching her advance. With his right hand he dug a small stone from the stream bottom and threw it at her weakly. She twisted to avoid it and kept advancing. She was fifteen feet away from him, past the deepest part of the stream.

His eyes fell on the fishing rod lying within arm's reach upstream from him. The hook of the brown streamer fly was still embedded in the cork handle above the reel. He reached for the rod with his right hand, rested it on his chest, and pulled the hook from the cork. He grasped the handle of the rod, and raised the tip into the air. The feathery lure floated free.

He moved the reel toward his face until the loop of green line coming off it was near enough to take between his lips. He gripped it with his teeth and pulled the reel away. It gave off a series of clicks as line came off it. He flicked the lure in the air and pulled away more line with his teeth.

She was lifting the pole above her head. He could see that it was thick and rusty. He snapped the rod back and whipped out line to his right. She saw what he was doing and tried to move toward him more quickly, but the water prevented her. The fly fell in the water short of her. He cried out and whipped it back.

He cast again, flicking his wrist sideways with all the strength he had left. The fly whistled through the air and wrapped itself around her raised left arm and her head. He snapped the rod back and to the left. Crying out, she slapped at her neck with her left hand. He yanked. She yelled and lunged at him. He could see that the hook had caught in the skin of her neck.

He gave the line slack, and snapped the rod back again. He had hooked her solidly.

She was within striking distance of him, but she was staggering off balance. With her right hand, she lifted the bar to hit him. He let go of the rod and took hold of the line. He yanked it as hard as he could, roaring at the top of his lungs. She howled and fell a body's length away from his feet.

Digging with his heels, he rotated his body until he was lying perpendicular to her. The slope of the stream bed allowed him to roll over onto his stomach. He found the strength to push himself up onto all fours. He began to crawl toward her, keeping the line taut as he got closer. She was on her hands and knees in the water, with her head bowed down. He could see blood running from where the hook was embedded in her neck.

He yanked at the line again. She pitched forward into the water. With the pressure of the hook eased for an instant, she rolled onto her side to face him. He crawled forward and fell on her. He thrust with his right hand and grabbed the hair at the back of her head. Yanking her hair he pulled her head underwater.

Her eyes stared wildly at him from beneath the surface. Bubbles streamed from her mouth. Blood rose from her neck in a wispy cloud. She thrashed, but his weight kept her pinned. He became aware that he was yelling hoarsely. He bore his weight down on her. He could see her eyes closing. Her arms waved feebly in the current. He shoved her down harder. Her eyes opened again. They began to roll upward.

He let go of her hair, and her head bobbed to the surface. He arched his body back and punched her in the diaphragm with his right fist. Water streamed from her mouth and she coughed weakly. He punched her again. She vomited water and gasped. Blood kept streaming down her neck.

He shouted at her, "You were going to kill me!"

She kept her eyes closed and shook her head weakly.

"You want more?" he screamed, and shoved her violently back into the water again.

Her arm came weakly up and plucked at his sleeve. He pulled her out again. "You want to tell me anything?"

She nodded and coughed. "Hook out," she gasped.

He rolled off her and sat up in the water. He looked at her. Her head was down. She looked faint. He turned and saw two figures on the opposite shore. One of them approached the stream and began to wade toward him, splashing loudly. As it came closer, Nick saw that it was the fat man. When he was beside Nick he reached and grasped the collar of Leila's sweatshirt with his right hand, and dragged her closer to the shore.

Nick slowly moved around to her left side, kneeled down beside her, and examined the hook in her neck. It would take a pair of wire-cutters to remove it from her flesh. The wound was only oozing now. He extended the set of clippers that hung from his vest and snipped the leader from the hook eye.

"We'll get the hook out later." He took her left hand. "Tell me, what was supposed to happen next?"

She panted. "I tell them you drowned."

Nick let her hand go and stood up.

The fat man was smiling at him. "You okay?"

Nick swallowed to catch his breath. "More or less."

The fat man looked down at Leila, then back at Nick. He frowned and shook his head.

Nick took another deep breath. "I wish you'd gotten here sooner."

"Yeah. She slipped by us when she came back."

Nick stood in the stream next to the fat man. His legs were shaking. He waved a hand at Leila. "She tried to kill me."

"Who sent her?" the fat man said.

"I don't know."

"We'll look after her good now. Maybe she'll tell us a few things."

Nick stopped to catch more breath. "See if you can get the hook out of her neck." He waded back toward the shore and retrieved his fishing rod from where it was lying in the shallow water.

As Nick began to cross the stream again, the fat man stopped him with his arm. "Your head is bleeding. Let us help you to the cabin." He turned and signaled the figure on the shore.

"I can make it," Nick said. He set off slowly through the shallow water at the tail of the pool.

"Can you see?" the fat man called after him.

"Enough," Nick said without looking back.

When he got near the cabin, he could make out someone standing on the porch steps.

"How was the fishing, Senator?" It was Lenny.

Nick shook his head but said nothing. He walked unsteadily to the bear's throne. He leaned his rod against the tree, dragged off his vest with his right hand, dropped it onto the stone table, and began to remove the suspenders of his waders.

"Could you use a beer?" Lenny called out.

"No."

"Hot coffee with a shot of brandy?"

"Might help." He slid the waders to his knees, sat down and tried to pull off the boots. He found that he was too weak.

Lenny approached with a steaming mug. Nick took it and set it down on the ledge.

"One of you guys could help the Senator get his boots off," Lenny called out. "Also a change of clothes." He turned back to Nick. "They'll find clothes upstairs?"

"In the bedroom," Nick said. He felt the cloth of his pants at his thigh. It was dry. "All I need is a shirt and sweater."

"Bring a towel," Lenny yelled.

"I lost my glasses," Nick said. "There's another pair in the top drawer of the dresser."

Lenny nodded and moved off toward the house. A tall man Nick hadn't seen before approached, kneeled in front of him, and expertly slid off his waders. He took the vest and rod and started off toward the house.

Lenny came back, brushed off one cinder-block ledge of the fireplace and leaned back against it. "They're getting your stuff."

"Thanks." Nick tried to lift his left hand, but he found the effort too great.

"You had a close call."

Nick blew on his coffee and sipped it. "She stripped the felt from the feet of my waders." He put the coffee down and reached across the top of his head with his right hand to feel the left side of his scalp. It was tender to the touch. He looked at the tips of his fingers and saw a smear of blood.

"The scalp heals quick," Lenny said. "Leave it alone."

The tall man returned with a bundle of clothing, a camp chair, and a small folding table. He set down the table and chair and handed Nick the clothes. Then he removed a pair of glasses from his shirt pocket and gave them to Nick. When Lenny had seated himself facing Nick, the man placed the table between them. Nick put the glasses on.

"Good," Lenny said. "You can see now. We're going to have a little breakfast. What would you like?"

"Toast will be fine." Nick grunted with the effort of putting on the sneakers with his right hand.

"Rye, white, pumpernickel?"

"Rye." He began to remove his damp upper clothing.

"Your arm hurts."

"Shoulder."

"You need help dressing?"

Nick took a towel from the pile of clothing and rubbed the back of his neck and shoulders with it. "I can manage, I think."

"The fat man will give you a shot for the pain. You want eggs?"

"No."

"Fruit? Melon? Strawberries?"

"Okay, some melon."

"Cantaloupe? Honeydew? Casaba?" Lenny was grinning brightly.

Nick laughed mirthlessly. "Cantaloupe, please."

Lenny nodded at the tall man, who went off. "Now, we'll talk a little, if you're up to it."

Nick stood up, tucked his shirt in, and began awkwardly pulling the sweater on. "Go ahead."

"That looks painful."

"I'm okay." He pulled the sweater down around his waist and sat again.

"More comfortable now?"

"Much." He looked off toward the stream. "But I'm having trouble keeping things straight in my mind."

"Well, let me help."

Nick swallowed. "I don't know who to trust."

"I can understand that."

"How did you know they'd send me here?"

"Just a hunch."

"Bullshit."

Lenny looked away. "There's things I can't tell you. We all have trade secrets." He looked back at Nick. "You have them too."

"Mine are legal."

"Look." Lenny scratched his ear. "You have to ask yourself, Why would *we* want you dead?"

Nick sneered. "Maybe not you yourself—"

Lenny waved his hand. "Don't start thinking that way."

"I don't like the way you operate."

"Just tell me, could she have thought that up all by herself?"

"What?"

"Tampering with your boots."

"I don't know," Nick said. "I guess only a fisherman would know that."

"So who do you think put her up to it?"

Nick shook his head. "You tell me—with your trade secrets. I don't even know who she works for."

"Don't worry, the fat man will get it out of her."

"I thought he didn't beat up on women."

"Oh, he won't get rough, don't worry. She may know something about your boy. Meanwhile, you got any idea at all, Senator?"

"Of who's behind everything? I've got some hunches." He put his fingers over his eyes and rubbed them. "It's either someone who doesn't like my talking with you, or someone in the Drug Control Department." He looked at his watch.

Lenny nodded.

Nick half rose from his seat and fell back. "What am I doing? I've got to get Matty back."

"Easy does it, Senator." Lenny put out his hand.

The tall man arrived with a tray of food and placed it on the table he had set up. Lenny dismissed him with a nod. To Nick he said, "Why do you mention the Drug Control Department?"

Nick sighed. "It's a couple of things." He closed his eyes. "The woman Leila, for one thing. They're the ones who assigned her to me."

"Continue."

"Then there's the things we talked about before," Nick went on.

"The weapon in the tree when we were down here in June. The license plate numbers of the hearses."

Lenny looked puzzled.

"I brought it up when we were walking around Wheelersville—when was it?—Sunday. Yesterday! God! It seems like last month. The license plate numbers matched a diagram that one of my assistants accidentally intercepted from the Drug Control Department. Over the Internet. My daughter had the same numbers in her autograph book, so that ties it all together."

"Where did she get them from?"

"I don't know. From the hearses?"

"Why?"

"That's the big mystery."

Lenny nodded slowly. "Why didn't you tell me all this before?"

"I wasn't sure about it. And why should I trust you?"

"Why didn't you want us to go into the building?"

Nick sipped his coffee. He felt nauseated. "When we talked last night I didn't know. . . . I had a vague idea that there might be something in there that I didn't want falling into a stranger's hands, if you'll forgive me."

"No problem."

"I learned that there's a safe in there."

"Did you get into it?"

"No. I thought I had the combination but it didn't work."

"Do you have any idea what's in it?"

"It's supposed to be something dangerous . . . dangerous to me, to my family. That's what my daughter told her grandmother. I can't imagine—"

"Her grandmother?"

"Yes. My mother."

"Then you found out she's alive?"

"Yes."

Lenny nodded. "Do you want us to open the safe for you?"

"No, don't go near it. The building is being watched and I don't want to stir them up anymore."

Lenny took a forkful of scrambled eggs and chewed thoughtfully. He brought his hands down on the arms of his camp chair. "I can understand if you're anxious."

Nick noticed that Lenny had a small piece of scrambled egg on his upper lip.

"Let's try to figure out your next step," Lenny said.

Nick touched his own upper lip. "You have a piece of egg here."

"Thank you," Lenny said. He wiped his mouth with his hand and flicked the egg away.

"I'm sorry. I can't concentrate," Nick said. "It's Matty. Matty. Matty. I should call the FBI. I should call *somebody*."

"But you don't know what they want yet. Your shoulder is hurting you?"

Nick shivered and yawned. "It's okay. I should be doing *something*."

"Let's speculate. Suppose she had succeeded, the woman?"

"She would have called somebody to tell them I had drowned."

"So they don't know what happened yet," Lenny said. He stared off into space and rapped his knuckles against the arm of his chair. "We know they took your boy to get you here. But why do they want you dead? That's the first question."

"At first I thought it was the drug legislation. Now I'm convinced it's to keep me from finding out about the red house."

Lenny nodded. "And now they're waiting to hear if you're drowned. When do you have to show your face again?"

"What do you mean?"

"Be out in public."

"At the budget vote. That'll be sometime tomorrow."

"Don't worry, it won't happen until late tomorrow night or early Wednesday. You'll stay here meantime. Rest up. We'll get you back in time to vote."

"How?"

"We'll have a chopper standing by up in the East Meadow."

"How will we know when to go?"

"C-SPAN. There's a dish antenna over at Camp Hoover. We'll run a feed from there."

"You work fast. Why are you doing all this for me?"

Lenny lifted his eyebrows. "I want you to be able to vote for the amended budget resolution. I want you to get drugs legalized." He waved his hand. "And who knows? Maybe we'll have other business sometime."

Nick looked at him. "Just help me get my son back."

Lenny passed his hand over his face. "I'm thinking it may not be as bad as it looks."

"Please convince me of that."

"Let's think about it some more. They took him to get you here, right?"

"I guess. I can't see it in perspective anymore."

"Well, that was the message: Go to the fishing camp. You went. If the girl had, you know, drowned you, they would probably have let him go. There's no point in hurting him."

"God, let that be true!"

Lenny sighed. "But they don't know what happened to you. So they have to wait and hold on to him. Time is on your side right now."

Nick leaned forward. "You're just guessing!"

"I'm reasoning. What else can we do? When they find out you're still alive, they'll either let him go or think up something else to make you do."

Nick nodded, closing his eyes.

"Either way, your boy is probably okay for the time being."

"But I can't just sit around and wait." Nick stood up. "I better call my wife."

"How much does she know?"

"Nothing. But she suspects something."

"Can you stall her anymore?"

"Yes. But not beyond tonight."

"Okay," Lenny said. "And there's something else you can do."

"What's that?"

"Do you think Secretary Frankfurt has any idea what might be going on in his office?"

Nick stared at the ground. He looked at his watch again. "I doubt it. I guess I ought to warn him."

Lenny looked off toward the cabin, lifted his arms, and pantomimed dialing a phone.

Nick turned his head to look. The tall man was descending the stairs with the cellular phone in his hand. Nick looked back at Lenny. "But I have to meet with him. This is something I can't do by phone."

"Why not? This one has a digitized scrambler."

"Emery's people have been eavesdropping on you. They'll know I'm talking to him."

Lenny laughed. "What makes you think they're bugging me?"

"He told me himself months ago. That's how he knew you were trying to meet with me."

The tall man stood waiting at a discreet distance.

Lenny said, "We got rid of that bug about the time we cleaned up this place. But suit yourself. Set up a meeting with him. Just remember that his people might try to stop you if they get wind of it."

"Could you get me to the basement of the Capitol safely?"

Lenny shrugged. "You go by elevator and corridors to get there, right? No open areas?"

"Right."

"Then it shouldn't be a problem."

Nick stood up and looked at his watch again. "Emery should be available now." He took the phone and walked on the soft forest floor to the edge of the stream. The day remained gray. The sun had not broken through. He looked at the stream. The water rushed by, churning white where it was normally placid.

He took a deep breath and dialed, then switched the phone to his right hand.

"Delta one-niner."

"I'm been trying to reach Secretary Frankfurt."

The line went dead. Nick waited. He tried to find a less painful position for his shoulder.

"Yes?" It was Emery.

"Emery, it's Nick."

"Nick! What a surprise! All's well?"

"I'm fine."

"Splendid. What can I do for you?"

"We need to meet, Em."

"After the budget vote."

"Something's come up. Something urgent."

Nick could hear Emery breathing. "What is it, Nick?"

"I can't talk on the phone. Can we meet tonight?"

"Tonight? Difficult."

"Emery, this is literally a matter of life and death."

"I see. Where would we meet?"

"How about my hideaway again? Please, Emery."

"All right. I can shift some things. We'll have a late bite. Say ten?"

Nick nodded to himself. "Ten on the dot."

The line clicked.

He used his thumb to disconnect. He turned and walked slowly back toward the cabin. The fat man was standing with Lenny beside the grill.

"So how did it go, Senator?" Lenny said softly.

"Tonight at ten." He went to the bear's throne and put the phone down on the stone shelf.

"The fat man and a couple of guys will keep you company." He turned to the fat man. "You'll protect him. It shouldn't be a problem."

The fat man closed his eyes.

"Then we'll fly you back here until the vote," Lenny said.

"Maybe. It depends on what happens with my son." He looked at the fat man. "What did the woman have to say?"

The fat man looked at Lenny. Lenny put his hands together and bit his lower lip. "That didn't work out so good."

"She wouldn't talk?"

Lenny shot a glance at the fat man, then looked back at Nick. "She killed herself."

"She's dead?" Nick said. "Just like that?" He took a step toward the fat man. "How could this happen?"

Lenny touched his companion. "It wasn't his fault. She ate something. Cyanide, most likely. She had it on her. She was trained."

"You didn't kill her?"

"No," Lenny said. "We don't do that."

"We can't hide this," Nick said. "We have to inform the police."

"Don't worry, Senator. It's being taken care of."

"How can it be taken care of? This could be big trouble."

"Don't worry," Lenny said. "Your name will never come up."

Nick went to the bear's throne and sat down. He lowered his head and ran his fingers through his hair. "Don't you understand? We can't go public until I get my son back. My God!"

Lenny picked up the camp chair, set it down next to Nick, and sat in it. He touched Nick's arm. "Look, you're tired and you're hurt. You're not thinking so clearly. Listen to me."

Nick steepled his fingers and rested his forehead against them.

"The girl will not be connected to you or your family until the right time comes," Lenny said. "Believe me."

Nick shook his head. "I'm afraid I do believe you."

"All right," Lenny said. He looked at his watch. "It's ten-thirty now. You got the day to kill."

"I have to get some sleep somehow."

"The fat man will give you something. Then we'll fly you up after dinner."

Nick stood up with an effort.

"The fat man will give you something for your shoulder too."

"I feel bad about my wife."

"I think you should keep her in the dark until you know more. How can knowing help her? What can she do?"

"I can't stand lying to her."

"It's a lie to save her pain."

Nick turned and headed slowly for the cabin. Inside the house there was the smell of bacon and hot bread. His nausea had subsided. Three men were standing in the kitchen. The tall man stood in the doorway. Nick climbed the stairs stiffly.

At the head of the stairs he turned and went along the hallway past the rooms that belonged to Lore and Matty. He paused at the entrance to the master bedroom, then turned right and went down the hall. Out of a window at the end he could see Lenny conferring with two of the men.

To the right was a small room meant to be Josie's study, though she had rarely used it. He entered and looked around. He opened the window a crack. A breeze wafted the gauzy white curtains.

He had never spent any time in the room. He could be in a stranger's house.

He pulled a wooden chair away from a small writing desk that stood against the wall and sat down in the chair. Using his right hand only, he worked off his sneakers and socks. He stood up and stripped down to his underwear, draping his clothes over the back of the chair.

After using the small bathroom across the hall, he pulled back the spread on the narrow bed next to the desk. It was made up with a quilt, a blanket, and white sheets. He pulled them loose, but instead of climbing into the bed, he sat down at the desk. On top of a dark green leather-framed blotter he found a notepad and a ballpoint pen. With the pen he drew a rough sketch of Lore's two cannons facing each other.

He studied the sketch.

What was the right question to ask?

He heard footsteps coming slowly down the hall. There was a tap on the door. "Come in," Nick said.

The fat man stood in the doorway, breathing heavily. He held a small black leather bag in his hand. "Let me look at that shoulder, Senator." He helped Nick remove his undershirt, lifted the injured arm gently, and moved it to various positions.

"What's your name, Fat Man?" Nick asked.

"Dominic." He took gauze and adhesive tape out of his bag and began to bandage Nick's shoulder. "You're bruised real bad—you could even have a muscle tear." He was holding up a syringe.

"What is that?"

"It'll help you sleep."

"I think I'll pass."

He handed Nick a small envelope. "These'll be just as good. A couple of codeines. Take it easy with them." He dipped his hand into his bag again, unfolded a length of black cloth and expertly fashioned Nick a sling for his arm. "That oughta be more comfortable." He inspected Nick's scalp, touching the hair around the wound lightly. "That's gonna be okay," he said. "We don't even have to dress it."

He packed his bag and stood in the doorway. "Maybe you better stay outta fights with the ladies for a while." He kept his face frozen in deadpan, turned away, and closed the door behind him.

Nick got into the bed. The sheets smelled damp but clean. He lay on his right side and looked out the window. Wind tossed the tops of the hemlocks.

"Let Matty be all right," he said. "Please God, let Matty be all right."

He closed his eyes. He felt the water dragging him. He saw the woman coming at him with the metal bar over her head.

Above the wind and the whisper of the stream he could hear the throb of a helicopter in the distance.

15.

The Conspiracy

The elevator shuddered to a stop at the basement level of the Capitol. The door slid open. With a glance at the fat man, beside him, Nick stepped into the vestibule. He looked to his left, out onto the concourse where the Senate subway cars arrived and departed. Except for a uniformed guard standing at the foot of the escalator, there was no one in sight.

As Nick set off to his right, he could hear the fat man laboring behind him. Beyond the inner entrance to the vestibule, where a sign pointed the way to the House Office Building, Nick turned left and strode through the yellow corridor that led to his hideaway. The motion of walking made his left shoulder ache. The pain medication was wearing off.

After several turns he came to the corridor where his hideaway was. When he looked down the hallway he saw a man in a black watch cap leaning against the wall just beyond the entrance. When the man saw Nick he gave a thumbs-up signal and gestured for him to come ahead. Nick nodded and waited. The man looked familiar, but Nick couldn't place him among the many strangers he had met in the last few days. He looked at his watch. It was five minutes to ten. The fat man came up beside him, breathing heavily.

"Is he one of ours?" Nick asked, tilting his head toward the man up ahead.

The fat man growled affirmatively.

"Then I think I'm okay from here," Nick said.

The fat man nodded.

Nick set off down the hall. He could hear the whisper of steam in the tangle of exposed pipes that ran along the ceiling. When he reached the entrance, he awkwardly removed the keys from his left-hand pocket, grunting from the pain in his shoulder, and opened the door. He looked back at the fat man and nodded.

He stepped inside and closed the door behind him. In the dark he could smell cigar smoke. He moved to his desk, felt for the lamp, and snapped the switch. The room remained dark. He tried the switch again. Nothing. He felt for the light cord with his hand and began to follow it to the wall behind his desk to make sure it was plugged in.

Out of the corner of his eye he saw a tiny point of light moving in the dark across the room. It stopped and glowed brighter. It was the burning tip of a cigar.

"Who's there?" Nick said. He turned to face where the smoker seemed to be sitting. The sound of a throat clearing came from Nick's right, at the other end of the room. He turned his head in the direction of the sound. He saw another cigar tip glowing. "Who are you?"

"It's all right." The voice came from the direction of the second cigar. Though hoarse, it was clearly Emery's.

"Emery, is that you?"

"It is."

"May I turn on a light?"

"Just tighten the bulb of the desk lamp."

Nick felt for the desk lamp again and twisted the bulb until the light came on. He looked to his left where he had seen the first cigar tip glowing. The mirror from the wall behind his desk had been propped on a chair at an angle to reflect Emery's cigar toward the door.

Nick turned to Emery. He was leaning against the pillows of the couch, staring up above the door where the TV monitor was mounted. The shadows under his eyes looked like caves. He was wearing a tuxedo. His jacket was pulled back far enough to reveal his gun harness. His feet were up on the coffee table, next to a bottle of scotch and a half-filled tumbler. A black overcoat and hat lay next to him on the couch.

"How in God's name did you get in here?" Nick asked.

"I have master keys to the Capitol." Still holding the cigar in his right hand, Emery rubbed the heel of the hand against his temple. "Get yourself a glass."

"No, thanks. I'm not drinking."

"Then sit."

With his good arm, Nick dragged the chair from beside his desk and placed it facing Emery on the other side of the coffee table. Still using only his right hand, he eased off the leather jacket he was wearing and draped it over the back of the chair.

He sat. "I thought we were to meet on the dot of ten."

"I couldn't risk that."

Nick stared at him. "Risk what?"

Emery lifted his head and scanned the room. "I wanted to make sure this place wasn't wired." He leaned slowly forward, placed his cigar in an ashtray, and took the glass from the table. "Just being cautious." He smiled, took a drink of scotch, and leaned back again.

"Why the mirror trick?"

"An old ruse. In case anyone got too excited."

"What are you talking about? Are you all right?"

"I'm simply protecting myself."

"From what?"

"Your friends."

"My friends? But I set up this meeting. Surely you trust me?"

"How many of your friends came with you?"

"Uh, two . . . three."

"There you are. I came alone."

"I'm sorry, Emery. I thought I needed protection too."

"I agree that you do. But I don't think you realize from whom."

"What do you mean by that?"

"You've gotten pretty tight with these Scordia people. Do you have any notion who they are?"

"Yes. I have a good idea."

"Don't you think you're taking unnecessary risks?"

"I have my eyes open."

"They're running a bluff. They're a tiny breakaway splinter group, and they're about to be destroyed. Do you seriously believe that organized crime is going to tolerate a move into legal drugs? The source of their greatest profits?"

"I've . . . wondered about that. But Lenny Scordia seems at liberty."

"Is that what he's led you to believe? He's famously charming, but he's fooling himself. If he feels free to do what he's doing, it's because they're giving him enough rope to hang himself."

Nick leaned forward. "So far he compares favorably to your people, if I may say so."

"That's only because he's being set up. Listen to me, Nick. I've been following this situation for years. Scordia is a tiny cipher in the larger scheme. But he's making too much trouble. And he'll shortly be stamped out. What worries me is that they're using *you* to do it."

Nick shook his head slowly. "How?"

"I mean that something will happen to you. They'll make it happen."

"Who will?" He waved away cigar smoke.

"The families. And then this Scordia group will be blamed. Your Lenny will be the fall guy, and everybody else will look good. Do you follow me?"

Nick nodded slowly. "I'm going to get some soda." He got up and moved across the room. He took a tumbler from a shelf inside the cupboard, and a large can of ginger ale and some ice cubes from the small refrigerator next to the liquor cabinet. He came back to his chair and poured some of the ginger ale. He took the envelope of codeine pills from the pocket of his shirt, tapped a single tablet into his mouth, and washed it down. "Look, Emery—"

"Tell me about your mother, Nick."

"My mother?"

"Yes. Tell me about Marian."

Nick shook his head. "That's not what I called about."

"First, I'd like to hear about your mother."

"How did you know I saw her?"

"She called, of course."

Nick nodded. "Yes, I see." He took a deep breath and held it. "It was quite a shock . . . finding her."

"Of course it was."

Nick waved his right hand. "We talked. We talked about my father."

"What about him?"

"About his dying. About the disagreement over the drugstore."

"What about his dying?"

"How he drank himself to death. Took drugs."

"What else?"

"Well, about . . . you and her." Nick lowered his head.

"Yes?"

Nick let out a little breath.

Emery lifted his feet from the table and sat up. He rubbed the back of his neck. "About your father's death, it was a terrific blow. To all of us, but I've always felt a degree of complicity, if you must know the truth."

"Why?"

"As Marian told you, there was the drugstore business. That was no small issue. Among other things at stake was your grandfather's approval. I'm afraid I won that particular prize."

"And you won my mother."

Emery made a dismissive gesture with his hand. "And I have to confess I was something of an enabler with respect to your father's dependence."

"How do you mean?"

Emery narrowed his eyes. "I wrote the odd prescription over the years. The pressure of the moment . . ." He shook his head. "Tragic. It's weighed on me heavily, I can tell you."

"And then you took his wife."

Emery shook his head. "That wasn't part of it. I never wished your father harm."

"Is that why the records are missing?"

"Which records?"

"The prescription records in the basement of Eckert's. A couple of years from around that time are missing. They're also missing in Harrisburg, apparently."

Emery's eyes moved away from Nick's and narrowed. "I wasn't aware of that. I certainly would never have taken them." He looked back at Nick. "They wouldn't be incriminating anyway. The pattern and frequency were reasonable. And he died of cirrhosis of the liver, I believe."

"Pneumonia, I thought."

"Perhaps that was the story given out." He moved the ashtray closer and carved away the ash of his cigar. "As for your mother, what can I say? She was a beautiful woman. Still is. It's good we're talking about this, Nick."

"Why didn't you ever tell me?"

"What? That your mother was alive? I didn't think this was up to me to tell you. You were a child when the decision was made not to."

"Why didn't you marry her?"

Emery nodded, as if to himself. "I don't know. Your mother and I are still good friends."

Nick waited for him to go on.

"Why didn't I marry her? I suppose children never mattered all that much to me. Perhaps my own lack of a present father." He tapped his cigar on the edge of the ashtray. "Excuse me for a moment."

"Sure."

Emery stood up, removed his jacket and laid it carefully on the couch. "I'm sorry this meeting got off to such a bad start. The mirror business and so forth. We'll talk properly now. You'll tell me what's on your mind." He removed his pistol harness, folded it, and placed it on the end of the coffee table. "I won't be a minute."

When the bathroom door closed, Nick leaned forward, slipped the pistol from its holster, and examined it. On the right side of its butt were the words "SIG SAUER." Along the stainless steel barrel was "40 S & W" and "P229." He turned it over. It was made in Germany. The safety seemed to be off; he slipped its lever forty-five degrees to On. He depressed the catch to release the magazine and slid it halfway out. He could see through an opening that it was at least half full of cartridges. Their tips were puckered, hollow-pointed. They could tear a terrible hole in you.

He pushed the magazine back in again until it clicked, and slid the weapon back into its holster. He heard the toilet flush and the sound of water running in the sink. He poured himself more ginger ale.

When Emery came out of the bathroom, he took his place on the sofa without putting on his harness and jacket again. "What's happened to your arm, Nick?" he asked.

Nick felt sweat on his forehead. "Emery, Matty's been kidnapped. I'm going crazy."

"Kidnapped! What do you mean?"

"I mean kidnapped."

"Good God, Nick! What's going on?"

"It isn't clear yet, why or who."

"Why didn't you tell me at once?"

"I tried to, but—"

"I didn't give you a chance."

"I called you last night and early this morning."

"Start from the beginning. What happened?"

"They left the farm while I was out. He and the people who were looking after him."

"When?"

"Yesterday evening."

"Who exactly was with him?"

"My executive secretary, Abby Stevens. And a man—"

"But Nick, I know Abby. She's been with you for years."

"Yes, but there was someone else. A new bodyguard we got for Matty. He could have forced Abby to go along with him."

"Are you certain it's not all some misunderstanding? Maybe Josie has him."

"I've talked with Josie." Nick shook his head slowly. "They've disappeared. Matty never made it home."

"Josie knows?"

"Not yet." Nick wiped his forehead. "I've been stalling her."

"Have you contacted the FBI?"

"Not yet. I wanted to give whoever has him some time to contact me first."

"And?"

Nick hesitated. "There's been no real word."

"What about the police in Wheel'ville?"

"I've talked to Don Ebright, unofficially."

"But why would anyone take the boy? Who do you think's behind it?"

Nick drained his ginger ale and rattled the ice cubes in his glass. "That's why I called you. I think it's part of a much bigger thing."

"Surely it's connected to your drug legislation."

"Maybe. But I think it's more likely this red house I've been telling you about."

"What about it?"

"It's the center of an illegal drug operation."

Emery stared at Nick. "In Wheel'ville? I find that hard to believe," he said.

"It sounds crazy, I know. But there's a processing lab hidden inside it."

Emery shook his head.

"They smuggle in the stuff inside corpses. There's a secret underground passage from Belcher's mortuary to a secret room inside the red house. I've seen it. That's why they took Matty. I'm convinced of it."

Emery put up his hand. "Nick, you're telling me that you've stumbled onto an illegal drug operation and that in retaliation they've kidnapped your son?"

Nick stood up. "That's exactly what I'm telling you."

"Sit down, Nick. Don't you see?"

"Don't I see what?"

"Sit down. Listen to me."

"For God's sake, what is it, Emery?"

"It's what I was saying before. You're being used for the destruction of this Lenny Scordia."

Nick shook his head rapidly. "No. No. That's not where the evidence points."

"Where does it point then?"

"That's why I had to meet with you tonight, Emery. Where it points is to your people."

"My people? What are you talking about?"

"Believe me, Emery—"

"That's incredible!"

"Emery, I have the evidence."

"Why don't you tell me what it is, Nick? Let's sit down and go over it systematically."

Nick sat down again and combed his fingers through his hair. "It all begins with Lore's dying message. The letters that all but spelled out red house."

"Go on."

"Then there was finding that doll. And the killing of John Holden."

"Yes, yes, I know," Emery said. "But what do those things have to do with the DDC?"

"Everything. Just listen."

"Why, we agreed last spring that the mob was probably behind them. They were part of why we set up that sting."

"And then there was the gun in the tree," Nick said.

"Which we have every reason to believe was put there by Scordia's opposition."

Nick closed his eyes and massaged them with his fingers. "There's been so much. I have to think."

"So far you're not impressing me, Nick."

"Then there was the Arab driver your people got for me. Leila. She tried to kill me today! To drown me, to be exact. Early this morning. She set me up with what she claimed was a message about Matty."

"Then they got to her somehow. Where is she now?"

"She's dead. She killed herself."

"How do you know?"

"She took cyanide."

"You saw her do this?"

"No. I was told."

"By whom?"

Nick looked at Emery. "By Lenny Scordia's people."

Emery leaned back. "This is your evidence? Go on."

Nick stood up, walked to the sideboard, and got himself more ginger ale. He stood with his back to Emery. "Lenny Scordia has carefully gone over every detail of the red-house operation with me. He's been meticulous, methodical, and reasonable. And he's been right. He's assured me that the mob has nothing to do with it."

"And you believe him?"

Nick turned to face Emery.

"You're going to accept the word of a gangster that some major undercover drug scam has no criminals involved?"

Nick slowly nodded.

"Nick, you're letting your emotions undermine logic." Emery sank back into the couch.

Nick let his breath out. "Of course I have *some* doubt." He moved back toward Emery, then stopped. "Wait, there was something else. The license plates."

"Nick, I know Abby Stevens. She's completely trustworthy. She would have to have been forced. Where did the bodyguard come from?"

"I haven't a clue. What do you mean, you know Abby?"

"She used to work for me."

"Abby worked for you? She never told me. Why wouldn't she have told me that?"

"It was many years ago. In Harrisburg."

Nick tripped as he came back to the chair. "Harrisburg?"

"My office there. It's not important. What about these license plates?"

"Dave Segal has been on the computer network with a guy in your office. Someone named Merced, I think. To send over those poll results you wanted. A few weeks ago there was some kind of glitch and Segal got this list of numbers on the screen. He printed them out for me."

"What does this have to do with anything, Nick?"

"Wait. When I was out in Wheel'ville this past weekend, I happened to notice something strange about the license plate numbers on the hearses. Listen, Emery, they match some of the numbers on the screen. How would you explain that?"

Emery shifted his eyes. "I can't imagine." He shrugged. "They could be a code for designating dealers."

"Why were they coming from your office?"

"Some undercover operation."

"I don't think so."

"How can you be so sure those numbers were intended for this Merced? There are millions of terminals hooked up on Internet."

"What are you suggesting? That they were just floating around Internet? Come on, Emery!"

"It's very possible that it was someone trying to alert us to something. An anonymous tip. That's our business, after all."

"Fine! If someone is telling you about these numbers, then they know who's behind the red house. Let's track them down. Call Merced. This could be the key to getting Matty back!"

Emery looked away. He sucked on his dead cigar.

Nick sat down and leaned forward. "Emery, this is solid. We can prove it. The rest—all your stuff on the mob—is just speculation."

Emery relit his cigar. He continued to rock his head slowly from side to side.

"Are you thinking what I'm thinking?"

"What is it you're thinking, Nick?"

"That we're both right. That the mob may have reached people in your agency."

Emery drew on his cigar.

"This fellow Merced. Do you know him?"

"Julio Merced. Yes, I know him."

"Let's talk to him. Let's get to the bottom of this."

Emery seemed to deflate. He uncrossed his legs, leaned forward, uncorked the scotch, and poured himself more to drink. "Please sit down, Nick."

Nick turned the chair around and straddled it.

"Do you mind if I light myself a fresh cigar?"

"Go ahead."

"Thanks." Emery removed a cigar from a case in the breast pocket of his jacket and went through his lighting ritual. He blew out a stream of smoke and watched it disperse. Finally he looked at Nick. "It's possible that you're onto something here, Nick."

"I'm sure I am. I knew you'd see it."

Emery looked away and picked an invisible fleck of tobacco from his lower lip. "You cannot conceive of what it's been like trying to pull together the various agencies in the DDC. Justice, Treasury, Customs, IRS, ATF, DEA, even elements of the FBI and CIA. An unending nightmare."

"I've heard stories."

"The truth makes them pale." Emery shifted his focus to Nick. "The petty rivalries, the jealousy, the backbiting. The whole point of the mission gets lost in the fury of bureaucratic wrangling. It's beyond belief."

"What's that got to do with this operation we've uncovered?"

"Let me give you a telling instance. Recently we went back to the old tactic of infiltration. Forget the thousand-kilo busts, the dealers on the street, the powder on the table. That's always been meaningless. The idea has been to penetrate the major crime families along with their dummy companies and the offshore banks that service them. Use the old Nixon laws to convict them. Enforce RICO, the Bank Secrecy Act."

"I still don't—"

"Wait. Unfortunately, it's worked all too well. We've set up our own dummy corporations and gained control of several billion-dollar empires."

Nick nodded. "The IK Corporation of Scranton, for instance?"

Emery shrugged and waved away smoke. "The problem is, everybody wants glory. A former department head who's now a field agent feels slighted and begins to brood about the injustice of it all. They're not wonderfully compensated, these people. Suddenly they've got a list of grievances a mile long and a thousand kilos of pure powder at their disposal. Who'll know the difference? And the corruption rises up the chain of command."

"If you know this, why can't you just put a stop to it?" Nick asked.

"Don't be naive, Nick. These people understandably resent being caught with sticky fingers. They try to protect themselves. And if the person trying to rein them in should be vulnerable in any way—"

"What do you mean?"

"Believe me, you don't want to know more about this than you need to, Nick."

"Are you talking about blackmail?"

"Let's just say my powers of command have their limits."

Nick stared at Emery. "Would those missing prescription records have anything to do with this?"

"Who knows? I really can't estimate the dimensions of what I'm up against." Emery picked up the ashtray from the table and leaned back. His face disappeared into shadow. "In the course of a career you take certain steps, develop certain attachments, make certain judgment calls. They can come back to haunt you."

Nick leaned forward. "I'm not sure I'm following you."

"There are things that could be dangerous to all of us."

"Are you saying this—this corruption—could involve the mob? Could it be one big conspiracy?"

Emery sighed. "It's possible. I don't know how deep or wide it goes. My view is limited to the levels I happen to deal with."

Nick took a deep breath. "Emery . . . Can you help me get Matty back?"

Emery's face came out of the shadow. He sat up, put the ashtray down, and picked up his drink again. "Let's think."

"I can't keep this from Josie any longer."

"I understand."

"She's jumping out of her skin."

"Of course she is."

"Do you want some more ice in that?" Nick asked.

"Please."

Nick got up and went back to the refrigerator. He brought the bucket back to his seat and set it on the table. He put two cubes in his own drink and poured more ginger ale over them.

Emery leaned forward, groaning at the strain, and added a couple of ice cubes to his drink. He sipped it. "Let's go back to fundamentals. Why do you think Matty was kidnapped?"

"The same reason Lore was killed. The red house."

Emery nodded slowly. "What led you there?" He drew on his cigar.

"Chronologically, it began with the clues Lore left. I've told you about those."

"You mean the . . . blood."

"Yes. And others."

"Go on."

"Well, I found the red house last summer, as you know. I went inside it. It was strange."

"How?"

"All these beautiful objects. I told you at the time."

"I meant how did you get inside?"

"Oh." Nick looked away thoughtfully. "Lore scrawled the numbers of the padlock combination on one of her drawings. Em, how is this going to help Matty?"

"I'm trying to reconstruct what's happened from the point of view of whoever took Matty. If it was this past summer that you found the drug lab, haven't they been awfully slow to respond? Maybe Matty's disappearance is completely unrelated."

"No. I didn't find the lab until yesterday."

"You went back inside?"

"Yes."

"Why?"

"Because when I finally figured out how the whole thing worked, I wanted to confirm that the lab was really there."

"And that's what you think triggered the abduction of Matty?"

Nick shook his head. "No. I went back *after* they took Matty."

"Was that really wise?"

"Probably not. But I was after something else."

"What was that?"

"Maybe it was stupid, but I thought I could gain some leverage."

"What sort of leverage?"

"There's a safe in there. I thought I had the combination to it. And I thought if I could get hold of whatever was in it, I might have something to bargain for Matty with."

Emery nodded slowly. "I see. What made you think there was something inside it to begin with? Where did you get the combination?"

"Another of Lore's clues. It was just a guess."

"And what did you think you'd find inside this safe?"

"I didn't have the faintest idea, Emery. But Lore was following the same trail when she died. I believe it's why she died. Why she was killed."

"Killed, Nick?"

"Yes. I no longer think she took her own life. I believe she was murdered because she discovered what was going on in the red house. That's why she wrote that message with her own blood. She may not have known who her killer was, but she knew it had something to do with the red house."

"This is incredible. Why didn't you tell me before?"

Nick shook his head. "I didn't know before. I only put it all together last night. And it's Matty I've got to worry about now."

"We may be onto something useful here. Lore gave no indication of what might be in the safe?"

"No. Just the combination. And I could even be wrong about that. I got it from the catalogue numbers of some stamps she took from my collection."

"But you had no idea what you were looking for?"

"All I knew was that she had discovered the red house. And then Marian told me that Lore had learned some dangerous secret. 'Dangerous to the family,' she said."

"Nick, those are almost my words."

"Yes, but she used them too."

"Maybe it's not a coincidence."

Nick stared at Emery. "You think Lore could have found out what those people are . . . uh . . . using to pressure you?"

Emery rubbed his hand against his temple. He looked at Nick vacantly for a moment.

"Anyway," Nick said, "the combination didn't work."

Emery's eyes came slowly back into focus. "I see."

"I tried it twice."

"Then maybe it's for some other safe?"

"That occurred to me."

Emery brought his hand softly down onto his knee. "Nick, I'd like . . ." His mouth remained open. "Where do you think this other safe could be?"

"I don't know."

"I'm very curious."

"Why?"

Emery looked down at his drink. "I don't know. I'm part of the family. If it's as dangerous as you say, then it affects me too. It affects all of us."

"Are you saying it might help you with . . . these people who're pressuring you?"

Emery looked at Nick vacantly, then began to nod. "Yes. That's a possibility. Yes, it might help me."

"There's one more clue I haven't figured out."

"Tell me."

"It's a drawing of two guns."

"What sort of guns?"

"You know, the old-fashioned kind on wheels. Like Civil War guns."

"Cannons!"

"Yeah, cannons."

"What does it mean?"

Nick shook his head. "I haven't the vaguest idea."

"And you think that clue might lead to this other safe? To whatever's so dangerous?"

"I'm just guessing."

Emery seemed to wake up. "I have people who are good at these things. People I can trust. What's the combination to the safe?"

"How is this going to help Matty, Emery?" Nick hit his knee with his fist. "Time is passing!"

Emery looked at Nick. "How? I'm not sure but I just think it might. I'm going to make a call."

"What do you mean?"

"If my office is involved, there's someone there who'll know."

"Then for God's sake, call him now. I'll give you the combination." He reached for his wallet and removed the slip of paper with the stamp numbers on it. He stood up, went to his desk, copied them down on a piece of paper, and handed it to Emery.

Emery studied it. "It does look like a combination." He folded it and stuck it in his shirt pocket. "Cannons! Cannons in Wheelersville." He stood up. "I'll use your telephone."

Nick stood up and moved his chair aside. "I don't get it, Emery."

"Wait, we'll see." Emery went behind the desk and sat down. He picked up the phone receiver, gazed into the distance for a moment, and then quickly punched in numbers.

He waited.

Nick stood and watched.

"Yes," Emery finally said. "Let me speak to R dash six." He looked at Nick blankly, then lowered his gaze to the desktop. "Hello, Saul. . . . Yes, I am. . . . Fine. . . . On the matter we discussed: How does that stand?" He lifted his gaze to the far corner of Nick's study. "I have reason to believe your badger, as you call him, was trapped. . . . Don't tell me more. . . . Just this. Are there possible terms?"

He listened, lifted his hand as if asking for silence, then lowered his gaze again.

Abruptly he hung up.

Nick waited.

Emery finally lifted his eyes and looked at him. "Yes." He nodded.

"What!"

"There are terms. A bargain can be struck."

Nick gaped. "Who was that?"

Emery spoke without emotion. "Don't ask any questions. Your son can be returned after the budget vote. He'll be in the Senate gallery, in the family section."

"Oh, my God!"

"On one condition."

"Anything! Anything!"

"You must have your language removed from the budget resolution."

"What do you mean?"

"The amended tobacco appropriation. Drugs for medical use. Your little deal with Senator Bodine."

"What does that have to do with Matty?"

"Nick, I'm telling you what they want. Those are the terms for his release."

Nick shook his head. "It doesn't make sense."

"Do you want to debate them? Or do you want your son back?"

"Just like that. You call them!"

"Do it now. Call Bodine. It's what everybody wants. The President too."

"Don't tell me he knows about this."

"Not the details. But he's strongly opposed to your amendment. He wants it out. Make the call." He stepped away from the desk.

Nick nodded dumbly and moved to the desk. His shoulder had begun to throb with pain again. His limbs felt heavy. He opened the middle drawer and took out his personal phone directory. He looked at Emery again.

Emery nodded.

Nick picked up the handset slowly. He tapped in the numbers. The phone rang softly.

"Bodine residence." A woman's voice, stiff but servile.

"Is the Senator available? I'm sorry to disturb you at this hour, but it's an emergency. This is Senator Schlafer."

"I'm sorry. Senator Bodine is not at home."

"Do you have a number where I can reach him? It's quite urgent."

"The Senator is on the way back to Washington."

"Can you give me the number for his car phone?"

"He's flying, Senator. I can try to contact him, but—"

"Would you, please? It's an emergency."

"I'll do my best. Where can you be reached?"

Nick looked at his watch. It was twenty to midnight. "I'm not sure where I'll be. I'll call you again around one A.M."

"Very well, Senator."

"Thanks." The line disconnected. Nick put the handset back and looked over at Emery. He had put on his harness and jacket and was slipping into his overcoat. "You'll have to trust me on this," Nick said.

"If the language is removed, Matty will be in the gallery," Emery said. "That's my understanding." He put on his hat and adjusted his collar. "In the meantime, Nick, I would make every effort to disengage from Lenny Scordia. It's evident he's at the bottom of this. I'll do what I can from my end."

"What guarantee do I have?"

"Don't ask so many questions, Nick. I've made you a deal." He put his hat on. "We're playing with dynamite here." He moved to the door and grasped the handle. "You do your part and all may be well. Meantime, we'll find that safe." He opened the door and was gone.

Nick stood up, went to the coffee table, and poured himself the last of the ginger ale. He took the glass back to his desk and sat again. He stared into space.

What was Matty feeling now?

And what about Abby?

He looked at his watch. A quarter to twelve. Almost thirty hours since Matty left the farm.

He shook himself out of his reverie, took out two more codeine pills, and washed them down.

He picked up the handset of the phone again and tapped in numbers. It rang once.

"Yeah?"

"This is Nick Schlafer. Is Lenny available?"

"Wait, Senator."

Nick put the phone directory back in the desk drawer.

"Senator?"

"Yes."

"How'd it go?"

"It's hard to say exactly."

"What about your son?"

"I don't know yet. It may be all right."

"That's good. You want to talk?"

"Do I want to talk? Yes, I want to talk."

"Go with the fat man. He'll drive you to the chopper, have you back down here in no time. Then we'll have a talk."

Nick tapped with his fingers on the desktop. "Yes. All right."

"Did you call your wife?"

"I'll do it from down there."

"Your mobile phone's been ringing. We're not answering."

"Good. It could be anyone."

"Don't worry. Everything's gonna be okay."

"I hope you're right."

The line went dead. Nick hung up. He stood, removed his windbreaker from the back of the chair, slipped his right arm into its sleeve and pulled the other side of it over his left shoulder. He put the cap back on the bottle of scotch, returned it to the cabinet, and put the two glasses in the bathroom sink.

He went back to his desk and snapped the small lamp off. The darkness still smelled of cigar smoke.

He pulled open the door and stepped outside. The man in the watch cap was gone. The fat man was standing at the end of the corridor.

Nick tried the door to be certain it was locked and then turned toward the fat man and made an upward circular motion with the index finger of his right hand.

The fat man nodded and waited to fall in step with him.

16.

Cannons

From the bear's throne, Nick watched Lenny poke a stick at the fire. Nick sipped the hot chocolate he had accepted as a compromise between booze and coffee. The thick liquid scalded his tongue.

"A campfire is a good place to talk," Lenny said.

"Well, it's not really a campfire," Nick said.

Lenny spread his arms. "It's a fire."

"It's a barbecue. It's for charcoal briquettes, not wood."

Lenny slapped his left hand against his side and sat down on a folding chair next to Nick. "We've settled in pretty good. Don't worry."

"So long as we don't get any more surprise visitors," Nick said.

"You're *f'tootsed* that we've taken over the place. It bothers you to see us hanging around where your grandfather used to . . . y'know."

"I'm worn out. And I've got a lot to figure out. No offense."

"Well, we'll talk now," Lenny said. His glasses glinted in the dark. "Hungry?"

"No, not now."

"You want to talk about your meeting?"

"I don't know. I feel a little light-headed. I'm cold too."

"I won't keep you long." He was looking over Nick's shoulder toward the house.

Nick turned his head. He could see Rizzo on the steps to the porch holding the cellular phone.

"Bring it here, Sal," Lenny said.

Nick stood up quickly. "This will be Emery Frankfurt. Thank God!" He hurried to meet Rizzo halfway and took the phone. He put it to his ear. "Hullo, Emery?"

"Please hold for Senator Bodine," a woman's voice said.

Nick walked past Lenny toward the stream cradling the phone.

"Senator?" Bodine said.

"Thanks for getting back to me, Rick. I was going to try you again. How did you find me?" He kept walking into the darkness until he felt he was out of earshot.

"It doesn't matter," Bodine said. "What's on your mind, Senator?"

"I have to ask a very big favor."

"Hope we can oblige. What is it?"

"I have to ask you to cancel our agreement."

"You better spell that out, sir."

"I'd rather not. I'm asking you to remove the tobacco amendment we agreed on last Friday."

"Well, now! The budget vote's tomorrow."

"I know, but this may be a life-and-death matter. You've got to take my word for it."

"Oh, I do."

"I realize this puts you in an awkward position. That you've made promises and now you're reversing your field. I understand that, and I'll make it up to you someday, if I can."

"What about your support of the budget?" Bodine said.

"That stands. I couldn't back down if I wanted to."

"Okay then, Senator."

"You'll get it done?"

"I'll do what I can."

"Will that be enough?"

"We'll see."

"Will you let me know?"

"I can't promise that. Let's say you'll know before the end of the vote."

"I'm not giving up on my drug legislation," Nick said. "I just have to buy some time."

"I understand, Senator."

"I'm in your debt."

Nick took the handset away from his ear and stood in the dark. He was damp with sweat. He turned and headed back toward the fire.

Lenny was still sitting in his chair. "You don't look so good."

"I think I'm getting sick."

"It might be your shoulder. So what did the Secretary say?"

Nick put the phone on the stone shelf. "That wasn't him. It was Senator Bodine."

"About the amended tobacco allotment?"

Nick looked at him. "How did you know?"

Lenny shrugged. "It's my business to know things."

"You're in touch with Bodine's office then?"

Lenny bobbed his head from side to side ambiguously.

"I'm trying to get the amendment cut out. Maybe you can help me."

"Now why would you want to do a thing like that?"

"I'm doing it to get my son back." Nick sat in the bear's throne.

"Did Secretary Frankfurt say that you'd get him back?"

"Yes."

"How can he promise that?"

"I don't know. He talked to somebody under him." Nick moved forward to the edge of his seat.

"Then it was his people took your son?"

Nick looked at Lenny. His expression hadn't changed. "I didn't push too hard for explanations once he offered me a deal. But the picture I got is of some extensive illegal operation involving both people in the DDC and rivals who are out to get you."

"To get me?" Lenny said. He pulled up the collar of the brown leather jacket he was wearing.

"He made a plausible case that you're isolated from the other crime families and that, frankly, your days are numbered."

Lenny nodded. "Interesting notion."

"It didn't quite add up. He blamed everything that's happened on your enemies. But when I gave him some concrete evidence that his own people were involved, he had to back down."

"So." Lenny poked at the ground with his stick. He turned his head to look back at the house. "Do you believe any of this?"

Nick shook his head. "I don't know what to believe at this point." He sipped his hot chocolate.

"I don't really blame you. I'm not gonna argue with the Secretary. Let's just see how his deal with you plays out."

"It's the only thing that matters at this point."

"But I gotta remind you of what I told you at the start: that the families are losing in the drug business. That's why we want to go legal."

"Yes. That's what you said."

"And you got no solid evidence that anybody connected in any way with me has done anything to you."

"That seems to be true. But I'll have to withhold judgment."

"That's fair, Senator. Tell me, did he seem shocked by all the stuff you know? The red house and everything?"

"Not really." Nick thought a moment. Something in the fire popped. "He seemed more interested in a meeting I had with my mother."

"Why would he care about that?"

"Partly it might have been because they were once lovers."

"Your *mother* and the *Secretary?*"

"That's right."

"Where does this guy come from?"

"He was a poor boy in Wheelersville. He went to work for the family drugstore when he was about eighteen. When I was a kid. My grandfather took him in. He became part of the family."

"When did he take up with your mother?"

"At some point they fell in love. It's probably what destroyed my father."

Lenny stared at the fire and shook his head. After a time he looked back at Nick. "So he says he can get you your kid back by having you kill the budget amendment?"

"Yes."

"Isn't that a lot to ask without some kind of guarantee?"

"I can't afford to look at it that way."

"What else did he say you could do?"

Nick stood up and went to the fire, which was burning low. He took a fork that lay on the back of the grill and poked the wood until the flames flared up again. "I'm desperate, Lenny. Not thinking clearly."

"That's okay, Senator."

"This wasn't part of any deal. But do you recall the safe I mentioned this morning?"

"The one in the red house."

"Not that one. I mean the one I've got the combination to. I don't know where it is, but there's something in it that both my daughter and Emery Frankfurt say is 'dangerous to the family.' Emery implied that his enemies in the DDC are using whatever it is that's in there to blackmail him. He said that if he could find the safe—find what they have on him—then he could move against them."

Lenny stabbed the ground with his stick again. "Tell me something, Senator—do you trust this man?"

Nick came back to his seat. "Of course I do. I gave him the combination."

"Then you just have to sit tight, Senator, until he finds this safe."

"It could be somewhere in the red house. Or it could be someplace else where the conspiracy is operating."

"So how are you going to find it?"

"Do you remember those clues my daughter left?"

"Yeah."

"Well, I've got them all solved now except one."

"What are these clues telling you?"

"Various things. About the red house, about my mother. What I don't understand is why if Lore was being threatened she didn't call directly for help. Why did she go to such bizarre lengths to lay a trail?"

"What is the remaining clue?"

"It's a drawing of guns. Two of them, facing each other."

"What kind of guns?"

"Artillery pieces. Old-fashioned cannons."

"What do you make of it?"

Nick said nothing. Another ember in the grill popped softly, showering sparks. "I don't know."

"Isn't the plural cannon?"

"Cannons. Cannon. Who cares? Both sound right."

"Anything else on the page?"

"The words 'You have to ask the right question.' That's to tell me it's a treasure hunt. I used to tell her that when she was a child."

"Cannon," Lenny said. "Could it mean something else?"

"The towel people?"

"What does that suggest?"

"Towels? Sheets? Washcloths? Rags maybe?"

"Is there a special place you keep things like that?"

"Sure. A linen closet. We've got several of them. In each of our houses. But it's too vague. In our game a good clue lit your mind up like a light bulb."

"You have to ask the right question."

"Right." Nick suppressed a yawn.

"Who makes guns?"

"I don't know. Remington? Colt? Smith and Wesson? Winchester?" Nick paused. "Sigarms?"

"Those are mostly small-arms manufacturers. Didn't they teach you in the army that you don't call a rifle or a pistol a gun?"

"The British call them guns," Nick said.

"Who makes *guns?*"

"Maxim?"

"Machine guns. Who's the German guy? You know, Big Bertha." Nick banged the side of his head with the heel of his right hand. "Von something. Krupp!"

"That's the idea. Who else? A British outfit named Whitworth and Armstrong made field guns used in the Civil War."

Nick stood up. "Son of a bitch! Krups!"

"What?"

"Krups. The coffee machine. See, it's a pun. Two guns are Krupps. The maker of the coffee machine is Krups. It's the one your men tried to use that put out the lights last summer. And Lore installed that coffee machine!"

"You better check it out."

"But if it's here, how could the drug dealers be using it?"

"Maybe you'll find the answer."

Nick turned and strode toward the cabin. Lenny followed him.

"What's happening?" asked Rizzo as they entered the living room.

"Nothing," Lenny said. "It's okay."

Nick went into the kitchen. Two of Lenny's men were sitting at the table at the back. The fat man was working at the stove. Nick turned to the cabinet to the right of the entranceway, swung its door open, and kneeled down. He reached inside with his right hand, grasped the base of the coffeemaker, and pulled it toward him. It resisted for a moment, then came free with a soft pop as its rubber supports unstuck, and slid easily forward. When he got it to the front edge of the shelf, he tried to use his left hand as well, but a stab of pain in his shoulder stopped him.

"Lend a hand, someone," Lenny said.

Nick rocked back onto his feet and duckwalked to one side. The fat man leaned down and easily lifted the machine away from the shelf. Nick kneeled in front of the cupboard again and peered into its depths. "There's a flashlight on the counter," he said. Half a dozen men were now standing in back of him watching. Lenny handed him a small flashlight. Nick flicked it on and aimed it into the darkness. The weak beam picked up a wall of cobwebs.

"I need a dish towel, please."

The fat man handed him one from the sink. Nick reached inside the cupboard and flicked the towel from side to side. Clouds of dust billowed out.

When the dust had begun to settle, he peered in again, playing the flashlight beam around. Near the back wall was what looked like a bread box with a small dial and a brass handle on it. He turned again to the fat man, who stooped, reached into the cupboard with a grunt, lifted the box out easily, and set it on the countertop.

Standing again, Nick pressed down on the handle, but it refused to give. He removed his wallet, laid it open on the counter in front of him, and found the slip of paper with the stamp numbers. He spun the dial through the numbers. When he arrived at the final 5, he reached for the handle and depressed it again.

It rotated forty-five degrees, then gave a satisfying click.

He pulled on it, and the front of the container swung open to Nick's left. At the back of it lay what looked like a book. Another book. He reached in and pulled it out. It was a black-bound volume about an inch and a half thick with several rubber bands around it.

"Your daughter was very secretive," Lenny said beside Nick.

Nick shook his head, bewildered. "I need to look at this alone."

"Sure," Lenny said.

Nick left the kitchen and mounted the stairs. He went down the hallway and into the room where he had napped earlier. He snapped on Josie's desk lamp and sat on the wooden chair.

He removed the rubber bands, laid the book on the desktop, cracked it open, and flipped through it.

The writing was in black ink. Two pages were filled with what looked like brief entries. The first words to catch his eye read:

Dull day at drugstore. Movies with Frankie. Home late. Another argument with G.G. Helene.

Nick checked the date: Friday, June 14.

With the tip of his index finger, he measured about a quarter-inch thickness worth of pages and flipped ahead. The capital letter E caught his eye.

Tues., Oct.18: E (Dinner)

the entry read, and was followed by a solid block of writing. He flipped back halfway to his original position and found the sentence "E talked about himself." It was dated "Fri., Sept. 6."

He worked his way back a few pages. He saw more references to E. And then: "Fri. Aug. 16: Another interview w/Emery. He's cool."

Turning pages from left to right, he went back through August and July. He passed references to Emery, Frankie, Helene, and Marian, until Emery's name seemed no longer to appear.

SCORED GRASS. Interviewed G.G. Helene. Good in some areas; holds back in others. Still finds it hard to talk about Big Stash, who's been dead three months now. I can't tell if she misses him. Maybe old people mourn in different ways.

Then he moved forward again until he found what he was half consciously looking for, the full name Emery Frankfurt. The entry was dated Wed., July 3. It read:

Great-looking older man came into Eckert's this A.M. Silver hair, black eyes, tall and lean, in terrific shape. I did double-take when I realized it was Emery Frankfurt, who's a very big deal in Wash., head of CIA (I think). We haven't seen each other in years—school—but he's an old old family friend, was close to G.G. Helene and Big Stash and Dad. Can't believe he's in late 60s. Looks 50. I bet he knows some family stories.

He caught me looking at him and gave me a big smile. Does he recognize me? (I've changed a lot since I saw him last.) Or was he coming on to me? Wish I could have gotten up nerve to ask him for interview about my project.

Running his eyes over the pages, he moved past references to movies, Frankie, and work until Helene's name stopped him.

> *Sunday, July 7: Slept late, breakfast in town, hung out until late afternoon. Interviewed G.G. Helene again. G.G. said she's thinking about telling me something "extremely confidential."*

That's going to be about Marian Showalter being in East Berlin, Nick thought. He skimmed ahead.

> *Wed., July 10: E.F. came into Eckert's again. Has some business going on w/Ms. E. I wonder what it is. He was looking at me while he talked to her. I'm sure he was asking about me. He looked surprised. Now I'm sure he didn't know who I was until she told him.*

> *Mon. July 15: E.F. again. He went down to cellar with Irene. Ms. Eckert wasn't in. Smiled and waved to me.*

Looking at the old prescription records? Nick wondered.

> *Wed., July 17: E.F. again. This time he came over to the soda fountain and introduced himself. Said he remembered me from when I was little. I felt tongue-tied. Am I supposed to treat him like an uncle, or what? He said he was giving a barbecue next Sunday and would I come and bring a friend. His house is in Park Hill.*

> *Abby called from Dad's office about money. Do I have enough? I do with salary and savings.*

> *Sun., July 21: . . . Evening in Park Hill. Drove over with Frankie. E.F.'s house overlooks Susquehanna. Great view. Fancy barbecue w/ 100 people; I hardly knew anyone. Half-dozen waiters in white jackets. We felt out of it. But E.F. friendly and gracious. I actually got up courage to ask if I could interview him about family and he said Sure, he'd be delighted. I should call him during the week.*

It pleased Nick that Emery had been willing to help Lore. But why had he never mentioned their meeting? His eye ran on.

> *Tues., July 23: More tension w/G.G. over what time I have to be in at nite. I love her but it's a real drag living here. She's just too old to be cool about things. She's thrilled about my interviewing E.F. Says he's "Great man," or "will be when his time comes." Also told me there's a member of the family I must meet. Bet who it is is the "confidential" thing she mentioned before. It's someone named Marian Showalter who lives down near Gettysburg. I'm supposed to call her.*

> *Fri., Aug. 2: Interviewed E.F. Never known anyone like him before. He knows all about me, not just usual family stuff, schools, camps, etc., but my feelings about things, the trouble I got into at Hill. He's non-judgmental. Insisted I call him Emery. If only he wasn't old enough to be my grandfather!*

> *Good stuff on family, stuff G.G. hasn't talked about. About Dad's father, Little Stash, who I barely knew existed until now. (See Project). E is such a great storyteller and mimic. He makes everyone come alive, like they're in the room with us. I mentioned this Marian Showalter who GG told me about. He looked a little surprised, but said "by all means" I should get in touch with her.*

> *Sun., Aug. 4: Finally reached Marian Showalter this evening. Didn't sound too happy to hear from me, but suggested meeting her for supper in Gettysburg this coming Friday. Guess I'll go.*

> *Wed., Aug. 7: Lunch w/Emery F (See Project).*

> *Fri., Aug. 9: Dinner w/Marian S. Holy Shit! She's Dad's mother! Dad has a mother who's alive! My grandmother! It's so weird. It throws everything out of whack. Very distant at first, but turned out she's terrified of embarrassing Dad. Feels guilty about leaving him when he was a child. Afraid to approach him now. I said I'd do something if things weren't so bad between me and Dad. She began to tell me story of her marriage (See Project).*

Wed., Aug. 14: Lunch w/ E (See Project).

Fri., Aug. 23: Dinner w/ E (See Project).

Fri., Aug 30: Great evening w/ E. He's so eloquent it makes me want to write better. I can actually see being a writer. He sez I have original outlook on things. That I'm smarter than I realize. B.S? Who knows! Mostly he's dry and ironic about things, so I guess I believe it when he talks straight. He talks in paragraphs. It's so funny. Understands my problem w/ Helene, need of a place to get away. He sez everyone should have some place to escape to. Whaaaat?

Talked about Marian a lot. He knew her pretty well, he sez. Her husband, my grandfather, was a weak man, an "emotional cripple," he sez. Was drag on growth of drugstore biz. (See Project.)

Mon., Sept. 2: Dinner w/ Marian in East Berlin. (See Project.) Good evening but she won't talk about Emery Frankfurt!! Stone wall.

Fri., Sept. 6: Dinner w/ E. Talked about himself.

They were having dinner every Friday now, Nick noticed.

It's really an amazing story. He came from nothing. No father; mother worked as a telephone operator. A Depression kid. Barely enough to eat. Then after World War II he goes to work for Schlafer's Drugstore and Big Stash makes him member of family. Like some old movie script.

Sat., Sept 7: Hung out w/ Frankie. He claims I haven't been seeing him, and he's pissed. Home late.
GG complaining again!

Sun., Sept 8: Dinner w/ Marian (See Project.) She says I should think about moving back to farm. Tates there. Says GG too old to understand my lifestyle.
When I got home I discussed moving w/ GG. She wouldn't hear of it. Said we should try harder to get along.

Fri., Sept. 13: Dinner w/ E. It's verrry weird, but I'm actually sort of turned on by him. I think he sort of senses it. We had dinner at Penn-Plaza in Park Hill. Encouraged me to be writer. Talked more about himself.

Wed., Sept. 18: E dinner, Penn-Plaza again. E. told me something strange. Sez he has trouble translating his feelings into "appropriate conduct." I said I didn't know what he meant. He got all quiet and said certain feelings just "froze" him. I said his success certainly made it look like he was good at knowing what he wanted. He said that wasn't what he meant.

Fri., Oct. 4: Dinner w/ E (See Project).

They skipped a Friday, Nick noticed.

Fri., Oct 18: Dinner w/ E.

Sat., Oct 19: Dinner w/ Marian in G'burg. Running out of things to talk about.

Fri., Oct. 25: Dinner w/ E. Long silences. Maybe I'm turning him off now. He says he still wants to meet and talk. But he keeps going away in his head. I can't get past his irony.

Fri., Nov. 8: E. restless again. We talked about Little Stash and drugstore. (See Project.) He's getting bored w/ Project, I think. "Enough of Schlafers."

He was quiet for long time. Then suddenly he began to talk. He told me that a while after he started working at the drugstore they wanted him to rent space for the increasing inventory and drugstore records because the basement not big enough. He found this old building with a lot of space in it. He liked that you could be inside it and look out and see whole center of town, but from the outside it looked like nothing.

At first he just stored spillover stuff there. Then he decided to make himself some living space there and would occasionally sleep there! It was place he could stay when he worked late. Then after he began to travel for drugstore business, he turned it into his only place to stay when he was in town. Now had place to store things he had begun to collect as he made more money. It amused him to keep it a secret, so while

he fixed up inside, he kept it the same run-down way outside!
He even started a rumor about a midget living there.

I said that was sort of weird.

He said it was a metaphor of what he meant by not being
able to act on his feelings.

I didn't know what he meant.

He said inside different from outside.

Oh!

I asked could I see this place some time.

Maybe.

Mon., Nov. 11: Abby calls about Thanksgiving. Mom and
Dad not coming out. Dad too busy. Mom preparing for book
tour. Matty going on ski trip to Canada with friend. Will I be
okay? Reassured her I'd be with GG.

I asked about Xmas, and she said, they were both coming
to the farm. I told her I'd like that. I'd like to make peace with
Dad. Feel ready for that. As cool Xmas gift, I could get him
good stamp for his collection. I know where he keeps the
combination to the safe in the closet behind his desk. Must be
a dealer in Harrisburg. Remember to ask Abby, or Mom.

Nick skimmed the next few pages until he saw the word
"Thanksgiving."

Dinner at GG's. I felt lonely. Miss Mom and Dad. Things
have got to be patched up for Xmas.

Then, on the next page, he saw the words "other place."

Finally got E to show me his "other place." I came home late
a little drunk and had this argument with GG. Called E at
home to complain, like he told me I could. He listened to me
carry on for a while, and then told me to meet him down-
town in front of Eckert's. He took me down Arch Street to
this nothing red building next to the railroad tracks. . . .

Wait, Nick thought. He double-checked the date, Friday, Nov.
22. That was when Emery was still at the CIA. Yet he had access to
the red house. More than access. Whatever happened to the building

later, the red house was originally his! He had known about it all
along!

His eye ran down the page:

> . . . *big chess pieces* . . .
> . . . *old paintings* . . .
> . . . *a large bed high on a platform* . . . *white
> canopy* . . . *creepy* . . .

The writing changed to brownish-red ink.

> *I bet I know why he fixed the place up like he did! He likes to
> bring his dates there. He really likes women, I'm beginning to
> see! He has a lot of them, too (I know from things that Mar-
> ian has hinted without realizing it).*
>
> *Wed., Nov. 27: Fantastic dinner at red house w/ E.
> Gourmet meal. Great! Wouldn't let me help. Said somebody
> would clean up later. Seemed a little distant and distracted.
> Why do I feel responsible for him?*
>
> *Fri., Dec. 6: Dinner at red house w/ E.*

There followed four blank pages. Was she planning to fill in the
details later? Did something happen? He felt a hollow ache in the pit
of his stomach.

He turned the next page.

> *Fri., Dec. 13: I guess I should have seen it coming. I guess I
> sort of asked for it. (They all say that, don't they?)*
>
> *I'm trying to be honest. Here's what happened. I was sup-
> posed to meet E at the red house for dinner, but he called to
> say he would be late, I should go there by myself and wait for
> him. He gave me the combination to the padlock on the front
> door—4711—I'll never forget it as long as I live.*
>
> *I got bored waiting for him and started snooping around.
> Fun! He arrived without my hearing him and caught me. At
> first he seemed only a little irritated, but gradually his face
> got red and a vein started sticking out at the side of his fore-
> head. He was enraged, a completely different person. Why? I
> started crying and saying I was sorry, I shouldn't have*

snooped around, I didn't know what I was doing. He said in
this clipped way that it was quite all right, I should go and sit
on the couch while he got us something to drink. I turned and
began to cross toward the couch. I was still crying. I felt a little panicky. Jesus.

Then I heard this roar and something hit me and I fell
down. Suddenly E. was on top of me with his arm against my
throat. I couldn't breathe but I tried to scream and he
grabbed my mouth and jaw so hard I couldn't move them.

I have to describe this exactly.

I was lying on the rug with my head and shoulders under
the glass coffee table. E's other hand was tearing at my skirt
and underpants. Then I suddenly knew what was going to
happen and I started crying again and deep inside I found
myself wishing I could get soft and wet so it wouldn't hurt so
bad, but I felt as if I was being torn apart. His face was
pressed against the surface of the table just above my eyes—
one cheek and part of his nose and the socket of his eye
pressed flat, and his eyeball sort of out and magnified—and it
looked so horrible that somehow I managed to get my hands
free and shove the glass back so that the whole table tipped
away and went crashing down. Now his face was next to
mine and he was heaving and I thought I was going to black
out, but I could scream now and move my arms and—oh,
God—my hands closed around a vase or something, a round
glass object. I lifted it up far away from me so I could bring it
down on his head with all my might, and then suddenly he
stopped heaving and collapsed on me with his face to the side
of me and . . . now he was crying. Letting out these howls.
God, I was frightened. Yet I just couldn't hit him. I just
couldn't. I wish I had now but I couldn't then. I even felt a
stab of pity for him—it makes me sick to admit it. So I lowered the vase to the floor and let it go and raised my arms
again. But I couldn't stand to rest them on him, so I held
them above the both of us, my hands bent at the wrists and
floating up above us like birds. Then rage went through me
again and I grabbed at the back of his neck and dug my nails
into his flesh and scratched him as hard as I could.

He pulled my hands away and lifted himself off of me
then, and I just closed my eyes and covered my face with my

hands and cried out. I hurt so much I thought I was broken. I
just lay there. When I finally opened my eyes again, he was
gone. I never even heard him leave.

Nick stopped reading. The words on the page were a blur. The
hollow feeling in his stomach grew.

He put his left hand over his mouth and forced his head back
until he was looking at the ceiling. With his fingers and thumb he
squeezed his cheekbones until they hurt.

A prickling stole over his face, like going under anesthesia. The
desktop rushed up and slammed his face. He lifted his head with an
effort. The room was spinning slowly.

The son of a bitch! The filthy, lying, hypocritical son of a bitch!

His mouth tasted of acid. What did anything mean? He brought
his head forward again and forced himself to read.

Now what do I do? I know it's crazy, but I still feel it's sort of
my fault for flirting with him. I was coming on to him. So
what did I expect?

I have to tell somebody. I can't go to the police. I know
there's been progress with women's rights and rape, but who's
a jury going to believe between a Senator's drop-out daughter
and the biggest shot in the community? Emery outranks Dad.
What was I doing alone with him to begin with, in the middle
of the night in his apartment?

No chance.

He turned another page. She had switched to pencil. The writing was barely legible.

Sun., Dec. 15: Had dinner with GG tonight and tried to tell
her. I really did. Brought up subject of Emery. She went into
her usual raptures. I said he maybe wasn't so great. She
stopped me in my tracks. "I will not hear a word of criticism
from you, young lady!" No way she's going to believe me.

Marian might, but what can she do? Besides, I get this feel-
ing it could blow up in my face. She's terrified of Emery, I
think.

I guess I could tell Frankie, but I haven't seen him in a
month and he would really freak out, which wouldn't help.

Fri., Dec. 20: Beginning to feel a little better, at least physically. I don't ache so much. But still have trouble sleeping and when I do I have bad dreams. Plus I have this terrible feeling that people at work know and are looking at me and judging me. I feel watched. Paranoia.

What's going to happen to me? I've got to tell someone.

Nick jumped ahead.

Wed., Dec. 25: Xmas eve, 1:30 A.M. Up late at GG's after Xmas eve w/ Mom and Dad and Matty at farm. What started great turned into disaster. I got there early to help out. Frankie was coming later, after supper. Dad was great—welcoming w/ no comments or recriminations. Amazingly warm for him. He loved the stamp. Was surprised I knew it was one he wanted. If he was concerned about what I paid for it, he didn't let it show. He made me feel so close to him I told him I had something I wanted to tell him later.

But then Emery arrived. It was unreal. I thought I was going to pass out. He acted like I wasn't there. I felt like I had done something wrong. He finally maneuvered me into a corner and hissed that I had better be careful—he said that if I said anything, it would be just my word against his. He said what I had done—my snooping around the red house—was dangerous to the whole family. The rest of the evening seems like a waking bad dream. I feel so helpless.

Nick skimmed ahead two pages.

Mon., Jan 6: More trouble. My period late by 3 weeks. I went and got this home pregnancy test and it showed positive. I can't panic. I made an appointment w/ Dr. Jagiello.

Wed., Jan. 8: Stupidly I tried to call Emery, but the number I've always used for him doesn't work anymore. I keep getting a recording of some doll-repair factory! One of those multiple-option messages. I tried three times since I know I didn't misdial. It was scary.

Thurs., Jan 9: I went to this pay phone up the street on my coffee break this morning and called Mom in Washington.

Got her answering machine. I forgot, she's off on her book tour—in Pittsburgh, I think. I didn't have her itinerary with me.

Then I called Dad's office and got Abby. Told her it was an emergency. She said she would get the message to him and that she was sure he would call right back. I didn't think I would cry, but I started to and she asked me what the matter was. I said I was in trouble.

It's late at night now and Dad has not called back. Is he still pissed at me for all the trouble I've made, despite Xmas?

An emergency call from Lore in January? He had no recollection. Could he have forgotten? Not possibly, especially since he had still been trying to figure out what went wrong at Christmas.

Could Abby have neglected to tell him? He coughed and fought an impulse to retch.

Sun., Jan 12: Bad weekend. Stayed in my room. Don't feel like seeing Frankie. GG bugs me all the time, especially since I can't talk to her about Emery. I've got to get out of this place.

Nick glanced ahead.

Fri., Jan. 17: Showdown w/ GG. I told her I was going to move back to the farm. She took it well, considering. In fact, I think she's secretly glad.

Sat., Jan. 18: Frankie helped me move my stuff to farm. Feel a little better to be back in my own room.

Wed., Jan. 22: Mistake to move, it looks like. I feel worse. Feel I'm being watched and I'm convinced someone's been searching my room. I brought it up w/ Dorothy Tate. She looked at me funny and said it was impossible—she and Tom always around and she sleeps in the house when none of us are here.

Fri., Jan 24: I went through all my stuff tonight and I know my room has been searched by someone. Proof? I keep this autograph book in my top desk drawer. It has a hair

scotch-taped inside its clasp to keep Matty from sneaking a
look at the list of boys I used to keep. I happened to check it
out of curiosity last weekend when I moved back in and the
hair was still there. But it's broken now and Matty hasn't
been here since Xmas.

I think I know what they're after and I'm beginning to re-
alize I'm in much bigger trouble than I even thought. I didn't
describe this before because I knew it was risky to, but I'm
now beginning to think this diary may be my only way of
telling someone what happened.

While I was waiting for Emery that evening I got to won-
dering again why the room inside the red house is shorter
than it looks from the outside . . .

Nick's eyes raced ahead gathering up the words "chess pieces,"
"refrigerator," "hidden entrance," and coming to rest at last on
"sealed-off room."

His skin felt cold. The secret operation had *preceded* Emery's
appointment to the Department of Drug Control.

It was clear now:

Emery had wanted to know about the safe so he could destroy
any evidence against him that Lore might have left behind. And Nick
had naively tipped him off. What did that mean for Matty? He forced
his eyes back to Lore's pages.

While I was in the sealed-off room, I found a diagram of the
red house that included what looks like an underground pas-
sageway that goes across the street! There were a couple of
copies of it, so I took one and put it in my bag. Later, when I
looked at it more carefully, I discovered the diagram also has
a bunch of serial numbers listed on it. I don't know what they
mean, but I bet that's what they want back from me. They
discovered a copy missing. Maybe if I leave it where they can
find it, it will make them forget about me.

Sun., Jan 26: I'm now sure I'm being followed. I had
Dorothy Tate drive me out on the Iron Rock Road this after-
noon to look for foundations of the early settlers' cabins.
When I came back to the clearing where we parked there was
this small dark-skinned woman in a black jumpsuit standing

Lenny sat quietly in the dark.

"Why would he rape her?" Nick looked at Lenny. "He only caught her in the drug lab."

"She could have exposed him, and he . . . An animal."

"What I'll never be able to forgive myself for is that I never saw a hint of anything like this in Emery. How could he do this to us? To *her*? My God, after what my family did for him."

Lenny spoke softly. "There's an insect that lays its eggs inside other insect larvae. The ichneumon fly. Charles Darwin once wrote about it. He said he couldn't believe that God would have designed the ichneumon to feed within the living bodies of caterpillars. That's not exactly what he wrote but you get the idea.

"Well, Darwin was wrong about his God."

"Perhaps. There's also a Sherlock Holmes story called 'The Crooked Man' where a character says that some people call mongooses ichneumon, but—I call them snake-catcher. What are *you* going to do about your snake?"

"I've got the goods on him now. We still have the DNA samples of Lore's fetus." Nick moved to the grill. The briquettes were barely glowing. "I'm going to expose him." He struggled to swallow a sob.

"You better go slow," Lenny said. "He's still got your son."

Nick turned. The dying fire reflected in Lenny's glasses. "Yes, he does. He's the one behind it all, isn't he?"

"So it would appear, Senator."

"Holden's death. The dummy. The Arab woman. The gun in the tree. Everything. Why?"

"Are you kidding? He's at the top of a huge pyramid. Everyone gets paid off right up the chain of command. If even a small percentage of his underlings are sharing their profits with him, he's making millions. Maybe more than a billion. You only have to ask yourself why he kept running a tiny operation like the red house."

"According to Lore's diary, that's where he got his start. It was a hiding place for him. A world of his own where he could get away."

"Right," Lenny said. "And there are now probably hundreds of red houses around the country."

"And legalized drugs would destroy the whole thing. No wonder he came after me. He thought I might have gotten onto him through my mother. That's why he was so interested to hear about my meeting with her."

"And then when it turned out you didn't know about what he

did to your daughter he switched the terms for getting Matty back."

"Yes. And it accounts for why he was so interested in solving her cannons clue and getting the combination to the safe." He took a step toward Lenny. "Let me have the phone. I have to somehow reassure him that I don't know."

"You better be careful."

"I'll walk a tightrope."

"You can handle it?"

"Yes. I'm under control."

"Okay." Lenny handed him the phone.

Nick walked into the darkness, feeling his way with his feet until he came to the stones near the edge of the stream. When his eyes had adjusted, he tapped out Emery's number.

"Emery."

"Nick! What's the news?" His voice sounded strained.

"I've reached Senator Bodine and arranged for the amendment to be removed."

"That's good, Nick. Matty will be in the gallery when the budget resolution passes. I can virtually guarantee it."

"Thank God, Emery."

"I'm looking into these charges of yours, Nick. There's going to be a major cleanup. But it will have to be done quietly and over time. We must meet again soon. I want your thinking."

Nick took a deep breath. "I found the safe."

"Really! Where?"

"It was hidden down here at the camp."

"And?"

Nick waited. Then: "Nothing. It was nothing."

"Nothing?"

"Absolutely nothing. A wild-goose chase."

"That's disappointing." The sound of his breathing came over the phone. "Then . . . what was the point? Why the elaborate clue?"

"Who knows? Maybe she was planning to hide something and she never got around to it. Or maybe she never even found what she hoped to be hiding."

"Perhaps." Breathing hard. "But why the safe . . . and the combination . . . all the details . . ."

Nick stared into the dark, trying to see the surface of the stream. "You misunderstood me. It wasn't Lore's personal safe. It was just an old strongbox we kept at the camp for valuables. She knew the combination. But she never got to put anything in it herself. Anyway, the safe was empty."

"I see," Emery said.

Nick waited.

"Yet you still think she was killed?"

"Yes. Yes, I do."

More breathing. "Then who do you think did it?"

"I . . . I think it's just like you said. The mobsters who are behind the red house."

"Yes, yes." He cleared his throat. "And let me warn you, Nick, they are capable of striking again." His voice sounded almost cheery. "I can bargain with them, but I can't control them. Some of them would be happy to see you dead yourself for the disruption you're causing. Don't give them an excuse to murder you. See that the amendment is out."

Nick said nothing.

"Goodbye, Nick."

The line went dead.

Lenny was waiting on the porch. "You were careful?"

Nick nodded. "I told more lies in that conversation than get told during a year in the Senate." He sat down on the inner bench of the picnic table.

"Did he believe what you told him?"

"I think so. He certainly pretended to. He promised I'll get Matty back if the drug amendment is out."

Lenny said nothing.

"He also threatened me."

"How so?"

"He said there are people he can't control who would like to see me dead and that I shouldn't give them an excuse."

"What would an excuse be?"

Nick stared at the tabletop. "I'm too beat to think. I'm afraid if anything goes wrong with the amendment, they might take me out right in the Senate. It sounds nuts but it would be easy enough to do."

Lenny put his hand on Nick's shoulder. "We'll send the fat man to look after you. Don't worry. Get some sleep. Matty'll be all right. Someone will wake you in the morning. You'll have some breakfast and see where things in the Senate stand. We got the feed from the dish at Camp Hoover, so it's all set up for you to follow things on C-SPAN. We'll fly you up when it's time to vote."

"I should go to Washington now."

"But there's nothing you can do there till the vote."

Nick rubbed his eyes. "I guess that's true. Lenny, one thing. About Frankie Tonelli."

Lenny stiffened.

"I was wrong to suspect him. I know he was never involved."

"No, he wasn't. He knew something was going on in the morgue, but he was clean. He needed the job. It's been tough for him. He's a good boy."

Nick massaged his left shoulder. "I certainly had that one wrong."

"Get some sleep."

Nick stood and picked up the phone. "I better call my wife now."

"What are you going to tell her?"

Nick sighed. "The truth. The whole truth. With a promise that she'll have her son back tomorrow night."

"You sure you wanna call her?"

"She already knows something terrible is going on. This can't be much worse."

Nick pushed open the screen door, and went slowly down the steps and into the dark. When he could see the phone dial by the light from the grill he began to tap in Josie's number.

17.

A Crooked Mile

Nick woke from fading dreams, his head throbbing, his mouth dry, his shoulder aching. He kept his eyes shut as he tried to recall the monster he had been chasing and trying to slay all night. His pursuit had been hindered by floods of water, by the fat man's grip on his shoulder, by images of Matty.

Matty!

He cracked his eyes open. The light came in like needles. He had to believe that Matty would be returned, but everything would have to wait until the budget vote. There was nothing else he could do just now.

He tried to push himself up and found the strain too great. His throat hurt when he swallowed. He felt feverish. He wanted to sleep. He allowed his eyes to close.

What time was it?

He opened his eyes again and brought his watch into focus. It was 8:56. The fourteenth. The day of the vote.

Bracing his left arm against his side, he rolled to his right. He saw the small television on the desk beside his head. A remote control lay in front of it. He struggled up and sat on the edge of the bed. The room swayed back and forth. Getting dressed and flying to Washington seemed beyond his strength and will.

He reached for the TV remote and pressed the power button. Even before the picture came on the sound told him that the channel selector was already tuned to C-SPAN.

A chaplain was praying: " '. . . and show thee great and mighty things, which thou knowest not.' Jeremiah, chapter thirty-three, verse three."

The camera was focused on the Vice President's desk at the back of the Senate well. The chaplain stood behind it and intoned:

"Eternal God, sovereign Lord of history, powerful as the Senators are, they have no power over time—either to hasten or delay. While they struggle, the clock ticks inexorably."

There was a knock on the door.

"Come in," Nick called out. His voice was a croak.

The fat man stood in the doorway.

"We pray in Jesus' name. Amen." The chaplain stepped down and was replaced by a gray-haired woman who sat at the desk.

"We let you sleep," the fat man said. He pointed at the TV set. "Nothing's gonna happen there for a while."

Nick put up his hand for quiet. The TV camera had shifted to the Majority Leader's desk. A tall balding man was standing on the left side of the center aisle holding a small microphone in the fingers of his right hand. In back of him were empty desks as far as the screen revealed.

"Madame President," the bald man said, "for the information of the Senators, I will be consulting momentarily with the distinguished Democratic leader and other members of the leadership. I will have an announcement shortly. In the meantime, I reserve the time of the two leaders, and I suggest the absence of a quorum."

As he leaned over and replaced the small microphone at the side of his desk, a voice off-camera said, "The clerk will call the roll."

Nick pressed the mute button on the remote.

The fat man stepped lightly into the room. "There's no one there to answer a roll call."

"It's just a formality to kill time," Nick said.

"Mmm. You want something to eat, Senator?"

"Just a glass of juice. I've got to lie down. I feel awful. I have to make a phone call." He tried to push himself up off the bed and winced at the pain in his shoulder.

"Stay put," said the fat man. He stepped closer and placed the back of his stubby fingers against Nick's forehead. "You got a fever. Lie down. I'll get you a phone." He turned and left the room.

Nick fell back on the bed. The room swam. He tried to line up his thoughts, but they kept breaking apart.

There was another knock at the door. The fat man again. He carried the phone, a thermometer, and the glass of juice. He set the glass and phone down on the desk and held out the thermometer. "Put it under your tongue until it beeps."

Nick sat up again, took the phone, and put the thermometer in his mouth. On the TV, the Majority Leader was speaking again; other people had gathered around him. Nick pressed the mute button to turn the sound back on.

". . . it is my intention that the Senate proceed to the consideration of the Continuing Resolution to fund the continued operations of the Government beyond the expiration deadline of midnight tonight contained in current law." He consulted with a woman standing next to him. "It was approved by the House of Representatives last evening, and it is imperative that the Senate approve that Continuing Resolution to permit continued funding of the Government until December thirty-first, by which time it is our fervent hope that the budget conference committee, working with the President and his staff, will have completed action on a proper budget."

He scanned a piece of paper that the woman had handed him, and looked up again. "Madame President, I now ask unanimous consent that the Majority Leader, after consultation with the Democratic Leader, may move to the Continuing Resolution, House Joint Resolution Number Thirty-six."

The thermometer began to beep.

"Is there objection to the request of the Majority Leader? The Chair hears none. It is so ordered."

Nick pressed the mute button, removed the thermometer and looked at it. "A hundred and two," he said.

The fat man nodded.

"It figures," Nick said. "No wonder I can't concentrate. I've gotta get up."

"No. Rest." He pointed at the TV screen. "Nothing's gonna happen there till tonight."

"Right. It'll be a long day of bull. But I ache too much to lie down anymore."

"Make your calls. Then take these." He handed Nick a small white envelope and a bottle of Advil.

"What are these?" Nick said, rubbing his thumb against the envelope.

"Seconal. Take three. They're a hundred milligrams each. And a couple of Advil. Sweet dreams." He went out and closed the door behind him.

Nick took the phone and tapped the numbers. His call was answered on the first ring.

"Yeah!"

"Segal?"

"Who else? Where the hell are you *now?*"

"Back at the camp. Watching C-SPAN. When do you figure they'll be voting?"

"Tonight. Late. After eleven. When are you coming in, for God's sake. Josie's here."

"How is she?"

Segal was quiet.

"You can't talk," Nick said. "Is she hysterical?"

"Not really."

"Is she calm?"

"Not really."

"Put her on in a minute. First do me a favor. Call Bodine's office and see if you can find out if he took out the amended tobacco appropriation. They'll know what you mean."

"Took it out? I thought you wanted it in!"

"I can't explain now. Call me at the camp as soon as you find out anything."

"Uh-huh."

"And for God's sake, don't tell anyone where I am."

"Okay. Here's Josie."

Nick waited.

"Hi," Josie said. She sounded surprisingly cheerful.

"How are you?"

"I'm okay, Nick. I have to be."

"He's going to be all right. I know it's a long wait."

"I know. I'll make it. How are you?"

"Running a lousy fever. I'm going to try to sleep it off and fly up at the last possible minute. You better fill Segal in on what's going on. Just the barest details. And keep it between the two of you."

"I will. You'll stay in touch? It makes it easier."

"I'll call on the hour."

"I love you."

Nick hung up, tapped three capsules from the little envelope, and washed them down with a mouthful of the orange juice. He slid back under the sheets. The bed swallowed him.

Somewhere in a dark tunnel the telephone was ringing. Nick threw himself toward it hopelessly and found to his surprise that he could reach it without pain.

"Hullo?" he said.

"It's Segal. Are you okay?"

"I think so." His head spun. He kept his eyes shut. "What time is it?"

"Four in the afternoon."

"Christ!"

"Nothing's happening yet. On your tobacco amendment: I checked with Bodine's office and with other sources. Far as I can tell the new language was never introduced."

"You're kidding!"

"I swear. It never came up. Not even during the markup."

"What do you think that means?"

"Just that they never did it."

Nick forced himself to a sitting position and opened his eyes. On the silent TV screen the Junior Senator from New York was speaking.

"It's funny," Nick said. "When I last spoke to Bodine, he sounded as if he'd done it."

"Did he say he had?"

"No. But he didn't say he hadn't. I don't get it."

"What does it matter?" Segal said. "Long as he didn't."

"I guess so."

"Do you feel any better?"

"Well, I just wish I could be sure what that tricky bastard is up to."

"No, I mean physically better."

"Oh." Nick widened his eyes. His mouth was dry. "Maybe a little."

"Are you coming in now?"

"It's four? Not yet."

"Aren't you going to make a statement about the resolution? Explain why you're supporting it?"

Nick sighed. "The way I'm feeling, I'd only make things worse. I'll see you around ten. Unless I hear from you."

"I'll keep snooping."

"Good. Put Josie on."

"She's down getting coffee in the cafeteria. She told me what's going on. She's keeping my spirits up."

"I'll call again."

He lay down, and slid back into a restless sleep.

The phone was ringing again. Nick came awake more easily. It was dark in the room, except for the glow of the TV screen. He lifted his right arm to look at his watch. It was 7:20. He picked up the phone and pressed the talk button. "Yes?"

"Have you got the TV on?" It was Segal.

"No, why?" Nick looked at the screen. The camera was on Bodine. He was standing at his seat and reading from a piece of paper in his hand.

"What's he doing?" Nick asked.

"I don't know. He just introduced some amendment. Oh-oh."

Nick unmuted the TV. The camera switched to the rostrum in the Senate well, where one of the clerks was reading aloud. "The Senator from North Carolina, for himself and Mr. Lanning, proposes an amendment numbered thirty-one, twenty-six."

The camera went back to Bodine. "Mr. President," he said, "I ask unanimous consent that the reading of the amendment be dispensed with."

"Without objection, it is so ordered," a voice said off camera.

"Mr. President," Bodine continued, "this amendment is really a group of amendments, *en bloc*."

"I don't like this," Nick said into the phone.

"They provide that the rate of operations for programs and activities of the Federal Government shall be continued through December thirty-first, 1997, at the lower rate . . ."

"This is probably just boilerplate," Nick said, lowering his feet to the floor.

"Then why bring it up at all?" Segal said.

". . . amendments would also change the amount to be available for the programs funded under the Department of Agriculture appropriations bill during the period."

"There!" Nick said. "That's where it is if he's doing it."

"I ask unanimous consent that the amendments be agreed to *en bloc*. But before I do that, I yield to Mr. Migdal and Mr. Calder for such statements as they care to make."

Nick muted the TV again. "What's going on, Dave?" He stood up stiffly, and snapped on the desk lamp. "What's that slick son of a bitch up to now? Is he double-crossing me?"

"I don't have a clue. Those amendments could be anything. What reason would he have to double-cross you, other than for the fun of it?"

"Because he has his own people to worry about. Can't you find out what's in the amendments?"

"Not really. I'm getting stonewalled by Bodine's office. The only way is to go down to the rostrum and read the language. And only you can do that."

"Well, I'd better get my ass up there, hadn't I?"

"You might as well. The vote's coming up anytime now. You feel any better?"

Nick looked out the window. In the dark he could still see the hemlock boughs tossing. "Yes. I can make it."

In the basement of the Russell Senate Office Building, Nick, accompanied by Josie and Segal, stepped onto the back of the subway car. Other members were sitting on board.

"I still think you can run a bluff," Segal said. He spoke in a low monotone.

The car started up smoothly. Nick held Josie's hand. Her face was pale despite makeup.

"I don't get you, Dave," Nick said.

Josie looked at them both with wide, empty eyes.

Segal leaned closer and raised his voice above the sound of the subway. "Our latest count says the vote is this close." He held up his hand with his thumb and middle finger pressed together. "If you find out the language is in Bodine's amendment, you can threaten to switch your vote. You'll take some members with you. You'll take Swain and Baron, for starters. That could easily do it."

"There isn't time. They'll be voting any minute now."

"If the Continuing Resolution's defeated, the whole government comes to a stop. They're running scared. All you have to do is tell 'em you're switching. I've got it all set up."

The subway pulled to a stop. The three of them got off. "I can't switch again," Nick said. "I'm locked in."

They stepped onto the escalator. Josie leaned against Nick.

"I'm saying you can run a bluff. Get 'em to gut the amendment."

"We don't even know that it's there. I have to believe it isn't."

"All I'm saying is, You can do it."

"You're dreaming, Dave. Everybody thinks I'm for it. They'll think I've gone over the edge."

They approached the second elevator on the right and waited in front of the closed doors. A bell somewhere in the vestibule rang once.

"There it is," Nick said. "Fifteen minutes to the vote."

"You could—"

"Forget it, Dave. *I can't.*"

The elevator doors opened. They stepped inside. Others crowded aboard. The doors closed and the elevator started up.

Nick glanced at the faces of the other passengers. He recognized no one, except the Senior Senator from Minnesota, who nodded at him absently, eyed Nick's slung arm, and lifted his eyebrows. Nick shrugged helplessly. He looked at Josie. Her lips were moving wordlessly.

The elevator stopped and the doors slid open. Nick took Josie's arm and followed Segal out. The vestibule was crowded with people coming and going. Nick immediately sighted the fat man hulking across the way next to the far elevator. He returned Nick's glance and dipped his head in acknowledgment. Beside him stood one of the Capitol policemen. Nick stopped, patted his breast pocket with his right hand, and took a deep breath. He felt sweat on his forehead.

Segal stood beside him. "Forget something?"

"No. I guess I'm just nervous."

"Have you got a handkerchief?" Josie said.

"Yes."

"You don't look so great," Segal said.

"I'll be okay."

"We'll meet you here after the vote," Segal said.

"Good." Nick hugged Josie quickly. "We'll be fine."

She bit her lip. "I know."

Nick turned away, walked to the Republican door of the Senate chamber, and pushed his way through. Inside he stopped and stood for a moment. A dozen or so members were already gathered down in the well. Others were moving up and down the aisles. A half dozen staff members were grouped in the far corner behind the railings.

The legislative clerk was calling the roll: "Mr. Bennett."

"Aye."

"Mr. Bennett votes aye. Mr. Bond."

There was no response.

"Ms. Boxer."

Nick looked at the back of the well. The Vice President was in his seat. So the vote was going to be close.

He began to move down the aisle toward the well. As he passed his own desk—the first one to the right of the aisle—he stopped and looked up over his right shoulder at the family section of the gallery, where Emery had promised Matty would be delivered. He could see only the front row. It was empty.

When he looked down again, he saw Lester Calder coming up the aisle toward him. Calder pointed at Nick's desk. "Sit down a minute, Senator. I want to have a word with you."

Nick slid into his seat. Calder lifted the top of Nick's desk and took a cellophane-wrapped hard candy from a large pile inside. He scraped with his thumbnail to unwrap it. "I don't like this agricultural amendment you're trying to get in, Nick."

Nick looked up at him. "What don't you like about it?"

Calder popped the candy into his mouth and sucked on it. "I know what you're up to. And I'm not the only one who doesn't like it." He rolled the cellophane into a ball with his thumb and fingers.

"Well, then, vote against the CR."

"You know I can't do that." He lifted the desk lid and flipped the cellophane ball inside.

"I don't know that the stuff you're objecting to is even still in there," Nick said. He saw Ted Diefendorfer coming up the aisle toward them.

"I heard it was going in," Calder said.

"When did you hear that?"

"Couple of days ago."

"That was a couple of days ago."

Diefendorfer joined them. "Don't be messing with my crew, Senator Calder."

"Good evening to you," Calder said stiffly. He moved off down the aisle.

"Why's he wearing foul-weather gear?"

Nick stood up. "A misunderstanding, Ted. At least I hope so." He looked beyond Diefendorfer and spotted Bodine down on the Democrats' side of the well.

"You still on board, Nick?"

Nick sighed. "I'm pulling my oar, I guess you'd say."

Diefendorfer put his hand on Nick's shoulder. "We may barely clear the rocks on this."

Nick looked down at his desk and then around at other desks nearby. "Where *is* the damn thing?"

"The budget resolution? It should be coming down any minute. It's a monster. *Nobody* knows what's in it."

"And let's hope they never will."

"Mr. Hollings," the clerk said.

"Aye."

"Mr. Hollings votes aye. Mr. Inouye."

"Nay."

"Mr. Inouye votes nay. Mr. Jones."

"What happened to your arm?" Diefendorfer asked.

Nick took a handkerchief from his pocket and blew his nose. "It's a boring story. Let's just say I slipped and fell. Will you excuse me, Dief?"

Diefendorfer stepped aside. Nick moved down the aisle to the edge of the well and began to work his way through the milling crowd toward the Democratic side. He felt light-headed.

"Greetings, Senator."

"What happened to the wing bone?"

"Good thing it's not the old casting arm. Right, Senator?"

Nick found Bodine, who was standing with one arm around the waist of the Junior Senator from Alabama. As Nick approached them, Bodine's dark eyes slid over to take him in and then drifted back to his companion. ". . . so I told him, I believe we can get it done. That seemed to satisfy him." His eyes returned to Nick. "Hey, there, Senator Schlafer! What happened to the arm?"

"Too much of the great outdoors," Nick said. "What's going on, Senator B?"

Bodine released his companion and spread his arms wide. "What's going on? Why, sir, all the senators are gatherin' here to see if they can keep the guv'ment going. Run up the deficit some more."

"What about our amendment?" Nick turned to Alabama. "Forgive me for intruding."

Alabama shrugged. "Don't give it a thought."

Bodine kept his eyes on Alabama. "We're tryin' in our way to scrimp and save where we can. A billion here. A billion there."

"I never heard from you," Nick said.

Bodine's black eyes sparkled. "No. It's been mighty busy. Mighty busy. These are desperate times."

"Were you able to . . . uh . . ." Nick looked at the Senator from Alabama. "A little bipartisan business I had with the Senator."

Bodine smiled at Nick. "The parties must stick together now, Senator. Party loyalty is the cement of our system."

Nick looked at Bodine levelly. "I guess I'm reading you."

Bodine looked away. "I have my constituents to worry about."

"Mr. Murkowski."

"Nay."

"Mr. Murkowski, nay. Ms. Murray."

Nick looked at Alabama. "Forgive me for breaking in." He looked back at Bodine. "Good evening, Senator."

Bodine kept his eyes averted. "Desperate times," he said, pumping his arms forward and back and bouncing on his heels.

Nick turned and began to push through the crowd toward the Republican side of the well. He looked up at the family section of the gallery again. He could see all of it. It was still empty. But of course Matty would not be there until after the vote.

If the amendment was out.

"What about the arm, partner?"

"Accident," Nick said. He made his way past the tables where the official Senate reporters were sitting, went up to the rostrum, and carefully rested his slung forearm on the marble counter.

Lewis, the legislative clerk, continued to call the roll. To his left—Nick's right—the assistant legislative clerk was talking to the Senator from Illinois. Nick looked at his watch. It was 11:19.

Illinois turned away and the assistant clerk regarded Nick quizzically.

Nick leaned toward her. "I'd like to check some language in Senator Bodine's *en bloc* amendments."

"There's a lot of it. Language, I mean."

"The amended agricultural appropriation."

"Okay." The assistant clerk reached for a thick stapled-together volume and flipped it open. Beside her, Lewis looked over and pointed to a slimmer volume that lay on the counter between them. "Mr. Rockefeller," Lewis said into his microphone.

"Oh, yes, the amendments," the assistant said. She began to turn pages. "Which part?"

"Mr. Schlafer," the clerk called out.

Nick looked at him, shook his head, and mouthed the words "I'll wait." He turned back to the assistant. "The tobacco allotment, if you can find it," he said.

"Tobacco. Tobacco." She ran her fingers down the pages. "Bup, bup, bup. Tobacco. Here!" She stabbed a page with her index finger and rotated the binder for Nick to see. He peered closer and read: "Title III—Amendment to the Rural Development, Agriculture, and Related Agencies Act . . ."

As Nick read, more bells began to ring. There were five of them. *Seven and a half minutes to go.*

He read on:

"Section 201. Technical Amendments: (B) in subsection (c) by inserting after 'broadleaf finest,' the following paragraph: '10 percent of the foregoing sums shall be set aside for the cultivation of cannabis, hemp, Erythroxylon coca, Papaver somniferum (opium poppy), digitalis purpurea . . .' "

Nick closed the binder and stood with his hand resting on its cover. He was sweating again.

"That answer your question?" the woman asked.

"Mr. Warren." There was no response. "Mr. Wellington."

Nick nodded. "Thanks." He looked up at the empty gallery.

"My goodness, Nick. What happened to that arm?"

Nick looked down unseeingly at the Junior Senator from California. "Excuse me," he said. He forced his way through the crowd. Faces turned toward him. He went up the aisle that led to the Republican cloakroom.

Diefendorfer was blocking his way. "Problem, Nick?"

Nick stared at the broken capillaries on Diefendorfer's nose. The man's crewcut hair had gone from gray to white in the few years Nick had known him. "What makes you think there's a problem, Ted?"

"You look like you just swallowed a gallon of bilge water."

"Mr. Warner."

"Nay."

"Mr. Warner, nay."

Diefendorfer looked toward the well. "That ends the roll call," he said.

Members continued to move down the aisle and gather in the well.

"Mr. Bond, aye," the clerk said.

Nick looked at his watch. It was 11:22. "I've gotta get to a phone before I vote." He moved around Diefendorfer.

"Hurry back." Diefendorfer looked at his watch. "You got about seven minutes. It could still come down to your vote."

Nick moved up the aisle. "Rest easy," he said over his shoulder.

When he reached the entrance to the cloakroom, he was nearly jogging. Inside he turned to his left. A young woman with straight blond hair was seated behind the counter at the end. She was reading a magazine, *National Review.* Nick went by her to the bank of phone booths to the left. He hesitated, picked the third one, stepped into it, sat on the leather upholstered seat, and pushed the sliding door shut. A fan began to whir above his head. He lifted the handset and looked at the mouthpiece.

He put it to his ear, listened for the dial tone, and took his notebook from his breast pocket. He laid it on the shelf in front of him, and turned the pages until he found the number he wanted. He tapped the buttons on the wall console.

"Yes?"

"This is Schlafer. Is Lenny available?"

"Sorry, Senator. He's tied up."

"Well, I have to speak to him."

"He's in a meeting."

"This is an emergency."

"Sorry, Senator, but he left instructions not to disturb him."

Nick took a deep breath. "Listen. I'd like to keep this nice and polite. But get it straight in your mind that you are all still guests on my property and I insist that you call him to the phone. I'll be glad to make a stink about it, if you want."

There was an unintelligible sound, and the line went dead. Nick waited.

The line came to life again. "Senator. How's it going? Where are you?"

"There's a problem."

"What's that?"

"The language is in the budget resolution. That bastard Bodine went and put it in."

There was a brief silence. "Yeah. I know."

"I thought I had a deal with Bodine. I thought you were going to help me get the language removed!"

"No, that you got wrong, Senator. You asked me, but I never answered you."

"You mean you knew all along it would go in?"

"I knew Senator Bodine wanted it in very much."

Nick put his hand on a notepad lying on the shelf beneath the phone. Across the top was printed in blue letters "United States Senate—Memorandum." He cleared his throat. "I thought you were helping *me*."

"I have been helping you. That's why I sent the fat man to keep an eye on you. You gotta understand—my main interest is legalizing drugs. Or decriminalizing as a first step. I put that on the table from the start."

"Well, my interest—my only interest now—is getting my son back."

"You still don't have your boy?"

"You know fucking well I don't."

"Take it easy."

"I was to get him back after the vote. If the language was out."

There was soft breathing on the line. "You're not seeing this clearly, Senator. Last night you had a deal with Bodine. I never said I would help, because the bottom line is I want the amendment to go through."

"But we're talking about my son's life here!"

"Well, I really thought you had yourself a deal with Bodine and Frankfurt. So, maybe it's time to take stronger steps. Use what you found in your daughter's diary."

Nick felt his eyes stinging. "It's a little late."

"I can't help that."

"I thought you were with me."

"I am, I am. But I have my own interests to look after. Just like Bodine does. Anything else I can do, give me a call. Goodbye, Senator."

Nick slowly hung up. He took a pen from his breast pocket,

thought a moment, and wrote down on the memo pad the number Emery had made him memorize. He lifted his hand and punched in the numbers. Had he recalled them correctly?

There were four prolonged rings. Then a high-pitched child's voice answered: "Hello, you have . . ."

"Hello, hello," Nick said. "Is Secretary Fr . . ."

The child was still speaking. ". . . reached the doll hospital. Is your baby broken? We can fix up him or her. Maybe you would like a new doll to look after. If you are using a Touch-Tone phone you may press the following numbers. For repairs, press one. For purchases . . ."

Someone was tapping on the door of the phone booth. It was a Senate page, a short redheaded woman. Hanging up the phone, Nick opened the door of the booth.

"They need you, Senator Schlafer. Senator Diefendorfer sent me. You have about four-plus minutes."

"Thank you." He stood up slowly and stepped out of the booth. He began to move toward the exit of the cloakroom, then stopped. He looked at the woman behind the counter.

"Is anything wrong?" she asked brightly, looking up from her magazine.

Nick looked at her. "No," he said. He shook his head. "No, nothing's wrong." He forced a smile, felt for his wallet, and drew it out of his pants pocket. Opening it and digging into one of its pockets with his index finger, he began to move back toward the phone booths. When he felt the folded scrap of paper, he slipped it out. He looked at the woman. She was back in her magazine. "Excuse me. Are these phones absolutely secure?"

"No. They're like phones anywhere. If you want to make a secure call, you can use the extra phone in the far booth on the right." She waved her magazine. "But I'll need to get Security to unlock it for you."

Nick looked at his watch. It was 11:26. He had about three and a half minutes. "Never mind," he said. "No time."

He went to the fourth and last booth, stepped inside, pulled the door shut, unfolded the scrap of paper, and studied the numbers on it. He looked up and saw the larger telephone console mounted on the wall above the standard one. He shrugged and unhooked the handset on the phone below, and brought it to his ear. Squaring his shoulders, he began to tap the numbers.

There was a single ring. A male voice answered, "Yes?"

"Uh. This is Senator Nicholas Schlafer speaking."

"Yes?"

"I was given this number to call."

"Yes?"

"I was given it by the President."

"Yes?"

"May I speak to him, please?"

"Hold the line." There was a muffled sound and the murmur of voices.

The line seemed to clear. A voice away from the phone said, "Tighten the screws on Bradley." Then the voice came louder: "Hullo? Nick? How's the fishing?"

"Hello, Mr. President."

"Why aren't you on the floor? They're winding up the vote."

"I'll be there in a minute."

"I understand you're supporting us. It's close." His voice went away. "What's the score now, Frank?"

"You have my vote, sir," Nick said. "But I have an urgent problem."

Something subtle in the sound on the line changed. Then the President came back. "I'm sorry to hear that."

"When I saw you in April—"

The President cut in. ". . . I told you to call me if you ever needed my help. What can I do for you?"

"Thank you for remembering."

"Aw, come on, Nick! We go back a long way. How can I help?"

"Can I speak confidentially?"

"Is your line secure?"

"No, but I'm alone in the cloakroom. No one can overhear me."

"Then go ahead."

"Okay. What I'm calling about is this: as you probably know, I'm unable to deliver my end of the deal."

"I don't think I'm with you, Nick. What are we talking about?"

"Killing the amendment to the agricultural allotment."

There was silence on the line. "Are you talking about growing experimental drugs? It's an interesting idea. A good compromise for you. But I don't know about any deal. Fill me in, Nick, and make it quick."

"Secretary Frankfurt indicated to me that you were strongly opposed to it."

The President laughed. "Oh ho! He did, did he?"

"Yes, he did."

"Good old Emery. He plays hard ball, doesn't he?" The President cleared his throat. "Yes. Well, of course I back him completely on that, Nick."

"But the language is still in, Mr. President. And you surely can't veto the Continuing Resolution."

"What is this all about?"

"It's been a *very* rough game Emery Frankfurt has been playing."

"It sometimes goes that way."

"This is going to sound crazy to you. But I have very strong reasons to believe that Emery was involved in my daughter's death."

Silence. Then softly: "That's a stunning accusation, Nick."

"And he's taken my son. Kidnapped him. He's holding him hostage till I get the drug language removed. He's led me to believe he has your backing."

The President's voice boomed heartily in his ear. "Senator, I want to discuss this more fully. Let me go to another extension."

There were muffled sounds on the line, then static. Nick stared through the glass of the phone-booth door at the floor of the cloakroom. There was another click on the line, then breathing. "What do you want, Nick?" The voice was cold.

"I want my son back."

"Where is he?"

"I don't know. That's the point. But Emery made it frighteningly clear that if the drug language got in, I would never see him again. And that my own life might be in danger."

"This is pretty strong stuff, Nick. What do you propose I do?"

"Mr. President, do you remember when we talked about my daughter's death?"

"Of course."

"Do you recall that we discussed her pregnancy and possible DNA samples?"

"I do."

Nick struggled to keep his voice level. "Mr. President, I know whose DNA will match the sample we took from Lore's corpse. Who the father is."

"Oh, Christ, Nick. Are you suggesting Emery Frankfurt is involved? How can you possibly believe that?"

"I found the diary she wrote and hid before she . . . *died*." The word stuck in his throat. "I'm telling you, Mr. President. I intend to go public with this just as soon as the vote is over. Whether or not I get anywhere with it, I'm going to shout it in every television and newspaper reporter's ear until there is not a soul left in the goddamned country who doesn't know about it."

There was silence on the line. The page appeared outside the booth. Nick nodded at her.

The President was speaking again. "Do me a favor, Nick. Hold off a little on this until I can look into it." His voice was dry and distant.

"The meter starts running as soon as the vote is final," Nick said.

"I understand that. Give me half an hour. Can you hold out that long?"

"I hope so."

"I appreciate that. I'll talk with Secretary Frankfurt now." The line disconnected.

Nick stood up and put back the handset. He pulled the door open and stepped out. Diefendorfer was standing just inside the cloakroom entrance. "Come on, for Pete's sake. You have half a minute. It's fifty to forty-nine against. Your vote will throw it into a tie, which the Vice President will break in our favor."

Nick stopped in front of the third phone booth, leaned into it, tore off the top page of the memo pad, and crumpled it in his pocket. He moved toward Diefendorfer. "You're saying I could kill the resolution, Dief?" He forced an exaggerated smile.

Diefendorfer looked at him and rolled his eyes up. "Belay there, Nick."

Nick followed him back into the chamber. Members were still crowded in the well and the aisles. He looked up at the family section of the gallery. There was an old woman sitting with her two hands clutching the knob of a cane that stood between her knees.

Still no Matty.

Nick moved down the aisle behind Diefendorfer's shambling figure. He raised his hand in the air with his thumb up.

"Mr. Schlafer, aye," Lewis intoned.

A few cheers went up. The chamber buzzed. Behind the rostrum, Lewis shuffled papers. "The vote stands at yeas fifty, nays fifty. Senators voting in the affirmative . . ."

As the names were called out, Nick looked across the aisle for

Bodine. He had broken away from the crowd in the well and was moving up the aisle toward the Democratic cloakroom.

The clerk went on reading names. "Mr. Calder, Mr. Campbell . . ."

Nick swung his head quickly to the left and looked up at the family section again. The old woman was moving slowly toward the exit at the back.

Nick went to the aisle that led to the Republican door and started up it.

"Good show, Senator Schlafer."

"Take care of that arm."

He found his way blocked by Diefendorfer again.

"Good to have you on board, mate."

"You'll have to excuse me, Ted." He pushed past Diefendorfer and found himself up against the stubby body of Senator Calder.

"You think you've pulled one off," Calder said, "but you haven't heard the last of this."

"That's fine, Les," Nick said. "But you've gotta let me go now."

Calder stood his ground. "You'll pay for putting that amendment in."

Nick put his hand on Calder's shoulder and pushed him firmly aside. He brought his face close to Calder's. "Go screw yourself." He turned, hurried up the aisle and went through the door. Just outside, Segal and Josie were waiting for him.

"Where's Matty?" Josie said as Nick hugged her hard.

He moved his head back and studied her worried face. He spoke to her softly, closing his eyes. "We have to hold together. The next half hour will tell. It's going to be rough."

She nodded stiffly. Tears flooded her eyes. Nick separated from her and began to move toward the elevator bank. Josie and Segal fell into step with him. Nick saw that the fat man was still standing next to the first elevator on the right. "Let's go to my office." He caught the fat man's eye as they went past him.

People were clustered at the far end of the hallway. A uniformed policeman stood in front of them. As Nick approached the last elevator on the left, a man in the group called out, "Would you answer a couple of questions, Senator Schlafer?"

Nick stopped beside the guard. Faces regarded him curiously. "Sure, I'll take a couple of questions." He turned to Josie.

"Nick . . ." she said.

He put his thumb under his chin and lifted it. Then he turned back to the reporters. Several voices spoke at once. Nick caught the eye of a middle-aged woman standing to the right of the cluster. She was holding a microphone. Nick nodded at her.

"Senator," she said in an unnaturally loud voice. "Are you still trying to legalize drugs?"

Nick moved closer to the microphone but kept looking at the crowd. "The question was, Am I trying to legalize drugs? As you know, I have introduced legislation to that effect. But my bill hasn't gotten out of committee. Members were opposed. At this time I have no further plans to push the issue."

"Come on, Senator . . ."

"Although I should add that I believe a growing segment of the American people would support at least decriminalization and an end to the wasteful drug war."

"Senator, what about a clause in the budget's agriculture allotment that provides for the cultivation of drug crops for medical use? Are you aware of this?"

"Yes, of course." Nick glanced back over his right shoulder. The fat man was still standing on the other side of the vestibule. He was watching the traffic on and off the elevator next to him. Nick backed away from the microphone and positioned himself so that he could see the reporters on his left and the fat man off to his right.

"Do you support Senator Bodine's amendment?"

Nick looked at the crowd. "I just voted for the budget resolution." He forced a grin. "Did it pass?"

A few people in the crowd laughed. Someone in the back said, "The Vice President just voted aye."

"Surprise," Nick said.

"Were you responsible for the amendment?" It was a man's voice.

"I didn't write it, if that's what you mean, or lobby for it."

Nick looked at the fat man. A tall young man with long ash-blond hair was standing in front of the elevator looking around. He wore a black T-shirt, dungarees, and dark sneakers. His face was as pale as his hair, and his eyes were dark hollows. His glance alighted on Nick.

Was this one of Emery's thugs? Nick wondered.

"Isn't the amendment a Trojan horse?" It was the woman with the microphone again.

The fat man was approaching the light-haired youth.

"A Trojan horse?" Nick said. "If by that you mean a sneak attack on prohibition, then no, it's not. The amendment is just what it says: a provision to grow a limited amount of drugs strictly for medical experimentation."

The blond man was tilting his head as if to listen to the fat man.

"Seriously, Senator," a man in the crowd said, "isn't this the thin edge of legalization?"

The blond man was nodding and talking. The fat man looked over at Nick, turned the corners of his mouth down, and shook his head dismissively. Nick turned back to the crowd. "Would you repeat the question, please?"

"Isn't this the thin edge of legalization?"

"Look," Nick said, "it's no more than what it appears to be. And it won't become anything bigger until the American people demand that it does. That's really all I have to say on the subject."

Two or three reporters moved away from the crowd and hurried off down the hallway to the right. At the same time, a man and a woman joined the crowd. The woman pushed her way closer to Nick with her hand raised. She had a wide heart-shaped face and wheat-colored hair that had obviously been dyed. Light glinted in her octagonal glasses. "Bonnie Satin of Heritage Radio," she said. She had a high-pitched voice, like a little girl's. "Isn't it true, Senator, that your legislation violates family values? Have you considered its implications for children?"

The light-haired man joined the crowd behind her and began talking to another man.

"I'm not sure this is the time to talk about drug decriminalization," Nick said.

A buzz of talk had started up in the crowd.

Bonnie Satin raised her voice. "You have a son, Senator. I'm here to represent the family and your answer doesn't satisfy me."

"Well, I'm sorry, then," Nick said. He looked over her shoulder and gestured at the far side of the crowd.

A young man with dark curly hair lifted his hand for attention. "Senator, would you care to comment on the news—the rumor about Secretary Frankfurt?"

Nick shook his head. "What rumor?"

"That Secretary Frankfurt is dead."

Voices began to come at Nick.

"Can you confirm that, Senator?"

"Wasn't he a member of your family?"

"Could you give us some background on this?"

Nick struggled to focus his thoughts. He covered his face with his hands, then lifted them with his palms out. "This . . ." He swallowed and closed his eyes. "This is the first I've heard of this. I don't know any more about it than you." He turned to look at Segal and Josie. Segal shrugged and shook his head. Josie's face looked like a mask of tragedy.

Nick looked at the curly-haired man. "How is he supposed to have died?"

"Suicide. Gunshot."

The crowd stirred. "Care to comment, Senator?"

"No. I really can't help you. How do we know this happened?"

"Somebody who works for him found him and called the President. The word is he left a note." Several reporters broke away.

Nick turned his head to look for Segal behind him. He was standing by the Senators' elevator. He shook his head at Nick and shrugged in bewilderment. Nick looked back across the vestibule at the fat man, who was partly hidden by people crowding off the elevator near him. He was leaning over and gesturing with his hand in Nick's direction.

"One more question, Senator?" a reporter asked. Nick craned his neck to see who the fat man was talking to.

"Dad," a child's voice cried out. The fat man was nodding and smiling.

Nick took a step in the direction of the voice.

Matty burst out of the crowd surrounding the fat man. He stopped to look at Nick, then lowered his head and charged, his arms pumping. Nick crouched down and caught him in his arms. He felt the solidness of Matty's body and breathed in the warmth of his hair. He shut his eyes. He felt Josie kneeling beside him, joining them in the embrace.

"Senator, could you give us some comment on what is happening here? We're in the dark."

Nick lifted his stinging eyes to look at Matty's face. It was smudged with dirt. In the distance beyond, a female form swam into view. Nick blinked to focus his eyes.

"What's the matter with your arm, Dad?" Matty said, looking down.

The woman was moving closer. It was Abby. She was smiling. Nick looked at Matty. "It's nothing," he said.

Abby stopped behind Matty and smiled at Nick. She was dressed in a gray running suit. A light-brown leather bag was slung over her shoulder. She was carrying a yellow-and-red coffee tin in her hand. A little behind her the fat man came waddling.

Nick stood up and pulled Matty around to his right, where Josie, still kneeling, continued to hold him.

Abby stood some five feet away, holding her smile stiffly. "I have to talk to you, Nick."

Nick took a step toward her. "Thank God you brought him back. Are you okay?"

Abby took a small step back. "I have to talk to you alone, Nick. Now."

"There's a room we can talk in just over there." He pointed behind her, beyond the vestibule to the Mansfield Room, S-207. "Will that do?"

She nodded woodenly without moving.

Nick turned back to Josie and Matty. "Go to my office with Dave. Don't talk to anyone. I'll be there in a few minutes."

Josie continued to hug Matty. She was pale and wide-eyed.

"Dave," Nick said. "Get Matty something to eat, if he wants it."

Segal stood beside Josie and Matty. "Okay. They'll be fine, Nick."

Nick could see the puzzled faces of reporters in back of them. He turned back to Abby. She began to walk in the direction he had pointed. Her face was still turned toward him, her expression unreadable.

The Mansfield Room was filled with dining tables set up for a breakfast meeting. Nick moved to a table just to the right of the door, turned, and leaned against the back of a chair. He was damp with sweat.

Abby closed the door and moved toward him. She stopped ten feet away. "Nick, I've just come from Emery."

"Abby."

"You've got to help him, Nick."

"What do you mean? I thought Emery . . ."

"Listen." She moved a few steps closer. "I was the one who decided to bring Matty back to you. It was *my* decision, do you understand? They didn't want me to."

"What about Don Fox?"

"He was never part of it. I took Matty."

Nick stood up and took a step toward her. "You, Abby? Why?"

She lifted her chin. "To protect Emery."

Nick lifted his hands toward her. "Why?

"You were a threat to him."

"*I* was a threat to *him!*"

"Yes."

"I can't believe this. Do you have any idea what Emery was doing to me? What he did to Lore? What he did to my father and mother?"

"I know everything."

"Then for God's sake, Abby!"

"He was building a whole empire."

"Yes, Abby—a drug empire!"

"That was just a step, Nick. The means to an end."

"You're not making much sense." He moved toward her.

She took a step back, putting up her right hand in warning. The coffee tin was braced under her left arm.

He stopped. "Don't you see, Abby, it couldn't go on. Even without my finding out."

She leaned toward him. "Well, it's all beside the point now. When he got that call from the President . . ."

"Yes. I'm responsible for that."

"The President told him something. Something terrible. I never saw him like that before. He fell apart in front of me. He went to pieces." She moved closer and reached for his good arm. "You have to help him."

"I can't."

"Call the President, Nick." Tears brimmed in her eyes. She pressed against him. "Nick, he's a human being. I can't let this happen to him."

Nick grabbed her by the shoulders. "Abby, do you have any idea what he's done?"

Her head trembled. Tears ran down her cheeks.

He shook her. "You never told me Lore called me for help."

She bit her upper lip. "What are you talking about?"

"That she telephoned. The Christmas before she died."

"I would never have kept a message from you."

"You're lying, Abby." He pushed her away.

She shook her head rapidly.

"Do you know what Emery did to Lore?"

She stared at him.

"He killed her, Abby." His voice broke. "He raped her and then he killed her."

She brought her hand to her mouth. "No, Nick, *he* didn't kill her. He lost control of his people. It was Leila who killed Lore." She moved close to him again.

"That's his lie, Abby. He never lost control of anything. He was behind everything."

"No."

"Abby, he was a glorified drug dealer."

"No. Emery and I . . . The President can give him another assignment, Nick. You have to help him. He's all I have."

"Abby, I always trusted you."

"Always trusted me! What are you talking about? You never even trusted yourself."

He let his breath out. "I can't help you."

Her face twisted. "You owe me, Nick. I brought Matty back on my own. Emery didn't want it." Her face was almost touching his. "Call the President. Say you made a mistake. Tell him you won't make any public accusations."

He shook his head. "I can't, Abby. It's too late."

She screamed at him. "It's not too late. For once you can do something." She raised her fist in the air and sobbed. "You can show some feeling."

He grasped her by the wrist. "No, Abby, it's too late. Emery's dead."

It was as if he had struck her. Her mouth opened slackly. She backed away. "No. How could you possibly know that?"

"The reporters out there."

She backed farther away, her mouth forming an O. She appeared to slump, but Nick saw that she was working the top off the coffee tin. He stared in fascination.

The tin and its lid flew away from her. A pistol was dangling from her fingers.

Nick lunged for her and fell to his knees. She moved clear of him.

"Abby, no! Don't!"

She kept backing away. She had the gun in both hands and was holding it slightly above her head. Nick stayed on his knees. He braced himself for the pain.

"Emery was a great man, Nick." She was backing toward the door and lowering the gun. She clenched her teeth. "He had a vision someone like you wouldn't ever understand."

Nick saw the door open slowly behind her. She was aiming the gun directly at him. The fat man moved into the room behind her.

"He can't be dead!" she cried. "He was so alive!"

Nick dove to his left. He heard an explosion and the sound of glass shattering. He landed on his hands and knees and rolled. His head and back slammed against furniture. Searing pain shot through his left hand.

A buzz of voices filled the room.

He flinched as hands touched his ankle and back. He tried to turn his head, but the pain in his shoulder made it difficult. He was being lifted gently to a chair.

Faces surrounded him. Josie was stooping by his side. He looked down at his left hand. A shard of clear glass jutted out of his palm. Blood welled at its base. His bad shoulder throbbed with pain.

He cradled his wounded hand with his free one, and looked up. "The shot. Was anyone hurt?"

There was unintelligible murmuring all around him. Someone reached for his hand and began to do something to it. His hearing seemed to grow hollow. The fat man's face swam into his view. "Everything's okay, Senator," he said. "The only shot she got off went wild. Nobody was hit."

Nick tried to steady his head. "Where is she?"

"It's okay. The Capitol police have her."

"The coffee can. Why?"

"To get the gun past security."

When he looked down at his hand again, the shard of glass was gone and the palm was covered with a bandage. Josie was talking to him.

"Are you okay, Nick?"

"Where's Matty?"

"With Dave."

Nick studied her face. Her pallor was gone. "There's a lot to explain," he said.

"Don't think about it now. You have time."

"I'd like to . . . I'd like to come back to you to do it."

"Why, Nick?" Her eyes searched his face. "Are you finished mourning?"

"Because I'm ready. Because I . . . love you."

She remained stooped at his side. She pressed her cheek against his thigh.

"Will you let me come back and explain?" he said.

She looked up at him, closed her eyes, and nodded. "You don't have to explain anything."

He looked down at his hand and pressed it against his stomach. Despite the bandage he could feel the sticky wetness of the blood on his palm.

"We can heal now, Josie. Let's go home."